KAT MARTIN

PERIL

ALEXANDRA IVY
REBECCA ZANETTI

ZEBRA BOOKS
Kensington Publishing Corp.
www.kensingtonbooks.com

ZEBRA BOOKS are published by

Kensington Publishing Corp.
119 West 40th Street
New York, NY 10018

Copyright © 2023 by Alexandra Ivy, Rebecca Zanetti, and Kat Martin

Redemption copyright © 2023 by Alexandra Ivy
Rescue: Hero Style copyright © 2023 by Rebecca Zanetti
One Last Kiss copyright © 2021 by Kat Martin

One Last Kiss was originally published as a Zebra ebook in 2021.

This book is a work of fiction. Names, characters, businesses, organizations, places, events, and incidents either are the product of the authors' imagination or are used fictitiously. Any resemblance to actual persons, living or dead, events, or locales is entirely coincidental.

All rights reserved. No part of this book may be reproduced in any form or by any means without the prior written consent of the Publisher, excepting brief quotes used in reviews.

To the extent that the image or images on the cover of this book depict a person or persons, such person or persons are merely models, and are not intended to portray any character or characters featured in the book.

If you purchased this book without a cover you should be aware that this book is stolen property. It was reported as "unsold and destroyed" to the Publisher and neither the Author nor the Publisher has received any payment for this "stripped book."

All Kensington titles, imprints, and distributed lines are available at special quantity discounts for bulk purchases for sales promotion, premiums, fund-raising, and educational or institutional use.

Special book excerpts or customized printings can also be created to fit specific needs. For details, write or phone the office of the Kensington Sales Manager: Kensington Publishing Corp., 119 West 40th Street, New York, NY 10018. Attn. Sales Department. Phone: 1-800-221-2647.

Zebra and the Z logo Reg. U.S. Pat. & TM Off.

First Printing: June 2023
ISBN-13: 978-1-4201-5418-4
ISBN-13: 978-1-4201-5545-7 (eBook)

10 9 8 7 6 5 4 3 2 1

Printed in the United States of America

CONTENTS

REDEMPTION

ALEXANDRA IVY

CHAPTER 1

Tessa Ralston was methodically searching through a stack of files that included twenty-year-old tax returns, bank statements, and financial transactions when her phone dinged. This wasn't her favorite part of being in the cold case unit. She usually spent her days reviewing witness interviews and scouring court records. She had a talent for picking out subtle clues that had gone unnoticed by other detectives. Her boss claimed she had a nose for sniffing out lies.

Numbers tended to give her brain a cramp.

Eager for a distraction, she grabbed her phone and glanced at the text on her screen. She'd expected a message from her mother. Or perhaps one of her fellow detectives wanting to grab lunch.

If it was work related, they would call or send an email.

A minute later she was jumping from her chair, punching her fist in the air as a jolt of anticipation sizzled through her.

She was hastily shutting down her computer and clearing her desk when the door to her office was shoved open and Rachel Fisher Evans stepped in.

At a glance the two women could pass as sisters. They were both tall with lean, muscular bodies, strong features, and dark hair that they kept pulled into a tight braid. But a closer look would reveal that Rachel's eyes were blue while Tessa's were a dark brown and flecked with gold. Plus, her skin was kissed with gold despite the long Wisconsin winters.

"Is everything okay?" Rachel asked, studying Tessa with blatant concern.

Tessa was momentarily confused by the question; then she wrinkled her nose. "Oh. I screamed, didn't I?"

"Loud enough to wake the baby," Rachel said, placing her hand against her still flat stomach. She'd only discovered she was pregnant a couple weeks ago, but she happily used every excuse to remind everyone of the babe.

Tessa smiled. "Sorry."

Rachel chuckled. The two had been working together for the past five years, and Tessa had watched her friend change from a workaholic who had no interest outside her job to a smiling, relaxed woman who understood that life was about balance.

And all because she'd reconciled with her husband, Zac Evans, who was the sheriff in a small town north of Madison, called Pike, Wisconsin.

Sometimes Tessa envied her friend, but most of the time, she was happy to concentrate on her career.

"I'm hoping that very enthusiastic screech is related to a case you're working on," Rachel said.

"Not a case." A hard smile curved Tessa's lips. "*The* case."

"I don't . . ." Rachel's words trailed away; then with a gasp realization abruptly hit. "Deacon Mitchell?"

Deacon "Deke" Mitchell was a hardened criminal who'd murdered Tessa's partner when she'd been a rookie at the Denver Police Department.

"I just got a text from his ex-girlfriend. She said she heard from Deke and he's returned to Denver."

"Have you contacted the Denver Police Department to let them know he's in town?"

"I'll give them a call on my way home to pack a bag."

Rachel watched as Tessa looped her canvas satchel over her shoulder before grabbing the Milwaukee Bucks sweatshirt that was hanging on the back of her chair. It was the end of June, but inside the station it always felt as if it was hovering around the freezing point. She wasn't sure if it was because northerners took pride in braving the cold or if they just enjoyed the frigid blast of air from the A/C.

"I'm guessing you're headed out west?"

"As soon as I can get a flight." Tessa grimaced, sending her friend a regretful glance. "I'm sorry to bail on you on such short notice, but—"

"I understand, and I'll clear it with the boss on this end. I'll also give a call to Denver to make sure you have access to their resources," Rachel promised, instantly comprehending that Tessa would insist on personally working the case. She hesitated, her expression tightening. "But that's not going to stop me from worrying about you."

Tessa flinched. Her wounds were still raw despite the time that had passed.

"I'm not the same cop I was five years ago."

"That's not what I'm worried about."

"Excuse me?"

Rachel moved close enough to grab Tessa's free hand. "You blame yourself for what happened that day."

"Of course I do." A shudder of horror raced through Tessa. She would never forget the moment she'd stepped into the shadowed alley, looking for her partner, Colt Maddox. He'd had his back to her, but over his shoulder she could see Deke Mitchell. The criminal had his hands in the air, but as Tessa had rounded the corner, Colt had glanced around to see who was there. In that moment,

Deke had grabbed Colt's service gun and pulled the trigger. Time seemed to freeze for Tessa, as if her brain had simply shut down. Then in shocked disbelief, she'd watched as her partner had crumpled to the filthy ground, blood pouring from his wound. With a shake of her head, Tessa tried to force away the image seared into her brain. "If I hadn't blundered into the alley that day, then Colt would still be alive."

"First of all, you did not blunder into the alley. You were following a lead." That was true enough. Tessa and Colt had been investigating a string of robberies in the area, and she'd discovered information that one of the perps was planning a break-in that evening. "And second, you have no idea if Officer Maddox would be alive or not."

"I distracted him," Tessa stubbornly insisted. "And Deke took the opportunity to gun him down and escape."

Rachel squeezed her fingers. "I'm not going to try and convince you to keep your emotions out of this—we both know it's impossible. But I'm begging you to use your incredible instincts. Think like a detective, not a woman who is seeking revenge for the past. Deke Mitchell has already proved he's willing to kill without conscience. I don't want you to be next."

Impulsively, Tessa pulled Rachel into a hug. Neither one of them were touchy-feely sorts of women. They were more take-charge and kick-ass. But Rachel had been more than just a mentor over the past few years. She'd become Tessa's best friend, and it felt good to know that she was worried about her.

"Take care of yourself and that baby." Tessa stepped back, sending her companion a warning glare. "And don't work too hard while I'm gone."

"Me?" Rachel blinked in pretend shock. "Work too hard?"

"I'm texting Zac to warn him I'll be gone a few days,"

Tessa said, not teasing. She really was going to let Zac know. Although Rachel was much better about her hours at the office, she would have more on her plate with Tessa gone. "He'll keep an eye on you."

Rachel smiled, her eyes sparkling with wicked amusement. "He keeps more than an eye on me."

Tessa deliberately glanced down at her friend's stomach. "So I noticed."

They shared a chuckle, and Tessa even managed to hide her stab of envy. How would it feel to be so completely loved? To be the very center of another's life?

Heading for the door, Tessa halted as Rachel called out behind her. "Tessa. If you get yourself shot, I'm going to be super pissed."

"Don't worry," Tessa assured her.

Rachel shook her head, her expression tense. "Too late."

Ian Sullivan stood in front of the window of the small conference room at the Denver Metro Police Department. It was not only one of the few spaces that offered privacy, but it had an unimpeded view of the parking lot. The perfect spot.

He'd been waiting for the past half hour, but he didn't notice the passing time. Not until the door behind him silently slid open. A wry smile curved Ian's mouth as he turned to watch the large male step into the office. He was dressed in tactical gear that marked him as one of the elite SWAT team.

Owen "Striker" Sullivan was Ian's older brother by three years and a lethal sharpshooter with the special weapons and tactics division. He was tall, almost as tall as Ian, who stood six feet four. He also had the same broad shoulders and narrow waist that came from hours in the gym. His head, however, had been shaved bald while Ian wore his copper hair long enough to curl over his ears and cover the base of his neck. In addition, Striker's green eyes were several shades darker than Ian's bright emerald.

The biggest difference between them, however, was the fact that Ian was wearing a silver-gray suit with a white shirt and blue tie with soft leather shoes that had been custom-made in Italy. The tailored clothing made him appear almost civilized, despite his bulging muscles and bluntly chiseled features.

Striker would never look civilized.

"How long have you been staring at that parking lot?" Striker demanded, moving to stand next to Ian. In answer, Ian lifted his hand and offered his middle finger. Striker made a sound of disgust. "If you were so anxious to see Tessa Ralston, then why didn't you pick her up from the airport?"

That'd been Ian's plan. As soon as the chief had called him into the office to say that Tessa Ralston was returning to Denver to track down Deke Mitchell, Ian had leaped at the opportunity to spend as much time with Tessa as humanly possible. Just the mention of her name had sent his pulse racing with anticipation. He'd missed her. More than he'd even realized.

But he'd known better than to reveal his excitement, and had merely shrugged when the chief revealed that Tessa would arrive at the station sometime this morning.

"She wanted to rent a car and get checked into her hotel first," he told his brother.

Striker wasn't fooled by Ian's offhand tone. "Leaving you hanging?"

"Don't you have somewhere else to be?" Ian sent his brother a chiding glance. "Shooting bad guys? Driving around in your SWAT-mobile?" His gaze lowered to the heavy boots. "Adding another layer of gloss to blind the bad guys?"

"Jealousy is an ugly emotion, bro."

Ian rolled his eyes. "Seriously, go away."

"After I say what I came here to say."

Ian moaned. Their dad had been a fighter pilot in the air force who'd tragically been shot down during the conflict in Iraq when Ian was just a baby. And while their mom had been a strong single mother who'd devoted herself to her boys, Striker had instinctively taken on the father role.

Sometimes Ian appreciated his concern; other times he wanted to punch him in the face.

"If it's some sort of brotherly advice—"

"It is. So shut up and listen," Striker rudely interrupted.

"Fine." Ian folded his arms over his chest. It'd be easier to stop a speeding freight train than Striker when he was in this mood. "Spit it out."

"I like Tessa."

Ian arched a brow at the clipped words. "That's it?"

"No." Striker paused, as if considering how to get his point through Ian's thick skull. "Tessa Ralston was a helluva cop even as a rookie and a good addition to the station. Honestly I thought she would work her way to chief someday."

"She's still a cop," Ian couldn't resist pointing out.

Striker ignored the interruption. "My only concern was your obvious interest in her."

Ian frowned. "Why would you be concerned?"

"Workplace relationships are dumpster fires. Especially between cops."

Striker wasn't wrong. Ian had been around long enough to see several of his friends destroy their marriages with affairs. Or end up hating their partner when they allowed the endless hours they spent together to become overly intimate.

"Nothing came of it," he reminded the older man. He'd never revealed what had happened between him and Tessa the night before she'd fled town. Not even to his brother.

"No, but I don't think you've ever forgotten her. I also think that she's the reason no other woman could ever satisfy you."

Ian's lips twisted. It was unnerving to think that Striker had sensed his frustration with dating. Of course, the two of them were closer than most brothers. Not only had the death of their father drawn them together, but they worked and even lived together.

"I'm not going to lie—I wanted more than a working relationship with Tessa when she was here," Ian admitted. "And a part of me is hoping like hell that she's still unattached."

Striker's jaw tightened, as if he was clenching his teeth. "Which means you're going to be distracted."

Ian lifted his hand. "I'm not going to forget why she's here. Or that Deke Mitchell killed one of us," he assured his brother. "There's not one officer in this city who's going to be satisfied until he's in jail. Or in a grave."

"I vote for grave," Striker growled. Any cop who'd been around five years ago had mourned the loss of Officer Colt Maddox. And harbored a burning desire to get their hands on the bastard who'd shot him. "And I hope you're right, Ian. Deke Mitchell won't hesitate to pull the trigger if he feels cornered."

Ian understood his brother's concern. A cop's life could hang by a thread. One wrong move, one moment of distraction, and he was dead.

"I'm past the age of allowing my dick to control me," he said, talking to himself as much as his brother.

Sure he was anxious to spend time with Tessa, but he wasn't going to do anything stupid that might put her, or himself, in danger.

Striker snorted. "The famous last words of every man."

Ian heaved a resigned sigh. "Shut up and go away."

"Fine." Striker pointed a finger directly in Ian's face. "But if I think you need an intervention, I'm going to haul your ass to Mom's house. She'll set you straight."

With his warning delivered, Striker turned and headed for the door.

"God save me from older brothers," Ian muttered.

CHAPTER 2

Tessa was buzzing with impatience as she made her way through the Metro Police building. It'd taken longer than she'd expected to arrange for a flight and battle through the red tape so she could officially work for the cold case unit in Denver. But at last she'd arrived and checked into her hotel. Now she was headed to meet her temporary partner so she could get on the hunt for Deke.

Walking down the hallway that led to the back of the building, Tessa occasionally caught sight of a face that seemed vaguely familiar, but she didn't stop to chat. She had one reason for being in Denver. And nothing was going to distract her from that mission.

Reaching the door at the end, Tessa pushed it open and stepped into the conference room. She'd expected to find her partner seated at the long table that was arranged in the middle of the carpeted floor.

When she realized there was no one there, her gaze swept toward the window, where she could see the outline of a man. A hiss escaped her lips as she felt a blast shock slam into her. It wasn't fear. Even though the sun slanting through the glass put the man's face in shadow, she didn't need to see his features to know exactly who was standing there.

Ian Sullivan.

During the flight, she'd had more than one renegade thought about the deliciously sexy cop. They'd worked in the same district, and he'd gone over and above the call of duty to give her advice when he sensed that she was struggling. Or simply a pat on the back to reassure her that she was doing a good job.

His kindness meant more than he would ever know.

And, of course, she'd been seriously in lust. The second he'd walked into the room, her heart would race and her palms would start sweating. As if someone had cranked up the temperature to high.

Not her fault. He was gorgeous with features that looked as if they'd been sculpted by an artist and the brightest green eyes she'd ever seen. Plus he had the sort of body that made a woman fantasize about stripping him naked so she could explore it in intimate detail.

The only thing that had kept her from making a fool of herself had been the promise she'd made to herself on the day she'd graduated from the police academy. Her parents had scraped and saved every penny to send her and her brother to college to ensure that they could have a better life. Tessa wasn't going to screw up everything they'd sacrificed for her because of a man.

And she hadn't. Not until that last night . . .

Licking her dry lips as the memory of hot, naked bodies pressed together seared through her mind, Tessa rearranged the satchel strapped across her body and sucked in a deep breath. She hadn't been expecting this encounter, or she would have made an effort to prepare herself.

"Ian," she finally murmured, pleased when it didn't come out as a croak.

"Hello, Tessa." He stepped forward and she had her first good look at his face. He hadn't changed much. There might be a few lines fanning from his stunning eyes, and his copper curls were longer. Oh, and he was wearing a suit that was a serious upgrade from his uniform. But he hadn't aged in the past five years. "It's been a while."

"Yes. I didn't mean to intrude." She was forced to halt and clear the lump from her throat. "I was told to wait in here for my partner."

He spread his arms. "The wait is over."

"I don't understand . . ." Her heart abruptly slammed against her ribs, and Tessa glanced around the empty conference room. As if hoping she'd overlooked an alternative choice. "You?"

It wasn't that she didn't think that Ian was a good cop. Everyone in the station knew he was one of the best. But she was there for one purpose, and this man could definitely make her forget that purpose.

He took another step toward her, and Tessa was suddenly surrounded by the clean scent of pine. It teased at her nose, reminding her of the times that Ian had stopped by her desk, bending over her to help her write up a report.

She loved the smell of pine.

"Is that a problem?" he asked.

With an effort, Tessa tried to gather her scattered thoughts. "Do you work cold cases?"

"No. But a cop killer is never considered a cold case. And I'm the detective with the most experience in Deke's old neighborhood."

"Detective? That explains the suit." She didn't add that he'd always had an air of fierce authority that sizzled around him. So did his brother. She assumed they came out of the womb like that.

"Someone has to do it," he said.

"It's a demanding position. You must have a very patient wife."

The words were out before Tessa could halt them, and she felt heat crawl beneath her cheeks. Where the hell had that come from?

A slow, knee-weakening smile curved his lips. "There's no wife. Not even a lover to complain when I work long hours and fall asleep on the couch." He held her embarrassed gaze. "What about you?"

She battled back her blush. "I'm still concentrating on my career."

"Are you happy in Wisconsin?"

"I like my job. And the people I work with are wonderful."

He tilted his head, the sunlight shimmering in the copper strands of his hair. "We're pretty wonderful here, too."

"You are," she agreed without hesitation. She loved Denver. And she loved this police department. They had taken her in as if she was a member of the family. "I just had to get away."

"But now you're back."

Simple words, but they sent a strange tingle down her spine. "Until Deke is found and locked away." She wasn't sure if she was talking to Ian or herself.

Thankfully, her words seemed to remind Ian why they were standing in the conference room.

"The chief said you had a tip that the bastard was back in town, but he didn't go into any details."

"I don't have many. Not yet." Tessa glanced toward the large clock that hung on the wall. It was an old-fashioned type with a face that had yellowed and black hands that revealed it was later than Tessa had realized. "I have a meeting with my contact in half an hour. Want to join me?"

She made the offer already knowing he would insist on riding along. He didn't disappoint.

"Absolutely. From now on we're joined at the hip." With a lingering smile, Ian strolled toward the door. "Orders from the chief."

Tessa pressed her hand to her stomach. It'd been a long time since a man had given her butterflies with just a smile. Actually, no other man had ever given her butterflies, she reluctantly conceded.

Just Ian.

In silence, Tessa followed her companion out of the building and into the parking lot. She needed a few minutes to collect her composure. She had a terrible fear that she was acting like an awkward teenager. Not exactly the professional image she prided herself on.

Heading directly for the white SUV, Ian sent a glance over his shoulder. "I'll drive."

"I remember you like being in charge," Tessa said dryly. He hadn't been arrogant or pushy like many of the men in the station, but there'd never been a doubt he was a natural leader.

Ian turned to face her. "It's been a while since you lived here. Plus I have a lot more firepower in my vehicle."

He was right. Although the vehicle was unmarked, she didn't doubt it was fully loaded, in more ways than one. And not only would it have weapons, but it would be equipped with a computer system that they would need to tap into police records.

Her rental car didn't have any of that stuff.

"Okay," she agreed, moving to climb into the passenger side of the vehicle.

Ian quickly joined her and switched on the engine. The

scent of pine filled the interior of the SUV as he opened the map app on his phone.

"Where are we headed?" Ian asked.

"Rosie's Café on Pennsylvania Street."

He tossed his phone onto the charging pad, obviously not needing GPS to reach their destination.

"I remember that place." He confirmed her theory. "I used to drive by it on my way to the district station."

They pulled out of the parking lot and headed south. Tessa shifted in her seat to study the familiar buildings passing by. She caught sight of the golden dome on top of the capitol building that glowed in the afternoon sunlight. Next to it were a few skyscrapers and apartment buildings, along with the towering spires of a church. But it was the distant silhouette of the mountains that tugged at her heart with a bittersweet lure.

She'd been born and raised in this city, and she was absolutely convinced that nothing could compare to the epic beauty of the Rockies. Mother Nature had really outdone herself here, she silently acknowledged.

"Why Rosie's?" he asked as they entered the mostly residential neighborhood.

"I used to eat lunch there," she explained. When she'd set up the meeting, she wanted someplace that was familiar. And just as importantly, someplace that would be quiet at this time of day. "It was far enough from the office so I wasn't surrounded by a bunch of cops, but close enough to mingle with the locals."

Ian sent her a quick glance. "You always understood the need to be a part of the community."

Warmth flowed through Tessa at his soft words. Ian had a gift for making others take pride in themselves.

"It wasn't only about the job," she murmured, smiling as

she caught sight of the apartment building where she used to live. The area hadn't been the safest place, especially for a young woman on her own, but Tessa had enjoyed the diverse community. "After my parents moved to California, I didn't have any family close by. And most of my friends had gotten married." She waved a hand to indicate the neighborhood. "The people around here became my family."

"Have you ever thought about moving back?"

"No." She shook her head. "There are too many bad memories."

"They can't all be bad," he protested.

They weren't, of course. She had endless memories that were bright and happy. But she'd shut them all down when she'd left town. It was the easiest way to deal with Colt's death.

"Park here." Tessa pointed toward a small lot attached to an empty auto shop. She didn't think anyone would be following her. Or care if they noticed she had returned to Denver. But she didn't want to take any chances of spooking Deke in case he was keeping an eye on his ex-girlfriend. "We'll walk the rest of the way."

With a sharp turn, Ian pulled into the lot and shut off the engine. He paused to check the gun he had holstered beneath his suit jacket before grabbing his phone and shoving it into his pocket. With a nod, they both climbed out and he locked the vehicle before heading toward the wide, currently empty street.

In less than five minutes they'd reached the corner, where Rosie's Café was draped in the shadows of a nearby oak tree. It was an unassuming building with white-washed bricks that were beginning to fade, adding to the old-world charm in the art deco pattern above the large window that was painted with gold letters. They strolled past the wrought iron tables on the wide sidewalk and barrels filled with flowers that framed the glass doorway.

The warm breeze tugged at Tessa's braid and the short-sleeved yellow sweater she'd matched with her black slacks. It also brought with it the warm scent of freshly baked bread.

Ian sniffed the air. "Something smells yummy."

"They make their own bread every morning."

Tessa's stomach rumbled. She had been too eager to get to the airport to bother with breakfast, and she hadn't had time for lunch.

Ian sniffed again. "It smells like home."

She sent him a startled glance. "Your mother baked homemade bread?"

"She made everything from scratch. She claimed that feeding me and my brother was too expensive to buy frozen dinners or take us out for fast food," he said wryly. "You can't imagine how I longed for a Happy Meal."

"I've seen you and Striker eating. Your mother has my deepest sympathies."

He arched a brow. "I remember you could pack away a healthy portion."

She smiled. She'd never been ashamed of her large appetite. "My mom said I never met a food I didn't like." She grimaced. "I'll admit I've had to cut back on the second helpings and run an extra mile in the morning."

"Me too." He patted his flat stomach. "Getting old sucks."

He looked fabulous, but she didn't doubt he worked hard to keep in shape.

Together they entered the café and paused to allow their eyes to adjust to the shadowed interior. Despite the art deco vibe outside, the dining room looked as if it was stuck in the fifties. Up front there was a glass counter filled with a selection of pastries and muffins along with an ancient cash register. The floor was tiled in a black-and-white-checked pattern, and the room featured a tin ceiling and old framed movie posters on the wall.

Tessa swept her gaze over the booths next to the wall, easily spotting the young woman with long, brown hair wearing a casual sweatshirt. If she hadn't been nervously watching the window, Tessa might not have recognized her. The last time she'd seen Kaye Breckwell, the woman had bleached blond hair, false eyelashes a mile long, and a thick coating of makeup.

"That's my contact in the corner," Tessa said.

"Diva Delight?"

Tessa sent Ian a startled glance. Diva Delight had been Kaye's stage name when she'd been a stripper, and she'd kept it when she'd moved to work for the various escort services around town.

"You know her?"

He shrugged. "I've busted a couple of parties where she was the entertainment. She might be more willing to talk if I make myself scarce."

"That's probably for the best."

"I'll grab us some coffee to go." He nodded toward the counter where a uniformed waitress was watching them with a curious expression. "Black, right?"

Pleasure tingled through Tessa. He'd remembered how she took her coffee. Granted, it wasn't complicated, but still . . .

"Yep." Her stomach did another rumble. "And maybe a blueberry muffin. They're worth every calorie."

"I'll keep that in mind."

Tessa headed toward the back of the café, trying to put the thought of blueberry muffins and Ian Sullivan out of her mind. Both were the sort of temptation she usually tried to avoid.

Sliding into the bench seat, she studied the woman seated across the table. She appeared far younger without her usual makeup and garish clothing.

"Hi, Kaye."

"Hey, Ralston. Long time no see."

Tessa wrinkled her nose at the subtle dig she'd earned for fleeing Denver. "I needed a change of scenery."

"No shit," Kaye said dryly. "I'd leave here, too, if I could convince my mother to go."

Tessa swallowed a small sigh, glancing around the familiar posters on the wall. Ian had been right. She did have good memories. And a part of her would never think of anywhere but this place as home.

"Honestly, now that I'm here, I realize I've missed it," she ruefully acknowledged.

A knowing smile curved Kaye's lips as she nodded toward the front of the café.

"Missed this place or him?"

Tessa didn't have to ask whom Kaye was referring to. Only Ian could inspire that dreamy expression.

"Dangerous question," she muttered.

"The best ones always are."

Tessa cleared her throat. Time to get down to business. "You said that Deke contacted you."

With a grimace, Kaye reached into her purse and pulled out a phone. "Not directly. He contacted my old escort service and left a message. They knew I was trying to avoid the creep, so they forwarded it to me."

"Can I listen?"

Kaye placed the phone on the table between them and touched the screen. There was a dull click as the call was connected, followed by a muffled thudding; then Deke's disembodied voice floated through the air.

This is Deke. Tell the Diva, I'm passing through town. I wanna hook up and have some fun. Don't disappoint me.

Tessa refused to react to the sound of the bastard's voice. Rachel had been right to warn her that it was vital to approach this case like a detective. She needed her training, not her anger, to capture Deke.

Leaning back, Tessa tapped her fingernail on the metal strip that ran around the edge of the table.

"Passing through," she repeated Deke's words. "He's not back in town to stay."

"Thank god." Kaye shuddered, genuine horror darkening her blue eyes. "Otherwise I'd be packing a bag or buying a gun. Deke Mitchell is never using me as a punching bag again."

Tessa had been the one to find Kaye after Deke had beaten her to a pulp and left her on the street. She'd had a fractured cheekbone and two broken ribs, but she'd been terrified to stay in the hospital in case Deke came to finish her off. Tessa had promised to remain at her side until the doctors said it was okay for her to be released. Afterward, she'd driven Kaye to her mother's house. It'd been then that the other woman had revealed that Deke was not only an abusive bastard, but also the leader of a crew that was responsible for the series of robberies plaguing the area. She'd also revealed the location of the next break-in they had planned.

Neither of them could have predicted the dire result of Tessa's attempt to stop the burglary.

"If you see him or he tries to contact you again, call me. Day or night." She pointed toward the phone. "Can you forward the message to me?"

"Sure." Kaye plucked her phone off the table and tapped in Tessa's number. Then, grabbing her purse, she slid out of the seat and straightened. Obviously, she was in a hurry to leave. "I have to bounce—my mom has a doctor's appointment."

Tessa glanced up at the woman who'd been through more than anyone should have to endure. Despite her tension, there was a confidence on her pretty features that hadn't been there before.

"You look good, Kaye," she said.

"I'm feeling good." She glanced toward the window. "Or I was."

"I'm going to find him, and I'm going to lock him away forever," Tessa promised.

"I pray to God you do. Maybe then I can stop looking over my shoulder."

Tessa watched as Kaye hurried out of the café and disappeared from view. She sympathized with the woman's desire to get Deke out of her head. Tessa hadn't been terrorized by the man as Kaye had, but she'd spent the past five years searching every crowd for his face and waking up in the middle of the night drenched in sweat.

She wanted to bury him in the past where he belonged.

She shivered as a shadow fell over her, and she glanced up to watch Ian take Kaye's place in the seat across the table. With a smile, he slid a large blueberry muffin directly in front of her and kept one back for himself. Instantly a flood of heat replaced the cold chill that had settled in the pit of her stomach.

Rosie's blueberry muffins and Ian Sullivan?

Temptation overload.

"That was quick," he said, placing a disposable cup with a lid next to the muffin.

Tessa unwrapped the muffin and took a large bite. She

had to suppress a moan as the sugary goodness hit her tongue.

"She didn't actually have any contact with Deke, but he left this message with her old escort service."

Licking her fingers, she pulled her phone out of her satchel and searched for the voice message that Kaye had forwarded to her. She hit play and handed the phone to Ian so he could listen while she sipped her coffee. Rosie's coffee was almost as good as her muffins.

"Passing through." Ian frowned. "Why risk coming to town if it's only going to be a fleeting visit?"

That had been Tessa's first question as well. "I doubt he's here to catch up with friends."

"Bullies like Deke don't have friends. Certainly none who want a cop killer sleeping on their sofa."

"Agreed." She took a bite of her muffin. "They have to know that anyone who carries a badge would recognize Deke's face."

"Does he have any family?"

She shook her head. As soon as Kaye had shared Deke Mitchell's connection to the crime spree, Tessa had returned to the station to run a background check on him.

"Not in Denver. His dad is in jail in Texas, and his mother died of an overdose years ago. I couldn't find any trace of brothers or sisters."

"So why is he in town?"

"Someone has to know." Tessa took back her phone and dropped it in her satchel, then polished off her muffin and took another sip of coffee before she was sliding out of her seat. "Let's start with the bars where he used to hang out."

CHAPTER 3

Deke Mitchell was leaning against the edge of the kitchen table when he heard the front door to the squalid apartment open and a male voice call out.

"Yo, Vince."

"Yo, Max," Deke called back, his lips twisting into an ugly smile as he heard the muffled curse.

A second later a familiar man charged into the kitchen, a gun in his hand. Max Stoddard wasn't large, but had a hard, wiry body beneath his black T-shirt and jeans. His black hair was messy from the breeze and lack of combing, and his arms were covered in tattoos.

Skidding to a halt, Max ran a startled gaze over Deke. He frowned as if it was taking him a second to recognize the man who'd once been the leader of his crew. Perhaps not surprising, Deke wryly acknowledged. There were streaks of gray in his reddish brown hair and he'd grown a beard to try to disguise his too-familiar features before returning to Denver. Not to mention the addition of wrinkles to his weathered face.

At last, Max slowly lowered the gun. "Deke."

Deke blew him a mocking kiss. "Did you miss me?"

The younger man didn't answer. Instead, he glanced around the kitchen, which was rancid with stale take-out containers and dishes that hadn't been washed in days. Maybe weeks.

"Where's Vince?"

"I told him to take a hike while the big boys discussed business," Deke said. "The dude might have the brawn, but he's severely lacking in brains. I don't want to repeat myself over and over."

Max cleared his throat. "I didn't expect to see you again."

"How could I come to Denver and not hook up with my old pal?"

The man looked less than excited by the reunion. Had he forgotten they'd once been besties? Deke snorted. They'd never been friends. Just business partners who used each other to survive.

"What are you doing in town?" Max demanded.

"I'm getting the band back together."

"What?"

"I'm in need of some quick cash."

"I don't have any."

"Christ, I know that." Deke curled his lips in disgust. "If I thought you had anything of value, I would have shot Vince and taken it before you got back."

Max furrowed his brow. "Then I don't understand."

"You never do. I found you in the gutter, and without me that's exactly where you returned." He folded his arms over his chest. "Thankfully I'm back to save you."

"Look, just tell me what you want," Max snapped.

"Money," Deke answered, his tone sharp. "Enough money so I can lay low for a while."

"You're in trouble?"

"Always." Deke felt a genuine stab of fear in the pit of his gut. It was one thing to be in trouble with the law. The cops were a bunch of idiots who wouldn't know their asses from a hole in the ground. But it was another kind of danger to owe money to the sort of people who would chop off body parts when you were late with a payment. "This time I might have pissed off the wrong people. I need to disappear."

"You need to disappear, and you come back to a town where you killed a cop?" Max looked genuinely horrified. "You think they just forgot what you did?"

Deke shrugged. He'd hesitated to travel to Denver. He didn't doubt that he was still on the most-wanted list.

"I came back to a place I'm familiar with, and more importantly, where my old crew is still living," he pointed out. Not adding the most vital reason he'd chosen Denver. "I'll be in and out of this shit-hole before the cops even know I'm here."

Max shook his head. "This isn't the same town, Deke. Since you left, they've wired the entire city with cameras. You can't take a piss without showing up on someone's computer screen."

Deke shoved himself away from the table, his hands lowering as he stepped forward.

"Why, Max, I'm starting to suspect you've turned into a scared little bitch on me. Or have you switched sides?" With a sudden flurry, Deke charged forward, pinning Max to the wall before the man could brace himself for the attack. "Are you a snitch?"

Max's breath came out in a pained gasp, but his expression was hard as he glared into Deke's face.

"No, I'm not a damned snitch."

Deke didn't think he was. He wouldn't have risked coming to the apartment if he feared for a second the man would stab him in the back. But it was an easy way to manipulate the fool.

"Prove it," he growled.

"How?"

"You're going to help me get the cash I need to vanish."

"Fine." Max conceded to the inevitable. "There's a couple of convenience stores south of town that should be an easy score."

Deke glared at the man in disbelief. Had he seriously just suggested they rob a gas station as if they were a couple of teenagers in need of weed money?

"If I wanted a cheap-ass score, I wouldn't have come back here." Shaking his head, Deke stepped back, releasing the man from his crushing hold. "Next you'll be offering to steal lunch money from some kid. Or cash your granny's social security check."

Max wisely remained pressed against the wall. Deke had an unpredictable temper. "It was just a suggestion."

"A stupid one. I need something big."

"A jewelry store?"

"No, numnuts." Damn. Did he have to spell it out? "If you want cash, you go to where they keep it."

Max looked confused. "The mint?"

"The mint? You stupid . . ." Deke's words trailed away. "Hmm. That's not bad." He considered the possibility. He didn't know much about mints beyond the fact that they made the money. Was it just coins? That seemed like a wasted effort. Plus he wasn't sure there was still a mint in Denver. He shook his head, dismissing the sketchy idea. "No, I'm talking about a bank."

Max snorted. "You always said that bank jobs take too much planning."

"They do if you want to do them right." Deke shrugged, careful to disguise his unease behind a casual confidence. If Max suspected that he was making this shit up as he went along, the jerk would bail on him. "It's going to be a smash and grab."

Max was predictably suspicious. "It sounds risky."

"Christ, when did you turn into such a puss?"

As Deke hoped, the younger man was instantly diverted by the insult. "Don't call me that."

"Then strap on some balls. I need you and Vince."

"Need us for what?"

"Vince has the muscle in case things go south. You, on the other hand, have the contacts to get me some weapons. I'm talking serious firepower." A humorless smile stretched Deke's lips. "See? Everyone has their job."

"What are you going to be doing?"

"First, I'm going to track down our driver."

"Who?"

Deke had already decided on who he wanted. "Ricky J."

Max made a strangled sound. "You can't be serious."

"Do I look like I'm joking?"

"Ricky J is a freaking lunatic."

No arguing with that. Ricky had always been wild. He'd started stealing cars when he was in elementary school, and things had only gone downhill from there. At least as far as his mother was concerned. Every criminal in the city wanted him behind the wheel.

"He's the best in the business."

"He used to be. Over the past few years, he's gone from edgy to *over* the edge. I heard it had something to do with his cousin."

Deke dismissed Max's concern. He had enough to worry about.

"I trust him. Which is more than I can say for you. Here." Reaching into the pocket of his jeans, Deke pulled out a burner phone he'd picked up before returning to Denver. He tossed it to Max as he headed toward the doorway. "Use that if you need to contact me. Oh, and clear your stuff out of your room. I'll be using it while I'm in town."

"What about me?" Max protested.

Deke never slowed. "You'll be bunking with Vince."

CHAPTER 4

Ian stood outside the narrow brick building that was squashed between a tattoo parlor and a laundromat. His hands were on his hips as he tilted back his head to study the roof, which was sagging as if it was one stiff breeze from collapse.

"I can't believe this place hasn't been condemned," he muttered.

Next to him Tessa appeared unfazed by the large windows that hadn't been washed in years and the shallow stoop that was stained with old chewing tobacco.

"It's looked like this for the past twenty years," she pointed out.

Ian grimaced. "That's not helping." He turned his head to sweep his gaze over Tessa's profile. His heart missed a beat at her powerful features. She'd always reminded him of a warrior queen. A female born to protect and care for others. It was no wonder she'd become a cop. "I'm guessing you've been in worse."

Her lips twitched. "There were times I *lived* in worse."

There was no bitterness in her voice. Ian didn't know a lot about Tessa's family, but she'd never hidden the fact that she'd grown up poor. Her father had been a farmhand, and her mother waited tables. Despite working hard, they'd struggled to keep a roof over their heads.

"How are your parents?"

As always, the mention of her family brought a smile to Tessa's lips. "Good. My brother built a new house with a detached cottage for them in the backyard."

Ian arched his brows. Tessa had mentioned that her older brother had gone into software programming and moved to California. Obviously he was doing well.

"Generous."

Tessa chuckled. "Not really. He has three young kids now, and keeping Grandma and Grandpa close by saves him a fortune on babysitters."

Ian was captivated by the sparkle in her eyes. Her family might have been poor in wealth, but they'd obviously grown up with an abundance of love. Luckily he'd been equally fortunate.

"I remember you saying he was a genius," he teased.

She pursed her lips as if considering his words. "I think I said he got the brains and I got the beauty."

Heat blasted through him as his gaze dipped to her smiling lips. He knew from delicious experience that they were just as satin soft as they appeared. And they'd melted in pleasure when he'd claimed them in a passionate kiss. Ian shuddered, battling back his intense urge to wrap her in his arms. She fit perfectly against him, but now wasn't the time to recall the precise feel of her slender body spread beneath him.

"I think you got both," he murmured, savoring her unexpected blush before he stepped forward to enter the cramped space.

He halted as he gave his eyes time to adjust to the dim interior. At last, he could make out a U-shaped wooden bar with a brass railing in the middle of the planked floor and the few tables scattered along the edges of the long room. There was fake wood paneling on the walls and a line of fluorescent lights on the low ceiling.

Tessa moved to stand at his side, her composure intact as she glanced around.

"I'll chat with the bartender if you want to question the customers," she said, taking control of the situation.

Ian shrugged. He didn't mind. As much as he wanted to take a cop killer off the streets of Denver, capturing Deke was personal for her. Besides, if she was in the center of the room, it would be easier for him to keep an eye on her back.

Crossing toward the tables, he was absently scanning the worn, faded faces of the customers crowded in the shadows when he heard his name called out.

"Sullivan, what the hell are you doing here?" There was a harsh laugh. "I heard you got some fancy promotion a couple years ago. Did you already get busted back to the beat?"

Ian swiveled to study the man who was seated alone at a table. At first glance, he couldn't place the narrow, heavily wrinkled face and red-shot gray eyes. Then he caught sight of a familiar tattoo of a badge on the man's upper arm, which was left bare by his T-shirt. Ah. Officer Jack Radcliff.

He was several years older than Ian, but he'd been a mentor when Ian had first joined the police force. A damned shame that his love of the bottle had driven him into an early retirement.

"Not yet," Ian said with a genuine smile.

"A matter of time," the older man teased.

"I'm not going to argue with that."

Jack touched the bottle of beer on the table in front of him. "Are you here for a drink?"

"Not today. I'm on the hunt."

Jack glanced toward the bar, arching brows that were gray and bushy in direct contrast to his nearly bald head.

"Is she tall, dark, and edible?"

That familiar shiver of anticipation raced through Ian. The man had to be talking about Tessa. He must have seen them walk into the bar together.

"Nope, he's a dirtbag who looks like this." Grabbing his phone out of his pocket, Ian pulled up a mugshot and turned the screen to show it to his companion.

"Deke Mitchell?" Despite a brain fuzzy with alcohol, Jack instantly recognized the picture. Another reminder that it made no sense for Deke to risk coming back to Denver. Not without a compelling reason. "He hasn't been around here since he killed Officer Maddox."

"Word is that he recently returned."

"Seriously?" Jack turned his head to spit on the ground in disgust. "He hasn't been here. If he had, I would have called." Jack reached to touch the tattoo on his arm. "I might not carry a badge, but I'm still a cop."

Sympathy tugged at Ian's heart. Jack was a great guy with a demon that had taken everything from him.

"I know that, Jack," he assured his old friend. "Is there anywhere around here that Deke might be welcome?"

"Try a couple blocks south. Those places are filled with scum."

"Thanks." Ian slid his phone back in his pocket.

"You might want to check on your girl," Jack abruptly warned, his gaze once again on the bar. "Clive is a nasty piece of work."

Ian turned, watching as a middle-aged man with a beer paunch and ruddy complexion shuffled behind Tessa, who was leaning against the brass rail as she chatted with the female bartender. He wasn't tall, but he was beefy enough to be twice Tessa's weight. Still, Ian didn't rush forward to deal with the drunken fool. He had a gun if things got out of control. A highly unlikely possibility.

"She can take care of herself," he assured his companion. "Watch."

The man managed to get close enough to Tessa to cup her ass in his hand. Epic mistake. Whirling around with the elegance of a dancer, Tessa smashed her elbow into the perv's chin. He grunted, his eyes rolling back in his head as he crumpled to the ground.

Jack released a low whistle. "Yours?" he asked, his voice edged with envy.

Ian squared his shoulders as a burst of determination raced through him. This woman had slipped away once. It wasn't going to happen again.

"Yes."

He was walking toward the bar when Jack called out behind him. "Be careful, Sullivan. Deke already killed one cop."

Tessa stared down at the man who was lying like an awkward lump on the floor. She hadn't intended to knock him out, but when she'd felt his fingers grabbing her backside, she'd reacted on instinct.

No one touched her without permission.

No one.

"Done playing?" Ian teased as he prodded the snoring man with the tip of his shoe.

Tessa shrugged. "Some things never change."

"Let's check out the bars south of here."

With a nod, Tessa followed him out of the building. The bartender had been adamant that she hadn't seen anyone but locals in the bar over the past few days, and Tessa believed her.

They headed down the block, moving in silence as they both kept an experienced eye on the clusters of people who huddled in doorways or leaned against the cars that were parked along the curb. Most of them were just wasting time, but there was no doubt a few were selling drugs or looking for an easy victim. They wouldn't be happy to discover a cop in their territory.

Drifting into one bar after another, Tessa and Ian searched for any hint that Deke Mitchell had been hanging around. It was nearly three hours later that they conceded defeat and headed back to Ian's SUV.

No one had been willing to admit to seeing Deke around, and the one person who claimed they might have information had been so high, they wouldn't have known if they'd seen their own mother.

Climbing into the passenger seat, Tessa pulled on her seat belt and heaved a sigh of frustration.

"Nothing."

"He might not even be in town yet." Ian drove out of the lot and headed east. "Or maybe he's smart enough to avoid his old hangouts."

Tessa grimaced, barely noticing the passing buildings as Ian weaved his way through the traffic. She hadn't expected to stumble across Deke. Her luck wasn't that good. But she'd had high hopes that someone in the neighborhood would know something about his return to Denver.

"We're screwed if he decides to lay low," she muttered at last, speaking her worst fear out loud.

Ian picked up speed as he hit the interstate, his expression impossible to read.

"I have faith he'll do something stupid," he assured her. "This evening we'll check out the strip clubs."

Tessa nodded her agreement. There was no point in aimlessly driving around Denver. Until they had a firm lead, they were stuck waiting. "You can drop me off at my rental car if you want," she said. She needed to unpack her bag and check her email. Rachel had promised to check with the credit card companies for any account in Deacon Mitchell's name. "I'm sure you have other cases on your desk."

"They've been given to other detectives. Tracking down Deke is a top priority."

Tessa wasn't surprised. Few things were more important than taking a cop killer off the streets. That didn't explain, however, where they were going.

"This isn't the way back to the station," she said, pointing out the obvious.

"That blueberry muffin wore off a long time ago. I need some fuel."

On cue, her stomach rumbled, reminding her she hadn't had a decent meal since yesterday.

"Good idea." She glanced around. They were heading in the direction of Aurora. "If you take the next exit, there used to be a restaurant a couple blocks from here that had the best fajitas."

He slowed, veering off the interstate, but he sent her a mysterious smile. "I have something better than a restaurant."

"You're not going to cook, are you?" she asked.

Halting at a stoplight, he sent her a glare of protest. "I'm not that bad in the kitchen."

She wrinkled her nose. "I've had your coffee."

He chuckled. "Trust me."

"I do," she said without hesitation.

And she did. Ian Sullivan was a man who could always be depended on to do the right thing. No matter what the cost to himself.

The light changed and Ian pressed on the gas pedal, then turned into a small subdivision that appeared to have been built in the sixties. The homes were all ranch style and squeezed together on small lots with neatly trimmed hedges and large trees that provided plenty of shade. They traveled toward the end of the neighborhood before he pulled into a narrow drive.

A strange tingle of excitement raced through Tessa as she studied the house with faded green siding and a recently replaced roof. There was a lamppost in the yard that was framed with a flower bed and a gliding chair on the cement porch. It was small and past its prime, but someone obviously spent a lot of time caring for the place.

Although they'd worked together, she had rarely spent any time alone with Ian. And never in the privacy of his home. The thought was . . . unnerving.

"Is this yours?" she asked, relieved when the words came out in a casual tone.

"No. I share a condo with my brother near downtown." Ian nodded toward the door, where a small woman dressed in white slacks and a tiger print shirt was standing. "This is my mother's place."

Ah. Tessa abruptly recalled that they were near the old air force base. It'd shut down in the nineties, but when Striker and Ian had been young, Mrs. Sullivan would have wanted to be close enough to use the on-base services. Her husband had, after all, paid the ultimate sacrifice.

Tessa unhooked her seat belt and climbed out of the SUV. She didn't know if she was disappointed or relieved to know she wasn't going to be alone with Ian. Either way, she was definitely eager to meet the woman who'd managed to raise two such incredible boys on her own.

"Hello." As Ian and Tessa stepped onto the porch, the woman tilted back her head, her warm smile revealing deep dimples.

She looked like a teenager with bright green eyes and her

honey blond hair curled to flip at the shoulders. It was only the faint lines on her round face that revealed she was old enough to have grown sons.

"Hey, Ma." Ian leaned down to brush a kiss over the older woman's cheek.

"It's about time," his mother said in dry tones. "I thought you forgot where I lived."

"I was here a couple weeks ago," Ian complained.

"Too long."

"Noted," Ian conceded, placing his hand on Tessa's shoulder. "This is Tessa Ralston."

"Tessa?" The woman blinked, sending her son an odd glance. "Really?"

Not sure what silent communication was going on between the two, Tessa held out her hand. "Hello, Ms. Sullivan. Sorry about just dropping in on you."

"Please call me Deanna." Deanna grabbed her hand, but instead of shaking it, she gave Tessa's fingers a slight squeeze. "And my door is always open to you, Tessa."

Wondering if the woman was usually so welcoming, Tessa was distracted when Ian loudly cleared his throat.

"I was hoping you might have something on the stove."

"Of course I do." Stepping back, Deanna waved them inside. "Chicken and dumplings with fresh-baked bread. There's also a banana cream pie in the fridge. How does that sound, Tessa?"

"Like heaven." Tessa pressed a hand to her empty stomach. She was terrified it would give a loud gurgle of appreciation.

"Good."

Deanna beamed in obvious pleasure, leading them through the square living room that had a floral couch with matching love seat and end tables that were crowded with framed pictures of her sons. On the far wall was a large portrait of a man attired in a flight suit standing next to a fighter jet. Tessa didn't have to guess that this was Ian's father. The man had the same strong features and coppery hair as his son, with a charming smile that must have made him irresistible. There was also a folded flag that was carefully preserved in a glass box. Tessa suspected it had been draped over the coffin when it arrived from overseas.

Deanna headed into the dining room, which was detached from the kitchen. It was a narrow space, but there was an oval table with four sturdy chairs and a matching corner hutch.

"Have a seat at the table and I'll bring in the food," the older woman commanded before disappearing into the adjacent kitchen.

Obediently sliding into one of the chairs, Tessa sent Ian a warning glance as he settled beside her.

"My mother would have whacked me with a wooden spoon if I brought by a guest without giving her a heads up," she muttered.

He appeared genuinely confused by her reprimand. "You're not a guest. You're my partner."

Tessa's heart clenched. But for the first time in five years, it wasn't in pain at the memory of losing her last partner. She felt a perilous thrill at the mere thought of spending her days—and nights—at this man's side.

"Temporary partner," she forced herself to say. She needed the reminder that her time in Denver, and with this man, was fleeting. It was terrifyingly easy to feel comfortable in his presence.

Well, maybe *comfortable* wasn't the right word. And it wasn't just the memories of their one, scorching night together.

There was a tingly awareness that made her feel as if a

thunderstorm was coming. She couldn't deny a feeling that they . . . fit. Yes. That they fit together.

"Besides, my mom loves feeding people." Ian thankfully interrupted her dangerous musings.

"That's obvious." She smoothed her palms over the hand-crocheted tablecloth as she deliberately glanced toward the salt and pepper shakers that matched the silver sugar bowl in the center of the table. It was clear that Deanna Sullivan was always prepared for guests.

"My dining table is piled with stacks of files and laundry that needs to be folded."

"At least you have one," Ian countered.

"It's not mine. My apartment was furnished when I moved in."

"Ah."

They shared a smile of mutual sympathy. Being a cop meant that life was put on hold when you were working a case. Sometimes Tessa barely remembered to eat, let alone set a table and wash the dishes. Only another officer would understand.

Ian reached out, covering one of her hands with his as he allowed his gaze to linger on her mouth. Was he recalling the taste of her lips? Tessa struggled to breathe as she silently willed him to lean forward and reignite the explosive passion that smoldered between them.

The moment was shattered as Deanna entered the dining room carrying a large tray of food.

"Here we go."

She cast her son a knowing smile as she handed out the large bowls of chicken and dumplings and placed a platter of bread on the table. She disappeared again, only to quickly return with another tray. This one held a pitcher of homemade lemonade and three chilled glasses.

Any regret that she hadn't discovered whether Ian's

kisses were still as sizzlingly addictive as she remembered was forgotten as the delectable aroma of chicken and noodles wafted through the air. The delicious scents made her mouth water.

Grabbing a spoon, she dug in with an appetite that had Deanna beaming in pleasure. It'd been a very long time since Tessa had enjoyed a homemade meal. And an even longer time since she'd been surrounded by the sense of family.

Ian and his mother were obviously devoted to each other, with an easy relationship that Tessa had discovered was unfortunately uncommon. She'd been close to her own parents, and it had been astonishing when she first started on patrol to realize not every family was happy.

Savoring the warmth in the room, Tessa listened to the chatter flying between the two as they discussed the animal shelter where they both volunteered. Tessa's heart melted. Why did they claim women liked bad boys? As far as she was concerned, there was nothing sexier than a good guy.

And this one was epically sexy.

Polishing off a large slice of banana cream pie with whipped cream, Tessa speculated on the possibility of giving in to her escalating desire. The memory of her partner's death hadn't been the only thing that had haunted her over the past five years. She'd dreamed of this man and their sizzling night of sex on more occasions than she wanted to admit.

Maybe she could achieve two goals at the same time. Throw Deke Mitchell in jail, where he belonged, and scratch the itch that Ian had created deep inside her. It might purge the last of her connections to Denver so she could concentrate on her new life in Wisconsin.

It wasn't as if there would be any complications, right? Just searing desire being mutually satisfied.

Thankfully unaware that Tessa was mentally stripping Ian of his clothes and licking him from head to toe, Deanna rose to her feet and began gathering up the empty plates.

"I'll clear this away and make a pot of coffee. You two go in the living room."

Tessa jumped out of her chair. "Let me help."

"Nonsense. You're my guest."

"But—"

"As a warning from someone who's known this woman for thirty years, you're wasting your time trying to argue with her," Ian cautioned Tessa as he stood, tossing his napkin on the table. "The best thing to do is concede defeat with as much grace as possible and mount a strategic retreat. That's my motto."

Deanna rolled her eyes at her son's teasing. "Go. And Tessa, there are some photo albums under the TV stand if you'd like to see Ian during his goth years."

With a sweet smile at the sound of Ian's choked cough, Deanna sashayed her way into the kitchen. Shaking his head with wry resignation, Ian led Tessa back into the living room.

"Goth, hmm?" Tessa inquired with raised brows.

"Full goth. I even pierced my tongue. Most painful experience in my life." He came to an abrupt halt as she pulled her phone out of her satchel. "You're not calling for an Uber are you? You don't have to look at any pictures."

She shook her head, locating the voice memo that had been forwarded by Kaye. "I want to listen to Deke's message again. Maybe I missed something."

"Good idea."

Ian stepped close enough to wrap her in the warm scent of pine, leaning down as she hit play. Deke's voice floated through the air, sending a sharp flare of anger through Tessa, but this time she ignored her instinctive reaction. Instead, she concentrated on the muffled sound in the background.

She replayed the message. "There." She glanced up at Ian. "Did you hear that? It sounded like a car backfiring."

Ian furrowed his brows. "Or fireworks."

"In June?"

Ian released a harsh breath, straightening as he reached into his pocket to pull out his own phone.

"Coors Field."

Tessa was momentarily baffled. She knew what Coors Field was, of course. She'd spent several wonderful evenings watching the Rockies play baseball and enjoying the fireworks. It was yet another thing she missed. But she couldn't imagine what that had to do with Deke Mitchell.

"You don't think that he would go to a game . . ." Her words trailed away as she realized that you didn't have to be at the baseball stadium to hear the fireworks. They boomed and echoed through the entire neighborhood. "Oh. Union Station," she said with a hushed breath.

"Yep." Ian pressed his phone to his ear.

"What are you doing?" she demanded.

"Getting a warrant. I want to see the closed-circuit TV footage; it would show if Deke came in on a train and if anyone picked him up."

CHAPTER 5

Ian finished his call to his current partner at the station and slid the phone back into his pocket. Then, heading into the kitchen, he gave his mother a kiss goodbye, deftly avoiding her whispered demand to know if Tessa was staying in Denver and when he would bring her around for another visit. Deanna Sullivan had suspected five years ago that he had been captivated by Tessa. And that he'd never put her out of his mind.

He didn't have any answers for his mother. Not yet.

Besides, he hadn't missed Tessa's attempts to hide her yawn when he'd been on the phone or the shadows beneath her eyes. She was obviously exhausted.

Returning to the living room, he discovered Tessa pacing the beige carpet. Anxious energy hummed around her, but her shoulders were stooped. She turned her head to watch him approach.

"I don't suppose we're getting the video any time soon?" she demanded.

He shook his head, pulling open the front door and urging her out of the house. "The process is started, but it's going to take a while."

She made a sound of impatience. "Even for a cop killer?"

"Even for a cop killer."

In silence they climbed into the SUV and pulled out of the driveway. The sun was setting over the city skyline, bathing the towering buildings in shades of orange and dusty purple. With a sigh, Tessa settled back in her seat and forced her tense muscles to relax.

"I forgot," she said in rueful tones.

"Forgot what?"

"The frustration of working a case with a ticking clock," she clarified. "My job now is usually reviewing evidence that was collected years ago and applying fresh eyes or new technology to discover any overlooked clues. This is . . ."

"Frustrating," he echoed her own word with a small smile.

"Yep."

"I think it's worse because you're anxious and tired. I'll take you back to your car and we'll call it a night."

She sent him a startled glance. "I thought we were going to check out the strip clubs?"

"They'll be there tomorrow."

"I hate to waste time. We don't know how long Deke will be in Denver."

"It would be wasting time to get sloppy and allow him to slip through our fingers," he pointed out in reasonable tones. "Or worse."

"I hate to admit it, but you're right. I'm running out of steam." She snuggled into the soft leather seat, patting her flat stomach. "Plus I ate too many of your mother's dumplings. There's no way I could chase down a suspect."

"Sit back and relax," he urged. "You're in good hands."

"Thanks."

She settled in, and by the time he reached the interstate she was sound asleep.

Warmth spread through Ian as he reached down to lower

the volume on his police scanner. Yes, Tessa was obviously drained from her long day, but she was a trained professional. She would never have fallen asleep unless she fully trusted him.

It was a start.

Returning to the downtown station, Ian pulled into the parking lot and put the SUV in park. Then, unhooking his seat belt, he swiveled to stare down at his companion. Darkness had fully descended, but the light from the nearby street lamp spilled over the stark beauty of her features. Tessa had never been traditionally pretty, but she possessed a compelling beauty that would age like a fine wine.

He reached to brush his fingers over the satin-soft skin of her cheek. As much as he wanted to sit there and savor the sight of her sleeping, she needed to be tucked into her bed. Plus staring at a woman while she was unconscious was a little creepy.

"Tessa." He spoke softly. "We're at your car."

Her eyes slowly opened, revealing the golden flecks in their dark depths. Ian had a vivid memory of those flecks glowing like golden fire as he'd moved inside her with powerful thrusts.

For a second she looked confused, as if she couldn't quite place where she was or what was happening. Then, with a slow, heart-churning smile, she reached up to trace his lips with the tip of her finger.

"Ian," she whispered.

Heat blasted through Ian, clenching his muscles in searing anticipation. Her touch was nothing more than a feather, but it was creating jolts of electric pleasure.

"Are you awake?" he asked, his voice oddly husky.

"I'm not sure." Her fingers drifted to stroke down the line of his clenched jaw. "Are you real?"

"Very real." Unable to resist temptation, Ian reached over to unhook Tessa's seat belt. "And currently off duty."

She tilted back her head in silent invitation. "Me too."

"Good." Wrapping one arm around her waist, he tugged her toward the low console that separated them. At the same time, he used his free hand to tug her hair from its tight braid. He ran his fingers through the silky strands. "I'm going to kiss you. If it's not what you want, tell me now."

"I want it," she assured him, her hand sliding to cup his nape so she could tug his head down. "I want you."

"I never forgot you, Tessa." He pressed a soft kiss to her lips, tasting the sweetness of banana cream pie and pure female temptation. Ian shuddered as the desire he'd suppressed for five years crashed over him like a tidal wave. He nibbled a path of kisses over her cheek to the hollow behind her ear. "You've been in my dreams since you left."

Her fingers tangled in his hair as she pressed herself against his chest. "And what exactly were we doing in those dreams?"

He nipped the lobe of her ear. "A little of this." He slid his lips down the curve of her neck, lingering on the pulse that fluttered at the base of her throat. She trembled, revealing her own arousal. "A little of that."

Tessa released a breathy chuckle, sliding her hand beneath his suit jacket to unknot his tie and tug it off. Then she slowly unbuttoned his shirt.

"I'm a big fan of this and that."

Ian made a strangled sound as her fingers spread over the bare skin of his chest. Her touch was branding him. As if she was claiming him as her own.

And he was okay with that. More than okay.

"Which do you like better?" he asked, allowing his hand to skim down her shoulder before cupping the soft weight of her breast. "This?" He used his thumb to tease her nipple to a hard peak beneath the soft sweater. "Or that?"

"This," she murmured, pressing kisses along the line of his collarbone, her hand exploring down his body to the tightly clenched muscles of his stomach. "And definitely that."

Ian groaned, turning his head to claim her lips with a hunger that he made no effort to disguise. His entire body was rigid with the need to haul her across the console and have her straddled over his thickening cock. He wanted to strip off her sweater and taste the rigid nipple that he could feel beneath his fingertips. He wanted . . .

Everything. The word whispered through the back of his mind.

Her body. Her heart. Her very soul.

It was only the realization that they were most certainly in view of the cameras, along with the refusal to have their long-anticipated reunion a quickie in the front seat of his SUV, that gave him the necessary strength to lift his head and gaze down at her flushed face.

"Will you be okay to drive back to your hotel?"

She blinked. "I'm fine."

Reluctantly he pulled back, swallowing a groan as his body protested at being denied the release it craved.

"You're so tired you can barely keep your eyes open," he murmured.

She heaved a sigh, but her smile was one of drowsy acceptance. "Another thing that has to wait for tomorrow night?"

He reached to touch her lower lip, his heart doing a strange flop in the center of his chest. It wasn't just lust. He'd felt that plenty of times. This was rare and wonderful and so very elusive. The sort of sensation that a man could spend his life hoping to experience.

"I want you fully alert to appreciate my efforts," he told her.

Her eyes smoldered with anticipation. "There's going to be effort?"

"Magnitudes of effort," he assured her.

"Then I'd better get my beauty sleep."

"You could never be more beautiful than you are in this moment." He bent his head to place a last, lingering kiss on her lips. "Be careful."

With a soft sigh, Tessa opened the passenger door and crawled out of the vehicle. As if she was as reluctant as he was to end their evening together.

Ian watched as she headed to her rental car and climbed in. Then, waiting until she'd pulled out of the lot, he followed her. Was she cussing him out for being overprotective? She was, after all, a cop. But the thought she might be pissed off wasn't enough to keep him from traveling to the local hotel and idling in the parking lot until she had let herself into one of the rooms and closed the door behind her.

Satisfied that she was safe, he drove out of the lot and headed to the condo he shared with his brother. Parking in his underground spot, he jogged up the back stairs and entered the living area through the sliding glass doors.

The recessed lights were dimmed, but it was easy to make out the heavy leather furniture that was scattered over the ivory carpet and the large-screen TV hanging on the wall. The stark lack of decorations and doodads in the room would no doubt reveal that it belonged to bachelors, but it was ruthlessly clean with everything put in its place. The men in their lives had been their dad's military buddies who'd taught them how to drive, how to shoot, how to hunt, and the belief that a tidy house was necessary for a tidy mind.

Ian slid off his jacket and neatly folded it over the back

of a chair along with his tie, which he'd found on the floor-board of his SUV. A welcome reminder of Tessa's impatient fingers as she'd tugged it off him. She could rip off his clothing anytime she wanted.

Busy recalling each glorious moment of holding Tessa in his arms, Ian was interrupted when his brother appeared from his bedroom wearing a loose pair of running shorts and nothing else. He'd obviously just finished his workout. They had a full gym built into one of the guest bedrooms.

"Alone?" Striker asked, deliberately glancing around the empty room.

Ian sent his brother a pointed glance before heading toward the built-in bar. "I wish."

Striker blew him a kiss. "I love you, too, bro. Any luck on the hunt for Mitchell?"

Pouring himself a shot of whiskey, Ian dropped in two ice cubes and turned to face his brother.

"No one's seen him in his old neighborhood, but it's possible he arrived in town on the train. I'm waiting for a warrant to get access to the video surveillance."

"Did Tessa's informant give you any leads?"

"Nothing beyond the fact that Deke is just passing through."

Striker's brows pulled together. He was a member of SWAT, but that didn't mean he didn't possess the mind of a detective.

"Why would a criminal pass through a town where he's wanted for killing a cop?"

Ian took a sip of his whiskey. "That was my question."

"Did you come up with an answer?"

Ian shrugged. It was always possible that Deke Mitchell was too stupid to realize that the cops would still be looking for him. Most criminals weren't renowned for their brain-power. But he didn't think that was it.

"My guess is that there's something in Denver he needs," Ian said. "Or wants."

Striker nodded in agreement. "That makes the most sense."

"What I don't know is if it's something he left behind or something he has yet to get."

Striker paused, considering Ian's words. "If he left something behind, it would be easier to slip in and out of town without anyone knowing," he at last pointed out. "There'd be no need to stay long enough to try and hook up with an old girlfriend."

"True." Ian took another sip of whiskey. "So what could he want?"

"Drugs? Money? Revenge?"

"Questions without answers. At least for now."

Ian polished off his whiskey and set aside the empty glass. Tessa wasn't the only one who was exhausted. He'd started his day at four a.m., and he would be up at the same time tomorrow. Unless he got called in tonight. He wasn't on duty, but that didn't mean anything. Being a detective meant you were always on the clock.

"And Tessa?" Striker asked as Ian headed toward the door of his bedroom.

Ian reluctantly stopped to glance back at his brother. Striker wasn't going to let him rest until he had the answers he wanted.

"What about her?"

"Is she married with a herd of kiddies?"

A tiny shiver raced through Ian. He hadn't really thought about children. His job had always come first. Now it was terrifyingly easy to picture a baby snuggled in his arms. A baby who had brown eyes flecked with gold.

"Not yet," he murmured, feeling oddly bemused.

"Is she engaged?"

"Not yet."

Striker folded his arms over his broad chest. "Careful, bro. Tessa came back to Denver to track down the bastard who killed her partner, not to find her happily-ever-after. When that's done, she's gonna bail on you again."

He couldn't argue with his brother. Tessa had been very clear that her time in Denver would be temporary. That didn't mean, however, that Ian was going to accept defeat.

"This time I'll follow." The words were out before he had time to consider the implication of what he was saying. Then a smile curved his lips. From the moment he'd seen Tessa again, he'd known that she was destined to be in his future. "Wherever she goes."

Deke stifled a yawn as he leaned against the storage shed. He'd been up at the crack of dawn to find the perfect spot to keep an eye on the brick building across the road. He wanted to watch the workers arrive at the small branch bank he'd chosen to rob. He didn't have a lot of time to spend casing the joint, but he wanted a general idea of how many employees worked there and how much security they had.

Unfortunately, he wasn't a morning person. Hell, he hadn't been up before noon since he was a five-year-old kid. Back then his mom would yank him out of his bed and toss him outside. She didn't care if he went to school or not, she just wanted him out of their apartment. Once he got a little older, he was able to fight back. The bitch learned that he would get out of bed when he wanted.

Battling another yawn, Deke was watching the uniformed guard enter through a side door. He was the second one to arrive. Deke shrugged, not particularly concerned.

He had a masterplan.

CHAPTER 6

Tessa spent the day in her hotel room after Ian called to say he'd been unexpectedly called into court to testify in one of his cases. In the past she would have driven around the streets to hunt for her prey; now she used her laptop to search through old police files. Not just the ones that included Deke Mitchell, but any that might connect him with known associates. Five years ago he had a crew. It seemed more than likely he would be seeking them out if he intended to commit a crime. If nothing else, he might be staying with one of them while he was in town. That would at least give her a direction to start her search.

She also spent an hour chatting with her parents, who were over the moon happy with their new cottage and full access to their grandchildren. Tessa missed having them close, but she couldn't be more pleased that they were comfortable in their retirement. After years of struggling to make sure their children had what they needed to thrive, they deserved a little pampering.

Making a mental note to put in for a vacation so she could fly out and visit California on her mom's birthday, Tessa jumped in the shower before dressing in a pair of gray slacks with a pink, sleeveless sweater. She pulled her damp hair into a braid, not bothering with makeup. Then, holstering her gun around her waist, she grabbed her satchel and headed out of her room to find a place for lunch and to make a quick sweep of Deke's old neighborhood.

It was nearing dinnertime when she received a text from Ian telling her that they had received the video surveillance from Union Station. Driving to the downtown station, she arrived just as Ian was jumping out of his SUV. Parking beside him, she easily matched his long strides as he hurried toward the building.

"How was court?" she asked, allowing her gaze to roam over the gray silk suit that was tailored to fit the muscled perfection of his body.

He'd been gorgeous in uniform, but the elegant clothing emphasized his rugged beauty. Plus the setting sun shimmered against his hair with a coppery sheen while adding a hint of mystery to his emerald eyes.

Tessa swallowed a groan. She'd done her best to avoid dwelling on the memory of being in this man's arms the night before. Not because she regretted their kiss. Just the opposite. She couldn't wait until they had an opportunity to explore the combustible desire that smoldered between them. But she couldn't let it consume her thoughts. Not when she needed to be focused on capturing Deke Mitchell.

Ian sent her a grimace. "Horrible as always. It's the one part of the job I dread."

"Agreed."

Tessa didn't have to go to court nearly as often as she would if she was a detective, but she did have to give testimony on occasion. Like Ian, she always dreaded being grilled as if she was guilty of inventing evidence.

Together they entered the building and headed up the back steps to the computer forensics department. As they entered the narrow office that was crowded with high-tech equipment, a young man jumped to his feet and waved for them to follow him to a back corner.

Tessa's lips twitched as she silently wondered when she'd reached the age that rookies looked so young. It was an unexpected reminder that the years were slipping past. Perhaps quicker than she realized.

"You got it set up?" Ian asked.

"Yep." The officer leaned over an empty seat to tap on the keyboard of the computer. "I located the cameras that cover the arriving trains. What time do you want the video to start?"

"I called the stadium on the way over here," Ian said. "The game ended at nine thirty-seven and the fireworks started approximately twenty minutes later." He considered for a second. "Start around nine and we'll take it from there."

"Gotcha." The man brought up the video on a large monitor set on a separate desk. There were eight small squares that covered various sections of the train station. "Here's a remote that will run the video." He handed Ian a small, black object. "I'll be at the front desk. Just let me know if you need anything."

"Thanks."

Ian stepped back to allow the younger policeman to slide past him, then together he and Tessa moved to study the monitor. The video was in black and white and occasionally flickered in and out of focus, but it was clear enough to make out the hordes of people who spilled out of the trains and hurried toward the main section of the station.

Standing shoulder to shoulder, they watched the video in silence, both too intent on the faces that rushed past the cameras to notice the muffled sound of activity that hummed through the building. It didn't matter that it was dinnertime for most people. A police station was always busy.

At last, Ian muttered a low curse and hit the pause button on the remote.

"There he is," he said, pointing toward the square in the lower left corner.

Tessa leaned forward, her jaw clenching as she caught sight of a man in a flannel shirt and worn jeans carrying a backpack. His reddish brown hair had more gray than she remembered and there were deeper lines on his weathered face, but there was no mistaking his identity.

Deacon "Deke" Mitchell.

Pure fury blasted through Tessa. How many lives had this man destroyed?

"He's grown a beard." She made a sound of disgust. "Like we wouldn't recognize him."

Ian absently nodded, touching the play button on the remote so they could watch Deke stroll toward the center of the station.

"He's traveling light," Ian murmured, referring to the backpack.

"And he's alone." Tessa frowned as Deke briefly disappeared from view before being picked up by the next camera. "At least so far."

"He's not meeting anyone," Ian said with absolute confidence.

Tessa sent him a startled glance. "How can you be so sure?"

"Look there." Ian tapped the screen where a group of travelers were standing next to the wall swiveling their heads from side to side. "Those people are scanning the crowd, waiting for whoever is picking them up."

"You're right." Tessa returned her attention to the screen,

which revealed Deke walking straight toward an exit. "I think he's heading for the bus terminal."

Without warning, Ian turned toward the keyboard, tapping. "I requested all the video from Union Station, so the bus concourse should be on here."

Tessa arched her brows as Ian easily searched through computer files to discover the video he wanted.

"You're a lot better at this than I am," she said.

"I doubt that CCTV is used much in cold cases."

"Unfortunately, no," she agreed. Most of the crimes she investigated had occurred before video was widely available. Then she wrinkled her nose, recalling video of another sort she'd investigated for Rachel. She'd had nightmares for weeks. "Although we recently had a case that involved old VHS tapes. A serial killer in Pike, Wisconsin."

Ian continued to tap on the keyboard. "Do you like your job?"

"I do," she said without hesitation. There were times she was so homesick she could barely breathe, but she never regretted taking her job in cold cases. "It doesn't have the same adrenaline rush as working patrol. Or even as a detective. But I enjoy the sense of being on the treasure hunt."

He released a startled laugh. "Treasure hunt?"

"That's what it feels like. I'm combing through the past to discover a truth that's been hidden." She knew that she wasn't explaining herself very well. She was a woman of action. She left the talking to others who had the skill. "And if I do my job right, I can bring justice to families who've waited a very long time."

She could see Ian still, as if her words had struck a chord deep inside him. Turning his head, he sent her a smoldering glance.

"I'm glad you haven't lost your passion."

"Excuse me?"

Awareness prickled in the air between them, reminding Tessa of the sizzling pleasure of his touch. Her breath tangled in her throat as she battled back the urgent need to lean down and kiss him. *Not now*, she sternly chastised her renegade desire.

"Your passion for your job," he clarified, then ruined his attempt at innocence with his wicked smile. "And other things."

"Hmm. Maybe you should concentrate on *your* job," she suggested.

"Probably."

Returning his attention to the computer, Ian at last discovered what he'd been searching for. The monitor went black before it flashed back on with a new set of camera angles. Tessa leaned forward, watching the crowd move through the long concourse.

"There he is," she abruptly announced, nodding toward the upper square that revealed Deke impatiently bullyingly his way through the passengers to head into a side gate.

Ian paused the video and enlarged it to read the sign over the opening. "That bus goes directly to Deke's old neighborhood. I can get a warrant to pull the video footage, but I doubt it will be much help."

Tessa pursed her lips, considering the information they'd gained. "We are now certain that Deke didn't drive here. Which means he doesn't have easy transportation. And that he headed into the area where we suspected he would go. That narrows down the possibilities."

Ian nodded in agreement. "He has to be staying somewhere in the old neighborhood."

Tessa reached into her satchel to pull out the list of names she'd discovered earlier that morning.

"I have the identities of his known associates from five years ago, but I don't have their addresses."

"I'll get my partner to track them down when he comes in tomorrow." He took the list and tucked it into the pocket of his jacket. "In the meantime, let's check out the strip clubs."

She chuckled. "How could I resist that invitation?"

He stepped toward her, cupping her chin in his palm as he gazed down at her upturned face.

"I always know how to show a woman a good time."

Delicious heat curled through the pit of her stomach. "I remember."

With a groan, Ian pressed his thumb against her lips. "You're killing me, Tessa Ralston."

"Good."

The word was muttered with a throbbing sincerity. She was on fire with desire for this man. It was only fair that he should do a little suffering of his own.

He gave her braid a gentle tug before he headed out of the office. Tessa quickly caught up with his long strides, as eager as he was to resume their hunt for Deke.

The parking lot was shadowed in the purple glow of dusk as they crossed it toward Ian's SUV. Tessa felt a small twinge of surprise. She hadn't realized how much time had passed. Was it because she was consumed with the case? Or because she was consumed with Ian Sullivan. Probably both.

Disturbed by the thought, Tessa took her place in the passenger seat and pulled on the belt. It was one thing to lust after Ian. What woman wouldn't? He was gorgeous, crazy sexy, and despite his tremendous strength, utterly gentle. Perfection. But the sensations tugging at her heart weren't just about their one night of screaming-hot sex. It was working side by side and sharing dinner at his mother's and . . .

Tessa shook her head, dismissing the powerful images.

Instead, she forced herself to concentrate on the passing buildings. They gradually became more faded and decayed as they entered an area that had seen better days. Then the SUV turned onto a street that glowed with garish flashing lights.

Tessa grimaced at the sight of the women in tight skirts trying to capture the attention of drunken customers stumbling out of the nearby bars and the men who hid in the shadows to pass along drugs.

"Let's try this place first," Tessa said, pointing toward a narrow building with windows that had been blacked out and a canopy over the door. "It's where Kaye used to strip. Deke might look for her there."

Ian pulled to a halt on the corner, turning on his flashers before they exited the SUV with the engine running. Any criminal with hopes of carjacking the expensive vehicle would realize that it belonged to a cop. Or a drug dealer. Either way they would leave it alone.

Ensuring the SUV was tightly locked, Ian moved to stand close to Tessa as they entered the dimly lit bar with a raised dance floor at the back of the cramped room.

They both looked around with a shudder of disgust. The nasty stench of stale beer, cheap perfume, and unwashed bodies hung thick in the air along with an acrid hint of marijuana. Despite the smell, the small tables were crowded with customers who were watching the naked girls gyrate around the poles stuck into the floor.

"I haven't been in this place since I busted the owner four years ago for selling drugs," Ian muttered. "I swear those are the same greasy tables and mustard yellow carpet."

"There's a real possibility it hasn't been cleaned since you were here," Tessa warned.

Ian held out his hands and stepped away from a nearby chair where there'd no doubt been a thousand lap dances.

"Touch nothing."

Tessa snorted. She didn't need his warning as her gaze roamed over the crowd of men who were already craning their necks to look in their direction.

"I don't suppose you could look less like a cop?" she demanded, the words loud enough to be heard over the music that thumped and crackled through the speakers. "You're scaring the pervs."

"Nope. I was born looking like a cop."

"I believe that."

Tessa headed toward the side of the room. Any customer who was carrying illegally or had a warrant posted for their arrest would try to keep a low profile. Well, as low a profile as you could keep in such a public space.

Acutely aware of the glares from the crowd who watched them with blatant suspicion, Tessa resisted the urge to lay her hand on her gun. She didn't want to provoke violence if it could be avoided. Just having Ian at her back was enough to make the men shift uncomfortably in their seats.

They were nearing the counter that ran along the edge of the stage where there were a dozen high stools for an up-close view of the dancers, when a movement out of the corner of her eye caught Tessa's attention. Turning her head, she watched a slender man with dark hair scurry toward a nearby opening. He was wearing a ribbed tank that revealed the serpent tattoo on his arm. Tessa sucked in a sharp breath. She'd seen that tattoo before.

"There." She grabbed Ian's arm, nodding toward the man who was disappearing from view.

"Did you recognize him?"

"Max Stoddard. He was a member of Deke's crew."

A hard smile curved Ian's lips. "We should probably have a word with him."

"There's a door at the end of the hallway that opens into an alley," she warned, recalling chasing a perp through the strip club. She'd assumed she had him cornered only to discover that he'd slipped away.

"I'll go out the front and circle around."

"I'll make sure he doesn't come back this way."

With a sharp nod, Ian turned to jog toward the front door. Once alone, Tessa cautiously entered the hallway. Now she allowed her hand to hover over her weapon. The only light came from a flickering exit sign that cast a weird red glow. It was difficult to make out more than the ghostly outline of doors leading to the bathrooms. If anyone was hiding in the shadows, she wouldn't see them until it was too late.

She was nearing the door when it was abruptly thrust open and her perp darted out of the building.

"Max Stoddard!" she called out loudly, running forward. Cautiously, she paused at the door to glance into the alley before stepping out. She wasn't going to rush into an ambush. Once assured there was no one but the man she was chasing, Tessa stepped out and watched him scurry toward the front of the buildings. "Stop."

Max paused, glancing over his shoulder to make sure she wasn't pointing a gun at him. "You've got the wrong guy, bitch."

"I just want to talk," she said.

"I told you. You got the wrong guy."

She took a step, but he was already back in motion, sprinting forward with surprising speed. "Ian, he's headed your way," she called out, her flare of panic easing when she saw a large form move to block the front of the alley.

There was no way Max was getting past that solid barrier. Convinced they were about to have their first major lead in the effort to track down Deke, Tessa cursed when she caught sight of another form that appeared from a parked car behind Ian. The stranger was just as wide as Ian, but several inches shorter.

She ran forward, her gun in her hand. "Ian, look out."

Ian immediately lunged to the side, but it was too late. The stranger was already swinging a weapon that looked like a tire iron. It hit Ian's skull with a loud crack, and with a low groan he fell to his knees. Tessa ran forward as the man lifted his arm, clearly intending to hit Ian again.

"Police," Tessa shouted, her weapon lifted to take a shot.

The man muttered a curse, throwing the steel rod in her direction. Tessa was forced to duck as the weapon whizzed past her head. She quickly straightened, but Max and the stranger were already jumping in the nearby car and squealing away.

"Shit," she muttered, holstering her gun and rushing to crouch next to Ian. "I'll call for an ambulance."

"No." He slowly turned his head to send her a frown. "I'm fine."

"You were hit on the head." She reached up to touch the back of his skull, easily finding the lump that had already formed. "You're not fine."

"I've had worse."

Tessa had no problem believing that Ian had been thumped on the head. Striker had probably smacked it more than once. But she wasn't going to forget watching as the perp slammed his weapon against Ian's skull. She'd been genuinely terrified that it was a killing blow. Now she needed reassurance that he was going to be fine.

"That's not the point," she insisted. "You could have a concussion."

As if sensing the fear that simmered just below the surface, Ian reached up to grasp her hand, tugging it away from his head to press her fingers against his lips.

"Tessa, I played football from the time I was six years old. I know when I have a concussion," he assured her in firm tones. "I just need to lie down for an hour or so."

"Stubborn." Accepting that he wasn't going to listen to her advice, she held out her hand. "Give me your keys." Trying and failing to hide his grimace of pain, Ian dug into his pocket to pull out his fob, dropping it onto her palm. Tessa wrapped her arm around his waist. "Lean on me."

Together they struggled to their feet, Ian accepting her assistance as he swayed and nearly fell back to his knees. She gave him a moment, bracing him with her body as he regained his balance. She'd never been so thankful that she weight-lifted several mornings a week. Otherwise, she would have been crushed. Instead, she managed to guide him to the waiting SUV. Using the fob to unlock the doors, she made sure that Ian was safely strapped into the passenger seat before she hurried to take her place behind the steering wheel.

Without asking for his preference, Tessa headed to her hotel. She wasn't going to be satisfied unless she could keep a personal watch on the man. At least until she could be sure that he didn't need to go to the hospital.

Ian didn't argue when they parked in front of her room. He even managed to get out of the SUV and walk to the door with a confident stride that helped to ease some of Tessa's concern. Still, his features were tense, as if he was trying to disguise his pain.

Using her key card, she pushed the door open and steered him toward the large bed pushed against the far wall. He cautiously eased onto the edge of the mattress.

"Make yourself comfortable." Tessa moved to the dresser to grab the bucket that was next to the TV. "I'll get some ice."

Leaving the door open in case Ian called out for help,

Tessa hurried to the machine at the end of the building. Within a couple of minutes, she had the ice and was returning to the room. As she entered, she discovered that Ian had moved to stretch out his legs, with his back propped against the headboard.

"You don't happen to have some aspirin?" he asked as she closed and locked the door behind her. She didn't think they'd been followed, but she wasn't going to take any chances.

"I'm a cop," she said wryly. "I always have aspirin."

Tossing aside her satchel, she grabbed a bottle of water out of the tiny fridge and the pain relievers out of her overnight case. Then, handing them to Ian, she went into the bathroom to locate a washcloth to wrap around a handful of ice.

Returning to Ian, she climbed onto the bed to press the icepack against the back of his head.

"Thanks." He heaved a sigh of relief. "Did you see who hit me?"

"Just a glimpse." Anger speared through her at the memory. "It wasn't Deke. He was too big."

"Another partner?"

Tessa nodded. She'd been giving thought to the names she'd pulled up earlier in the day.

"I'm guessing it was Vince Nolan. The police records indicate that Max and he were partners in petty crime long before hooking up with Deke."

Ian frowned, as if trying to place the name. Then he gave up with a grimace. "The question is whether they were waiting there to lure us into a trap, knowing that we're searching for Deke. That seems doubtful considering how many dives and sleazy clubs he was known to frequent. Or if we just happened to stumble across them."

"Either way, you need to call in the attack to the station."

He cautiously swiveled his head, as if wary of sloshing his aching brain around. "Do I have to?"

She arched her brows at his reluctance. "If we can locate them, it might lead us to Deke. Not to mention the fact they need to be in jail for the attempted murder of a cop."

He snorted. "I'm pretty sure it was more panic than attempted murder. Plus I'm not eager for the entire station to know I was taken down by a petty criminal who has at least ten years on me."

Tessa shrugged. "It happens to the best of us."

"You don't know Striker. When he finds out, he'll never let me live it down. But you're right, I need to call it in."

Tessa shifted on the mattress until she was facing Ian, her hand still holding the ice to the back of his head.

"The two of you are close, aren't you?"

"Very close," he instantly agreed. "I don't have any memory of my dad. He died when I was a baby. Striker took on the role of father figure."

Tessa studied his profile. Her brother had been a couple years older than she, but she'd always been the one who felt the need to protect him from the sketchy neighborhoods they lived in as they bounced from one sad apartment to another. He spent his life with his nose stuck in a book, unaware of the dangers that surrounded them. And that's what she loved most about him.

Striker and Ian, however, were remarkably alike. Neither would be willing to accept the authority of the other.

"Did you resent him trying to tell you what to do?"

"Absolutely." His features softened with an affection he made no effort to disguise. "But I never doubted he loved me and wanted me to succeed."

"Did you consider joining the air force?"

"No." The word was emphatic. "My mother honored my

father's memory, but she didn't make it a secret that she wanted us to choose careers outside the military. She was worried about us."

Tessa didn't blame Deanna Sullivan. She'd lost her husband; it would be unbearable to consider sacrificing one of her sons. But Tessa was puzzled how their chosen careers had eased the older woman's mind.

"So you both became cops?"

"Yep." His expression was wry as he no doubt recalled several stern lectures meant to prevent him from joining the police force. "She finally accepted we were never going to be nine-to-five guys." He blinked as Tessa abruptly burst out laughing. "What's so funny?"

"I'm trying to imagine you or Striker sitting behind a desk."

"No shit," he muttered. "Just the time I spend in the office now that I'm a detective gives me hives."

Tessa's gaze lowered to the suit that had managed to survive the attack with only a few stains on the knees.

"You might not like the office, but you do look fine in your suits," she assured him.

His eyes darkened as he reached up to grab the hand holding ice against his head. He gently tugged it down, pulling the washrag out of her hand and tossing it on the floor.

"I look fine out of them, too."

"Yes, you do." Tessa had a vivid memory of each delectable inch of his body. He'd looked like a statue sculpted out of marble with a broad chest and sleek muscles that flexed beneath his smooth skin.

He leaned toward her, his eyes blazing with sudden hunger. "It's been a while. Would you like to make sure nothing has changed?"

Heat swirled through her, a tingle of anticipation inching down her spine. Yes. She very much wanted to strip off that suit and explore every inch of his body. With her hands, her lips . . . and her tongue.

Unfortunately, she was close enough to see the lines of pain that tightened his features.

"I would bet my brother's new house that you haven't changed by so much as an inch," she assured him in dry tones. "But more importantly, when I do get you out of that suit, it's going to be when you're not suffering from a head injury."

He scowled. "I'm fine."

Tessa clicked her tongue. Ian was too stubborn to admit he was in no condition for more than sleeping in her bed. She would have to convince him to be sensible.

"You promised maximum effort, remember?" She reached up to cup his cheek in her hand. "I'm not going to be satisfied until you're one hundred percent."

Turning his head, Ian pressed his lips against her palm. "Why do I feel like fate is deliberately keeping you away from me?"

Her heart forgot how to beat as she was snared by the emerald fire in his eyes. "Fate isn't going to keep us apart. At least not tonight." She leaned forward, pressing her lips lightly against his mouth. Desire spiraled through her, but another, far more dangerous emotion settled in the center of her heart. "I'm going to be right here. I promise."

She indulged in one more kiss before she was reluctantly pulling back. Ian wasn't the only one who was frustrated. The urge to wrap her arms around him and drown in their hunger was nearly irresistible. What she needed was a distraction.

Sliding off the bed, Tessa moved to grab her satchel and pulled out her phone.

"Hey, you just promised to be right here," Ian grumbled.

"I will be," Tessa assured him. "Just as soon as I order a pizza. And you make that call to the station."

"Pizza?" Ian groaned, pressing a hand against his flat stomach. "Oh hell, yes. I'm starving."

CHAPTER 7

Ian woke to find the morning sunlight streaming through the window. Where the hell was he? And how late was it?

It took a minute before the memories flooded back. He'd been with Tessa. Yes, that was right. They'd been chasing a suspect out of a strip club when he'd been hit over the head. After that . . .

He had a vague memory of coming to this hotel and demolishing a large pizza before shedding his jacket and shirt and giving in to the painful need to slip into unconsciousness.

Releasing a deep sigh, he tugged Tessa even closer. He couldn't remember the last time he'd slept so deeply. Or so peacefully. Was it because of the blow he'd taken to the head? After all, it'd hurt like a bitch. No. He hadn't lied when he said he knew when he had a concussion. He'd had a headache, but no permanent damage.

That meant his restful night had to be due to the woman who was currently snuggled in his arms.

Carefully turning onto his side, Ian had every intention of kissing her awake. Instead, his brows snapped together as she twisted her head from side to side.

"No," she whimpered, her hands lifting to press against his chest. "No, no, no."

"Tessa, it's me. Ian." Rolling onto his elbow, Ian pressed his lips against her forehead. "You're safe."

He felt her stiffen as she jerked awake, clearly as confused as he had been to discover someone in her bed. Then she released a shaky sigh and tilted back her head to meet his worried gaze.

"I'm sorry. I was having a bad dream."

"Do you want to talk about it?" he asked, watching her expression tighten at his suggestion. Obviously, she wasn't eager to reveal the terror that haunted her dreams. "It might help," he urged in soft tones.

She hesitated before answering. "I was dreaming about the night that Colt was murdered."

"Not surprising." He brushed a strand of hair from her cheek, studying her pale features. Tessa was always so strong and controlled, it was rare to glimpse the hint of vulnerability beneath the surface. "Hunting down Deke was bound to stir up the memories of that night."

She grimaced. "I've never stopped having nightmares."

"A lethal shooting is a traumatic experience for any cop to endure. Especially a rookie. It would be a miracle if you didn't suffer from PTSD."

Her eyes darkened, as if she was battling back unwelcome emotions, wondering if they could be part post-traumatic stress. "It's not just the shooting."

"Then what?"

"I blame myself for Colt's death."

"It wasn't your fault," Ian said, wincing at the lame words she'd no doubt heard a thousand times over the past five years.

The truth was that he didn't know how to ease her guilt.

As if to drive home his lack of skill, she sent him a wry frown. "That's easy to say, not so easy to believe."

He held her gaze. Maybe if she talked about what had happened, it would help to purge the self-reproach poisoning her soul.

"What happened in that alley, Tessa?"

Her lashes lowered, as if trying to hide the pain in her eyes. But she answered.

"I'd spoken with Kaye earlier in the day. I took her home from the hospital, and I think she was terrified that Deke was going to show up and finish what he'd started. She told me that Deke was responsible for the string of robberies we were investigating in the hopes that I would arrest him."

"Did she tell you where he would be that night?"

"She said that he intended to rob the jewelry store on the same block as the other robberies. It was supposed to be his big score." Her jaw tightened. "I assumed he would go in through the back door, and I was hoping to get there before he showed up so I could catch them committing the actual crime."

Ian frowned. Deke Mitchell had been considered a petty criminal who preferred to rob stores at night so he could avoid direct confrontation. But that didn't mean he wouldn't be dangerously violent when cornered.

"Alone?"

He felt a shiver race through her body. "I called Colt, but he didn't answer his phone. I left a message, telling him what I'd discovered from Kaye."

"But you didn't wait for him to call you back?"

"No. I was too impatient. And Colt . . ." Her words trailed away.

"What about Colt?"

She hesitated. Did she regret exposing her inner pain? Or was she considering her words?

"He was a good cop and he treated me okay, but he was old-fashioned in a lot of ways."

"Because you were a woman."

Ian didn't have to guess what she meant. Colt had been very vocal in his displeasure when he'd discovered he was going to be partnered with a female rookie. And he wasn't the only one in the station who'd been sour at the thought of women in uniform.

"Yes. He claimed he didn't mind girls on the force." Her lips twisted as Ian's brows flicked upward. "His words, not mine," she clarified. "But he wasn't convinced they belonged on patrol."

"Things are changing, but it's slow."

"Beyond slow." Her words revealed that she still ran into discrimination. "And it annoyed me that Colt would leave me behind when he had a meeting with a confidential informant or when he was questioning the local gangs. He thought he was protecting me, but I felt as if he was deliberately hindering my ability to move up the ladder."

"I don't blame you," Ian said. He hadn't faced the obstacles that had been put in Tessa's path, but that didn't make him blind to the internal biases that affected others. "Office politics suck."

"No crap."

"So what happened?" he asked, returning the conversation to the night that her partner was shot.

"I arrived at a time I thought would be early enough to find a good spot to watch for Deke and his crew without being seen." He felt her body tense as she forced herself to dredge up the bad memories. "But when I got there, Colt already had Deke cornered."

"Were you surprised?"

"I was furious," she admitted with blunt honesty. "Looking back, I realize he was just trying to keep me out of danger, but at the time, I thought he was using the evidence I'd gotten to make the collar without me."

Ian brushed his fingers over her cheek, which had flushed as she revealed her reaction to finding Colt trying to take the credit for her hard work.

"What did you do?"

"I went into the alley, determined to be a part of putting Deke into custody." Her features hardened with self-disgust. "Instead, I watched my partner die in front of me."

"You had every right to be there, Tessa," he said in firm tones. "Colt should have taken you with him. It was your intel that located the perp. You deserved to be there for the arrest."

She was shaking her head before he finished speaking. "I shouldn't have been so ambitious."

"Never apologize for being ambitious." His voice was harsh, but the thought that this fabulous cop might have her talents ignored because she happened to be a woman infuriated him. "I don't."

She stilled, as if surprised by his words. Then lifting her lashes to meet his fierce gaze, she allowed a slow smile to curve her lips.

"How are you feeling?" she asked, her hand reaching up to stroke her fingers through his tousled hair. "Any aches or pains?"

Easily distracted, Ian released a low groan. She'd changed into a tiny T-shirt and shorts that emphasized the slender perfection of her body.

"My head is fine," he assured her, skimming his palm down the bare skin of her arm. It felt as soft as satin beneath his touch and hot enough to soak into him with a sensual pleasure. "The rest of me is aching all over."

She turned onto her side, arching her back until she was pressing against his thickening arousal.

"The bed isn't the most comfortable," she murmured.

He gazed down at her, absorbing the strong lines of her face. The wide brow, the bold nose, the dark eyes that shimmered with gold, and the lush lips that he wanted exploring him from head to toe and all the erotic spots in-between.

With a small stab of surprise, he realized that they were as familiar to him as his own. As if he'd memorized them when they'd spent their lone night together.

"The bed isn't causing my aches," he growled, his voice thick with hunger. "You are."

"I don't know how you can blame me." A teasing smile curved those lips that he wanted to kiss with savage urgency. "I've been sound asleep."

"That's true," he agreed, allowing his fingers to slide back up her arm and along the scoop neckline of her T-shirt. "You have the cutest snore."

"Lies." She pretended to be outraged even as she shivered in anticipation. "I don't snore."

"It's not a trucker snore, but—"

She pressed her finger to his lips, an erotic fire burning in the depths of her eyes. "You take that back."

He abruptly rolled forward, trapping her slender body beneath him as he braced his arms against the mattress to keep his considerable weight from squashing her.

"Make me."

He eased his head down, giving her ample opportunity to tell him to stop. She didn't. Instead, she reached up to wrap her arms around his neck. It was all the encouragement he needed. With a low groan he found her lips and kissed her in searing need.

The sweet taste of her hit his tongue, setting off tiny explosions that pulsed through him to the straining length of his erection. It was a taste that had haunted him for five long years. Desire thundered through him, constricting his lungs until he struggled to breathe.

She tangled her fingers in his hair, her mouth parting in silent invitation. But even as his hand moved beneath the T-shirt to cup the gentle swell of her breast, Ian heard the unwelcome buzz of his phone.

He wanted to ignore it. Hell, he wanted to toss the stupid thing out the window and never see it again. Only the realization that Striker didn't know where he was made him pull back with a pained groan. The rumors that he'd been attacked at the strip club were no doubt by now the hot topic at the station. He didn't want his brother to be worried.

Rolling to the side, he grabbed the phone out of the pocket of his jacket, which he'd tossed on the floor.

A glance at the screen made his heart sink. This couldn't be good.

"Damn. It's the station." He connected the call and pressed the phone to his ear. "Sullivan."

Ian's brow furrowed as he listened to his partner. "Seriously? Did she give a name?" Ian hissed, shoving himself into a seated position as he leashed his desire. "Damn. Keep her there. We're on our way."

He ended the call and turned to discover Tessa was sitting upright, her expression concerned.

"What's happening?"

"Livy Maddox showed up at the metro building," he said. "She claims to have information about Deke Mitchell."

"Livy?" She blinked, as if struggling to place the name. Then her eyes widened in shock. "Colt's daughter?"

"Yep."

Despite occasionally seeing the younger woman around the station, Ian didn't know much about Colt's daughter. Nothing beyond the fact that she'd been in college when

Colt had died and that they'd set up a fund in the office so she could complete her education. Something in finance.

"What information?" Tessa demanded.

"She hasn't given a statement yet. I told them to keep her there until we could question her."

Tessa nodded, shoving aside the covers. "I'll hop in the shower first, then I can dry my hair and get ready while you're showering."

Ian made a sound of frustration as his gaze seared over her. He wanted those long, muscular limbs wrapped around him as he plunged deep inside her. He wanted her dark hair spread across the pillow and her mouth parted as she released tiny pants of pleasure.

He wanted . . . everything.

Rounding the foot of the bed, Ian cupped Tessa's bare shoulders in his hands, gazing down at her with blatant yearning.

"We could save time and shower together."

She tilted back her head, regarding him with raised brows. "Do you really think that would save time?"

Ian heaved a resigned sigh. If he got into the shower with this female, it would be hours before he recalled what they were supposed to be doing.

"Definitely not," he muttered, dropping his hands and stepping back. "Next time I'm turning off my damned phone."

Her lips twisted. "If you don't, I will."

Tessa followed Ian through the station to a private office where a woman wearing a white blouse tucked into a black skirt with matching black shoes was seated at a long table. She was short and square with bleached blond hair that had been bluntly chopped at her shoulders. The woman lifted her head to watch them enter the office, and Tessa caught sight of eyes that were somewhere between blue and gray.

A mixture of pain and regret twisted Tessa's stomach into a tight knot. Livy Maddox had always resembled her father, but the resemblance had intensified over the past five years. As if sensing Tessa's distress, Ian took command of the meeting, heading toward the table.

"Livy?"

The woman nodded. "Yes."

"I'm Detective Sullivan." Ian turned to motion Tessa forward. "And this is—"

"Officer Ralston," Livy said, eyeing Tessa with an expression that was impossible to read.

Regaining command of her shaken composure, Tessa crossed the room and slid into a chair across the table from the young woman.

"Hello, Livy. It's good to see you again."

Livy studied her with a steady gaze. It was impossible to know if the younger woman was pleased or angered to see her father's one-time partner.

"I thought you left town."

"I'm just here for a few days."

"Because of Deke Mitchell?" Livy asked.

Tessa and Ian shared a startled glance before he was smoothly moving to take a seat next to Tessa.

"How did you know?" he asked Livy.

"I saw him."

Ian made a choked sound of shock. "When?"

"This morning. I was walking to work and . . ." She halted, forced to clear her throat. "And there he was."

Ian laid his hands flat on the table, leaning forward as he visibly struggled to contain his excitement.

"Where?"

"He was walking down the street." Livy bit her lower

lip, her fingers nervously plucking at the tissue she had wadded in her hand. Had she been crying? "At first, I wasn't sure it was him. He had a scruffy beard and he looked older."

Tessa felt a surge of hope, recalling the image of Deke on the video surveillance they'd gotten from the train station.

"But now you think it was Deke?" she asked Livy.

The woman nodded. "I followed him."

Ian frowned. "That was foolish."

Livy hunched her shoulders, as if afraid she was in trouble. "I had to know if it was him or a figment of my imagination. He's haunted my dreams for so long."

"Understandable," Tessa said in soothing tones. They couldn't afford to have Livy regret coming in to talk to them. "What happened?"

Livy turned toward Tessa, as if relieved to have another woman to talk to. "When I first caught sight of him, I thought he was just aimlessly wandering around. Then I saw him go into an alley." Without warning, Livy reached for the purse she'd left on the chair next to her. A minute later she had pulled out a phone and was sliding it across the table toward Tessa. "This alley."

Tessa grabbed the phone and gazed at the screen. There was a picture of a shadowed passage with a man standing near the back of a building. It could have been any alley in the city, but Tessa's heart clenched as she caught sight of the broken neon beer sign and faded green awning in the background.

"This is where your father was shot," she said in a hushed tone, her mouth dry.

"Yes," Livy agreed.

Lifting her head, Tessa caught sight of the younger woman's pained expression. "Can I send this to my phone?"

Livy shrugged. "If you think it would help."

Tessa tapped the screen and typed in her number to forward the picture before handing the phone back to Livy. Then, opening her satchel, she pulled out her phone and pulled up the image to show it to the impatient man next to her.

"Why would Deke return to the scene of the crime?" Tessa asked, speaking her baffled thoughts out loud.

Livy shivered. "I didn't stay around long enough to find out."

Ian leaned forward. "It looks like he's doing something with the window."

Tessa forced aside her raw emotions. Right now, she was a cop, not a woman who had waited five long years for justice.

Ignoring Deke's smug face, she studied his hands, which looked as if they were sliding something underneath the sill of the window. She frowned, sifting through her memories to recall the various businesses in the area.

"Isn't that the old jewelry store?" she finally asked.

Ian absently nodded. "It closed down not long after you left Denver."

"It's reopening this weekend," Livy told them, swiping her finger over the screen of her phone to pull up a new picture. "I took this when I was leaving. I thought it might be important."

She held out her phone so Tessa could see the picture of the front of the store, which was draped in banners and balloons.

"Grand opening. Saturday morning at ten." Tessa read the words painted on the front window.

"Did you notice anything else?" Ian asked.

"Not really. I was too shocked at seeing that . . . that monster."

Livy abruptly rose to her feet, dropping her phone back into her purse as if she couldn't bear to look at the picture. Tessa didn't blame her. The ruthless criminal had taken away her father.

Both Tessa and Ian stood as well. "Thank you for coming in," Ian said.

Tessa stepped forward. "Livy. I never got the opportunity to say how sorry I am—"

"I have to get to work."

With a jerky movement, Livy was whirling around and heading for the door as if the devil was on her heels. Tessa grimaced, her heart plunging to the tips of her toes.

At Colt's funeral, she'd avoided his wife and daughter. She had no idea whether or not they blamed her for what had happened in the alley, but either way, she didn't want to intrude on their grief.

Now she felt as if she'd just been slapped in the face.

Obviously, she didn't have to wonder any longer. Livy did blame her for her father's death.

"Tessa." A strong arm wrapped around her shoulders as Ian turned her to meet his worried gaze. "We need to concentrate on Deke."

She squeezed her hands into tight balls. She wanted to scream that it wasn't fair. That she had never intended for Colt to die. Instead, she forced herself to take a deep, calming breath.

Ian was right. Nothing could change the past. What was done was done. But she could do something about the future. More specifically, she could do something about Deke's future.

"Right." Clearing the lump from her throat, she pulled

away from Ian's comforting grasp. Time to put on her big-girl panties. "It wasn't an accident Deke was in that alley today."

"Nope," Ian readily agreed, his concern fading as he watched her square her shoulders. "Was he looking for something? Or casing the place for a robbery?"

Tessa leaned toward the table to grab her phone, zooming in on the image of Deke's fingers. "I think he was prepping it," she said. "It looks like he's doing something to the window."

"It does." Ian furrowed his brows. "Deke intended to rob the store five years ago, right?"

Tessa flinched at the question, but she offered a firm nod. "Yes."

"Which means he would have spent time discovering the best way to sneak in and out of the building," Ian pointed out. "And unless they did a complete renovation for the reopening, he would know the exact location of the safe and the best way to bust it open."

"I agree," Tessa said without hesitation. "Deke could never be called a mastermind, but he did manage to pull off several robberies without getting caught. That means he had to have some skill in planning his jobs."

Ian folded his arms over his chest, considering the various possibilities of what they'd learned.

"That would also explain why he's in Denver. If he's familiar with the building and the best way to enter without triggering the security system, it would make sense to return if he heard the jewelry store was reopening."

Tessa wasn't sure how Deke could have learned about the reopening, but it was easy enough to get information off the internet. Or maybe one of his local buddies gave him a heads up.

"And the night before the big weekend extravaganza would be the perfect time to rob the place," she added.

Ian nodded. "The safe will be filled with inventory."

It was an opportunity custom designed for a thief like Deke Mitchell.

"So what's the plan?" she asked. She was a part of this investigation, but Ian was the lead detective.

It would be his decision how to handle the takedown.

Ian smiled. "We set a trap and catch the bastard before he can kill again."

CHAPTER 8

Ian hated stakeouts. He hated the boredom. He hated being trapped in his SUV. He hated the constant chatter from whoever his partner happened to be at the time.

Being with Tessa was certainly an upgrade to his usual stakeouts, Ian wryly acknowledged. They'd had ample opportunity to reveal embarrassing stories from childhood and to discuss their hopes for the future. He'd even discovered that Tessa's favorite color was red, that she hated bananas, and she loved soaking in a bubble bath and reading romance novels.

All fascinating and wonderful information.

But after ten hours of being stuck in the vehicle, his ass was numb and his legs were starting to cramp. Plus his stomach was rumbling for his long-overdue breakfast.

Shifting on his leather seat in an effort to encourage the blood to reach his toes, Ian was thankfully distracted as he watched a car pull into the alley.

"At last," he muttered, grabbing his suit jacket and slipping it on.

Not that he cared what he looked like. He was well aware his hair was tousled and his face roughened by unshaved whiskers. But he wanted to cover the gun he had holstered at his side.

He was opening his door when Tessa reached out to touch his arm. "There's a van following the car."

Ah. Better and better. Deke had obviously brought along his crew of idiots. It would be a perfect opportunity to lock all of them away for a very long time.

Waiting for the van to turn into the alley, Ian climbed out of his SUV and cautiously crossed the street. He wasn't going to ask for backup until he knew for sure that the robbery was going to happen. Too many cops hanging around tended to scare off the bad guys.

He could sense Tessa just inches behind him, her steps as silent as his own. Then, reaching the edge of the alley, Ian peered around the corner to watch the men climb out of the car and van. There were at least six of them, but Ian wasn't worried. One call and he'd have the place surrounded.

Reaching for his phone, Ian was halted as Tessa laid her hand on his arm.

"That's not Deke," Tessa muttered.

Ian frowned, watching as one of the men wearing a hand-tailored suit pulled out a key to unlock the back door. Within a minute they'd all disappeared into the store.

"No. Dammit. They have to be the owners." Ian shook his head in disgust. They'd wasted the entire night watching the alley. There was no way anyone had slipped in and heisted the jewels. "What time is it?"

Tessa glanced at her watch. "A little after seven thirty."

"Too late for a robbery."

"Unless Deke intends to come in and force the owners to hand over the jewels."

Ian had a brief flare of hope before he was shaking his head. "Deke wouldn't have needed to come back to Denver if he intended to use brute force."

Tessa gave a grudging nod. "Something's off." Reaching into her satchel, she pulled out her phone and tapped on the screen. She moved to stand in the opening, holding the phone up to compare the image with reality. "This is the same alley. And that's the window he was standing in front of."

Ian stepped next to her, studying the photo. "Yep."

"Maybe he intends to come tonight . . ." Tessa's words faded as she held the phone closer to her face, as if searching for something. "Wait."

"What's wrong?"

Pressing her fingers against the screen, Tessa spread them to zoom in on Deke. "Look at his shadow."

Ian leaned forward to study the dark outline that was visible against the brick building, then lifted his head to glance toward the jewelry store window. The sun hadn't penetrated the alley, and it wouldn't for several hours.

"You're right. Livy said she was walking to work when she followed Deke into this alley. That means it had to be around this time of morning when she took the picture. There's no way there could be a shadow."

"Plus she would have to be closer than this sidewalk." Still holding up the phone, Tessa moved until she was several feet inside the alleyway. "Here." She turned her head to send Ian a puzzled glance. "So why didn't Deke notice her?"

Ian silently judged the distance between the spot where they were standing and the window of the jewelry store. They were only a few feet away, not to mention the fact it was a narrow space with zero places to hide.

"There's no way he could have missed her."

"That means that Livy must have lied." Tessa sent him a baffled glance. "But why?"

It was a question that was searing through Ian. Not only had Livy wasted nearly twenty-four hours of their time, but she'd managed to make Tessa feel even more guilty for the death of Colt Maddox. He'd seen her pain at the younger woman's rejection.

The knowledge that Livy had been deliberately screwing with them sent jolts of white-hot fury through Ian.

"Let's ask her," he ground out.

"I have her number from forwarding the picture," Tessa offered.

Ian shook his head. He didn't know what was going on with Livy, and until he did, he didn't want to give her the opportunity to vanish.

"I'm not sure we want her to realize we know she lied to us," he said. "Not until we're face-to-face."

Tessa nodded, dropping her phone back into her satchel. "Can you pull up her information?"

Ian arched a brow. "I can tell you anything you want to know about Livy Maddox."

"I want to know why she lied."

"Except that."

With a rueful smile, Ian led Tessa back to the SUV and climbed inside. Once they were settled, he pulled an electronic pad from his glovebox and typed in Livy's name.

A second later, the information scrolled up the screen. "Olivia Maddox Howard. Twenty-six years old. Degree in accounting from University of Denver . . ."

"Wait," Tessa abruptly interrupted. "She's married?"

"Yep." With a tap on the screen, he brought up her marriage certificate. "Three years ago. Her husband is a bank manager, and she has a six-month-old baby."

"She used her maiden name when she came to the station."

Ian tapped the screen again. "And she lives on Murphy Street."

Tessa furrowed her brow. "I don't know where that is."

"At least ten blocks north of here."

"Does she work in the area?"

Ian flipped through the information, easily finding her employment records. "No." He was focused on the address and realization that she would have no reason to be walking by the alley, when his gaze caught sight of the name of her employer. "Damn."

"What is it?"

"She works as a loan officer at the same bank as her husband."

Tessa sucked in a sharp breath. "Do you think . . ."

"She must be working with Deke?" Ian waited for Tessa's small nod. "That's exactly what I'm thinking."

Tessa made a sound of disbelief. "The man killed her father."

Ian agreed it sounded improbable. But there was obviously some reason that Deke had posed at the window while Livy was taking pictures.

"Stranger things have happened."

"True." She shook her head. "But even if she is working with him, why would she come to the station and tell us lies?"

Ian paused, his brain churning through the various possibilities. "And why would she deliberately send us to this location?"

Silence filled the SUV as Ian continued to search for an explanation. None of this made any sense. They hadn't located Deke or traced his previous companions. In truth they didn't have a damned clue where to find him.

Why draw their attention to this place?

He grunted as the answer smacked into him.

"A distraction."

Tessa stared at him in confusion before her lips parted in horror. "The bank," she said and winced at the ruse.

Ian reached down to start the SUV, fierce urgency pounding through him. They'd been led on a wild-goose chase, and he didn't doubt for a second it'd been the work of Deke Mitchell.

The bastard.

"Call the station and let them know what we suspect," he told Tessa. "But warn them to come in quiet. I don't want to spook Deke if he's in there."

Concentrating on traveling through the maze of streets that were thick with rush hour traffic, Ian zigzagged his way north. It was a frustratingly slow pace, but there was no point in risking a collision when they didn't even know if his wild theory was correct.

Once he was a block away, Ian whipped into an empty lot and parked. They both climbed out and after ensuring the SUV was locked, Ian headed toward the nearby sidewalk.

"Where's the bank?" Tessa asked as she hurried to catch up to his long strides.

Ian pointed toward the low, brick building on the corner. "It's a small branch, but there are large windows. We should be able to look in without attracting attention." He grimaced. "I don't want to cause a panic."

She nodded in agreement, pressing close to the brick wall as they neared the huge panes of glass. Ian halted next to her, peering through the window over her head. He could see a narrow lobby with a handful of chairs arranged on the gray carpet and a long counter along the wall. Across the room was another counter. This one had glass partitions that formed cubicles for the tellers.

"Ian," Tessa warned in a soft voice.

Ian turned his attention to the people that were crammed into the lobby. Deke was easy to make out despite the fact that he had his back to them, his arm stretched out with a gun in his hand. Whoever he was pointing the weapon at was out of sight, but Deke was shifting from foot to foot as if he was extremely agitated.

Never a good thing.

Ian craned his neck to get a better view.

"Shit." He easily caught sight of two more men. One was the thin, dark-haired man they'd chased out of the strip club. And the other one was larger with stringy blond hair. Ian was guessing he was the bastard who'd given him the lump on the back of his head. "He's not alone."

He felt Tessa stiffen. "And there's Livy," she rasped, drawing his attention to the young woman who was standing close to Deke.

The woman was turned toward the window, and Ian swallowed a curse, suspecting she'd caught sight of them. But oddly she didn't alert the man next to her. Instead, she tangled her hands together and jerked her head to the side. As if she had a twitch.

"What's she doing?" Tessa demanded in confusion.

Ian ground his teeth together. "I'm guessing she wants us to go to the back of the bank," he said. "Either it's a trap, or there's something she wants us to see."

Tessa studied the men, who were waving around guns as if they were in a video game, not a bank with a half dozen employees. Thankfully it was too early for the bank to be open to customers.

"We can't go through the front. We might as well take a look at the back," she suggested.

Ian nodded, turning to cautiously make their way toward the narrow alley they'd just passed. Livy looked like she'd been crying, but she'd already proven to be a cunning liar.

He was going to assume that this was some sort of trap until he could—

"Careful," Tessa hissed, wrapping her arm around his waist and leaning her head against his shoulder as if they were two lovers strolling down the street.

Ian quickly laid his hand on her back, tilting his head down as if he was whispering in her ear even as he watched a car slowly roll past, the shadowed form inside hunched down as if trying not to be seen.

"At least the getaway driver is smart enough to keep moving," Ian murmured. Most amateurs parked in plain sight of the bank, giving the cops an opportunity to block them in.

Plus this driver was in a position to take off and save himself if things went south.

Once the car had crawled past, Ian ducked into the alley with Tessa close at his side. It was dark and smelly with a line of dumpsters that were used by the nearby businesses.

"Look there." Tessa pointed toward the heavy steel door. "It's open."

She was right. Although it appeared to be closed from a distance, there was an outline of light that revealed it hadn't been properly latched. Was this how the robbers had gotten in?

It seemed probable.

Ian pulled his phone from his pocket and made a quick call to the station. They'd gone from suspecting a bank robbery to witnessing one in progress. He wanted the officers to know they would be facing armed suspects and hoped to get an update on when they would arrive.

"Backup just left the station," he said in a tense voice, shoving his phone back in his pocket. "It's going to be a while."

She appeared frustrated by the wait, but she gave a quick

nod. They both understood it would be safer for everyone if they had extra firepower. But even as he prepared to leave the alley, a loud bang ripped through the air.

Both Ian and Tessa instinctively crouched down, recognizing the sound of a gunshot.

"Damn," Ian muttered. He didn't know what was happening inside, but it was obvious that the bank employees were in danger. "We can't wait."

Tessa nodded, pulling her gun. "I'm ready."

Ian had his own weapon in his hand as he cautiously pulled open the door. He placed his back flat against the back wall and tilted his head to glance inside.

There was a long hallway lined with doorways he assumed were offices. At the end, it opened into the front lobby. Perfect. And even more perfect was the fact that the hall was currently empty.

Silently Ian and Tessa entered the bank, leaving the door open for the backup. Then, holding their weapons in a position that would allow them to get off a quick shot, they crept up the passageway, pausing to peer into each office and ensure they were empty before moving to the front of the building.

Once they reached the end of the hall, they paused. They could hear Deke yelling at someone to open the safe, along with loud sounds of people sobbing in fear. Occasionally one of Deke's crew would shout a warning to the employees, who were no doubt struggling not to panic.

Ian's attention, however, was captured by the sight of the uniformed guard who was lying on the ground with blood pooling around his rotund body and seeping into the gray carpet. The man was less than a foot away from the hallway, and Ian assumed that he'd been in one of the offices and followed the intruders to try to stop them. From Ian's angle it was impossible to see the actual wound, but that much blood loss indicated it would soon be fatal if he didn't receive medical attention. Only the sight of the man's chest moving in shallow breaths revealed he was still clinging to life.

They had to get him out of there. Quickly. Ian's gaze moved to two women who were kneeling underneath the counter, clutching each other as they stared at Ian and Tessa with wide eyes. He was guessing they'd managed to hide when the robbers had first entered but had been too afraid to try to move when the bullets started flying. Probably for the best. One of the women was clearly pregnant and the other one was in her mid-sixties. They would have been easy targets if the gunmen had caught sight of them.

He felt Tessa lean toward him, pressing her lips against his ear as she whispered the words that he was dreading.

"You have to get them out of here."

He turned his head to glare at her. "Tessa."

She pointed toward the wounded guard. They both knew that Ian was one of the rare people who had the strength to carry the man to safety. Along with rescuing the two women.

Muttering a curse, he pressed a hard kiss against her lips. "Don't do anything stupid," he warned. "I have plans for our future."

CHAPTER 9

Tessa watched as Ian crouched low and inched into the lobby to grab the wounded guard by his ankles. Then, trying to cause as little damage as possible, he tugged the unconscious man across the carpet. They couldn't risk attracting attention to themselves. Not if they wanted to rescue the guard and the two women.

Staying low until he was back in the hallway, Ian scooped the man into his arms, his muscles straining as he rose to his feet. Tessa waved toward the women, urging them to follow Ian.

Not surprisingly the two were terrified to leave their hiding space, but while they didn't seem to trust Tessa's gestures, they both crawled forward when Ian simply turned and headed down the hallway. They didn't want the big man with lots of muscles leaving them behind.

Tessa waited for them to disappear before she crept toward the counter where the women had been hidden. She paused to ease her racing heart and slow her breathing. Adrenaline was great when you were being chased by a lion, but it sucked when you were trying to sneak up on an armed bad guy.

Once she was sure that her hands had stopped shaking, she placed her back against the counter and bent her head to avoid it being seen over the top as she crawled forward and peeked around the corner. There were Deke and his two henchmen along with Livy Maddox. There were also two men in suits and three women huddled in the corner. Tessa assumed they were bank employees.

Plus another guard. And like the first one, he was stretched on the floor with a bullet wound in his chest. A glance at his slack face and wide eyes staring blindly at the ceiling, however, revealed he wasn't as fortunate. He wasn't going to survive his wounds.

"Stop shooting people," Livy whispered in a shaky voice, pointing at the guard. "You said no one would get hurt."

Tessa grimaced. She hadn't wanted to believe that Livy was working with the murderous bastard, but obviously Colt's daughter had been fully aware there was going to be a bank robbery.

"The idiot shouldn't have tried to be a hero," Deke said, his tone indicating he didn't give a crap about the dead guard. "Your husband is going to be next if he doesn't get that safe open."

"I told you. It's on a timed lock." Livy heaved a weary sigh, reaching up to push her tousled hair out of her face. She looked as if she hadn't slept in a very long time. "It won't open until eight thirty no matter what Jack does."

Deke scowled. "Why didn't you tell me about this timed lock yesterday?"

"Because I assumed everyone knew how the security systems in banks work."

"Bullshit." Deke pointed his handgun directly in Livy's face. "You're trying to get me caught."

The woman hunched her shoulders, tears in her eyes. "If I wanted to get you caught, I would have told the police what you were planning when you forced me to go there."

Forced? Okay. Maybe Deke was somehow manipulating

Livy into helping him. Why else would she have risked the dangerous man's anger to indicate the back entrance of the building? And why hadn't she alerted him to the fact that the cops had discovered the robbery?

"I want that money." Deke turned to point toward the doorway on the far side of the lobby, where Tessa assumed Livy's husband was standing out of sight. The vault room? Probably. "I'm going to give you to the count of five to get that damned safe open. One. Two. Three. Four . . ."

"No, please," Livy sobbed.

Shit. Deke's face was flushed and his muscles clenched. He was getting ready to do something stupid.

"Police." Surging upright, Tessa pointed her weapon at the center of his chest. "Don't move, Deke Mitchell."

Every head in the room swiveled in her direction. Most appeared relieved that the police had made a sudden appearance. Deke and his buds, on the other hand, were visibly shaken.

Muttering a curse, Deke quickly regained command of his composure, smoothly turning to point the gun in Tessa's direction. It was exactly what she wanted. As long as he was focused on her, the hostages were safe. Unfortunately, the other two robbers continued to wave their weapons around in apparent distress.

"Officer Ralston. I didn't expect to see you," Deke drawled between clenched teeth, sending Livy a sour glare. "Obviously, someone lied when they told me you were going to be otherwise occupied this morning."

Livy licked her lips. "I repeated exactly what you told me to say."

"We spent the night staking out the jewelry store," Tessa hastily assured the jerk. "But when the owners arrived, we knew something was up. A quick background check revealed that Livy and her husband worked at this bank. We decided to check it out."

Deke glanced over her shoulder. "Where is the Neanderthal?"

"Outside." Tessa forced a smile to her stiff lips. "He's directing our backup into place."

Deke's companions instinctively scurried toward the window, peering out at the empty street.

"There's no one here, you idiots. Not yet," Deke snapped, shaking his head in exasperation. "Both of you go into the vault room with the manager. The second it hits eight thirty, I want you loading money into those bags or putting a bullet through his brain. Got it?"

Max nodded. "Got it."

The two men cautiously crept past a scowling Deke before sprinting through the open doorway, as if afraid he might decide to vent his frustration by using them as target practice. Probably a legit fear, Tessa silently acknowledged as the hardened criminal abruptly reached out to grab Livy's arm and jerked her until she was pressed close to his side.

"Don't do anything stupid," he growled.

Tessa studied the man as his gaze nervously darted from side to side. There was a layer of sweat on his forehead and a muscle bunched at the base of his jaw. He pretended he was in charge, but it was clear that he was as uneasy as his partners in crime. Deke Mitchell wasn't a bank robber. He was a petty thief who preferred to slip in and out of an empty store.

She needed to distract him from the fact that a whole bunch of cops were about to arrive and surround the bank.

"Why did you come back to Denver?" she demanded.

Thankfully his attention returned to focus on her. If he lost control, she didn't want him randomly shooting the innocent bystanders.

"Things were getting hot at my current location," he admitted. "I needed some quick cash to disappear for a while." He glanced toward Livy. "Luckily a few months ago, an old friend happened to send me a link to an article about Livy Maddox Howard, the daughter of beloved policeman Colt Maddox, and her promotion to loan officer at the same bank where her husband worked. It was a story that touched my heart."

"You don't have a heart," Tessa ground out in disgust. "You shot a cop in cold blood and then used his daughter to steal money from a bank. What kind of monster does that?"

"In cold blood?" Deke released a harsh laugh. "What the hell are you talking about? That bastard was going to make me vanish."

Tessa blinked. That was an odd thing to say. Was it some sort of street slang she hadn't heard before? Certainly her time in cold cases meant she didn't spend her days with local criminals.

"Vanish? You mean go to jail?"

Livy released a choked sob. "Don't."

"I mean . . ." Deke lifted his free hand to snap his fingers. "Vanish. That's what happened to criminals who were stupid enough to cross Colt Maddox. Joe Brooks. Gabby Samson. Kirk Jacobs."

Tessa frowned. She had a vague memory of seeing a file on Kirk Jacobs. He'd been a local drug dealer who'd disappeared a week or so after she'd started working with Colt. It was assumed that he'd moved to another city, despite the fact his mother had filled out a missing person report. It happened all the time.

"What are you saying?" she demanded.

Deke shook his head, his expression one of genuine disbelief. "You really didn't know, did you? Christ. You call yourself a cop?"

A strange sense of dread curled through the pit of her stomach. As if she sensed that she was about to open Pandora's box.

Of course, that didn't stop her. She'd become a cop because she had to know. No matter what was happening, what was hidden, what secret was being concealed. She had to know. That's why she'd figured out there was no Santa by the age of four, and why she'd been kicked out of the Girl Scouts when she dug up the time capsule that had been buried by the mayor. And why she'd known the second that her boyfriend kissed her best friend when she was a freshman in high school.

"Just spit it out, Deke," she muttered.

"Okay." Deke shrugged. "Colt Maddox was a dirty cop."

Tessa jerked as if she'd taken a blow. "No."

"So blind." Deke smirked in pleasure at her stunned expression. The bastard was enjoying this. "He was worse than dirty. He didn't just take bribes and steal drugs from the local gangs. He was a pimp who worked dozens of girls. He smuggled painkillers, and he ran crews of thieves through every neighborhood he patrolled."

"I don't believe you," Tessa rasped, her mouth dry.

"Just ask on the street," Deke insisted. "They all knew Colt Maddox. And feared him."

"Of course they feared him. He was a good cop," Tessa snapped.

"He was rotten to the core. Why else do you think he rotated through partners so quickly? He didn't want anyone interfering in his business." Without warning, he gave Livy a sharp shake. "Still, if you don't believe me, just ask his lovely daughter. She can tell you all about her daddy's naughty habits."

Tessa didn't have to ask. The pain of her father's betrayal was etched on Livy's face. The only question was whether the younger woman knew about Colt's supposed crimes when he was alive or recently discovered them. Tessa was guessing that Colt's family always knew. You couldn't just come up with random money without people asking questions.

And it would explain why they'd avoided her at the funeral.

With a shake of her head, Tessa shoved away the shocking revelations. Now wasn't the time to worry about her dead partner. Or his sins.

"What happened that night?" she instead demanded.

"Colt was the one to set up the jewelry heist," he told Tessa. "He said he was tired of nickel-and-dime stuff. He had college tuition to pay and a wife who wanted him to retire."

"Then what went wrong?"

"You, Officer Ralston." There was an edge of bitterness in the man's voice. As if he'd been brooding on her for the past five years. The thought was unnerving as hell. "I was all prepared for a big score when Colt called to ask me to get to the alley a couple hours early. I didn't think anything of it. Not until Colt pulled a gun on me." His eyes narrowed. "He said that you had managed to connect me and my crew to the recent robberies. He couldn't allow the possibility that I might get arrested and squeal like the proverbial pig. As far as he was concerned, I was a loose end that needed to be tidied up. With a bullet to my heart. I truly thought I was a goner until you appeared."

Tessa struggled to keep her expression smooth. The last thing she wanted was for him to sense her relief that she'd never told Colt her information had come from Kaye Breckwell. Who knew what he might have done to Kaye?

A shrill beep sliced through the awkward pause, and then

Max . . . or was it Vince—one of the dynamic duo—shouted from inside the vault room.

"It's open!"

"Get the cash," Deke shouted back. "Hurry."

Deke licked his lips, his gaze moving toward the huddled employees. Was he thinking about getting rid of the witnesses?

"Why did you send Livy to the police station?" she sharply demanded.

It took a second, but Deke eventually turned his head to send her a cold smile. "I heard on the street that you were in town looking for me and I liked the thought that you would be wasting your night. A petty bit of revenge. More importantly, I wanted you occupied while I completed this job and got the hell out of town." His gaze flipped down her with blatant disdain. "You have a habit of turning up where you don't belong."

Tessa pursed her lips, glancing toward the pale-faced Livy. "Why would you help him?"

"He showed up when I was coming into work yesterday." Her voice was shaky and fresh tears filled her eyes. She was at the point of snapping. "He said he would kill my baby if I didn't help him."

Tessa made a sound of disgust. "Nice."

Deke jutted out his chin, but before he could respond, Max and Vince were running out of the vault with several large bags that bulged with cash. Or at least that's what she assumed it was.

"We got it," Max muttered. "Let's go."

Tessa tightened her finger on the trigger of her gun as the men dashed out the front door, but she didn't pull it. There were too many bystanders to risk a shoot-out. She would have to trust that the backup was in place and that the robbers would be stopped before they could get out of Denver.

Frustrated with her decision, even though it was the right one, Tessa sucked in a sharp breath when Deke backed toward the door, still holding on to a terrified Livy.

"Release her," Tessa commanded.

Deke continued to drag the struggling woman toward the door. "Not a chance in hell. I don't intend to walk out of here without some insurance."

Tessa grimaced, then reluctantly raised her hands in the air. "Then take me."

"Forget it," Deke ground out. "I don't trust you."

"Please. I swear I won't do anything . . ."

Her words dried on her lips as she watched the terror twist Livy's features. The young woman had reached her breaking point, and the thought of being held as a hostage by the robbers was pushing her into a complete meltdown.

On cue, she jerked against Deke's hold, kicking out and screaming bloody murder.

"Let me go," she shrieked, continuing to kick Deke hard enough to make him curse in pain. "Let me go, you bastard."

Tessa winced. It was a certain way to get shot.

Unable to maintain his hold on Livy, Deke watched her stumble away with red-faced loathing.

"Bitch." He lifted his gun. "I'm going to send you to hell. Say hello to dear Daddy."

Tessa didn't doubt for one second that Deke intended to kill Livy. They were both in a panic and incapable of thinking clearly. She had less than a second to prevent disaster.

Swiftly calculating the distance between her and Livy, who was running toward the vault, Tessa realized she'd never reach her in time. Not to mention the fact that Livy was running straight in front of the other employees.

At least one person was going to die.

There was only one option. Bending her legs, Tessa gathered her strength and catapulted herself forward. She intended to smash into Deke and knock him on his ass. Unfortunately, he managed to jerk backward, avoiding the full blow. She did, however, hit his arm as he pulled the trigger, grabbing the gun when it fired. The bullet that had been intended for Livy lodged in Tessa's shoulder. The best of a bad situation, she wryly concluded as she fell to the ground.

At least this time she wasn't watching her partner die in front of her. And even if Deke managed to escape for now, it wouldn't be long before he was captured.

Pain radiated through her, pulsing like hot circles of fire. Or was it lava? Yes. That's what it felt like. Thick and fiery and unbearable.

Her eyes drifted closed as the blood gushed from the wound. She didn't think she was going to die, but she wasn't going to stay conscious for very long. Giving in to the inevitable, Tessa allowed her eyes to drift shut.

She was on the verge of going under when she felt arms scoop her off the floor and cradle her against a broad chest. Tessa didn't bother to fight the tight grip. In fact, she melted against the hard muscles. She already recognized the rich, pine scent.

"Dammit, Tessa," Ian's voice rumbled in her ear as he pressed a gentle kiss against her cheek. "I told you not to do anything stupid."

CHAPTER 10

It was later than he'd planned when Ian at last arrived at the hospital. First he'd been called into the office at the crack of dawn. And then he'd had to run by his mother's house when she'd called in tears after she'd heard on the news that he'd been in a shoot-out at a local bank. It'd taken nearly an hour to calm her down.

Now it was close to noon as he walked down the long hallway lined with patient rooms. He grimaced at the smell of antiseptic and the squeak of his leather shoes against the polished floor. He always felt awkward in hospitals. Like the proverbial bull in the china closet.

His discomfort was forgotten as he watched the door to Tessa's private room open and a familiar man appear, then walk toward the far end of the hallway. With arched brows, Ian headed into Tessa's room.

It was just twenty-four hours since she'd been shot, but already she looked better. She was still in the hospital bed with her shoulder heavily bandaged beneath the gown, but she was seated upright, and she had more color in her face. Best of all, the scary tubes and doodads that had been attached to her were gone.

"Was that the chief?" he asked as he stepped through the doorway.

Tessa nodded. "It was."

Ian crossed the floor. The room wasn't big. Just enough space for a narrow bed, a built-in sink with a mirror over it, and two leather chairs. But it had an attached bathroom and a beautiful view of the Rocky Mountains out the wide window.

"What did he want?" he asked as he laid down the huge bouquet of flowers he'd brought on the table next to her bed.

"To make sure I didn't leave town without coming by the station to make a full report."

Ian's brows inched higher. He had great respect for the chief, who'd proven to be a tough but fair leader who expected excellence in all his employees. But after earning his promotion, the chief didn't spend his days dealing with individual officers. He was the "big picture" guy.

"He drove down here to tell you he needs a report?"

An unexpected blush touched her cheeks. "He also had an offer."

"What sort of offer?"

"There's an opening in his cold case unit. He wondered if I would be interested."

Ian stared down at her, silently acknowledging that the chief must have been doing some digging into Tessa's track record with the Wisconsin Police Department and been assured she was a top-notch investigator. Add in the fact that she was currently being hailed as a hero by the local papers, and the chief would see the perfect opportunity for some great publicity for his office. Something they were going to need once Colt Maddox's treachery was revealed.

"Are you interested?" He kept his tone light, even as he struggled to breathe.

She paused before a small smile curved her lips. "Perhaps."

Ian lifted his hand to reach beneath his suit jacket and remove a folded piece of paper.

"Then I should probably wait to give this to my supervisor."

"What is it?"

"My resignation."

Her mouth fell open, as if he'd truly managed to shock her. "Resignation? Are you serious?"

Ian shrugged, tossing the paper onto the table. He'd typed it up when he'd been at the office earlier, but when his mother had called in a panic, he hadn't gotten around to turning it in.

"I'm not going to let you walk away again," he assured her, meaning every word. "Wherever you go, I plan to be at your side."

He braced himself for her response. He'd known the moment she returned to Denver that he'd been waiting for her. And that he wasn't going to allow her to escape again. But that didn't mean Tessa felt the same. He was fairly certain that she desired him. He could feel it in the burning heat of her kisses. But did she want an eternity together?

Tessa turned her head, as if deliberately avoiding his gaze. "The thought of leaving Denver isn't as easy as it was the last time."

Hope flared in the center of his heart, but Ian was careful not to leap to conclusions. There were lots of reasons she might not be so eager to leave.

"Because you discovered the truth about Colt?" He asked the most obvious one.

After all, it had been the overwhelming sense of guilt that had driven her away. Now that they knew Colt hadn't been an innocent victim, she could hopefully bury her bad memories.

"In part." She abruptly shuddered. "I'm still trying to process the fact that he'd been working with Deke."

Ian grimaced. That was why he'd gone into the office at an ungodly hour. They were all bracing for what was to come when word got out that Colt Maddox had been a dirty cop. Not only outrage from the public, but every criminal serving time would claim that Colt had framed them or forced them to commit their crime.

"Yeah, that unfortunate revelation is going to cause a shitshow," he said dryly. "I don't even want to consider the fallout."

She turned back to study him with a troubled expression. "You know there was always a part of me that sensed Colt was hiding something. I told myself that his secretive behavior was because of his discomfort at having a woman as a partner. Convinced myself I would eventually earn his trust." She shook her head in disgust. "I didn't want to believe it could be anything else."

"A lot of us missed what was happening. Even cops who worked with Colt for years," Ian pointed out. Tessa had been a rookie. The last thing she would have expected was that her mentor was a lying, thieving scumbag. "Like you said, we don't want to believe one of our own is dirty."

Tessa released a deep sigh before asking the question that had no doubt been preying on her mind for the past twenty-four hours.

"Is there any word on Deke?"

"Not yet."

Tessa muttered a curse. "I can't believe he escaped again."

Ian shrugged. There was a statewide manhunt for Deke and his crew. Ian was confident that the bastard wouldn't slip through the net again.

"It's just a matter of time."

"I hope so." The gold in her dark eyes flared with frustrated fury. "The thought that he's out there with all that money makes me want to punch something really, really hard."

Ian reached out to tuck her hair behind her ear. He understood her outrage. Deke Mitchell had haunted her for far too long. But Ian was eager to concentrate on the future.

"Let's talk about something besides Deke Mitchell."

She sucked in a deep breath, visibly forcing her muscles to relax. Then, settling back into the pillows behind her head, she sent him a teasing glance.

"Like what?"

His fingers moved to skim down the line of her jaw, the feel of her satin-soft skin creating tiny jolts of pleasure.

"You said that the truth about Colt was only part of the reason you weren't eager to leave Denver. What's the other part?"

Her eyes darkened with the awareness that sizzled between them. "I've missed the city. It's always been my home."

His thumb brushed her lower lip. "Just the city?"

She blinked, her expression overly innocent. "What else could I miss?"

Taking care not to bump her shoulder, Ian crawled onto the bed and stretched out beside her. He wasn't trying to start anything. Even if they weren't in a hospital, she was still in some pain and weak from her blood loss, but he wanted to hold her in his arms.

It was the only way he could reassure himself that she was alive and on the road to recovery.

"This," he murmured, gently scooping one arm under her back and pressing a light kiss against the top of her head.

"Ah yes." She turned to snuggle against his chest, her hand lying flat against his stomach. "I would definitely miss this."

"Tessa, it doesn't matter where we are. In Denver or in Wisconsin. I just want to be with you." He stroked his lips down her cheek. "Forever."

"Forever sounds amazing," she whispered.

The soft words hit him like a tidal wave, washing away the grinding fear that she would tell him she wasn't interested in a relationship.

"When I heard that gunshot . . ." A choking lump formed in Ian's throat as the memory of the day before slammed into him. When he'd charged back into the bank to see her lying on the ground with blood pouring from her shoulder and her face as pale as a ghost, he'd been convinced his life was over. How could he go on without Tessa in his world? Then he'd gotten close enough to see that she was still breathing, and he'd made several vows. Both to God and himself.

"Ian." She skimmed her hand up to rest over his rapidly pounding heart.

Ian smiled wryly. He'd done ten-mile hikes up the mountain without sending his pulse into such a crazy pace.

"I promised myself if you survived, I wasn't going to waste one more day before I asked you to be my wife," he forced himself to continue.

He wasn't sure what he expected. And that was the flat-out truth. He didn't know if she would be horrified. Or delighted.

What he wasn't prepared for was having her jerk her head back to glare at him in outrage.

"Ian Sullivan. You are not going to propose to me when I'm in a hospital gown and looking like a hot mess."

He stared down at her in confusion. "You look beautiful to me."

"I haven't even combed my hair."

Tightening his arm around her, Ian pressed his lips against the center of her forehead.

"Just say yes, Tessa," he rasped. "I promise I'll take you out for a romantic dinner at the fanciest restaurant in town as soon as they release you from the hospital." He struggled to think of some other quixotic gesture. "Or have the proposal written in the sky."

Her annoyance faded and her lips twitched as if she realized she was being a little overdramatic.

"Honestly, I don't need a fancy dinner. Or skywriting." She snuggled back against his chest. "Just some time alone with you."

A groan was wrenched from Ian's throat. "Yes, please."

"And some place to live," she added. "If I stay in Denver, then I'll be homeless."

"That's easy to solve," Ian assured her. He'd already started the process of sorting through his finances to ensure that she would have a very nice roof over her head. "I've been meaning to move out of Striker's place. This seems like the perfect time to look for a new home."

"A home," she murmured, a hint of wonderment in her tone.

"*Our* home," he assured her. "With a white picket fence." He stroked his lips over her brow. "And a dog." He nuzzled her temple. "And children—"

She abruptly reached up to press her fingers against his lips. "Let's just start with the house and go from there."

He chuckled, bending his head so he could capture her lips in a soft kiss. "And this."

Her hand cupped his cheek, her lips parting in encouragement. "Definitely this."

RESCUE: HERO STYLE

REBECCA ZANETTI

CHAPTER 1

Shooting tequila wasn't the best way to get over a man . . . but it wasn't the worst, either.

Ella Riverton tipped back her third shot of tequila and coughed as the liquid burned her stomach. Her eyes watered, blurring the entire world.

Her friend, Tara Webber, nudged her from the next bar stool over. "That looks like the good stuff."

Ella scrutinized the bottle behind the bar. "Yeah, it's a Grand Petron." Even though the liquor was sharp, the agave tasted rich. It was odd the Cattle Club had expensive alcohol, but as she examined the bottles lining the glass shelves, she saw it was all high end. "You should have a drink or two."

Tara laughed. "I'm our driver, remember? It's amazing Cami talked you into attending a party. This is the time for *you* to relax and have fun. It's been heartbreaking to see your, well, heart break the last few weeks." She leaned over and tugged Ella into a hug.

Ella smiled and then straightened. "You've been a good friend. I'm sorry I've cried on your shoulder and eaten all your ice cream."

Tara snorted. "My shoulder and freezer are always yours, and you know it."

Tears tried to gather in Ella's eyes, but she was done

mourning her relationship. One day she'd been happy with her fiancé, and then the next morning he'd disappeared, leaving her a goodbye note. She'd moved out of his place now, mostly, but still didn't understand what had happened. He'd had some sort of nightmare the night before leaving, but that couldn't have been it. The guy had even taken a sabbatical from being sheriff in their small town. "You're a good friend."

"Thanks."

Ella studied Tara. She'd worn jeans and a blue sweater along with wedges in a casual combination Ella would never be able to duplicate. With Tara's sandy-blond hair pulled up into a messy ponytail and her brown eyes barely enhanced by mascara, she looked like one of those curvy models who'd perfected the natural look after hours with a makeup artist. But Tara's beauty truly *was* natural. "You get asked out all the time. Why don't you go?"

"I get asked out by single dads who have kids in my classes. It's not a good idea to date them." Tara sipped delicately on her soda. "I had a very good marriage and don't see how to repeat that." Her eyes softened. She'd always seemed happy with Brian, who'd been a rodeo star. He'd died of cancer that they'd fought for three solid years. "I think I'm going to stay single."

Ella leaned over and hugged her again. While Tara looked as if she could grace a Nordstrom magazine, Ella looked like she shopped at a steep discount. She'd worn a hand-sewn blouse and jeans from the secondhand store. Even though she could afford to buy clothing now, old habits died hard. Plus with her plain brown hair and eyes, she'd never look like a model—even though she did have the height. She loved being tall.

Behind her, the party continued with people playing pool, darts, and just hanging out on the leather furniture.

"Hey, Tara," a female voice called. "Come play pool with us."

Both Tara and Ella turned to see Cami standing by the pool table with the twins.

Ella couldn't remember their names, but they were definitely twins, both tall, both dark, but with different scars on their faces. In fact, most of the Cattle Club men had scars. It was curious.

Tara waved at Cami. "At least she's not making out with him anymore. I thought they were going to hit second base."

Ella covered her mouth and tried not to chuckle. "Second base? They were rounding third." It was odd to see Cami loosening up so much. The woman had been in town for four years and hadn't dated a single man, and now she seemed nearly infatuated with Zachary, one of the twins. Maybe she'd found her soul mate. Cami was one of the kindest people Ella had ever met; she deserved happiness. The two had been over on the couch for quite a while, and hopefully Zachary was also falling for Cami.

Tara snorted. "I'll stay here."

Ella nudged her. "No, go play pool. I'm fine." She wasn't missing Caden at all. Nope. Plastering a bright smile on her face, she tried to convince herself of that fact.

Tara slid off the stool. "Fine. I'll play one game of pool, and then we should head on home."

Definitely. This had been a mistake. Ella turned back to her empty shot glass. A boisterous round of darts had started up across the room, and she thought about playing. But right now she was pretty comfortable on the bar stool.

Austin McDay, one of the owners of the Cattle Club and its acres and acres of ranch land, moved down from the other end of the bar and reached for the tequila bottle. "You want another shot?" he asked. The guy was edgily handsome with intriguing gray eyes and a hard-ass body.

"No, thanks. The world is blurry enough. You all throw quite the party."

"We try. It's your first time here, right?" Austin placed the bottle back on the shelf before turning toward her. "You can play pool if you want."

She shook her head. "I'm not in the mood." Once again, she glanced toward the door, not knowing why.

Austin followed her gaze. "I don't know your fiancé well, but he will be coming back, you know."

"He's no longer my fiancé, and I don't care if he returns," she said, not meaning a word of it. She did care and wanted to know where Caden was, needing to know he was okay. But since he'd been gone for six weeks and hadn't bothered to call or text, she shouldn't care. She had to stop caring.

Austin opened the fridge and drew out a bottle of water to nudge toward her. "Hydrate."

She started to reach for the bottle. "Thanks." Then she noted the partial tattoo visible below the dark sleeve that covered his muscled bicep. "You all have the same tattoo, don't you?"

"Yeah," he said softly.

She'd noticed it earlier when one of the Cattle Club guys had taken off his shirt. A snarling wolf wrapped each man's right arm and shoulder. "Why a wolf?"

Austin shrugged. "We had a buddy who was from Wyoming. We called him the Wolf, and he didn't make it home. I guess it fit." His gaze closed.

She frowned. "You know, you don't really seem like a cowboy to me."

Austin grinned. "I'm helping out at the sheriff's office for now, so not just a cowboy here."

"Yeah, but none of you really seem like cowboys. Tell me about the guy who died."

Austin shook his head. "Nah, darlin'. I've told you enough."

She took a sip of the water, noting how he used an endearment to provide distance. "Why are you all here? I mean, you just show up, you buy a bunch of land, you build this clubhouse. Why? There's no doubt you all served at some point. I can tell by the way you move." Her grandfather had been a soldier, as had her uncle, and they'd moved the same way the Cattle Club men did. "So, what's the deal?"

Austin reached for a soda on the counter and tipped it back. "There's no deal. We wanted a new life and we're creating one. We like it here in Redemption, and I figure that we'll all find the right path. I mean, look at Trent and Hallie. They found each other, right?"

"That's true." Hallie had been fleeing danger, and Trent had taken her right in. He was one of the Cattle Club guys and had always been kind to Ella when visiting the bank where she worked. Trent and Hallie's wedding had included the entire town, and it had been a lot of fun. She cocked her head. "What about you, Austin?"

He put down the can. "What about me?"

She grinned. "I don't know. I've been drinking here for three hours, and you haven't made one move." Unlike several of the other men who had come by to ask her to dance, offers she'd quietly and nicely turned down.

His eyes warmed. "Honey, there's no way I'd make a move on you."

"Ouch, that kind of hurt." She snorted and tried not to giggle like a dork. "Why not?"

He sobered. "Two reasons, and the first would be Caden

Scott. You're in love with that man, and anybody with partial eyesight can tell."

"Yeah, but he broke up with me. It's over."

"Oh, honey, I don't think it's over."

If the guy used one more endearment with her, she was going to throw something at him. "What's the second reason, cowboy?"

He sobered, losing the smile completely. "You're not my type."

"Fascinating." She blinked to keep him in focus. "What's your type?"

"Obedient."

She blinked. Was he joking? The guy wasn't smiling. "Seriously?"

"Yep." The guy was the president of the Cattle Club, or whatever it was, and he wore a gun strapped to his thigh, even when he wasn't helping out the local law.

"That's a little, well, unrealistic these days."

"I'm aware," he drawled.

"You could temper your expectations?"

He lifted one powerful shoulder. "Nope. I know who I am and what I want, and I ain't gonna find it around here."

Well, that was kinda sad. She took another sip of the water. "There might be a woman around here who doesn't mind a bossy butthead."

He reached for a rag and wiped down the bar, his grin a quick flash of teeth. "It's not a temporary situation with me, darlin'. Besides, I like being alone."

She studied him awhile longer. "I don't think you do." Yeah, it might be the tequila talking, but she could read people fairly well.

He shook his head. "Life is easier that way, believe me."

Something fell behind her and she turned to see one of the Cattle Club guys, she thought his name was Wyatt, making out with a blonde she didn't recognize. They were definitely rounding third base.

Austin caught her gaze and let out a short whistle.

Wyatt looked up from the sofa with the blonde sprawled over him, grinned, and stood, tossing her over his shoulder. "Sorry," he muttered, heading past the round tables and through the door to the private area with her trying to push his jeans down his butt.

Austin snorted. "Sorry about that. We've been trying to become more family oriented around here, but the guys haven't completely gotten the message." His expression cleared. "In fact, we'd like to plant some flowers around the place to make it seem homey, and you're good at that, right?"

She'd been transplanting native flora to soften her homes for eons. It was free and fun. "Yeah. I'd be happy to help."

"Thanks." Austin shook his head as a half-naked woman walked by. "We need to mellow things out here."

Ella forced a smile, but all of a sudden she felt like an old lady in the middle of a bunch of kids. She wasn't old enough to be an old lady, but this was what falling in love with Caden Scott had brought out in her. She straightened on the stool and nodded toward the tequila. "You know what? I'll take another shot."

The door flew open and a man burst inside, as if brought by the summer storm. Her gut dropped and her heart clenched. It was Caden. He looked at the bottle, he looked at her, and he glowered.

She glowered right back. "Austin, I said I want another shot."

Austin paused in pouring the alcohol and looked from her to the door and then back. "Ah, maybe you should take a break from tequila, just until those earlier shots take effect?"

Caden stalked through the crowd, straight at her.

Her breathing stopped, her lungs seized, and then they completely forgot how to work. "Austin, the shot," she muttered.

Austin dutifully filled her small glass again.

Caden reached her, and his woodsy scent came with him. He was six feet tall with blazing green eyes, a rugged, masculine face, and a body made of steel. "What the hell are you doing at a Cattle Club party?"

She jolted. He was angry? Seriously? "None of your damn business."

His chin lifted and his gaze clung to her face. She couldn't help but study him. He looked good. His color was healthy, and his eyes were mellower than she'd seen them in a long time.

She tried really hard not to notice how sexy he looked in his worn T-shirt and jeans with scuffed motorcycle boots. It was odd she hadn't heard his motorcycle drive up, as she was entuned to that sound. Maybe she was finally getting over him.

Caden leaned in and studied her eyes. "How much have you had to drink?"

She blinked, noting she'd had just enough to make him blurry. "Get lost, Caden."

He reached for her arm. "Come on. I'll take you home."

She jerked back, nearly falling off the stool. "You're not taking me anywhere."

His jaw tightened. "Ella, you are not staying at this party." As if on cue, a lacy blue bra sailed over his head and landed on the sign above the glass shelves holding liquor. The sign was handcrafted and said, "If it can be ridden, we ride it."

Austin snagged the bra off the sign and looked over her head. "Levi," he bellowed. "You have a suite. Take it to your rooms, damn it."

Movement sounded behind Ella, but she didn't turn around.

"Sorry about that," Levi called out, his voice trailing away.

Caden's eyes narrowed in a way that shot butterflies through her abdomen. "You are not staying here."

Fire burst through her until her ears rang. The man had lost the right to give his opinion about her life—or to turn her on. Darn it. "I am staying here, and there's nothing you can do about it."

He reached for her arm again.

Austin moved toward them. "Hey, we'll make sure she gets home, Caden. I can't let you take her."

Caden glared at the man. "The hell I'm not. Stay out of my way."

Austin shook his head. "Listen, man, you let her go. You cut her loose. If she was still yours, I'd be fine with you carrying her out of here and slapping her ass on the way. But she's not yours at the moment. You made sure of it."

Caden's eyes turned a darker green.

Oh, this was going south and quickly. Ella hopped off the stool. "I don't need any of you to make sure I get home."

Right then, Tara appeared at her side and grabbed her purse off the bar. "Looks like we're leaving."

CHAPTER 2

"Can you believe him?" Ella pushed herself along the booth, finally settling somewhere in the middle. The diner seemed to be tilting around her, so she flattened both hands on the worn tabletop. She'd left Caden in her dust at the Cattle Club, and she hadn't looked back. Well, more than twice.

Tara scooted in across from her. "It's not like Caden was acting any different from normal, right? He's always been a mite overprotective with you."

Her heart hurt. She missed that feeling of being safe. Ella reached for the glass of water that was already waiting at the table and drank most of it down. At this time of night, there were only a couple of farmers at the counter, both nursing coffee. The rest of the light blue booths were empty of patrons. "He has no right to act that way now."

"That's true," Tara said loyally. "That is definitely true."

Sandra bustled up and handed over menus. "Hey, I thought you two were going to the Cattle Club party tonight."

Ella looked up, noting that Sandra, for some reason, was tilted to the left. "We did go, and I might've had too much tequila."

"Ah," Sandra said, reaching for a water pitcher off the

counter. "You should probably start hydrating now." She refilled Ella's glass.

Ella tried to focus. "Thank you."

Sandra had moved to town a couple of years ago and purchased the diner, and she was probably the best cook in all of Wyoming. The woman was in her mid-twenties with natural red-blond hair. "I was wondering if folks would come wandering in after the party. They usually want pancakes."

Pancakes didn't sound appealing. "What else is good tonight?" Ella asked.

Sandra shrugged. "I have a steak sandwich that was real popular earlier."

Ella nodded. "I'll take that."

Tara spun the menu around on the table. "What do you have fresh for vegetarians?"

Sandra tucked a notebook in the pocket of her apron, which was tied tightly around her jeans beneath a plain white T-shirt. "Pretty much anything, although I will say that the substitute burger is exceptionally good right now."

Tara laughed. "I take it you need to get rid of a couple."

Sandra nodded. "They're still fresh, but they're only going to last a day or two more. So . . ."

"I'll take one," Tara said, reaching for her water. "And a diet soda, please."

"Coming right up." Sandra peered outside at the darkened night. "Please tell me that Cami didn't stay out at the party."

Ella winced. "She and Zachary seemed to be getting along well." She'd motioned to Cami when they were leaving, and Cami had indicated that she wanted to stay.

Sandra sighed. "He's going to break her heart."

Ella sobered. "I think he's into partying and messing around, and I'm afraid she wants more. Does she?"

Sandra pushed her strawberry-blond hair away from her face. "She really cares for him. It's so weird. She hasn't dated anybody since I met her, and now she's head over heels. That sucks when it happens so quickly."

"I didn't know you two were such good friends," Tara murmured.

Sandra nodded. "Yeah. With her owning part of the coffee shop next door, we collaborate quite a bit. She's smart and always kind. I wish I could help her."

Ella sighed. "Men suck."

"Amen, sister," Sandra said, turning to bustle around the counter and into the kitchen.

"Speaking of men . . ." Tara smoothed her napkin on the table. "Are you going to give Caden another chance? I mean, if he wants one?"

"No," Ella exploded. "He didn't just break up with me— he broke up with me without any explanation or promise to even try to work things out. You can't just continue after something like that." She wouldn't let herself go back after such treatment. She was a smart woman. If a guy hurt you once, he'd do it twice. She wasn't going to let that happen.

Tara sighed. "I don't blame you, but—"

"Nope," Ella said. "Don't tell me he had his reasons. Don't tell me he had his demons. Don't tell me anything. He had me, and he threw me away like I was nothing." She picked apart her paper napkin, feeling like the lost kid from the poor side of town she'd once been. "Besides, he never asked if I wanted to jump into politics with him— which I probably don't." Caden had a dream of becoming the governor of the state, and he'd probably need somebody sophisticated and experienced to help him. She was neither.

Tara winced. "Okay, fair enough. You're right, I won't bring it up again."

Just then something rustled and a man shoved his way into the booth next to Tara. "Well, hello ladies," he said.

Ella blinked several times, trying to focus. "Um, hello?"

The man smiled at her. He appeared to be a few years older than she was and had dark hair, dark brown eyes, and a cleft in his chin. "You don't remember me, do you?"

"No. Sorry, I don't," Ella said. Of course, the world was spinning, so her memories were fuzzy right now.

"That's okay." He held out a hand. "I'm RJ. I was a few years ahead of you in school."

Ella took his hand and shook it. "RJ. Oh yeah, RJ Jones." It had been a while since she'd seen him. She tried to remember anything about him. "You lived with your uncle?" Some of it was coming back.

"Yeah." He released her hand and sat back in the booth. "I came to live with my uncle my junior year because of some problems at home, and I stayed through graduation."

"That's right," Ella said. Hadn't he been suspended from school a couple of times? Either for drinking or smoking or something else? "Where did you go after graduation?"

RJ shrugged. "You know, around." He turned to the side. "We haven't met."

"Oh," Ella said. "I'm sorry. RJ Jones, this is Tara Webber. She grew up in Sheridan but was in the same grade as me."

"Hello," RJ said, holding out a hand.

Tara scooted a little farther away but still shook his hand. "Hi."

Ella's stomach began to lurch. "Uh-oh, too much alcohol."

RJ's brows drew down. "Are you okay?"

"Yeah," she said, reaching for the water and downing the entire glass. "Too much tequila."

RJ's eyebrows lifted. "I see. Well, I'll have to make sure you get home safely tonight." His eyebrows wiggled and his grin widened, showing a crooked front tooth that could be considered charming.

"I've got her," Tara said. "Thanks though."

RJ's eyes softened as he looked at Ella. "You were such a sad little thing in school, and I always hoped your life got better. Please tell me that it did."

She must still look tragic. Ella sighed. She gulped down air and tried to settle her stomach. Her father had taken off with the town librarian at that time, and Ella had been the poor girl from the trailer park whose daddy had run away. Her head started to pound. Tequila was a mistake. Always.

"I should've reached out to you, but I was in high school. I'm sorry about that," RJ murmured.

"No worries." Ella grasped her water glass, trying to sober up. The reminder of her father deserting her mother, of just leaving town and never looking back, was a good one right now. Caden had cut things off with her just as brutally, and it didn't matter that he was back in town again.

RJ smoothly planted a hand on the table and swung around to sit next to Ella, sliding an arm over her shoulders. "I remember when the middle school kids came over to the high school and spent a day in our classes. You were so cute and inquisitive. What do you do now?"

"I work at the bank." It was a job that provided security, and she needed it.

"Very cool. I heard through the grapevine that you and Caden Scott ended up together. Didn't he date Sherri Richardson all through high school?" RJ asked.

Ella nodded. Sherri had been a petite blonde who had looked perfect with Caden. She'd gone to Stanford and lived in Denver now. A mean little voice in Ella's head noted that wealthy and educated Sherri would be a much better governor's wife than a kid from the trailer park ever could. She sighed.

RJ drew her closer.

"You have about two seconds to remove your arm before you lose it," came a calm voice from behind Ella.

She closed her eyes. This was *so* not good. Somehow, the world kept spinning even though she'd stopped looking at it. So she wearily opened her eyes and tried to breathe in through her nose and out of her mouth the way she'd learned in Yoga.

RJ partially turned, nudging her breast with his elbow. "Excuse me?"

Caden moved up to the side of the table. "Unless you don't speak English, you understood my words. Don't make me start counting, because then I'm going to start punching."

Something in Caden's expression must have convinced RJ because the guy let go of her immediately. "Hey, we were just sitting—"

"No," Caden said. "I hadn't heard you were back in town, RJ. How's your uncle?"

RJ grinned. "Uncle Henry is happy to see me as always."

"Huh," Caden said. "I'll have to drive out there tomorrow and check with him."

"Feel free," RJ returned.

Ella's stomach lurched. She gulped, and everybody paused and turned to look at her. Oh man, this was not going to be good. "Move, move, move," she told RJ, trying to shoo him away.

He just frowned.

Caden clapped him on the shoulder and started to pull him out, but it was too late.

Ella turned and heaved wildly, losing all the tequila she'd imbibed as well as the pizza they'd eaten before going to the bar.

RJ bellowed and finally barreled out of the booth, covered in vomit. He slammed into a couple of stools across the aisle, sending them sprawling to the floor with a loud clatter. Frantically, he wiped at the pizza remains on his jeans and then slid through vomit, barely keeping his balance.

One of the burly farmers at the counter leaped up and spun around to stare at them. He settled on his feet and backed away, gagging. Then he turned and puked into the booth behind them, farting at the same time.

Tara took one look at the entire scene and burst out laughing.

Ella ducked her head. Oh man, this was terrible.

Sandra was instantly at her side, pulling her toward the ladies' restroom. "I've got her." She helped Ella inside, where Ella plopped onto one of two chairs in front of a quaint vanity.

Ella groaned. "I can't believe that just happened." She'd had many a fantasy about Caden returning; in them, she always looked both stunning and aloof, happy without him.

Sandra reached into a cabinet and brought out a vanity kit. "Not the first time, my friend." She handed it over. "There's a new toothbrush, makeup, and aspirin in here." She looked Ella over, head to toe. "Somehow, I don't think any got on you. That's fortunate." She moved toward the door. "Come on out and face that man when you're ready. Get it together and keep your head up, Ella." She opened the door, then shut it behind herself.

Ella never wanted to leave that restroom. Even so, she forced herself to stand and then brushed her teeth. Three times. Then she gargled with mouthwash. Two times. A quick look into the bag had her drawing out makeup to fix her face and then a brush to repair her auburn hair.

Then she straightened, took a deep breath, and forced herself back to the diner. Sandra had already cleaned up the mess, and Ella made a mental note to bring her flowers sometime soon.

Tara and RJ were nowhere in sight.

"I told Tara I'd take you home," Caden said, leaning against the back of the nearest booth, his ankles crossed and his gaze seeking. "You okay?"

"Fine." She couldn't believe Tara had left her.

Caden straightened, looming over her. She was a tall woman at nearly five feet nine, and yet he made her feel short. "I haven't even been to my place yet. I told Tara we needed to talk and that you'd text her when you decided to come back to my home. Our home."

In other words, he was a bossy asshat who'd made it clear he'd follow them until he got his way.

Her phone buzzed and she dug it free of her purse. "Hello."

"I'm right outside. If you want to kick him and head out, I'll take us home," Tara said.

Ella grinned. Now that was more like it. "On my way." She slipped the phone back into her purse.

Caden's gaze narrowed. "We need to talk."

"No. I don't talk to jackasses."

His lids half lowered.

Her breath caught, and anticipation rippled beneath her skin. "It's been a long night."

For once, he gave an inch. "Understood. Tomorrow, then?"

"There's nothing to say." She clenched her back teeth. "Obviously there was nothing good between us."

Shockingly fast, he curled both hands around her arms and yanked her to him, his mouth taking hers. Then he kissed her, pulling her even closer. Hot and firm, his mouth took her over, making her head spin. Liquid fire shot through her, zipping down her chest and making her entire body ache. She moaned into his mouth, lost in him.

He released her. "Oh, baby. There's a lot of good between us. I'll talk to you tomorrow." With that, he turned on those tough guy motorcycle boots and prowled out of the diner.

She put trembling fingers to her still tingling mouth. So much for aloof.

CHAPTER 3

The full moon illuminated the well-kept lawn in front of his log home. Caden parked his bike on the gravel driveway and let the silence center him. He'd purchased the property from a retired couple who moved away to chase the sun, but it hadn't become a home until Ella had moved in with him.

Even now, the cheerful flowers in the bright blue pots on his porch next to the new swing were all Ella. In fact, he was surrounded by flowers and plants that she had spent hours tending, and he wasn't sure he'd ever shown her how much he appreciated it. The woman had worked her sweet butt off to make a home for them, and he'd taken her for granted, too caught up in his own shit. In fact, had he ever really asked her if she wanted to go on the campaign trail and enter politics with him?

He needed to take a moment and appreciate life—as well as the people around him. Especially Ella. A lesson he'd learned from a camp in the mountains for ex-soldiers suffering from PTSD. The nightmares sucked but they didn't have to control his life.

Movement caught his eye as a figure crossed around the side of the garage. He swung his leg over the bike and stood upright. "Mac? What are you doing here at this time of night?"

He was the owner of Mac's garage and had been since the Cattle Club guys had moved into town six months ago. Unlike several of the others, he had dark blond hair and glacier blue eyes and looked like one of those Vikings from long ago. Except, once Caden had caught him coming out of his office at the garage after what sounded like a Zoom meeting, and he had black contacts in his eyes. When pressed, he'd said it was a joke.

It hadn't seemed like a joke, but Caden didn't have a different explanation. Mac scanned the area. "Just went for a run and thought I'd keep an eye on your place. Didn't know you were home."

Caden shook his head. "What were you doing behind my garage?"

Mac flashed a quick grin. His tank was sweaty and his running shorts loose. "Harley's back there, and I was trying to see what he was doing. We lost sight of him for a couple days, and I tracked him here where it seems like he's been hanging out on your back porch."

Caden's eyebrows rose. "The wolf is prowling around my house?" Maybe it was a good thing he'd sent Ella away. While Harley seemed domesticated, he was a wild animal and was far too dangerous to be around her.

"Yeah. Don't know why, but he seems intent on staying." The man shuffled his feet. "All right. I brought him something to eat."

Caden bit back a grin but couldn't help a chuckle. "Seriously. You brought a wild wolf something to eat."

Mac's ears turned red. "Shut up. You would've fed him, too."

Caden nodded. "Yeah, I probably would've."

Mac studied him, his gaze knowing. "You all good now?"

Caden stiffened. "I'm better than I was." Just what did Mac know about his trek into PTSD survival camp?

"Good. Talking about the problem is the only way to beat it. I've been there." It was an admission, and coming from one of the Cattle Club men, a big one.

Caden looped his thumbs in his jeans pockets. "You've been there?" The background check he'd run on Mac had shown the guy to have grown up in western Kentucky, attended a mechanics school in Pittsburg that no longer existed, and then wandered around for a few years. There had been no red flags anywhere, and nothing to show either military service or a traumatic event. "Mac?"

Mac began striding back down the driveway. "Glad it was a success. That girl of yours isn't gonna wait forever."

Caden paused. "Girl of mine? We broke up. She's not the forgiving type, and she's definitely not waiting for me." Although he was going to change that somehow.

Mac paused and looked over his shoulder. "I don't care what type she is. If you have a woman like that, you don't let her go. Trust me. I know what I'm talking about." Sorrow and a sizzling anger blazed in his light blue eyes.

Caden shifted his weight. "You wanna talk about it?"

"Fuck, no." With a halfhearted salute, Mac turned and jogged back down the driveway.

"You want a ride back to your place?" Caden called out.

Mac just waved and disappeared around the bend. Apparently, he hadn't been interested in the party going on out at the club.

Caden pushed his shaggy hair out of his face and shook off unease about the mechanic. For now, he had bigger problems. He strode into his log home and flicked on the lights. It was quiet, too quiet. Too quiet and too empty. He tossed his keys onto the kitchen table and just stood in the silence.

All life was gone from the cottage. Ella was gone. There were no flowers, no knickknacks, no scatters of paper from the notes she always left herself. No clipped coupons. He'd told her she didn't need to clip coupons all the time, but she'd been raised to do so and seemed to enjoy it.

It was as if the life had gone out of the home.

He rubbed a thick hand through his hair and dumped his backpack on the floor. Ella wasn't there to tell him to pick it up. Man, he'd really screwed up. He'd been six weeks away from home, and he'd learned a lot. He had worked hard in the PTSD program and the wilderness camp. For the last three nights, he'd slept without nightmares. Oh, he had no doubt he'd have nightmares again, but he was getting a handle on them. Why hadn't he attended the program before he told Ella it was over? It couldn't be over.

He wouldn't let it be over.

A picture of the two of them was still on the bookshelf near the kitchen, and just looking at her smiling at the camera was like being punched in the gut. She had the softest brown eyes and the cutest freckles across her pale skin. Her hair was a dark brown with natural blond highlights, and her smile was both impish and sweet.

He was a moron for letting her go.

Cursing himself, he moved to the fridge and drew out a beer, flipping off the top and taking a deep drink. Then his gaze caught on the little black box near the wine rack. It was like being stabbed in the chest, but he took it because he deserved it.

Slowly, he walked over to the box and flipped it open, seeing his grandmother's ring, the one that had looked perfect on Ella's hand. The happiest day of his life had been when she said yes, and now she had left him the ring in the box. The diamond sparkled at him as if even the stone was angry.

This was his fault.

Then he noticed the folded piece of paper next to the

box. He reached for it and took a deep breath. All right. What was he going to read? He deserved it. Whatever she said in that note, he deserved. Had she told him how much he'd hurt her? Probably. Had she waxed on about what a great life they could have had if he wasn't such an ass? Most likely. He'd earned every word. So he opened it, expecting tears or anger or recriminations.

Only two words stared back at him. There in clear, graceful, beautiful writing were two words: *Bite me*.

Only Ella. He chuckled, feeling better than he had in days. Bite her? Yeah, that could be arranged.

Early morning, sporting a pounding hangover, Ella wearily waved at Tara and used her key to open Caden's door with two empty laundry baskets beneath her arm. She'd packed most of her belongings, but she had forgotten the Christmas decorations stored in the basement. They were hers, and she wanted them back. It had taken her hours upon hours to painstakingly make each one the way she had as a kid since they couldn't afford to buy the glittery ones at the grocery store.

She turned and glanced at the flowers lining the driveway, a pang of sadness hitting her. She'd worked so hard to plant those native flowers, which was something she'd learned to do as a small girl because they were free. The yellow of the false dandelion looked stunning against the purple nodding onions and the blue sticky Gilia. Lately she'd seen Harley, the local wolf, hanging around. Maybe he just liked her garden.

Shaking off bittersweet emotion, she moved inside and shut the door. The place was quiet. No doubt Caden had already gone to the station; he usually liked to be there before six. Since she wouldn't have time to head home and change, she wore a blue suit and tennis shoes for now, since she always kept a pair of heels at the bank. Tara had agreed to pick Ella up in time for her workday. Her car was in the shop right now getting new tires.

She couldn't wait to reclaim her Christmas decorations.

The half-burned lavender candle still remained by their picture. Caden strongly disliked the smell, so she'd only burned it when he wasn't around.

An impish thought struck her. She shouldn't. Shrugging, she grabbed the matches out of the junk drawer and lit the candle. See how he liked that when he returned home. A sound in the other room stopped her dead in the living room. She paused. Was somebody there?

Caden padded out of his bedroom wearing only an un-buttoned pair of jeans. His hair was messy and his eyes mellow. "Hey, I thought you would come back."

"I'm not coming back," she said, taking two steps away, her nerves igniting at the sight of his bare chest. "I just wanted to get my Christmas decorations."

"Ella, you have to listen to me. I nearly choked you when I had that bad dream, and it scared me. A buddy of mine recommended a place to go to deal with PTSD, and I did. I should have talked to you about it first, but I just didn't think I could be helped."

She'd been sleeping blissfully and had barely noticed he'd touched her neck. When she'd mumbled his name, he'd instantly retreated. "You didn't talk to me—that's the point." She took another step away. "I'll come back when you're not here."

One of his eyebrows rose, giving him an arrogant look. "Oh yeah? How did you get here? Your car is at Mac's."

Darn it. Why did he know her every move? She fought

the urge to stamp her foot and instead met his stare directly. "I am so tired of you taking control of everything."

He looked formidable standing there in the morning light. "If I took control of everything, you'd be back here where you belong. The fact remains that you don't have a car, so you can sit your ass down and discuss this with me."

Fire swept through her, the anger finally banishing the pain. Desire was on its heels, and that infuriated her. She had to get out of there before she jumped his hard body. "I'll borrow yours." She claimed her candle, snatched the keys off the counter, and ran past the refrigerator into the garage. She leaped into his sheriff's Jeep, dumped her purse and the candle on the seat, turned the key, and punched the gas.

The Jeep reversed out of the garage, and she whipped it around.

Caden yelled after her and ran out behind her, his feet bare on the gravel. She didn't care. She was so over this. The police Jeep bumped along the country road as she wiped tears off her face. The roar of a motorcycle erupted behind her. She jerked. He was following her? Oh, no way. She grabbed the wheel with both hands and pressed down on the gas pedal as far as it would go.

She took a wide turn by the old oak tree and headed toward the small town of Redemption. The sound of the motorcycle pipes came closer. A quick glance in the rear-view mirror confirmed that Caden was on his bike—still wearing only his jeans and yelling something.

She hunched over the wheel and tried to go even faster. Yeah, this was probably grand theft auto, but if the sheriff wanted to arrest her, he'd have to do it as his last act before he resigned. Then he could run for governor and have a glamorous life without her holding him back.

He caught up to her, pulling up alongside the Jeep and gesturing wildly. She flipped him off and took a sharp right toward town. Trees dotted the fields along the way, and in the distance the mountains of Wyoming rose around them.

A light rain started to drop on the vehicle, and she took satisfaction—that she wouldn't be proud of later—knowing he was getting wet on his bike. She drove between the log archways that marked the main part of town and took another sharp left turn, headed toward the garage to claim her car.

Caden pulled up alongside her again and gestured her to pull over. She ignored him. Then everything happened too fast to track. A massive animal burst across the road, and it took her a second to realize it was Harley.

She slammed on the brakes, her body careening against the steering wheel. Pain cracked through her chest. She whipped the Jeep around, trying to avoid hitting the fire hydrant at the corner of Main and First. She struck it and the Jeep bounced back, sending a geyser of water into the air.

What had just happened?

She looked down at the still lit candle, her mind in shock and her ribs aching. Then, in slow motion, the candle slid off the seat onto a box on the floor. The box instantly ignited.

Fire flashed toward her and spread out, smoke spiraling shockingly fast throughout the vehicle.

Holy crap. She slapped at the flames.

Her door was wrenched open and rough hands yanked her out. She fought Caden, hitting him in the neck as panic and anger consumed her. In one smooth motion, he tossed her over his shoulder and started to run.

At the same time, people poured out of the restaurant on the corner and several businesses down the way. She slapped his legs as he jumped behind the massive cedar tree that stood at the entrance to the town park.

He set her down.

"What?" she snapped.

"Duck." He tackled her and dove to the ground just as an explosion lit up the entire street. They rolled several feet before coming to a stop. Her ears ringing, she slowly turned her head to see the Jeep engulfed in flames with the water from the hydrant pouring onto it. Steam hissed angrily and clouded the air.

Caden shot to his feet and pulled her up, scouting the area. "Is everybody all right?" he yelled.

There were several nods as people backed away from the disaster.

Caden sighed, his chest heaving.

Ella peeked around him to view the destruction. "What in the world?"

He shook his head. "The box on the floor? Those are bottles I confiscated from Chester's still before I left town. The fool nearly started the forest on fire again."

She gasped and wiped dirt off her face. "Those bottles are full of grain alcohol?"

"Yeah." Fury now lit his eyes for the first time that day. Ah, his "mad look."

"What?" she snapped as the fire crackled merrily and the water made steam hiss off the vehicle.

"I should arrest you," he muttered.

She put both hands on her hips. "Oh yeah? I thought you were going to resign."

His glare held as much heat as the fire. "I haven't decided."

She took another step away from him, happy to be wearing tennis shoes for now. "Well then, you'd better go do that, hadn't you?" With that, she turned and marched toward Mac's garage down the street. Caden could deal with his vehicle.

She had to get on with her life.

CHAPTER 4

Her feet were killing her, and she'd only been wearing the shoes for an hour. Ella shifted back and forth on the adorable kitten heels and glared down. Well, they were cute. They were bright yellow, and they complemented her blue suit perfectly. She finished counting the money in her drawer and shut it, looking around the quaint bank. The waiting area was empty as usual.

Cami worked behind her by the drive-through window. There was nobody outside the window, although it was still early in the morning.

As usual, it was just the two of them in the bank. The owner, Mrs. Thomas, acted as bank manager but rarely actually worked. Not that they needed her. Ella sighed.

Cami chuckled.

Ella turned around and crossed her arms. "What's so funny?"

Cami threw pure black hair over one shoulder and rolled her eyes. "You. You're waiting for something interesting to happen, and nothing ever happens in this town." Her eyes lit up. "Well, except for when my best friend blew up the sheriff's car in the middle of town a couple of hours ago. Now that was exciting."

Heat climbed into Ella's face. "You know that was an accident."

"Was it?" Cami asked. "Even so, it will keep everybody talking for at least a couple of weeks. What's your next move?"

Ella shook her head. "I have no next move. Caden and I have broken things off, and that's the end of it." She uncrossed her arms and reached for the candy bowl on the counter, finding one of the mints still in it. She'd eaten most of them already. "He left me when we could've worked on our problems together. That's the end of it." She plopped the mint into her mouth, her gaze catching on her now ringless hand. Man, she missed that ring. She had loved everything it represented, and now it was over.

Cami gave her a sympathetic smile. "I don't believe you two are calling it quits. You were just too strong together."

Ella shook her head. "Nope, it's done. He left me, and now I blew up his car. I pretty much think that's the end of things." The door opened, and she turned to see a stocky man stride into the small waiting area. He looked at the guest chairs and table covered with magazines depicting everything from football to fishing before he sauntered up to the counter.

"Hi." His gaze raked her from head to toe.

"Hello," she said, straightening her shoulders. "Can I help you?"

His smile was a little too quick to arrive. "You can definitely help me."

She wanted to roll her eyes, but she needed this job. "How so?" she asked.

He looked around again, and then his gaze landed on her chest. "I'm new in town, and I'd like to use a local bank. How do I open a checking account?"

She leaned down to reach a low shelf, located a brochure, and slid it across the counter. "We offer three checking accounts, one personal, one business, one kind of a hybrid."

He reached for the brochure, his fingers brushing hers. His hair was stringy and blond beneath a low cowboy hat, his eyes shielded by dark sunglasses, his beard full and bushy, and his muscles bulgy. The shirt he wore was about two sizes too small, as if he wanted to emphasize his strength. "I'm Vince. What's your name, pretty lady?"

She couldn't really think of a reason not to give her name, considering it was a small town and everybody knew everybody anyway. "My name's Ella. Would you like to open a checking account?"

He took the brochure in his beefy hand and shoved it into his back pocket. "I probably will, but I need to check with my business partners first." He looked around the bank again and then focused on her breasts. "Since I'm new in town, I was hoping to make a friend or two. How about I take you to dinner, and then you can show me around?"

Her smile even felt fake. "Thanks, but I'm seeing somebody." Anybody but this guy.

He lost the smile, and his sneer was creepy. "Fine, for now. It was very nice to meet you, Ella." He turned and strutted toward the door.

"What an ass," Cami whispered from behind her.

RJ Jones walked inside and collided with him.

Vince shoved him back. "Watch it, Ricky J. You dipshit." Throwing back his shoulders, he barreled out the door.

RJ's ears turned red. "What a jerk."

Ella nodded. "Right? I don't know what his deal was, but what a creep. I hope he banks somewhere else." Although there really wasn't anywhere else to bank in Redemption,

Wyoming. He would have to drive an hour or two to a bigger town. "Ricky J?"

RJ straightened his green flannel. "I bought some firewood off him yesterday. Guy was at the side of the road. Gave me the nickname and doesn't even know me."

Ella grimaced. "I hope he doesn't come back."

"Don't blame you." RJ tugged the jeans up his thin legs.

"I'm sorry about last night," she murmured, heat flushing up her neck to her face. "So sorry."

RJ chortled, looking boyish. "That's okay. We've all done it. I just wanted to drop by and see if you were okay."

That was kind. "I have a well-deserved headache, but I'll be fine." She could use another aspirin.

"Cool. So, would you like to grab lunch later?"

Oh man. She didn't want to hurt his feelings. "I have plans, and as everyone knows, I just ended an engagement. Or rather, it was ended for me." The last thing she needed was a man right now.

He gulped. "Okay. Friends, then." He winked. "Though I'll keep trying." He turned on well-worn tennis shoes and left the bank.

Cami dusted the counter by the window. "Please tell me you'll go to another party with me tonight. It's supposed to be a blowout at the Cattle Club as a salute to working people everywhere. We need to have more fun. All we do is work."

"All *you* do is work," Ella countered. Cami was buying out the current owner of the local coffee shop and worked there from five in the morning until eight, then worked eight to five at the bank, and finished off her workday five-to-nine at the coffee shop. "You have to be close to buying out Mrs. Silverton."

Cami sighed. "I'm a year away before I'll have enough

money. So take pity on me and come out and have some fun tonight. You have to stop wallowing, Ella."

Ella bit her lip. She really did need to stop wallowing, but it was hard. Caden was the man of her dreams, and they'd been together for almost a year. What was she supposed to do, just go find somebody else? It wasn't possible. There was nobody else like Caden Scott. Plus one night a year at a party like yesterday's was enough. "I'm staying in tonight. Also, I'm worried about you. Zachary is charming and sexy, but you're falling for him. I can see it."

Cami nodded. "I know. It's crazy, but he's so sweet and sexy at the same time. I want to see him again tonight."

"Just be careful, okay?"

"Of course. I'm worried about you, too. Promise you'll stop wallowing over Caden Scott."

Ella forced a smile. There was no end to wallowing over a man like Caden, but she could fake it, couldn't she? Even so, it was going to be a lonely night without him.

Considering she'd stolen and blown up his Jeep earlier, it was highly doubtful he'd want to talk to her again. Tonight would be the first of many lonely nights, she was sure.

CHAPTER 5

Mugginess filled the morning air as clouds tumbled high above in the promise of a heated summer storm. Caden had left Ella alone all of yesterday after the Jeep disaster, hoping to give her time to think things through.

But it had been difficult.

He hadn't slept, so he'd worked on his neglected home until mid-morning, when he couldn't stay away from work any longer. He was grumpy when he strode into the sheriff's office as he'd done a million times before and paused at the front desk. "Good morning, Ethel." The elderly woman had worked the front reception area for as long as anybody could remember.

She grinned, her hair a silvery gray and her lips painted bright blue today. "'Bout time you got home—even though it's mid-morning. You're usually here much earlier. The boys have done a good job, but I missed you. There are blueberry scones in the fridge with your name on them."

His heart warmed. Redemption was his home, and yet, he needed to do more, operate on a bigger scale. But he wasn't going to make any plans until he had Ella back where she belonged, planning her future with him. "You're the best."

"I surely am, and I'm glad you're done being a dumbass. Have you apologized to your girl yet?" Ethel's eyes narrowed behind her bright silver-rimmed eyeglasses.

"I tried, but she wasn't having any of it," he admitted.

"Good." Ethel sniffed. "You should have to earn it."

That was fair. His gut clenched at the thought that he'd hurt her. Even if Ella forgave him, he wasn't going to forgive himself. But he'd make it up to her. Somehow.

Ethel tapped a pencil on her notepad. "Well? Get to work."

He'd strapped his service weapon to his thigh for that very reason. "Yes, ma'am." He strode past the reception desk to the rooms in the back and his office. There he leaned against the door frame, surprised at the sight of Austin McDay behind his desk. "What the hell are you doing here?"

Austin looked up from behind the desk, appearing quite comfortable, even with Caden's pictures and trophies on the side shelf. "I covered for you last month, and the crew figured I should do it again."

Irritation clawed down Caden's spine. "I left several deputies on duty."

"Exactly. They're good, but they're young, and they still need a leader." Austin's gray eyes darkened. "You weren't here."

Guilt cut Caden deep.

Austin held up a hand. "I figured you were off doing something important, so don't feel guilty. You have your head on straight? No more nightmares?"

"How did you know about the nightmares?" He couldn't believe Ella would've confided in one of the co-op members.

"Eavesdropped on Ella while she was shooting tequila,"

Austin admitted. "Plus I've seen the panic in your eyes, and yeah, I've felt like that before."

"Your background check just showed a routine patrolman's job in a small town in . . . what was it?"

"Kentucky. Tiny little town that disappeared when the coal mines closed. Place was incorporated into the county." Austin lifted a shoulder in an "aw shucks" move that didn't fool Caden a bit. "Back to business, Sheriff. We had a burglary last night."

Caden straightened. "What are you talking about?"

Austin nudged a piece of paper across the littered desk. "Cami's café was robbed last night. The back door was easy to jimmy, unfortunately, and the thief got about two thousand dollars that should have been locked up in the bank."

Caden reached for the paper and looked over the police report. "Doesn't Cami live above her coffee shop?"

"Yeah, but she wasn't home. She stayed out at the Cattle Club with Zachary."

Caden studied the man he recognized as a fellow soldier but didn't know or trust. "Have you questioned Zachary?"

Austin's face revealed no expression. "Why would I talk to Zachary?"

Caden held on to his patience. Barely. "Because he might've been keeping her occupied while somebody else robbed her place. Your backgrounds are obviously fake, and I have to ask why."

"They're not fake. Feel free to investigate us all you want." Austin's gray eyes went flat. "Zachary was definitely keeping her occupied, but it wasn't for money. While two thousand might be nice for a petty thief, it doesn't buy enough hay to last us a week, and it's not worth it. In addition, Zachary would never use a woman like that." Austin shoved his black Stetson farther back on his head. "I figured you'd be better at reading people."

Caden could read people just fine, which was why he'd pushed Austin. The Cattle Club members were as close as any military unit he'd ever seen, and this was more proof of their hidden background. He had to figure them out. "Is Cami okay?"

"Yeah. She got to work and discovered the cash gone as well as a bunch of her dishes smashed to bits. It looked like the robbers had a field day breaking china. I took her report, and she was surprisingly calm. In fact, the woman went to work at the bank while we started dusting for prints, but it's unlikely we found any. We did discover a piece of a rubber glove caught in the doorjamb, and I texted Cami that she could start cleaning up around noon."

"What about her partner, Mrs. Silverton?" Caden had always had a soft spot for the elderly woman.

"She's visiting her niece in Dallas. They've been having teenagers cover the shop during the day. So at least Mrs. Silverton is safe, although we have no leads."

Caden shook his head. There weren't any CCTVs in the area. He'd been meaning to talk some of the local shop owners into installing security cameras, but the town was old-fashioned and people didn't want to change the quaint nature of downtown. Plus, nobody had the money to install a decent system. "Do we have deputies canvassing yet?"

"Two deputies are doing so now," Austin said. "The robbery had to have occurred around three in the morning, so I doubt there was anybody around. Sandra's closed down around midnight, and she's usually the last open in town, as you know." Austin pinned him with a gaze. "So are you coming back to be sheriff or—"

"Yeah, and your ass is in my chair," Caden drawled.

Austin stood. "Fair enough. Yet I've opened this case, and I've been deputized. I'd like to stay on this one."

Caden could understand. Plus having Austin close would help him to figure out the co-op men. If they were dangerous, he needed to take them down. Not that it'd be easy. "We can work this one together until we find the robber."

"Great." Austin crossed around the desk. "It'd be nice if we had a lead."

"We might. RJ Jones is back in town, and that guy is all trouble. It's no coincidence the coffee shop was robbed with him in Redemption." His suspicion was based on RJ's high school record, not the fact that the guy had been hitting on Ella the night before. Probably.

Austin strapped his weapon to his thigh. "Who's RJ Jones?"

Caden motioned down the hallway. "I'll tell you all about him on the way out to his uncle's ranch, but I want to check out the scene of the robbery first. For now, I'll have Ethel do a background check on him. I do wonder where RJ has been all these years."

"Sounds promising," Austin said.

Hopefully. Caden needed to find this thief and then get back to figuring out his life.

Somehow.

Ella dumped the bin into the garbage can and shoved her hair out of her face. Rain pattered gleefully against the windows, and the wind blew hard as the summer storm strengthened outside. "What a disaster," she muttered.

Cami, her hair up in a ponytail and dust on her nose, nodded. "I know, right? It was one thing to rob us but something else to break all these mugs. What was the point in smashing the coffee cups?" She stared at the now fairly clean room. "I appreciate your helping me clean up during our lunch hour. This is really nice of you."

Ella shrugged. "Of course I came to help." She'd been stunned when Cami had shown up at the bank to open and related the details of the robbery. "Tara would be here, too, but she had a migraine when I called."

"It's sweet of you," Cami said.

There was plenty of time before they had to reopen the bank after the lunch hour. "I'm so sorry about this, Cami."

Cami looked around at the few chips remaining on the floor. She grabbed a broom and headed toward the shards. "It happens." She quickly swept the remaining pieces to a corner. "Well, it doesn't happen here in Redemption, but it certainly happens other places." Changing the subject, she asked, "What are you going to do about Caden?"

"Nothing," Ella said. The man hadn't called her yesterday or last night, and that was that. "He said it was over, and it is."

Cami nodded. "I get that. I completely understand."

Ella dropped the dust bin to the ground. "I notice you didn't call Zachary after you found out you'd been robbed this morning."

Cami flushed. "Yeah. He made it pretty clear when I was leaving early this morning that there was nothing more than fun between us." Her eyes glimmered for a moment and then she steeled her shoulders. "I don't know what I was thinking. For a moment I let myself dream, you know?"

Ella let out a short chuckle. "Believe me, I totally know. I let myself dream for a solid year and look how well that turned out."

Cami snorted. "We kind of suck."

Ella laughed. "No, we don't. They suck. They're just stupid, and they're missing out."

Cami nodded. "Ah, good point. I should have known

when I left home that I wasn't going to find some white picket fence type of life in the middle of nowhere, but stupidity sometimes takes over."

Ella reached for a rag and started wiping down the counter, which still held traces of fingerprinting dust. "You know, you don't talk much about home or where you came from."

"No," Cami said. "I really don't, and I don't want to. The past is the past, right?"

Ella finished wiping down the counter. "Yep, exactly. You're right. The past is the past."

Just then *her past* walked through the front door in faded jeans with a dark T-shirt stretched across a mouthwateringly wide chest. "What are you two doing here alone?" Caden asked, his green eyes blazing.

Ella tossed the rag into the sink. "We're cleaning up. I assume you've already caught whoever the robber is, Caden. You are Superman, aren't you?"

A muscle ticked in his jaw, but he didn't react otherwise. Austin moved up behind him. Oh great. Now those two were working together. That's all Ella needed.

"I need to go out and speak with RJ. Besides him, have you seen anybody acting suspicious or any strangers around town?" Caden asked.

Ella shook her head.

Cami sneezed. "What about that jerk at the bank? The guy with the hat and full beard who flirted with you?"

Caden visibly stiffened. "What guy?"

Ella paused, having forgotten about him. "His name was Vince, and he inquired about a checking account and was kind of creepy."

Caden watched her the entire time, no expression on his rugged face. "He was wearing a hat?"

She grimaced. "Yes." Great. Here came the lecture. "And also dark sunglasses."

Caden rested his hand on his weapon in a familiar stance. "Ella."

"I know." Their bank, like most banks, had a policy of not allowing hats or sunglasses on patrons. There was a sign by the door, but in ranching country, there were so many cowboy hats that the rule was rarely enforced.

Austin cleared his throat. "Vince didn't give you his last name?"

"No," she said.

"And you didn't see what he was driving or if he was with anybody?" Caden asked.

"Nope," she said. There had been tension between Caden and Austin since the co-op had begun purchasing property all over town, but they worked well together. She had no doubt they'd both disagree with that assessment. "I just met him, and then he was gone." She tilted her head. "Though he ran into RJ, and he called him 'Ricky J.' RJ said they'd only met once."

Caden reached for his phone and quickly texted. "We can look at the bank's CCTV, but it sounds like this guy hid his appearance fairly well. I'll need to speak with RJ." He slipped his phone back into his jeans pocket and stared at Ella in that way he had. It was as if he wanted to say something or ask something, but he wasn't quite sure how to do it.

"What?" she snapped.

"You're coming home with me," he said. "Until we figure out who these robbers are, I'd prefer you stay at my place."

"I don't think so," Ella said. "Your place is no longer my place."

Austin cleared his throat. "I actually think Caden is right. We should probably be—"

"No," Ella said. "The answer is no."

Caden looked around the now clean coffee shop. "All right. How about I just drive you back to work? You and I need to talk."

She glared at him but knew that expression. It was what she'd dubbed his "stubborn and I'm not going to give an inch" face. She might as well get this over with. "I have to be at the bank in thirty minutes, and it's only two blocks away. You can drive me if you insist." It was a decent way to avoid the current summer storm.

His smile made her chest hurt. "Good. I have lemon doughnuts."

Darn it. Those were her favorite.

CHAPTER 6

Caden pulled away from the curb with Ella safely ensconced in the passenger side, happily munching on a lemon-filled doughnut.

"How are you feeling?" he asked. Last time she drank hard liquor, she'd had a hangover for three days.

"Much better," she mumbled around a big piece. "I knew not to drink tequila the other night, but oh well."

He deliberately drove away from the bank toward the other side of the park. She didn't complain because she was occupied with the doughnut. He cleared his throat. "Listen, Ella."

"Nope," she said around another mouthful of the lemon-filled delight. "I don't need to listen. There's nothing to say. We're good. It's over. Move on, Caden."

He'd always liked her stubborn side, but right now he couldn't remember why. "Let me explain."

"Nope."

He pulled into the gravel lot on the far side of the town park and cut the engine. The rain beat against the metal truck, tinging off the wide windows. "We're going to sit here until you listen."

She sighed, licking her fingers. "All right. Fine. Say what

you have to say, and then I need to go to work. The lunch hour is almost over."

Yeah, he really was not appreciating her stubborn side at the moment. "I was wrong to break up with you, and I'm sorry," he said, quite reasonably if asked.

She turned to him and smiled, her pink lips curving. "Okay."

He paused. "Okay? That's it?" Man, he hadn't thought it would be so easy. He'd forgotten once again what a sweetheart she could be.

"Yeah," she said. "You're forgiven. Now will you take me to work?"

Warning ticked at the base of his skull. "Hold on a second. So is everything okay?"

"Yeah." She eyed another doughnut in the container between them. "Everything's great."

His heart sank. "Ella."

She reached for another doughnut. "What? You apologized. I accepted your apology. We're good. Now I really do need to get to work."

"I know you're mad."

"Nope. Not mad." She took another bite. "I'm not mad at all. I was angry for about a week, and then I was sad for three weeks. Then I was fine. I'm fantastic now. Caden, it's good. We're good. We'll always be friends." Her tone was light, but her eyes had always given her away. She was furious. Man was she pissed, and she had every right to be.

"Darlin'?" He held on to his temper with both hands. "You've never taken me seriously, and I never quite understood why."

Her pretty brown eyes widened. "What are you talking about? I've always taken you seriously."

"No, you really haven't. I told you I had nightmares. I

told you I had PTSD, and I told you that you might not be safe with me. You blew it all off."

She blinked and then settled back in the cab. "I guess that's true. I'm sorry about that."

That was another thing about Ella. She always told the truth. He liked that about her. He liked that she also could admit if she was wrong, once in a while. This time it didn't seem to be working for him, however. So he paused, not sure how to go on.

She drew her light, knitted cardigan closer around her curvy body. "I know what you're talking about. The night before you left, you had a nightmare—you didn't know where you were. You're right. I wasn't afraid because honestly, Caden, I don't think you'd ever hurt me. Even when you grabbed my neck before you woke up, I wasn't really scared."

That was the problem. She should have been terrified if he woke up and was out of control. He needed her to at least know that she was in danger and to act appropriately. She should have stabbed him, for Pete's sake.

"Listen, you have to protect yourself."

"I am!" she exploded. "Why do you think we're not getting back together?"

He sat back, taking the punch to the gut. "I hadn't realized you thought I'd physically hurt you."

"I don't, you moron." She shook her head. Her curly hair escaped the clip that had been trying to contain it and fell around her shoulders, framing her pretty face. "I'm not afraid of you on any physical level. I know that you're trained and you're scary, and sometimes you have nightmares. I still don't think you'd hurt me. You didn't hurt me that night. I talked to you, and you immediately let go. Then you woke up and apparently freaked out all night instead of talking to me." She shoved the rest of the doughnut back into the bag.

"Okay, that's fair. I should have talked to you instead of breaking up right away, but honestly I just reacted." He hadn't been in his right mind.

She crossed her arms. "If you reacted that way once, you'll react that way again. I learned my lesson there."

He paused as the truck cab steamed up until the windows fogged over. Rain continued to punish the outside of the vehicle. "What do you mean?"

She looked down at her hands. "I know we've talked about when my dad left my mom, but I never told you that it wasn't the first time."

Caden sat back and tried not to grimace. This so wasn't good. "It wasn't?"

"No, he left her at least three or four times for different women. He'd always come back, and she'd always forgive him, and then she'd believe he wouldn't leave again." Ella swallowed and her face paled. "Every time he found some-body new and left again. In fact, you know what? I think if he showed up again today, she'd probably take him back, and it's been more than ten years." Disgust and sadness settled onto her expression.

Caden set one hand on the steering wheel. "Honey, I'm sorry about that. I really am, but I'm not your father."

She shrugged. "You ended things just like he always did."

It was like a kick to the groin. "Okay. You're right, but I was wrong, and it won't happen again." Even as he said the words, he heard how they must sound. Damn it. There was no way around this.

She looked at him, her gaze earnest. "I'm really glad that you seem to be better."

"I am," he said. "It was six weeks of wilderness and sur-vival training with a hard kick of PTSD therapy." He'd made good friends in the program and planned to keep in touch with them. "I think I can handle it, Ella. I wasn't doing so before, but I can do it now."

She reached out and patted his thigh. "I'm glad. I really am."

Those weren't the words he wanted to hear, nowhere near. "What can I do for you to give us another chance?"

She looked him directly in the eyes this time. The woman was so pretty his heart hurt. "Nothing. It's over."

He clenched his jaw. Not once in his life had he given up on anybody or anything. He didn't know how. Her eyes widened as if she caught his expression.

He smiled. "While I normally like your stubborn side, I think at the moment, you're just trying to teach me a lesson. I deserve that lesson, but how long are you going to hold out like this?"

Fire lit her face, and a bright pink washed over her high cheekbones. "Aren't you the arrogant ass?" she sputtered. "When I said it's over, it's over." Yet those pretty eyes couldn't lie. She looked as sad as he felt.

His patience was quickly thinning. "You know we belong together. I'll do whatever you want. If you want to stay here in Redemption, I'll stay here and be the sheriff. If you want to go on the campaign trail with me, I'd really like to run for governor, but only if you're all in. It's up to you."

She gulped. "You never asked what I wanted before."

"I was a jerk and just assumed you wanted what I did. What *do* you want?"

Hope glimmered in her eyes, and she quickly banked it. "Nothing."

Heat rushed through him. He could give her more time. "Regardless, I'm not letting you out of my sight until we figure out who robbed the coffee shop." Something in his gut told him it wasn't over. That it was the first crime of the week, and there would be more. He wouldn't let anything happen to her, whether she liked it or not.

Her delicate chin firmed. "I don't want or need your help."

That was it. Just plain and simply it. "Too damn bad."

The skies opened up with a furious rain as thunder rolled across the sky in a spectacular summer storm. Caden craned his neck to look out of the front window of Austin's truck after he'd dropped Ella at the bank, leaving his own truck right outside. "We're going to have some downed fences around the county."

Austin nodded. "Yeah. I already have my partners out, looking for problems." He flipped on the windshield wipers. "Although now they're going to have to wait an hour or two, aren't they?"

"Definitely," Caden said as they finally rolled to a stop in front of old man Jones's farmhouse. The guy had been a widower for more than fifty years, and the place looked like it. It was sturdy and livable but not exactly pretty or decorated.

Austin looked around. "We're going to need a painting party, aren't we?"

"Yeah," Caden muttered. He hadn't been out in too long; he should have checked on the old guy. Jones's ranch house had a wraparound porch, and the white paint was peeling everywhere. Two of the steps leading up to the porch needed repair, and a quick look at the nearest barn showed similar problems. "We're going to want more than a painting party," he said.

"I'll get the group together and see what we can do next week."

That's one thing Caden liked about the Cattle Club men:

they didn't hesitate to chip in if someone needed help. "You know, I ran background checks on all of you again."

"No kidding," Austin drawled. "I assume they came up the same as before?"

"Yeah," Caden drawled back. "That doesn't mean they're complete."

Austin shrugged. "Hey, keep looking, buddy. What you see is what you get."

Caden didn't have time to argue, so he jumped out of the truck and strode over the muddy ground and up the porch to knock on the door.

Henry Jones opened it, dressed in a flannel shirt, jeans, and mud-covered boots. "Hey, Caden," he said. "Come on in." He clasped Caden's hand in a firm handshake and tugged him into the interior of the ranch house. Jones was a barrel of a man with only slightly stooped posture, thick gray hair, and the bowlegs that came from an ancestry more comfortable on a horse than off one. Brown marks dotted his weathered skin from years spent in the sun.

Caden followed, noting that although the furniture was worn, the place was clean, as it always had been. He figured that even if old man Jones could afford new things, he wouldn't want to waste money on anything but feed for his cattle. "You know Austin McDay, right?"

"Sure," Henry said, shaking Austin's hand and also pulling him inside the quiet home. "What are you two doing out here during a storm like this?"

Caden kept his stance casual. "We were hoping to talk to RJ."

Henry sighed. "Yeah, RJ is back. He's trying to get his life on track again. Apparently, he was dating some woman and she dumped him up in Colorado, and now he's just trying to figure out what to do next." Henry shook his head and then ruffled his thick gray hair. "You know, he's a decent kid. He's just never quite found his path."

Caden kept his thoughts to himself. RJ was an ass and always had been. "We want to talk to him about a robbery that occurred in town last night."

Henry's eyes widened. "RJ didn't have anything to do with it. He was here all night." He pointed to the couch and a series of beer bottles on the table next to it. "We watched old movies well into the morning. It was like having the nice kid back before he got into trouble."

Austin tucked his thumbs in his jeans pockets. "You're saying RJ was here all night?"

"Yeah, he really was. Honestly, we got about an hour of shut-eye before I went out to feed the cattle this morning." Henry lifted his head and bellowed. "Hey, RJ. Get out here."

Movement sounded from down the hallway, and then RJ emerged from a bedroom with his dark hair tousled and his jeans lying low on his skinny hips. "I was just takin' a nap after lunch," he mumbled, zipping his pants.

Henry rolled his eyes. "We live on a ranch. There are no naps here unless you get thrown by a horse first."

RJ yawned widely and scratched his thin chest. An unruly trail of hair ran from the center of his torso, across his navel, and down into his pants with several R shapes shaved along the way. His gaze caught on Caden and Austin. "What's the law doing here this time of day?"

Caden cocked his head. "Your uncle told us that you were here with him all last night."

RJ snorted. "Of course, I was here all night. Last time I asked a chick out, she puked all over me."

Irritation clawed through Caden, but he hid it. "So you stayed in last night?"

"Yep, I watched old movies with my uncle. Why?" RJ jutted his chin out.

Man, Caden would like to take a punch at that chin, but it'd probably shatter and then Austin would have to arrest him. "Do you know a man named Vince? Ella said he recognized you at the bank."

RJ scratched a pimple on his chin. "The guy I bought firewood from? I think his name was Vince. He was selling cut logs by the side of the road, and I introduced myself before buying some. Guy was an ass."

Caden's gaze narrowed. "What do you know about the Espresso Oasis being burglarized?"

"Nothin'." RJ rolled his neck and a vertebra popped. "Do you think this Vince jerk robbed the café?"

"Not sure," Caden said. "But whoever did it will be caught."

RJ wiped his nose with a bare arm. "I'm sure you're up to it, Sheriff."

What a weasel.

Henry gestured to the door. "You boys have asked your questions, and now we have to get back to work."

Caden gave RJ a look. "Keep in touch."

"You too, Sheriff," RJ drawled. "Though you can't go around harassing everybody who flirts with Ella. She's a pretty girl, and rumor has it you cut her loose. That's on you."

Yeah. It was.

CHAPTER 7

The afternoon was surprisingly busy at the bank with everyone coming in and asking questions about the coffee shop robbery. Mrs. Thomas even stopped in, pretended to go through receipts, and then headed out for her bridge club.

After several hours, the crowd finally dispersed. When the outside door opened again, Ella looked up and smiled as a slender man with dark hair hustled toward her. "Can I help you?" she asked.

"Yeah," he said, tugging out a worn leather wallet from his back pocket. "My name is Max Lewiskowski, and my wife and I just moved about twenty miles from here. We bought the old Ramses property."

Ella smiled. "Oh, that's right. I forgot that was for sale. I didn't know somebody had purchased it."

He nodded. "Yeah, we've always wanted a farm. The property came up for sale and we thought, what the heck?" He shifted to the side, showing a serpent-like tattoo winding up his arm into his black tank top. He brushed rain off his flat stomach. "Do the storms always come on this quick out here?"

She nodded. "Yeah. It's rare to have a summer storm, but when we have one, it's dramatic."

Max laughed and brushed back his wet hair with his other arm, which had a tattoo of a skull and crossbones. He caught her gaze and looked down at his bicep. "I had a wild youth before I got married." Then he chuckled. "Jenny convinced me to grow up and here I am. We're expecting our first child in just a month."

Ella's heart warmed. "That's really sweet. Welcome to Redemption."

"Thanks. You know, I was looking around, and it seems like this is the only bank anywhere near our property."

"That's true. We pretty much service the town of Redemption and all of the outlying county," she said. "We're a full-service bank, and we are, of course, insured by the FDIC."

Max pulled out his license and pushed it over the counter. "Great. I'd like to open a checking account and a savings account. I'd also like to get a safe-deposit box, if possible. It'd be nice to get it all done today."

"Sure," Ella said, reaching below the counter for the necessary forms. "We'll fill this out and get you taken care of."

He rocked back on his heels and stuck one hand in his dark jeans. "That's fantastic. Thanks. Back in the city, it would've taken a week to get all of this done."

She chuckled. "There's not a lot going on in Redemption at this time of day. Let's see what we can do."

It took nearly an hour, but Ella finally straightened Max out and even took him to his safe-deposit box. "Our vault is an older Mosler with a time lock." She legally had to tell him that the walk-in vault was old. "The pivot bearings are bronze and the gear train is comprised of five gears."

"I assume it's pretty safe here in Redemption," Max mused.

"True. This vault is an automatic locker on a timer." She took him to his new safe-deposit box.

He checked it out and then nodded. "I think that's the right size. We just want to put some of my wife's jewelry in there to keep it safe. Thank you, Ella." He turned and walked out of the vault.

She followed him, making a mental note to dust inside the vault again.

He turned away. "Thanks again. I'll bring Jenny into town next week so she can start meeting people."

Ella noted that the late afternoon had turned bright outside as the sun began to beat down and dry the sidewalk. The storm had passed finally. "That'd be great. I'd love to meet her."

Max gave a quick salute and walked out into the now sunny afternoon.

"He was an interesting man," Cami said.

Ella filed the papers in a large metal filing cabinet near the wall. "I'm curious about his wife. She sounds like a nice person." In fact, Max had spent most of his time in the bank talking about her. "He seems like a guy in love." She'd had that once, but it was gone.

Outside the window, Max started walking toward a blue Ford Fusion truck and then paused. His shoulders went back, and his stance changed. Ella craned her neck to see what was happening. As she watched, another man approached from down the sidewalk. The other guy was taller and bigger with streaks of gray in his reddish brown hair. He wore an old gray flannel and dark jeans, and he had a full beard. The two seemed to argue about something, and then Max poked the other man in the chest, his face drawn in harsh lines. The other guy finally nodded and then turned and disappeared back up the sidewalk.

Cami stood next to Ella. "What do you think that was about?"

Ella shook her head. "I have no idea." Then she spotted

the truck across the street. Caden was no longer in it, but he'd left his rig right where she could see it, as if wanting her to know that he wasn't going anywhere.

Oh, they'd see about that.

After a full day of unsuccessful investigation regarding the robbery, Caden stopped his motorcycle in the horseshoe area of the Cattle Club driveway, noting once again the perfect symmetry of the three buildings. The views between them led out to open fields with mountains behind them, and yet, the placement of the buildings created a fortress that strategically protected the main clubhouse. In fact, now that he looked closer, there were ideal sniper positions not only on top of the three roofs but also in the surrounding trees. He couldn't have designed a defensive facility any better.

The breeze picked up and he paused a minute as more clouds rolled across the summer sky. Though the late afternoon had been sunny, another storm was moving in, and he probably shouldn't have left his truck at home. He'd switched out the truck for the motorcycle a little while ago.

After visiting Henry's farm, he and Austin had gone their separate ways. Caden had waited to come here until now, hoping to interview Zachary without Austin around.

The door to the main clubhouse opened, and two men walked out. It was Zeke and Zachary Snowden. As usual, the twins were together, which he had expected. What he hadn't expected was the quick sound of a foreign language being spoken between the two.

They saw him and stopped. What the heck was that language? He didn't recognize it. He studied the two, noticing how strategically they moved, as graceful as any soldier he'd ever seen. But they weren't soldiers, were they? Not according to their background checks. Yet something told him, once again, he didn't have the full story.

Zachary caught sight of him first and stepped forward. He was tall with light brown eyes and dark hair. His rugged face normally showed a good-natured expression, even though an old scar ran from behind his right ear and down his neck to disappear in his shirt. "Hey, Caden, what's up?"

Caden cocked his head and turned his attention to the other brother. "Zeke, what kind of language were you two just speaking?"

Zeke shrugged, his eyes not twinkling and his stance slightly more defensive than his brother's. He also had scars on his face, but these two showed deep slashes across his right temple. "Oh, you know, twin speak. It's a language we made up years ago."

Zachary kicked dirt off his cowboy boots. "What can we do for you, Sheriff?"

Caden looked around at the various defensive points in the compound. "You know, I never asked you guys, who designed this place?"

Zachary shrugged. "I can't remember. I think we did it all together. We wanted a clubhouse, and we needed buildings to hold the vehicles we all hoped to have. Now they're full and we probably require another building."

It would be interesting to see where they placed a new building. Caden would bet his left arm it would be over to the east and slightly up the hill where it could cover the entire property. He turned his attention to Zachary. "I heard you were with Cami the other night."

Zachary cocked his head. "Did you now?"

"Yeah," Caden said softly. "Her place was robbed, and I just need to double-check that she was here."

Zeke remained silent.

Zachary's stance remained relaxed. "I already spoke

with Austin about it. Camila was here all night, and I don't know anything about who would rob her." He lost the good-old-boy expression he usually wore. "I'll find out who tried to hurt her, don't worry."

Caden rocked back on his heels. "Are you making a claim?"

Zachary flashed a good-natured grin. "Nope. No claim here, but the woman was with me when somebody tore her store apart, so I will find out who it was."

The hair on the back of Caden's neck rose. "I can handle it." Movement to the side of the building caught his eye, and he turned to see the massive wolf walk around the side and flop down to watch them.

Zachary followed his gaze. "Harley has been missing lately. I heard he was around your place quite a bit."

"I don't know. I just got home," Caden mused.

Zeke watched the animal. "He's been following Ella. I saw him outside of the bank a couple times last week."

Well, that was interesting. Caden hadn't heard about the wolf. "Not for nothing, and I know I'm definitely not somebody to give romantic advice, but if you're going to go after whoever tried to hurt Cami, you'd better be making a claim. Otherwise, you're just going to confuse her."

Zachary lifted one dark eyebrow. "You're right. You're nobody to be giving romantic advice."

Caden wanted to say more, but what was there to say? There were shadows in that woman's eyes he didn't understand, and if Zachary wanted to take them on, it was his choice. But something told him Zachary was backing away from commitment faster than Caden ever had. He let the personal crap go. "Who do you think robbed the coffee shop?"

Zeke shook his head. "Dunno. Yet. Any news on who that Vince character was in the bank the other day?"

So apparently Austin had talked to his crew about Vince.

Plus strangers in town usually caught everyone's attention. "No, no idea."

Zeke started toward the building to the left.

His brother watched him go. "Well, Sheriff," Zachary said. "It's been nice seeing you, but we have several downed fences to repair. Let us know if you need any help figuring out who robbed the coffee shop."

"Zachary, you'll be the first person I call," Caden drawled.

CHAPTER 8

Ella pushed the half-eaten macaroni and cheese plate away and wrinkled her nose. There was a time she liked cooking or at least trying to cook, but it was no fun when she was only cooking for one. Tara had stayed late at the school, finalizing the summer school report cards, so Ella had come home alone after work. She couldn't even go outside and garden because another storm had erupted, and the rain was beating mercilessly against the flowers she had already planted.

She stood and paced back and forth by the window, watching the rain splat onto the river. This was ridiculous. There was no reason to eat microwave crap when there was a perfectly good diner in town. She hurried to the closet for her raincoat and then moved into the garage. It was a quick if muddy drive to town, and she soon was pulling up to the curb in front of Sandra's diner.

Yanking her hood over her head, she jumped out of the car and ran across the sidewalk with the rain battering her. When the storms hit, they really hit. She dodged inside, and the bell jangled over the door. A quick glance around showed that the diner was empty.

Sandra emerged from the kitchen. "Hey there. What are you up to?"

Ella wiped rain off her face. "I thought I'd grab something good to eat, but there's nobody here. You should close early and give yourself a break."

Sandra pushed her strawberry-blond hair over her shoulder. "It's a busy night elsewhere, I think. It's end of year at school, and I know they were having a picnic afterward. Plus there's also volleyball camp in Sheridan. Finally, I think there's a baseball camp going on. So anyway, nobody's here. I can still make you something to eat, if you want."

Ella shook out her wet hair as the thunder rolled high and loud outside. Lightning zipped down and illuminated the night. "No, really. I'm good." She glanced at the rotating pastry case on the counter. "You know what? I'll take a piece of apple pie to go." Apple pie counted as a fruit, and that was a good dinner.

"Sure," Sandra said, reaching for a to-go box under the counter.

The door opened, and Ella slid to the side, prepared to tell the person that the diner was closed. Her heart sank. It was that Vince from the bank, and he'd shaved his beard. She could still recognize him by his stringy hair, dirty hat, and sheer size.

He walked in and smiled. "Well, hello. I knew we'd meet up again. Most chicks don't turn me down so fast."

Her instincts were screaming for her to back away. "Sorry, but the diner is closed." How could she unobtrusively take her phone from her purse to catch a picture of him for Caden?

Vince's eyebrows rose. "That's okay. You can make it up to me." His grin was off-putting, to say the least.

She shook her head. "I don't think so."

Sandra placed the pie in the box on the counter. "I'm sorry, but we are closed early tonight."

Vince looked around again. "Cool." He shut the door behind him. "How convenient that nobody is here right now. Small towns, right? I think we'll have a little talk."

Warning trilled through Ella, and she stepped to the side. "Now, listen."

"No, you listen." Vince drew a gun from the back of his waistband.

Ella froze as shock dropped like an iced-over rock into her stomach.

Sandra stepped away from the counter.

Vince grabbed Ella by the arm and yanked her to him, keeping the gun pointed at Sandra. "You come around here and lock this door."

Sandra paused and then scurried toward the door, plucking her keys from her pocket.

Vince yanked Ella closer to the counter and shoved the gun into her side. "Lock the door and shut the shades."

Sandra hurried to comply and then backed away from the door, her eyes wide and her face pale.

"There we go," Vince said. "Where's the safe in this place?"

Sandra shook her head. "I don't have a safe."

"What do you mean, you don't have a safe?"

She gulped. "I take the money to the bank every day. It never made sense to have a safe when the bank is two blocks away."

Vince tightened his hold on Ella and prodded the gun farther between her aching ribs.

Pain flared along her side, but she didn't wince. "Vince, there's not a lot of money here," she whispered, trying not to cry out from the pain.

Sandra edged toward the counter again. "I'll give you

everything I have in the till, but it hasn't been very busy today."

Vince leaned in and sniffed Ella's hair. "Oh, I don't know. I bet I can find something else to make this worth my while."

Ella's stomach lurched, and she gagged. She gulped down panic.

Sandra moved behind the counter and pushed the button that opened the till. "Take the money and go."

Ella tried to ease away and lessen the pain in her side. "I take it you robbed the coffee shop?"

Vince nodded. "Yeah, and they hardly had any money, either."

"It's a small town. There's not a lot of money here," she said through clenched teeth. "Could you please pull the gun out of my ribs?" Was there a way to get to the phone in her purse?

He relaxed his hold a little bit. "Are you going to do what I want?"

Probably not. "The police know you robbed the coffee shop—you need to get out of town." It was a lie, but she couldn't think how else to convince him to leave.

"I'm not going anywhere," Vince said.

Sandra paused in the middle of pulling money from the till.

Vince pointed the gun at her. "Do you want to get shot?"

"No," Sandra said. "Here." She yanked bills out and threw them on the counter. "You can have it all. Just leave."

"I'm not going anywhere," Vince repeated. He grabbed the money. "There's only a hundred here."

"Yeah, I told you it was a slow day," Sandra said. "That's all the money I have."

"Well, then," Vince said, "I guess I'll have to take payment another way."

Ella caught Sandra's eye. She wasn't sure what to do, but the gun wasn't pointed at her, so she ducked her head and motioned for Sandra to do the same. Then she hit Vince square in the wrist, hoping he'd drop the gun.

The beefy guy barely moved.

Sandra reached under the counter, lifted a handgun, and fired wildly toward Vince. He dropped and tried to take Ella with him. She kicked him in the knee as hard as she could and shrank away. He howled and released her, crouching beneath the counter so Sandra couldn't aim at him. Something pierced Ella's shoulder and she cried out, falling to the tiled floor.

A truck screeched to a stop outside.

"Damn it," Vince bellowed, dodging toward Sandra and pointing his gun at her.

She ducked beneath the countertop.

He fired several times toward the wall. The bullets impacted the wall and destroyed a red clock, sending it smashing to the floor. "You'll pay for this," he yelled, rolling over the counter and barreling through the kitchen.

"Ella," Sandra screamed. She ran around the counter and reached Ella, pulling her to her feet. "Come on. We have to run."

Dizziness swamped Ella, and she leaned against her friend. Pounding came from the outside door. Sandra hurriedly unlocked the door and yanked it open.

Caden was there, already reaching for Ella. "Did I hear gunshots?"

The room spun around Ella, and her knees weakened. "I think I've been shot." Then darkness engulfed her, and she fell, barely noting when he caught her.

* * *

Caden paced outside the hospital examination room, fury roaring through his veins. Austin McDay rounded the corner, his hair and sweatshirt wet from the rainstorm. "You find anything?" Caden asked. He was becoming accustomed to working with the enigma of a man, and he needed to get over that and fast. After he found Vince and broke his face.

Austin shook his head, his gray eyes pissed. "Nothing. I have everybody out looking, and we're doing a full canvass, but we haven't found Vince anywhere." He dropped his hand to the holstered gun at his hip. "Anything?"

"No. I talked to Tara Webber, who teaches art at the school. As soon as Sandra and Ella are able, they can work with her creating a better composite of this asshole." Now that they'd both seen Vince without his beard and glasses, they should be able to give a good description. The moron had admitted he'd robbed the coffee shop. He'd also been inside the bank. Caden needed to up the security there. "What about RJ? Did Deputy Bixby Jr. go interview him?"

"Yeah. According to Henry Jones, his nephew was with him all day and well into the night and hasn't left."

Caden took a deep breath and tried to exhale all anger. He had to think. Henry Jones would not lie, not even for his nephew. "So maybe RJ wasn't involved and did just meet that Vince buying firewood."

"RJ told Bixby that Vince had the firewood in the back of an old purple Datsun. I think he's full of crap," Austin said. "It's the nickname. Seems too familiar."

Caden agreed. "I want to bring him in." Although he didn't have probable cause.

Austin scanned the quiet waiting room. "How is Ella?"

"The doc's with her now."

"Was she shot?" Austin asked.

Just the idea burned fury through Caden. "No. She took a ricochet from a bullet fired by Sandra, from the sound of it." There was no doubt Sandra had probably saved them both. She was sedated in the other room. "It looks like Vince shot at the wall and didn't try to kill them." Which wasn't going to save the jerk.

"Good."

"I want someone put on Sandra's door through the night while she remains in the hospital."

"Not a problem," Austin said.

Caden looked at him. "I mean one of my deputies."

"Ah," Austin said. "Okay. I'll call one in."

"Thanks."

Just then, Ford burst through the front door, his dark hair slicked back from the rain and his eyes an unfathomable black. Crimson darkened the olive tone of his skin and made the several white scars down the right side of his face stand out. "I heard Sandra was shot."

Caden paused while Austin did the same.

"No. She fired at a guy and missed him," Austin said, his gaze alert on his friend. "She's sedated, and we plan to put a guard on her through the night."

"I'm her guard." Ford stalked by them and turned the corner.

"Huh." Austin watched him go.

Caden didn't have time to worry about the involvement of another of the Cattle Club men. "Is he good?"

"The best," Austin affirmed. "She couldn't be any safer than with him at the door."

That would have to do for now. "Whatever you're all hiding from better not be the law," Caden growled.

"We're not hiding from anything," Austin countered, his expression deadly serious. "We're trying to build new lives because our old ones were taken away. We want nothing more than to work the land and protect this town. You have my word."

Ella emerged from the examination room with a Band-Aid across her arm and dark circles beneath her eyes. "Hey."

Everything inside Caden settled. She was okay. "Hi," he said. "How bad is it?"

"It's nothing," she said. "I mean, it hurts. The doctor only needed to give me a couple stitches and a pain pill." She opened her hand to show a small white capsule. "I don't want to take the pill."

"You don't have to take it," Caden said. He remembered that she had told him about an uncle of hers who had been addicted to pain pills. "How about an aspirin?"

She tried to smile but her lips trembled. "Yeah. I'll take an aspirin when I get home."

He didn't want to anger her, but she wasn't going home alone. "Just tonight, I want you to come back out to the cottage. You can have the bedroom. I'll take the sofa."

Tears filled her eyes. "I want to argue with you, but I also don't want to be alone. I was so scared, Caden." Twin tears slid down her smooth cheeks.

The outside doors slid open, and Nurse Ramber walked inside holding a large bouquet of the yellow wildflowers found all over the county. The woman was around eighty with thick gray hair tied in a bun. She'd ruled the hospital with an iron fist from the dawn of time. "There were flowers outside on the bench." She frowned as she ambled toward the unoccupied reception desk. "Where is everybody?"

Caden shook his head. "I don't know. There's been

nobody at the front desk all night, but Doc didn't seem to mind."

"Darn it," the woman muttered. "I'm going to fire that girl."

Caden had no idea who she was talking about and didn't really care. "I take it you're on night shift?"

The nurse gently placed the flowers on the counter and shucked off her raincoat. She wore a starched white nurse's uniform and always had. "I am. I got the call that somebody had been shot?"

Ella shook her head. "I took a ricochet, but I'm fine. It's just a slight cut." Her gaze moved to the flowers.

The nurse squinted at the yellow blossoms. "There has to be a note here somewhere." She reached inside and felt around before pulling out a folded piece of notepaper. "This is odd. Ella, your name's on it."

Caden took the note before Ella could and opened it. "Hey, Ella. Sorry about tonight. We'll definitely make up for it soon. XO, Vince."

Ella pressed a hand to her stomach as if attacked by nausea.

"Damn it," Austin said.

Caden couldn't take his gaze off Ella. "You're going to be okay. We'll find Vince and put him away."

She swayed on her feet.

That was it. He reached for her and lifted her against his chest. "It's time we headed home."

Austin paused. "Wait a minute. You need to give an official statement."

Oh, that was right. For a second, Caden had forgotten his job. He moved to sit in one of the cushioned waiting room chairs, still cradling her. "All right, let's get the full story, and don't leave anything out."

She took a trembling breath and then related the events

of the night. The more she talked, the angrier Caden became, but he kept his expression calm and his hold gentle. He was going to kill Vince when he found him. It was a miracle neither Sandra nor Ella had been truly hurt.

Austin winced. "Sandra fired at least three or four times?"

Ella nodded. "Yeah, I think she hit above the window. I don't remember any glass breaking. Vince fired at the wall and seemed furious that you showed up." She finally wound down but remained stiff in his arms. Two months ago, before he'd lost his mind, she would've snuggled right into his neck.

He looked up at Austin and let his rage show, although his tone remained mild. "I'm taking her to my place."

Austin nodded. "We'll continue canvassing for Vince's rig. Although I don't believe RJ's report that it was a purple truck."

"Agreed," Caden said. "I'll give you a call later." With that, he stood and carried Ella out into the rain.

CHAPTER 9

RJ Jones kicked back at the campfire with a series of crumpled beer cans littering the dirt around him. The clouds had finally parted, leaving the stars sparkling in the dark sky. Smoke rose into the air and scented the night with the smell of the campfire. It should be relaxing, but his fingers twitched with the need for speed. If he wasn't burning rubber down a road, fast as possible, then he wasn't happy.

Sad but true.

A figure slowly emerged from behind the nearest barn. "We good?" Vince asked.

RJ looked up at the mammoth man. His hair was stringier than usual, and a new Band-Aid had taken up residence above his left eyebrow. "We're good. I slipped the old man a couple of pills, and he got tired and headed to bed."

"Good." Vince dropped into the camping chair that had been vacated by RJ's uncle.

RJ looked at him. "Why are you always causing problems?"

Vince reached for a beer from the nearby cooler and popped open the top. "Are you sure Deacon's going to meet us? I don't trust that son of a bitch. I have no doubt he'd take the money from our score last week and head to Mexico with it."

RJ had had the same doubts, but Deacon didn't have the means to get to Mexico. "I'm pretty sure he'll pay us, or we'll turn him back in to that cop in Denver. He knows it; we know it. He's gonna give us our share." Nobody had asked RJ, but in his opinion, he deserved more of the bank robbery stash than the rest of the crew. Without him they never would've gotten away. He was the best getaway driver around, but he knew better than to say that to Vince. "What's your deal with women anyway? Why can't you just be a decent guy and ask one out once in a while?"

Vince shrugged. "I did ask pretty Ella out. She said no. I moved on to plan B."

Once again, RJ wondered if it was worth continuing with Vince, but the guy did provide the muscle they needed. Plus he couldn't think of a way to get rid of him. Maybe after they collected their cash from Deacon, he'd go find a new crew. This one didn't seem to be doing very well.

The deal had been that nobody would get hurt, but Deacon had lied. They'd killed a security guard and shot another one. That upped any potential consequences to a place RJ didn't want to go. "I understand getting rid of witnesses, but we're taking chances we don't need to take." He tried to use logic with the ape again.

Vince finished the beer, crumpled the can in one beefy hand, and tossed it on the ground. "You do your job and I'll do mine, Ricky J. Other than that, stop messing with me."

All right, RJ would just have to go along until he could ditch this group. Then he'd find a new one that didn't try to kidnap women and shoot guards. He had no problem killing if necessary, but in this case, it just didn't seem necessary. So why do it?

For now, he had to make sure he got out of this situation alive. "Vince, you need to listen to me just this once. I re-member Caden from high school, and even then the guy was unbeatable, at least on the football field. After school, he was in the service and who knows what he learned there. While I did hear that he got a little fucked up during missions, he's still not a guy who will ever give up. You need to forget Ella and move on."

Vince pushed back his greasy hair. "It's too late. Nobody says no to me, especially some hick twit living in the middle of nowhere. I can't let that stand."

RJ sighed. "Well then, at least be smart about it. If we're going to take her, let's not get in a shoot-out over it." There was no doubt in his mind that he was about a billion times smarter than Vince, though of course, so was the average garden slug.

"Good evening, gentlemen." A slim figure moved from the shadows and walked toward them.

RJ straightened in his chair. "Max, what are you doing here?"

"I heard about the shoot-out and thought I'd make sure our entire plan wasn't blown." Max looked around, spotted an overturned piece of firewood that hadn't been split, and struggled to roll it closer to the fire. "I have my schematics of the bank and am ready to come up with a plan if you two are." He sat on the log and looked up at the quiet ranch house. "Where's the old man?"

"He's out," RJ said. "He ain't waking up 'til early tomorrow morning."

"Good. Did he give you an alibi for Vince's latest fiasco?" Max slipped sideways and then righted himself.

Vince turned and smacked Max on the arm, knocking him clean off the log. Max dusted himself off and regained his seat, his eyes darting nervously toward the bigger man. "Seriously, Ricky J. Do you have an alibi?"

"Yeah," RJ said. "I was with the old man the entire time during the coffee shop robbery so Vince and I couldn't be connected. For tonight's fiasco, I didn't know Vince was going to make a move on Ella Riverton. It's a happy coincidence I was here drinking with my uncle until I drugged him." He glared at Vince but stayed out of striking range.

Max reached for a beer. "All right. Back to the plan. I have the schematics, and the interior of the bank is clear in my mind after spending an hour inside renting a safe-deposit box."

RJ scratched behind his ear. "I take it the fake ID held up well?"

"It definitely did," Max said. "We should use that guy again if we need him. It was no problem." He scratched his chin. "I really had that chick going with how much I love my pregnant wife and want to start a farm in this bumbfuck town in the middle of nowhere."

At least something was going right. "What's the plan? Do you really think there's enough money there?" RJ asked.

Max nodded. "There's enough to get us back to Colorado and keep us safe for a couple weeks until Deacon brings the money from our last job."

Vince crushed another beer can with his bare hands. "Are we sure Deacon is going to meet us with the Denver cash?"

"Oh yeah," Max said. "He stopped in town, and I let him know what would happen if he didn't. He doesn't have enough leash to get free of this without our help. So he will meet us, and he'll give us our cut. I made sure of it."

"I didn't know he was in town." RJ started planning the escape route after they robbed the local bank. "Glad you set him straight."

"No problem. He's already long gone, so we should have no problems with this current job." As Max detailed his plan for the robbery, even RJ had to admit the guy was pretty good. He might be a weasel, but he sure knew how to strategize. Plus without Deacon around, hopefully nobody would get shot this time.

"Okay," RJ finally said. "This is actually going to work." Adrenaline flowed through him at the thought of out-running Caden Scott.

Max's beady gaze flitted toward the quiet ranch house again. "This place is pretty nice. What's here? About fifty acres?"

"More like two hundred acres." RJ reached for another beer.

Max cleared his throat and his Adam's apple bobbed. "Are you the old guy's only relative?"

"Yep," RJ said, already knowing where Max's brain would go. "The property is mortgaged to the hilt, and if the old fart dies, the bank gets it all." It wasn't true. Not a word of it. But RJ had plans for good ole Uncle Henry to hit the dirt within the next few months, once he was clear of Deacon and these two morons.

"That's too bad," Max said, wiping his hand down his now dirty tan slacks. "It'd be easy to arrange an accident."

Which was exactly RJ's plan once he had a decent alibi set up somewhere. He hadn't realized until this trip back home that Uncle Henry had managed to pull the farm out of the red and create a nice nest egg. The property was now at high value in Wyoming, so RJ would need to move quickly within the next few months. He'd establish himself in Colorado, sneak home and kill Henry, and then get back before anyone noticed he'd been away. "Unfortunately, killing the old man wouldn't lead to anything good for me."

"Sad," Max lamented.

RJ kept his gaze averted. His uncle had enjoyed a good life, and RJ would make sure his death was relatively painless. Accidents happened all the time on the farm. But first things first. He needed distance from this place so the authorities wouldn't connect him to the death. He wondered who would contact him after his uncle's body was discovered.

Hopefully Caden Scott. That'd be a nice turn of events. "There's the annual summer football scrimmage against Tempest high tomorrow night, and most of the town will want to get there early and tailgate. We should hit the bank right at that time," RJ murmured.

Vince straightened, his eyes gleaming. "So long as you remember that Ella is coming with us." He finished yet another can and tossed it in Max's direction. "She has to be nice to a guy like me."

RJ sighed. "All right." He recalculated in his head. Once Vince was done with Ella, she wouldn't be any good to anybody. He should ask her out again first. The chick had to be nursing a broken heart after the sheriff had dumped her. "I'll make arrangements for a hostage. Are you sure this is what you want to do?"

Vince nodded. "Oh yeah. That bitch is coming with us."

CHAPTER 10

The rain pounded mercilessly on the now drenched earth as Caden sat on his deck beneath the heavy overhang with the night darkening his backyard. He had a cup of coffee in front of him. All he wanted was a bourbon, but he was on duty, and he had to keep Ella safe. He'd tucked her into his bed just an hour before. The one they used to share before he'd been such a colossal ass.

She'd been so terrified, it was all he could do not to slide into bed with her, but she deserved space.

A pair of light eyes flickered from the tree line, and he stiffened. Then the wolf moved into sight, his coat drenched. They stared at each other for a moment. Caden couldn't decide if the beast was a danger or not. He knew the men of the Cattle Club considered it a pet of sorts.

Movement sounded behind Caden, and the sliding glass door opened.

The wolf slowly turned and headed back into the forest.

Odd. Very odd. Caden looked over his shoulder, his body heating at the sight of his woman standing there. "Ella, what are you doing? Go back to bed." The idea that she could have been shot this evening still sent fire through his blood, and he needed to keep himself calm.

She wore one of his T-shirts, which was long enough to

hang almost to her knees, even though she was a tall woman. She looked small and defenseless with the slight bandage peeking out from the shirt.

"Caden," she said softly.

He shook his head. This wasn't a good idea. He had to protect her from herself, even if it killed him. "Go back to bed."

She steeled her shoulders and moved barefoot toward him as the rain continued to pummel the world around them. "I don't want to be alone tonight."

Everything inside him calmed, settled, and then heated. "Turn your sweet butt around right now. You've had a rough night and you need sleep."

She kept moving toward him, the scent of honey blossoms coming with her. In one smooth motion, she sat on his lap, facing him, her thighs on either side of his. Then she kissed him.

His body jolted but he couldn't pull away. Her mouth was soft and sweet, and he could stay there forever.

He let her wander and then finally tangled his fingers in her hair to still the torture. "Honey, this isn't just a 'burn off some tension thing' for me or a 'we had a rough night thing.' If you're in, you're all in. There's no more of this stubborn bullshit." He'd used the expletive on purpose to piss her off.

Instead, her eyes softened. "I know." She leaned in and kissed him again. Then she pulled back. "I don't care. I want you."

Yeah, his whole body was on fire for her, and his cock felt like it was going to burst through his zipper. So he kept his hands gentle and ran them down her arms, careful to avoid her stitches. "You need to go back to bed, and we'll talk about this in the morning."

"No." She leaned in and nipped his bottom lip.

Sparks flew from his mouth to land in his balls. "Ella, I ain't gonna tell you again."

"Good." Her soft hands spread out over his pecs, burning him through the shirt. She gave a soft hum. "I've missed you."

"I missed you, too," he managed to grind out. "But you need to stop pushing me." He was two seconds from taking her down to the worn porch, and that wouldn't do. His body rioted in disagreement, fighting his good intentions.

She leaned in again and nibbled along his jaw. "Caden, come inside." Her teeth sank into his earlobe.

Every muscle in his body tensed. "Baby—"

"No," she said, her mouth wandering across his again. "I want you."

He grabbed her hair and yanked her head back, forcing her to look at him. "If we're doing this, we're back on and we're back in. There's no getting out. You give yourself to me tonight, you're mine, Ella. Tell me you get me." He held his breath. Honesty was all he had going for him at the moment, so he gave it to her.

Her eyes softened. "I get you," she whispered.

His instincts roared to the surface, and he took her mouth the way he wanted. Hard and fast. . . and his.

Ella didn't care about the future, and she sure didn't care about consequences. She was lucky to be alive, and she wanted to live. It didn't matter what words she needed to say. The second her mouth touched his, she was all in.

He took over the kiss as she'd hoped, his mouth firm and his tongue wicked. She made a soft sound of need, and he tightened his hold, plastering her against him. How she'd missed this. Missed him. While the muscles beneath her palms were familiar, she'd thought she'd never get to touch him again.

The idea that she could have another night with him shot her from interested to fully aroused in less than a second.

Caden easily held her in place, taking control. Heat rushed through her, igniting every nerve, forcing her to rock against him. Right where they met.

Still working her mouth, he stood.

She tightened her thighs against his flanks and tunneled her hands through his thick hair as he walked inside the house and smoothly shut the door.

Air rustled against her, and then she was being lowered onto the bed.

He lifted his head, letting her breathe. His eyes had darkened to the color of a rare emerald, mysterious and deep. Hunger filled them. For her. "You're sure?"

Gulping, she nodded.

He didn't ask twice. In a heartbeat, he yanked off her shirt and then pushed her back.

She fell and laughed, joy and need singing through her. A quick snap at the side of her panties had them torn off.

Her gasp was full of hunger.

He dropped to his knees, and then his mouth was on her. Fast and hard and so wicked, he knew exactly how to please her. Within seconds, she was crying out his name.

Before she'd fully come down, he was pushing her up again, sliding one finger and then two inside her. This orgasm bore down and flashed lights behind her eyes.

Then he stood and slowly removed his clothing as if drawing out the moment.

Grasping her hips, he lifted her and set her farther up on the bed. Heat rolled off him, and she fought to get closer as he covered her with his powerful body. Caden was everything in that moment. He powered inside her with a possessive thrust, a sense of wildness in every touch. Pain and erotic pleasure swamped her, and she dug her nails into his chest, avoiding the scar above his heart.

When he was finally embedded all the way, he leaned down and gently kissed her. Then he lifted his head, and his eyes gleamed through the darkness. "Now we're gonna have a little talk," he murmured.

Her body was on fire. She needed him to move and right now. "Later."

"No." He ground his hips against her, torturing the desperate nerves inside her. "Now."

Her whimper would embarrass her later. She scraped her nails down his chest, and he instantly captured her wrists in one broad hand and secured them above her head.

Heat blew through her. There was an edge to him tonight. A new one.

He grinned. "You like that. Interesting." Slowly, he pulled out and pushed back in. "Now we're gonna get a few things straight."

She struggled against him, surprised when she couldn't move. Whatever had been unleashed in Caden surrounded them, stealing her breath. Fire blasted through her, making her ache. "Start to move, Caden," she moaned.

"Not yet." He kissed her nose, his big body holding her captive. "No more stubbornness, and no more forgetting we have a future. Tell me you're mine, sweetheart."

She liked being stubborn, and trusting him wasn't as easy as before. But she also knew him. He wouldn't move an inch.

What did she want? Definitely him. Her need was so great, she'd say anything to get him moving again. "Okay," she whispered.

"Good." He kissed her hard, going deep.

Her mind spun and her body rioted.

Then, finally, he began to move. He grasped her buttock with one hand, partially lifting her to him. The fingers of his other hand captured her hair, holding her in place for his kiss.

This time, there was no teasing. No seeking. No question in his kiss.

It was a claiming. Completely.

His body bunched; his muscles tightened. Then he powered into her, all of him giving to all of her. It was a complete possession, and she knew he'd never let her go.

Tension rolled through her, throwing her near that cliff. She clung to him, holding her breath, trying to reach the pinnacle.

His teeth grazed her shoulder and she spun into the un-known, crying out his name. The climax rolled over her, through her, taking everything she'd ever be.

Finally, she came down, her body relaxing. He kissed her hard, shuddering with his own climax. Then he lifted his head, his eyes glittering through the darkness. Lightning zapped outside.

"I'm holding you to this promise," he whispered. "Mine forever, Ella."

CHAPTER 11

What in the world had happened the night before? Ella sat at the comfortable table on the back porch, a steaming cup of coffee in front of her and the beautiful backyard with its colorful flowers spreading out in every direction. It probably wasn't fair to call the area a backyard, considering it bordered the national forest, and even now a deer peeked out at her.

What had she been thinking? She tried to muster up some concern, but her body was completely satiated. She hadn't felt this good since before Caden had left town. Something had been different the night before. He hadn't held back this time. Not at all.

As if conjured by her imagination, he slid open the sliding glass door and loped toward her, his hair tousled, his eyes mellow, and his gait graceful. He'd tugged on worn jeans that hugged his powerful body. As usual, his bare chest did nothing but intrigue her. The various healed knife wounds and the one bullet hole above his heart reminded her of the life he'd led and the danger he'd already beat back.

"Morning," he said, drawing out a chair and dropping into it.

"Hi. Before I forget, Tara is heading over, and I'm going

to describe Vince to her without the beard." She reached for her cup so her hands had something to do. "About last night—" she started.

"Nope," he said. "Last night happened. We're back on track."

She winced, even though a part of her sprang awake, happy with his declaration. "Caden, it's not that easy."

His gaze sharpened, so strong and green, caressing her face. "It is that easy, Ella. I gave you the choice, and you took it. Period."

She swallowed and tried to find a reasonable explanation for what had happened. "Listen, last night was, well, stressful, you know, with my getting shot and you being upset, and then, well, this happened."

One of his dark eyebrows rose. "Are you saying I took advantage of you?"

"No, no, not at all," she said. In fact, if anybody had taken advantage of anybody, she had taken advantage of him. Even though he was very good at masking his emotions, she couldn't help but see how furious he'd been that she'd almost been shot. His emotions had been closer to the surface than they ever had been in the year they'd spent together.

"I don't want to rush back into something just because we had one night." Yeah, it had been a fantastic night, and one she'd love to repeat, but she had to protect her heart.

"We had a year," Caden protested, looking big and broad in the morning light. Man, he was mouthwateringly sexy in the morning, especially with his grumpy look. It was so tempting to jump right back into his world and his arms. But she couldn't forget the lessons of the past.

As if reading her mind, he shook his head. "I'm not your father. I'm not going to break up with you again and leave you. I screwed up. I went and got my head on straight, and I'll know better next time. If I start struggling, I'll talk to you."

It was what she had needed to hear . . . more than six weeks ago. She paused with the mug halfway to her mouth. More than six weeks ago—wait a minute. A pit opened up in her stomach.

"What?" he asked, leaning forward. "Are you okay? Are you feeling all right?"

"Um, yeah," she said. "I, well, yeah. Huh."

Caden tilted his head. "I don't know what that means. Are your stitches intact?"

She probably didn't even need the Band-Aid on her shoulder any longer. "I'm fine. I just, well, huh. Hmm. I'm going to go get dressed."

"Oh no, you're not." Caden put a hand on her shoulder, effectively keeping her in place. "What just went through your head?"

She sighed. "Well, when you left, you know, I figured it was over. I decided I'd never date anybody again because men suck. So I, well, I went off the pill." She said the last on a rush as her mind started spinning faster than any globe ever could.

"Oh, okay." His shoulders settled and a lazy smile tipped his lips. "I'll go get your ring."

"No, no, no," she said, holding out her hands. God, she'd missed that ring. She had loved wearing that ring. "No, no, no, no, no. We are not going backward just because there was one night of . . ." Her voice trailed off. A night of what? Perfection? The best sex ever? A night she wanted again right now? She couldn't finish the sentence, so she didn't even try.

Caden's chin firmed into that solid-rock expression he

had, one that she had once dubbed his "I'm a rock face" look. "Oh, you are wearing that ring. Especially now."

She held up one hand. "Now listen. As much as I like your caveman routine, I'm not in the mood for it right now."

"Well, darlin'," he drawled. "That's unfortunate, because that's what you're going to get."

"No, I'm not," she said. "One night doesn't mean anything happened. And if it did, we'll figure out what to do when the time comes." For a solid year, she'd dreamed of building a family with him, of having his baby, or *babies* because she wanted a large family. Right now the idea was too tempting even to consider.

His gaze softened in complete contrast to the muscle ticking beneath his jaw. "Honey, I know you were hurt by your parents' marriage, and I know you're still angry with me and trying to punish me, which is understandable. But I'm about done with this."

She jolted back. "Excuse me?"

His voice remained patient, but he emitted an air of tension that she would've been blind to have missed. "I said I'm about done with this. All right? You want to be together; I want to be together. You're just hurting us both by being so pigheaded."

"Did you just call me a pig?" she asked, her temper flaring.

"Don't be silly. I said you're being pigheaded, and you know you are. You're being stubborn for no reason except that you want to make me hurt like you hurt. I get that. But like I said, I'm about over it." He reached for her mug and drank down half of her coffee.

"Hey, that's mine," she said.

"And you're mine," he retorted, setting the coffee down. "Deal with it."

At the far edge of the tree line, the wolf yipped once as

if in agreement. Then he turned and dashed back into the woods. Ella cocked her head. "Do wolves yip?"

"Apparently that one does."

A quick look at the wild male next to her confirmed that not only did he yip, but he was ready to bite. For some reason, the expression on Caden's face roused her defiance.

"Oh yeah, Sheriff? Bring it on."

Caden parked his truck in the lot by the sheriff's building, scanning the cars and knowing instantly who was inside. After the previous night with Ella, he felt better than he had in weeks. Yet he still couldn't get her to commit. Oh, he deserved her stubbornness. But at this point, she was in danger, and he could only allow her defiance to go so far.

The ring box in his pocket reminded him of how badly he'd screwed up, but he was trying to make things right. His mind flashed back to what she'd revealed that morning, that she was off the pill. The idea of having a child with her filled him with hope, but it was doubtful he could be so lucky. He also didn't want to use a possible pregnancy to push her back into a relationship with him.

He knew they belonged together, but unless she agreed, nothing could happen. For now, no matter what, he was going to keep her safe. Yanking his focus to the present, he made a quick call to the hospital. Apparently Sandra had been released earlier that morning. The woman had been in shock the night before, but the doc assured him she'd be okay.

The doc also informed him that Ford Campbell had taken Sandra home. Was there something going on between those two? Ford had never given any indication of being interested in the diner owner, and Caden felt responsible for her as sheriff of the town. He'd have to stop by the restaurant later and make sure she was okay. Plus the woman had probably saved Ella's life, although she'd been a terrible shot.

He should start a firearm training class for anybody in town who needed it. For now, he needed to stop by the office and then visit each business in town to be sure that everybody was on the lookout for Vince.

Caden stomped into the sheriff's office, bypassing Ethel, who was on the phone at the reception desk. He opened the door to his office to, once again, find Austin seated behind his desk, poring over documents. "You're way too comfortable in my chair."

Austin looked up. "Hey. Got the composite."

Caden was about done with this guy acting like a lawman when he had an undiscoverable past. Yet for now, the man was doing a good job. "They met at my house to do it— Tara is good. Did Bixby Jr. load it into the system?" Should Austin even have access to the system?

"Yeah. We don't have a last name or prints, so it's just a picture going out to sheriffs' offices throughout Wyoming. I'm not holding a lot of hope."

"It's better than nothing," Caden returned. "I have two guys covering Ella at the bank until we find him."

"Sounds good," Austin said, kicking back in the chair. "Did you get a ring back on your girl's finger?"

Irritation clawed down Caden's back. "Not yet." At Austin's smirk, he paused. "What? You'd do something differently?"

Austin shrugged. "My girl never would've dared take the ring off in the first place."

Caden crossed his arms. "Maybe that's why you're single."

Austin threw back his head and chuckled. "That's definitely why I'm single."

Interesting. "Your self-awareness is noted. Have you discovered anything about this Vince character yet?"

"Not yet. I did review the CCTV from the bank, and Tara's drawing is much better. You're gonna need to talk to your girl about enforcing the rules at the bank."

"Already did," Caden muttered. Repeatedly. He might have to make that lesson stick, and she wasn't going to like it.

"Understood," Austin said. "Also, Ethel ran a background check on RJ Jones, and there's no criminal record. He does have a juvie record, but you don't have enough for a warrant to get that opened." He cleared his throat. "However, I could get it if you want."

Caden paused. He had no clue what kind of resources Austin had, but he did know they weren't legal. "Let's hold off on breaking the law at this point," he said dryly. "Even if RJ has a juvie record, that was a long time ago, and it's doubtful anything in it would help us with this situation."

"We could bring RJ in," Austin offered.

Caden had already considered that. "Yeah, but why? Because he bought wood from a guy named Vince on the side of the road? Or at least he said he did."

Austin tapped a pen on the desk. "You and I both know he's probably lying. You give me ten minutes with him, and he'll talk."

Caden rested his hand on the weapon that was strapped to his thigh. "If you want to be a law-abiding citizen of Redemption, you can't be saying things like that, Austin."

Austin blinked. "Oh. Yeah. I guess that's true." His grin would probably be charming to most people.

Caden's phone buzzed from his hip, and he put it to his ear. "Scott," he answered.

"Hey, Sheriff. It's Deputy Bixby Jr. I'm at the bank, and RJ Jones just walked in."

Caden stiffened. "All right, I'll be right there." He cut off the call. "Maybe I'll see if RJ will voluntarily come into the office."

Austin's chin lifted. "Just remember that you *are* the sheriff with that whole law-abiding situation."

"Right," Caden muttered. Damn it.

CHAPTER 12

Ella's shoulder ached as she finished counting bills in her drawer. Cami was quiet behind her, working on monthly reports. It was nice and calm in the bank, even though there was a guard at the front door and one at the back. Caden was definitely going overboard to make sure Vince couldn't get to her, but she couldn't complain.

Besides, she had more pressing problems on her mind. What was she going to do about him? Was he right? Was she just being stubborn to hurt him the way he'd hurt her? If so, that made her petty. But she was also uncertain that he meant everything he said. The man had proposed to her. They had planned a life, and then he'd just broken up with her as if none of it had mattered. She wouldn't be a smart woman if she didn't at least stop to consider that situation and the possibility it could happen again.

Plus was she cut out for the political life she knew he wanted? She'd never been to a charity dinner, much less a political ball.

"All right, girlfriend. You've stewed enough." Cami stretched her back and moved away from the drive-through window. "What's going on in that brain of yours?"

Ella shuffled her papers to the side. "I spent the night

with Caden, and it was like old times. I feel like if I trust him again, I'm just making a mistake I already made."

Cami reached for a half-eaten cookie on the desk. "I understand that. But it's Caden. He's one of the good guys, right?"

"Yeah. I guess," Ella said.

Cami shook her head. "Listen, we've been friends a long time."

Ella laughed. "We've been friends for four years, since you came to town."

Cami grinned. "That's a long time for me. You have no idea."

"No, I really don't," Ella said. "You never talk about where you come from. All I know is you came from Florida, you moved here, and you said you started over."

"And I did," Cami said. "There really isn't anything else to talk about. I had a life, it was over, and I started a new one. That's all I've got, Ella."

"Okay," Ella said. They had become friends, and she trusted Cami. If Cami wanted it that way, then she could go on faith. "Just answer one question. Did you leave a man behind?"

Cami threw back her head and laughed. "I left a few behind, but nobody who really mattered."

"Okay. Fair enough." Ella eyed the plate of cookies to the left. "You have to stop bringing in baked goods. I think I've gained ten pounds since you started working at the bank."

Cami chuckled. "I'm sorry. I bake for fun."

Wouldn't that be great, to bake for fun? Ella shook her head. "Well, I appreciate it. I also appreciate that we're friends and will stop pushing you. To be honest, I don't know what to do about Caden. What about you and Zachary?"

"It's over. I mean, not that there was anything to start

with, but if there had been, it would be over." Cami's eyes lost their earlier sparkle.

Ella shook her head. "We're going to end up being nuns, aren't we?"

Cami snorted. "Um, I don't think I would make it as a nun, but you could. I'll fully support you if you want to don the habit and start telling people what to do."

Ella reached for the watering can by the side of the desk and lifted it to take care of the plants decorating the area. She'd slowly added different flowering plants, one at a time, knowing that Mrs. Thomas didn't like them. Mrs. Thomas only popped in once in a while, so she probably wouldn't complain. "So anyway, what happened between you and Zachary?"

Cami finished the cookie and dusted her hands off. "What happened was the condom broke. And yes, he freaked out."

Wow. They were kind of facing the same situation. Interesting. Ella scratched her chin. "Wait a minute. Zachary freaked out?" She'd met the cowboy several times, and he was the calmest person she'd ever noticed. "What's that like?"

"Well, he didn't exactly freak out. He more just, I don't know, turned to stone? Yeah, that's it. He went from being playful and fun to being a rock-hard, solid slate mountain. I don't think there's any real emotion in that guy."

"I'm sorry, Cami. I know you really liked him."

Cami brushed her dark hair over her shoulder. "Yeah, I did, and it was a mistake. I knew the first time he smiled at me with that dimple, he was trouble."

Ella finally gave in and took a peanut butter cookie. "What are you going to do?"

"I'm sure nothing will come of it, but if there are consequences, I'll figure it out at that point. Either way, Zachary

Snowden doesn't need to be involved." A truck rumbled up to the drive-through window, and Cami turned and flicked on the microphone. "Hi there, Mrs. Wallaby. What can I do for you today?"

The outside door opened, and RJ Jones walked in.

Ella stiffened, her entire body going cold. Caden had mentioned that he thought RJ and Vince might know each other, but what if he was wrong? RJ had been nothing but nice to her. "Hi, RJ. What's up?"

Today, RJ wore tan slacks and a button-down shirt from a golf course she'd never heard of. His dark hair was slicked back, and his face was clean-shaven. He walked up to the counter and pushed a check across. "Hi, I heard you were shot last night. I'm surprised to see you here," he said quietly, looking shyly away and then back.

"I wasn't really shot. There was just a ricochet." She leaned toward him, wanting to remember the kid he'd been at one time. "Do you know who that Vince was who tried to rob Sandra's diner? He could've killed us."

RJ threw up his hands. "No. I really don't, Ella. I needed some firewood to build a campfire, I saw a guy selling it on the side of the road, and I bought the firewood. It was this Vince guy and no, I didn't know him before this, and I didn't see him afterward. I'm so sorry that I even talked to that jerk."

Ella nodded. She didn't know RJ well enough to judge whether she could trust him or not, but he seemed sincere. If he was telling the truth, then it had to be difficult to be under so much scrutiny, especially when both Caden and Austin were involved. "Okay. So what do we have here?" She drew the check closer. It was made out to RJ from his uncle in the amount of a thousand dollars.

Her eyebrows rose. Henry Jones barely had twice that in his account right now.

RJ looked at the check. "I know. My uncle is paying me to help him around the farm. He's giving me an advance because I'm kind of broke."

She looked closer at the signature. It definitely was Henry Jones's signature. She'd been working at the bank for years and knew everybody's signature. "Just a sec. I'll have to get this kind of money from the back till."

She took the check, walked around the corner to the manager's office, and shut the door. Holding her breath, she made a quick call.

"Jones," Henry Jones answered.

"Hi, Mr. Jones. It's Ella from the bank."

"Hey, Ella. Hey, I heard you got shot last night. Are you okay?"

Sometimes living in a small town was just too much. "I didn't get shot, Mr. Jones. I took a ricochet and I'm fine. I only needed a couple of stitches."

"Well, that's good," he boomed. "Though, you know, a ricochet can be bad. You should take care of that."

"I did, sir. I saw the doc last night."

"Oh, good. If you need anything, you call me, and I'll come do it."

She smiled. "That's really kind of you, Mr. Jones." Henry Jones had always been one of her favorite people. "I'm calling to verify a check your nephew is cashing here. You know we always call to confirm amounts over five hundred dollars." That wasn't true, but she had no problem telling the lie.

"Oh, yeah. Of course. Yeah. I understand," Henry said. "I did give that check to RJ to help him get on his feet as he starts assisting me out at the ranch here."

Her shoulders relaxed. "Okay, Mr. Jones. I'll go ahead and issue the money. I just wanted to double-check with you."

"That's mighty sweet of you, Ella. I appreciate it. You have a good day now." Henry ended the call.

Ella took the check into the other room and opened her drawer.

One of RJ's narrow eyebrows lifted. "I thought you said you had to get the money from the back room."

She barely kept back a wince. She had never been any good at lying. "It turns out we don't have enough money in the back room. I'll just have to empty my till for ya." She tried to smile.

He sighed. "It's okay. I understand. I know nobody likes me or trusts me in this town."

A pang of regret hit her. The guy really hadn't done anything wrong. Sure, he'd been a little wild in high school, but a lot of people had been wild in high school. So far, all he'd done was return home and offer to help his uncle at the farm. There was no doubt Henry needed assistance.

She patted RJ's hand. "I'm sorry, RJ. I just really like your uncle and wanted to make sure he was being protected."

RJ brightened. "No, I understand. I really like my uncle, too. Don't worry about it, Ella. It's okay."

She smiled. "Okay."

RJ shuffled his feet. "So, I mean, I don't want to be too insistent or anything, but I want to ask again if you'd like to grab coffee with me sometime?"

She counted out the bills, making sure to give him different denominations. "That's nice of you, but I'm still nursing a broken heart here."

His eyes twinkled. "I understand, but the best way to get over a man is to find another one. Right?"

She laughed. "I don't think so. I think once a man has burned you, you cast them all to the depths of hell."

He grinned. "I ain't going to give up." He gathered the money and tucked it into his back pocket. "I'll see you real soon, Ella Riverton." Just then, the door opened and Caden stepped inside. RJ sighed. "Oh man, here we go again." He turned and walked toward the sheriff. "Are you here for me, or are you here for her?"

Ella started at the belligerent tone in his voice now, although she couldn't completely blame him.

Caden looked beyond RJ to her. "I'm always here for her, but you know, RJ, why don't you and I have a little chat?" He grasped the man by the arm and drew him outside the bank.

Cami popped up next to Ella. "This could get interesting."

CHAPTER 13

After dusk, Caden kept an eye on Ella as she sat in the bleachers with her friends. He strolled along the perimeter of the football field, watching as parents and friends poured to the fifty-yard line to congratulate the Redemption Wolves. The annual preseason scrimmage was often the highlight of the summer, and they'd won by two touchdowns. He kept his badge on his belt and made the rounds to keep everybody calm and in line. It was a pretty boisterous crowd, but he understood the excitement.

Austin met him halfway around the track. The guy already seemed to be acting like the sheriff, and Caden hadn't yet decided if he was leaving or not. "It was a good game."

"Yeah. That Simpson kid has a hell of an arm." Caden was becoming accustomed to having Austin around, but he needed the truth from the man.

Austin tucked his thumbs in his jeans. "Did you play football?"

"I did," Caden said. "I played quarterback in both high school and college before I enrolled. I blew up my knee junior year of college, so that was the end of it. How about you?"

Austin shook his head. "No, I didn't play football. I, ah, played soccer."

"Really?" Caden said, watching as a group of boys wrestled near the concession stand. They seemed harmless enough.

"Yeah. Are you sure you want to leave this place?"

The idea was both thrilling and sobering. "No," Caden said honestly. "I'm torn. I always wanted to do something more, but nights like this, Redemption feels like home."

"I get that," Austin said, nodding at a couple of farmers as they walked by talking about their glory days. "You could always keep a place here for vacations. For tonight, I can handle things from here if you want to get your girl home. She has to be sore from her wound."

"I'm gonna need the truth from you if you really want trust. Think about it." Caden clapped him on the arm. "For now, I appreciate it." He nodded at several of the townspeople and moved toward the bleachers, motioning for Ella to come down.

She gave him a look, but still said goodbye to Tara and Sandra, and then gingerly picked her away down the stairs. He held back a grin. How many times had he seen her trip down those very stairs? The woman was beautiful, but man was she clumsy. Yet another thing he loved about her.

She reached him. "Hey, great game, huh?"

"Yeah," Caden said softly.

She tucked her arm through his. "You're going to miss nights like this, aren't you?"

It hit him then finally, all of a sudden. Nothing really mattered if she wasn't with him. "I never asked what you wanted, and I only want to make you happy. You have to know that. I'm not going to go if you want to stay here," he said softly.

She jerked to a stop. "What do you mean? I thought you wanted to run for governor."

"I thought I did, too," he said. "But if you're staying here, then I'm staying here."

She paled and tried to take a step back, but he wouldn't let her. "You can't give up your dream because of me."

"You are my dream," he said. "If you don't want to leave Redemption, then we won't leave. If you don't want to be with me, then fine. I'm still staying here just to be close to you. That's a fact, Ella." It was as vulnerable as he could be with anybody, but she deserved the truth. She deserved all of him.

Pink flashed high across her cheekbones. "I don't know what to say." Her eyes glimmered.

He set his arm over her shoulders and pulled her through the crowd. "Come on, you need rest. We can talk about it in the morning."

"I don't want to talk about it in the morning. I want to talk about it now."

"Fine, but let's at least do it in the truck."

She nodded and they maneuvered through the crowd to his truck. He lifted her in and then shut the door, swinging around to the other side.

Then he settled back. "I'm sorry I pushed you to leave home," he said.

She turned toward him, tucking one leg beneath her in order to face him. "I thought one of the reasons you ended things with me was because you wanted to run for governor and you didn't think I would, well, help." She tucked her hair behind her ear.

He felt like such an ass. "No, that wasn't it at all. You'd be an excellent partner campaigning, and I think you'd be a hell of a first lady of Wyoming. I ended things because I was scared; I couldn't control the nightmares. That was the only reason." How could she even think he wouldn't want her at his side? "I'm sorry if I ever made you feel like I didn't value you or that you weren't good enough."

She scrubbed both hands down her face. "You didn't. My insecurities were my own. You always tried to build me up—I just wouldn't let you. I think maybe I need to build myself up."

He grinned. "That sounds pretty deep." His phone buzzed and he pressed the speaker button. "Scott."

"Hey, boss, it's Bixby Jr. There was just an explosion at the bank. I think it's being robbed."

Ella held on to the handle above the door as the truck careened around the corner, back toward the center of town. Caden switched on a siren, and vehicles pulled to the side to allow them to pass.

"Status," he barked into his radio.

"Big ass explosion, boss," Bixby Jr. yelled over the line. "We're headed that way now. There's a lot of smoke in the air."

Smoke filled the air above the downtown area. "All right. I'm on my way." The radio clicked off. He drove even faster and cut her a look. "I'm going to drop you by the station. I want you to run in, and then I'm headed down to the bank."

"No," Ella said. "It's my bank. I want to see what's happening."

"Don't argue."

She held the handle tighter. "Caden, I want to see what's happening at the bank. I've worked there for years."

"I don't give a shit," Caden said. "I've had deputies patrolling all of the businesses in town, but they can't be everywhere at once. Though maybe it's a good thing they weren't at the bank."

He took a turn so quickly, Ella lifted her knees to brace her feet on the dash. "I asked Mrs. Thomas for more security, and she refused. She also keeps way too much money there, but she won't listen to me. I think our vault is old but still effective."

Lights from the town came into view as he turned down Main Street and quickly rolled to a stop in front of the police station. "Go inside now. There are two deputies in there, and you'll stay until I return."

When she opened her mouth to argue, he reached over and released her seat belt. "Now, Ella. Go," he snapped.

Fine. She opened the door and jumped out, not having a choice. Fully knowing that he'd wait until she went inside, she ran as fast as she could and opened the door, dodging inside the station.

She paced back and forth in front of the wide door as more police vehicles rushed by, followed by a fire truck. She had to at least get out there and see what was happening, so she made a move toward the door.

"Excuse me, ma'am? Caden gave clear instructions for you to stay inside the station."

She spun around to face John Whitcomb, who stood behind the reception desk. "Did you just call me ma'am, Johnny?"

John turned red from his neck to the tips of his ears, until his skin matched his bright red hair. "Ella, come on. Help me out here." He lifted his phone in the air. "Here's my text from Caden. 'Keep Ella inside or it won't matter that you're a cop. It won't matter that I'm a cop. Things will not be good.'"

Ella threw her hands up. "Are you kidding me? You're going to listen to that?"

John sighed and set down the phone. "Listen, ma'am."

"Darn it, John, if you call me ma'am one more time, it's

not Caden you're going to have to fear." She stomped toward the counter.

John took a step back. Even in his deputy uniform, he reminded her of the kid two years younger than she who had always been late to every class because he was busy playing a video game in the hallway. "Please don't get me in trouble."

"Fine." The last thing she wanted to do was get Johnny in trouble. "But don't call me ma'am again."

"It's a deal," John said, looking relieved.

She moved past the counter. "I'm going back to Caden's office to listen on his radio."

"Fair enough," John said cheerfully. "I'll bring you coffee."

Ella didn't want coffee. She wanted to know what was happening at the bank. She moved down the hallway and into Caden's office, her gaze instantly catching on a picture of the two of them on the shelf to the right of his desk. It was placed front and center before several of his trophies, other pictures, and a stack of books on weaponry.

She crossed to the desk, sat in his thick leather chair, and flipped on the police radio. Another explosion shook the windows. For the first time, fear hit her dead center. Was Caden walking into more danger? She had figured the explosions and the robbery would be over by the time he got there, but now it sounded like they were still lighting up the night.

Johnny appeared in the doorway with a cup of coffee for her. "You have to trust that Caden knows what he's doing." The radio went silent.

She jolted, panic quickening her breath.

"It's okay," John said. "That's normal. It probably means they're worried whoever tried to rob the bank is listening. It's a good sign."

Yet another explosion rocked the world outside. Her heart started beating even faster, and she took several deep breaths.

"I have to go direct operations from the command center. I'll be right down the hall if you need me." He quickly disappeared.

She sat for several moments and then reached for her coffee, willing the radio to start sputtering again. Her cell phone buzzed from her purse, and she yanked it out. "Hello? Hello? Caden?"

"No. Ella, it's Mom. I just saw something on the news that there's been a big explosion in Redemption?" Her mom had moved to Sheridan for a job as a receptionist in an accounting firm with great benefits.

Ella sat back in the chair, her stomach turning. "Yeah. I don't know exactly what's going on. I'm in the sheriff's office, and I can't get down to the bank."

"Good!" her mom exclaimed. "Stay where you are. You don't need to be near any bombs."

"Yeah, but Caden's down there."

Her mom was quiet for a second. "Caden is trained to deal with explosions. You aren't. Anyway, what are you doing at the sheriff's office? You two broke up, right?"

"He's back in town and he wants to make amends." Right now she wanted nothing more than for him to be safe.

Her mom sighed. "He's an honorable man. You're in love with him, and you have been since high school. Don't you think you should give him another chance?"

Ella's temples began to ache. "Mom, I don't want to go through what you did for all those years."

"Oh, come on," her mom said. "I loved your dad. I probably shouldn't have accepted him back so many times. But you're not me, and you're not going to make the same mistakes. Caden isn't your dad. He's good and solid. If he says he'll stick around, he will. You're smart enough to know that."

Ella took a sip of her coffee. "Maybe, but he also wants to run for governor, and I don't want to hold him back."

"Why in the world would you hold him back?"

This was so difficult to explain. "Look at him." Ella had been careful not to voice any of her concerns before, because she already knew what her mother would say.

"Okay. What about Caden?"

"You know. He was the golden boy. Captain of the football team. He went to college, and then he was a hero in the service. Now he's the sheriff."

"So?"

"I didn't even go to college. I took that class in accounting, but Mom, we grew up on the other side of town, in a trailer park. I don't know how to be a governor's wife."

Her mom laughed then, the sound deep and true and happy. "That's the dumbest thing I've ever heard. All you have to be is you. You're smart. You're strong. You did graduate from that course, and you run that bank. You can do anything you want to, Ella. I can't believe you're harboring this kind of insecurity. I had no idea."

"I know. I just . . . I love it here in Redemption."

"Then stay in Redemption. Don't go with Caden. Or keep a cabin in Redemption and come home once in a while. If you want him, you could figure it out."

Her mom's confidence in her warmed her throughout. "Thanks."

"Besides, just think what you could do in the big city. I mean, if Caden is elected governor, what kind of platform could you have to do some of the things you want to do?"

Ella rubbed her chin. "I hadn't thought of it like that." She'd contributed to many charities, and she helped every chance she could during fundraisers.

"Just think about it. If you want to assist Caden, there's so much you could accomplish with that kind of platform," her mom said. "You could even create your own charity. Think of the people you could help. I know you have a drive to make a difference."

"That's true," Ella said. She might not be comfortable at fancy dinners or balls or whatever governor-type people did, but she really could do some good.

Her mom cleared her throat. "That's not a reason to be with him, though. If you go with Caden, it has to be for him and for you."

"You're right," Ella said. "Thanks. I think I needed to hear this."

"Sure thing. Let me know that he's okay, all right?"

"I will. I'll talk to you later. Love you." Ella clicked off.

Heat rose into her face. She had been thinking about this situation the wrong way. If she looked at the new opportunities as a way to do something good, the idea of moving to the city and even the governor's mansion wasn't so daunting. But her mom was right. If she chose Caden, it had to be for Caden and no other reason. Right now, she couldn't imagine her life without him.

Just then, another explosion rocked the world so hard, their picture fell off the shelf and shattered on the floor. Oh God, was he okay?

CHAPTER 14

The dust was finally settling as Caden crouched and brushed debris away from what was left of the bank's counter. "Something's not right here."

"No kidding," Silias Bixby Sr. said, crouching next to him. "Whoever planned this is a moron. Everything that could go wrong did." He looked at the demolished reception area of what used to be the bank. "They used dynamite, which did a great job of destroying the walls, the counter, and the furniture. But every idiot in the world knows that dynamite usually doesn't work against a bank vault."

Caden stood as particles of dust settled around him. "The one thing they did right was knocking out the cameras." The system in the bank was an old one that just recorded on a monitor in the back room. He'd been trying to get the bank owner to update for years, but Mrs. Thomas thought Redemption, Wyoming, was as safe as safe could be. It was an attitude Caden hadn't much appreciated.

Even so, he'd send what remained of the video to techs at the FBI.

"Thanks for coming out when I called," Caden said.

"Oh, of course," Silias Bixby Sr. said. He'd worked as a bomb expert in New York for years before retiring to

Redemption, where his son and grandkids lived. His son, Bixby Jr., was one of Caden's best deputies.

The second the bomb had gone off, Caden had called Silias to come help, even though it was pretty obvious several different bombs had been placed around the exterior of the bank, all made of dynamite. "Dynamite can be traced, right?"

"Well, sometimes," Silias said. "My guess is this is something old from an abandoned mine around here, and you're not going to learn anything interesting. What I can't figure out is what they thought they'd accomplish. They must have thought they could do a fast dash and grab?"

Caden nodded. "When it didn't work, they left the remaining bombs on a timer and just left? These guys were real idiots."

"Yeah," Silias said. "You know, I did see a report of a bank robbery in a small town in Idaho where dynamite actually did blow enough of a wall away that the robbers could get into the bank vault. That bank was even older than this one. But considering the exterior of this bank looks so old, I guess it's possible they thought they had a shot. Their grand plan just didn't work out."

Caden reached for his radio and lifted it to his mouth. "Hey, Johnny, do we have anything on the robbers and their escape yet?"

Johnny clicked back. "No, not yet. We do have the CCTV from Gatlan's Grocery at the edge of town, and we're going through it now to see if we can spot them. Nothing yet."

"Okay. Thanks." Caden clicked off. His phone buzzed. He lifted it to his ear. "Scott."

"Hey, it's Austin. I'm back at the Cattle Club. One of my guys was able to hack into the bank feed before the explosions, and I have video."

Before the explosions? That meant that the Cattle Club

men had hacked into the system a while ago. Caden paused. "Did you just say one of your guys hacked—pre-explosion? How long have you all been breaking the law in this town?"

"Do you want to make a crime of it now? Or should we talk about it later?"

Caden would deal with them later. "What do you have?"

"Two men wearing full ski masks that covered their entire heads placing the explosives around the bank. One is big and broad. One is shorter and wiry. It's impossible to see facial features or hair because of the masks."

"One sounds like that Vince guy."

"Absolutely," Austin said. "We're fanning out, and we're tracing the routes they could have taken to get out of town. There's no doubt they were headed east based on other CCTV that we may or may not have acquired."

In other words, the recording from the grocery store. Caden briefly shut his eyes. "All right. We'll talk about the hacking later. For now, let's get everybody looking for them. Did you ID their vehicle?"

"Yeah, we have a van from the flower shop on Main. It's their delivery van. It looks like it was stolen earlier tonight, and they probably haven't even noticed yet. I'll call Johnny to put out a BOLO right now."

"Thanks." Caden appreciated that Austin had initiated the "be on the lookout" alert. He paused, then coughed out dust. "I called Mrs. Thomas earlier, and she's already hired a security team from the city to come guard the bank. They pulled up a few minutes ago and are scouting the area."

"Good plan. Talk soon." Austin clicked off.

"This is crazy." Ella suddenly appeared behind him.

Truth be told, he was surprised Johnny had been able to keep her at the station so long.

She looked around, her eyes wide. "The entire reception area is destroyed."

Caden put his arm around her. "Not only that, the back office is a disaster. The only thing that survived is the vault."

"So they didn't get anything?" She was so pale, a light blue vein showed in her forehead.

"No."

She cuddled into his side. "Did you find out who they are?"

"Not yet," Caden said. "But the description fits Vince. He was with a shorter man, kind of a wiry guy. Have you seen anybody like that around here lately?"

"No," she said, rubbing her head. "Well, no, wait, there was a new guy, but he was really nice. His name was Max, and he was newly married."

Right. Caden texted orders for Bixby Jr. to start looking for a wiry man named Max in the area. "What's his last name?"

"Lewiskowski," she said. "I took a photo of his ID." She glanced around the rubble. "Somewhere."

They weren't going to find that photo. "Give me all the details on Max, and I'll check him out. Just in case. We don't have a lot of new people in town, and I don't like the coincidence of both those strangers being here and then the bank being robbed."

"Okay," she said, stumbling back and surveying the disaster. "Also, I saw Max argue with another man on the sidewalk. He had a bushy beard with gray in it and looked broad."

"Did you see his face?"

"Not really."

Caden turned her toward his truck. "Let's get you home. Then we'll figure out our next steps."

She looked up, a smudge of dust already on her forehead. "Okay."

At least she'd agreed for once.

* * *

The loud ding of a phone jolted Ella out of a dream-filled sleep. "What?" she muttered.

Caden leaned over and snatched his phone off the bedside table, his chest bare and his body warm beside her. "Scott." Then he sat up. "When? All right, I'm on my way. Get everybody there." He was out of the bed in a second, yanking on his jeans and tugging a T-shirt over his strong torso.

Ella sat up and blinked sleep from her eyes. "What time is it?" A quick glance at the clock confirmed it was nearly 7:30 in the morning. "Wow." She'd slept well. "What's happening?"

"It looks like the hardware store on the other edge of town was just hit." He strapped his weapon to his thigh and reached for his badge on the table.

She pulled the covers closer to her chest. "It was just hit? Like robbed or another bomb?"

He ruffled his hand through his hair. "Sounds like another bomb and a robbery. These guys want money and are probably heading out of town right now. Even so, I want you to stay here—I'll have Johnny head out to cover you. Keep the door locked until he gets here."

"Okay." She rubbed her eyes. "I'll get up and make some coffee for him." She slipped from the bed and quickly dressed in her comfortable jeans and a light blue sweater. Thunder rolled high outside, and lightning struck the ground. "Yet another summer storm," she muttered. "Be careful."

"I will." He leaned over and gave her a quick peck on the cheek and then hustled out the door.

She hurried to the attached bath to take care of business before heading to the kitchen to start coffee. The sky split open with a loud clack outside, and rain began to beat against the side of the house. She shivered and started the coffeepot. About ten minutes later, a quick rap echoed at the door. Oh good. Johnny was there. At least she'd be kept in the loop. She padded quickly to the door and opened it.

Then she stopped short.

"Well, hello there," RJ Jones said, smiling.

She blinked twice. "Wait, what?"

He grabbed her arm and yanked her out onto the porch. "We've got to go."

It took another second for her brain to kick in. "Wait. No. RJ, what are you doing here?"

His fingers tightened painfully on her arm. "What I'm doing here is leaving."

Panic licked through her. The sight of a foot in her flowerbed caught her eye, and she craned her neck to peer over the porch. Deputy Johnny Whitcomb was facedown in the mud, rain pounding on his now dirty uniform. "Johnny!" she yelled.

He didn't move.

RJ tightened his grip painfully. She had to get away from him. Turning slightly, she angled to kick him in the knee. But he was too fast. In a surprisingly quick move, he manacled her around the neck and cut off her air.

She struggled against him, but he was stronger than he looked. Darkness began to fall over her vision. Then nothing. She was out.

What seemed like seconds later, somebody was slapping her hard across the face.

"Ouch!" She lifted a hand to ward off the pain.

"Wake up. You've got to wake up."

She slowly opened her eyes and pain flashed behind her temples. "RJ?"

He smiled, his teeth crooked in the morning light. "There

you go. I've never choked anybody out before. I had no clue you'd be out this long."

Memory of his arrival flashed through her along with fear. "Where are we?" She looked around as her vision finally cleared and found they were at the rear entrance to the bank. Yellow crime scene tape cordoned off the damaged building. "What are we . . ."

He grabbed her hair and yanked her out of a truck she recognized as belonging to his uncle. It was an old farm truck, and nobody would think twice about seeing it in town.

"Come on." He jerked her beneath the crime scene tape.

"RJ, what are you . . ." Then it hit her.

"Oh, yeah." His wiry body was dressed in black, but he had left his face uncovered. Of course, the cameras weren't working. "Come on." He jerked her over a series of crumbled bricks to the still intact vault. Much of the outside wall remained standing, even though part of the roof had been ripped off. Rain pelted down on them. He glanced at his watch. "In about two minutes, the automatic lock is going to release and you can open this vault, right?"

She tried to jerk away, looking frantically around.

His grip was relentless. "Trying to find the security guards? My partners took them out."

She gulped. "They killed those men?"

"Nah. We're in enough trouble. They knocked them out and are dropping them outside of town."

Dust particles still filled the air, and she sneezed. "This is a mistake. You have to know Caden will never stop looking for you."

RJ smiled and the sight was garish. "He's not going to know it's me, Ella, because you're coming with me."

Her stomach lurched. "I'm not going anywhere with you."

"Yeah, you are. I promised Vince."

Her breath heated. "So you guys *are* working together." Anger poured through her.

"Of course we're working together. I'm usually the getaway driver, but we figured that wouldn't work in this case. So we came up with a second plan."

She looked at the torn cement floor. "You set off these bombs as a decoy?"

"Now you're getting it," RJ said. "Right now, Vince and Max have robbed the hardware store, which will keep the sheriff and all the deputies busy." His beady gaze darted to his watch. "In about two minutes, there's going to be an explosion out at the football field. Don't worry. Nobody will be hurt."

Ella finally jerked away, fury making her ears ring. "How could you do this to your uncle and the rest of the town?"

His bloodshot gaze narrowed on her. "This town never did nothing for me. I was sent here after a couple of minor car thefts, and my uncle tried to give me tough love and teach me to work a farm. Do I look like a guy who's going to work a farm?"

"No," Ella snapped. "You look like an asshole who's going to spend the rest of his life in prison." Her mind finally came fully awake. "Did you kill Johnny?" She hadn't been able to tell whether he was dead or alive.

"I wouldn't worry about that dork. You should probably be thinking about how to keep me happy so I don't turn you over to Vince—or kill you." The casual way he spoke of murder chilled her.

The vault lock released with an audible click, just on time. "There we go," RJ said. "Now, before anybody realizes the security guards are gone, you're going to open this puppy."

CHAPTER 15

Caden finished taking Hal's statement as the paramedic rechecked the elderly man's vital signs. Hal had owned the hardware store since the beginning of time and had to be pushing ninety years old. The idea that he'd been shoved around pissed Caden off to a new degree of fury.

Austin walked up after surveying the scene. "How much did they get?"

"About five grand," Caden said, shaking his head. Hal was known for distrusting banks, even the small one in town, so it wasn't a surprise he'd kept so much money beneath the counter.

Austin looked at the front door, which had been blown apart with dynamite. "Does this seem like overkill to you?"

"Yeah, and not only that, the explosion was triggered *after* these guys got the money."

Unfortunately, there weren't any CCTV cameras in the hardware store or outside of it, but the grocery store was only two blocks away. The stolen flower truck had been spotted with two men, still wearing full face masks, headed north of town. "Do we have a blockade set up?" Caden asked.

"Yeah," Austin said. "There are multiple turnoffs that go into the mountains, though. I'd be shocked if they kept to the main road. I have all the Cattle Club men out either on horseback or UTVs, trying to cover as many of those side roads as possible. We'll get them, Caden."

"I know." He had almost all his deputies out looking and was relieved to have the club's utility terrain vehicles as well. But there were innumerable paths from town through the mountains, and if they didn't find these guys soon, they never would. "Did you get a chance to view the video?"

"I haven't," Austin said. "Jesse took a look, and he said one of the guys was large and the other smaller and wiry. It's definitely this Vince."

"We haven't had any hits on the composite," Caden said. They'd already compared the CCTV from when Vince first came into the bank, but since he'd been wearing a hat and had a beard on his face, it was difficult to get a clear rendering of his features from those photos.

The earth moved slightly, and he paused. "Was that another explosion?" His phone instantly buzzed. "Scott," he answered.

"Hey, Sheriff. It's Bixby Jr. We're getting reports of an explosion out at the football field."

"Damn it," Caden said. Hopefully there weren't any kids beneath the bleachers meeting for "coffee and kisses," as the kids called it. "Let's go, Austin." He patted Hal on the shoulder. "You need to go to the hospital."

"I'm fine," the storekeeper grumbled. "I'm just pissed they took my money. We're going to find them, right?"

"Absolutely," Caden said. He nodded to the paramedic. "Take him to the hospital. He needs to be checked out." He left the paramedic to deal with Hal, then strode out the door with Austin at his side. His phone buzzed again. "Damn it. What?" he answered.

"Uh, Sheriff, it's Johnny," his deputy croaked over the sound of rain pinging off metal.

Everything inside Caden went cold. "What's going on?"

"I don't know. I got to your place and then somebody hit me from behind. I don't know how long I was out. Ella's gone."

Caden's call-waiting buzzed, and he clicked over. "What?" he barked. "Ella?"

"No. Hi, Sheriff. It's Sandra. I was opening the diner and . . . I don't know. This is probably silly to call you, but I saw Ella and RJ Jones in Henry's truck, and she made a face at me as they drove by that I—"

"Which way were they going?" Caden demanded.

"Um, they were going north on Main Street," Sandra said. "Should I have done something?"

"No, no, you're good. Thank you, Sandra." Caden clicked off.

Austin looked at him.

Caden went cold. "I think RJ has Ella." He shoved all emotion away. He had to act.

"Let's go." Austin clapped him on the shoulder, already snapping orders into his phone. "I'm sending somebody to the bank, and then everybody else will move to finding this truck. Tell me about Henry's rig."

Caden described the old farm truck. It was a light blue with rusted rims.

Austin's faced hardened. "They're headed north, which gives them multiple side roads and trails to take."

Caden's anger spiked along with panic. "We have to find her."

"We will," Austin said grimly. "I'll get everybody on it. For now, we'll forget Vince and his partner. We will get her."

Caden couldn't breathe. He couldn't lose her now.

* * *

Ella's hands were tied in front of her, and the seat belt was fastened over her arms, making it difficult to move. RJ had already driven onto a barely visible logging trail, careening over the dirt and through a series of trees. Her head pounded even more than it had earlier. How long had she been out? She couldn't even remember. "RJ, you have the money. Now let me go."

RJ drove too fast for the conditions, and the tires spun in the mud several times. The rain continued to beat down, limiting visibility. "Hey, I'm doing you a favor. You have any idea of what Vince wants to do to you?"

Her stomach clenched. "Yeah, I do. Are you taking me to Vince?" She had to escape this truck.

"No, I'm not taking you to Vince. I had no idea there'd be twenty-five grand in the bank." His eyes gleamed as he hunched over the steering wheel. "Seriously, I thought we'd get about five thousand."

She shook her head and immediately regretted it as pain pounded in her temples. Did she have a concussion? "What is your new, and no doubt brilliant, plan?"

"My plan is to take the money, hide it, and go tell my partners that there was only five grand there. So I'll keep twenty thousand for myself, and they'll never know it." He smiled gleefully. "This is the best day ever."

"What about me, RJ?"

He looked sideways at her. "I figure you and I will have some fun for the next couple of days, and then I'll let you go."

Something told her that he wasn't going to release her. "You don't seem like a killer to me."

"I don't like killing people. I think it creates problems further down the road. Plus I wouldn't want Caden to come after me forever." He laughed as if they were old friends.

Ella tried to force a smile, but it just wasn't happening.

"You know Caden's going to come after you, no matter what?"

"Yeah, I do know that," RJ said.

In other words, she was dead. If he was going to flee Caden, he wouldn't want a witness. "Enough people saw us in the truck together that everybody knows it's you," she said, trying to reason with him.

"Yeah, I know that, too," RJ said. "However, life on the run is easier than you think. My partners and I robbed a bank in Colorado, and they didn't catch us, and they're not going to find us now. All we have to do is disappear."

"Your partners must know you," she countered as the truck bumped over several rock outcroppings. "They'll guess you double-crossed them, and then they'll just kill you."

His fingers tightened on the steering wheel. "I'm smarter than all three of them put together. They'll never know I got this much money from the bank. As for you, they're just going to be pissed I couldn't bring you, but you will have unfortunately passed on."

He wasn't hiding the truth any longer. "Your uncle would be so disappointed in you," she said angrily.

"I've always been a disappointment to him," RJ muttered. "Don't worry, Ella. He's not going to be disappointed too much longer."

The breath caught in her throat. "What did you do?"

"I haven't done anything yet. After I get clear of this, I'll figure it out."

"You'll be a fugitive after this, you dumbass," Ella snapped. "They're not going to let you inherit anything, even if you do kill your uncle." She had to figure out a way to save Henry, if she could do nothing else.

"I'm well aware of that," he snapped. "I had a great plan, but now I've got to alter it. It's not that hard."

Could she somehow get her arms free and open the door? "Oh, really? What's your new plan?"

"After this mess, Henry will no doubt take me out of his will." RJ spoke slowly as if just coming up with a plan. "But I do have a couple of friends and a girlfriend, even, that Henry could leave things to. I just have to figure out the right way to make it happen."

"You're insane," Ella whispered.

RJ laughed, and the sound grated on her in the small truck cab. "My girlfriend will show up on his doorstep pregnant, needing help. Uncle Henry will bring her right in, and then my plan can go from there."

Ella thought she might throw up. Her stomach lurched and bile rose in her throat. "Do you really have a pregnant girlfriend?"

"No, but it's not like I couldn't find somebody who'd want to help. There are a lot of people out there who need money."

He was absolutely evil. "I hope you enjoy your time in hell," she muttered.

"Yeah? You're going there before I do," he said. "Of course, like I said, we're going to have some fun first."

Just then, a massive wolf bounded across the dirt road in front of them.

"Harley?" Ella shrieked.

RJ screamed and hit the brakes. The truck swerved wildly in the mud, spinning around several times and then smashing into an ancient spruce tree on the passenger side. Ella hit her head on the window, and sparks flashed behind her eyes with sharp bursts of pain.

Silence slammed in after the truck settled in the mud. A second later, two powerful UTVs roared out of the forest, and her gaze caught on Caden driving one while Austin steered the other.

"Caden!" she yelled. Her ears rang.

RJ reached over and released her seat belt, grabbed her arm, and pulled her toward his door. He pulled a gun from his waistband and pressed it to her neck, forcing her out into the storm and toward Caden's UTV. "All right, Sheriff. Get out of the UTV, and let us take it," RJ yelled through the pounding rain.

Caden gracefully leaped out and faced them. "Let her go, or you're a dead man."

CHAPTER 16

Caden settled into fighting mode as naturally as breathing.

Austin came up on his other side, his gaze intense on RJ. The rest of the deputies and the Cattle Club men were covering the other country trails and roads, so it was just the two of them. He'd used his best guess that RJ would take this way out of town, and he'd been right. The rain beat mercilessly down as Caden stared straight into RJ's eyes. "Let her go and I won't kill you."

Ella gave a small sound of distress, and it took every ounce of his self-control to keep from reacting. "I mean it, RJ. You don't want to die today." He kept his hand loose on his weapon, which was unholstered.

RJ's gaze darted around wildly. He had Ella in front of him with a gun pressed to her neck. "Just get out of my way. I don't want to kill her, but I will."

Caden had no doubt he meant what he said. It was a risky shot to take, but there was no way he was letting RJ go with Ella. "I'll give you one chance. Release her, and we'll let you have a UTV," he offered.

Austin stiffened next to him but didn't otherwise react. Caden didn't care. He'd do anything to ensure Ella's safety, even if that meant letting RJ go for now.

RJ must've pressed harder against Ella because she squirmed to the side and twisted her neck, wincing.

Her gaze met Caden's, showing trust and acceptance. She trusted him to save her, and he would.

Harley stalked from the tree line toward RJ, growling. The fur along his back was raised. His head lowered and he moved closer, menace in every line of his muscled form.

RJ shifted slightly, his eyes widening on the animal. "What the hell? The wolf is your pet now?"

Caden shifted his weight, trying to put himself closer to Ella. He had no idea what the wild animal was capable of and wanted him to back off. The last thing he needed was for the beast to attack. "Austin, get your wolf to halt," he muttered.

Austin moved away at an angle, and they began flanking RJ. "He's not my wolf," he muttered. "I have no idea what he's doing, but he seems to be trying to help your girl."

"Yeah?" Right now the wolf was making RJ twitchy. The idiot's gaze kept darting from Caden to the wolf and back. He was freaking out, and that wouldn't do. Caden needed him calm and thinking. "Back off, Harley," Caden snapped. The wolf paused, looked at Caden, and then sat in the mud.

When the wolf settled, for some reason, Ella started to panic. She began to struggle against RJ, her eyes widening. "Let me go," she yelled, shoving her elbows back into his gut.

"Stop it," RJ snapped. "Or I will shoot you."

"Ella?" Caden said as soothingly as he could.

She fought harder, her eyes unfocused.

"Ella," he commanded, putting bite into his tone this time.

Her eyes focused on him again. "I need you to stay

calm," Caden said. "Stop struggling. I will get you out of this. You're going to be okay. Trust me."

She stopped struggling, her body trembling. She put her hands down and remained still, although she seemed to be gulping in air. It looked as if she might hyperventilate, and the wilder her breathing became, the more panicked RJ appeared.

"That's good," Caden said, reassuring her. "Take a couple of deep breaths and let them out slowly. You're doing great. Just hold on."

RJ began hauling her toward the nearest UTV. "This is what's going to happen, Sheriff. We're taking the UTV, and when I'm clear of you, I'll leave your girl somewhere safe. But if you don't stop moving right now, I'm going to shoot her and take the consequences. I don't have anything to lose."

Caden's jaw firmed. "One last chance. Let go of Ella."

RJ almost had her to the UTV. They were so close. "She's coming with me, Sheriff." His eyes narrowed and his finger twitched on the trigger.

Soundlessly, Austin moved closer to RJ. "He's losing it," he muttered quietly.

Caden swallowed and settled his body. He exhaled. "RJ? Let her go."

"No," RJ yelled, his face turning red.

In one smooth motion, Caden raised his weapon, pointed, and fired.

One second RJ had the gun against her neck, and the next his body flew back to hit a sycamore tree. Ella screamed and started to run toward Caden, sliding in the mud but not stopping.

He caught her and wrapped one arm around her waist,

handing his weapon off to Austin. "You're okay. I've got you, baby," he said, holding her tight.

Her whole body shook so hard her teeth rattled. Tears streamed from her eyes. "I was so scared."

"I know." He leaned back and wiped her face with gentle thumbs, the pads of his fingers rough. "You're okay. I've got you." And he did.

She burrowed into him. "When I was at the house, I didn't know it was RJ at the door." All of her thoughts poured out of her mouth, and she couldn't stop them. Her teeth kept chattering. "Is Johnny okay? He wasn't moving in the mud, and I hope he isn't dead. Please tell me RJ didn't shoot him."

Caden kissed the top of her head, his hold still tight. "Johnny is fine. He's the one who called in your abduction. I'm sure he's at the hospital getting checked for a concussion, but he's okay."

She blinked away tears. "Did anybody else get hurt?"

"No. They blew up the bleachers at the high school, but no kids were around."

Thank goodness. "I gave RJ the money, Caden. I didn't know what else to do."

"You did the right thing, honey. I'm sure the money's in the truck. We'll get it back, and no money could ever compare to the value of your life. You have to know that." His breath was warm against her head, even though the rain continued to pummel them, throwing up glops of mud. "I'm proud of you."

She'd been terrified, and the only person she could think about was Caden. The thought that they wouldn't have a future together had burned through her brain. What if it had been too late? She snuggled closer to him. "I'm so sorry. I should have said yes right away. I do want to marry you. I didn't mean to be so stubborn."

"I like you stubborn. I've always liked you stubborn, and don't worry, I knew we'd get married." He tugged the ring out of his pocket. "This. On. You. Now."

She held out her hand, and he slid the diamond back where it belonged. She paused and tried to look over her shoulder. "Is RJ dead?"

Caden planted a hand firmly on the back of her head and kept her face pressed to his chest. "There's no need to look. Just take more deep breaths and hold on to me."

She'd hold on to him forever. Even so, she angled her face a bit to see Austin.

He looked up from crouching near the prone man. "Oh, yeah. RJ's dead. Clear shot center of the forehead." His gaze was appraising. "Looks like you had some sniper experience, Sheriff."

Caden just pulled Ella closer and held tight. "Austin, what do you think about being one of my groomsmen?" he asked.

EPILOGUE

It was the perfect day for a wedding. The sky was a cerulean blue, the wind slight, and the atmosphere celebratory. Ella double-checked herself in the long mirror again.

"Oh, you look beautiful," her mother whispered, tears in her eyes. "I knew my dress would fit you."

It was the perfect dress. It was white and long with short sleeves and a V-necked bodice that narrowed to a tiny waist surrounded by crystals. "I really do love the dress," she said on a whisper.

Her mom stood and fixed the veil. "You look beautiful, Ella. I'm so proud of you."

Ella hugged her mom. At nearly sixty, her mom looked forty, with just a few strands of gray strewn through her brown hair. She was as tall as Ella with similar bone structure. She'd arrived with her new beau, a guy named Phillip, who was from Alaska. The man had retired after working as a fisherman for several years. Ella had liked him immediately. He was rough and tumble, but he seemed like a nice guy.

"All right, I have to go take my place," her mom said, hugging her quickly. "I think it's very sweet that you're having Caden's dad walk you down the aisle. I've always really liked both Frank and Louise Scott." She winked. "They'll make wonderful grandparents someday, as will I."

Ella chuckled. She'd found out just a week before that she wasn't pregnant. She definitely wanted to have children someday, maybe after they finished campaigning for the governorship, which she knew Caden would win. She had so many grand plans, and she couldn't wait to start living them.

She glanced out the window at the outdoor venue. Though Henry Jones was still mourning for his nephew, the man had immediately offered his farm for their wedding setting. And it was perfect. They'd turned the nearest barn into a reception area and a couple of the Cattle Club men had built a gorgeous gazebo.

It looked as if Henry was onto something, creating a wedding venue at his farm, and she was happy to be the first to use it. Maybe he had found a new calling.

Sparkling lights twinkled around the barn, which had been opened and now held tables and a nice bar area. She noticed her bridesmaids gathering toward the end of the aisle along with the groomsmen. Caden's brother Jack had flown in to be his best man, and both Austin and Mac were serving as groomsmen. Caden had apparently sat the Cattle Club men down and questioned them about their lives, and whatever he'd learned seemed to have pleased him. He'd never break a confidence, but if he thought they were good for the town, then they definitely were.

She had Tara, Cami, and Sandra as her bridesmaids, and each looked lovely in lightweight, pale yellow dresses with flowers in their hair. Cami had been tight-lipped about her status or possible condition, and Ella hadn't pushed.

Her gaze caught on Mrs. Thomas, preening on one of the chairs. The two security guards had been found trussed up but alive, and the normally cheap woman had offered to pay their hospital bills. It was a surprisingly kind gesture.

Greg Simpson stood tall and broad by his nephews and niece over to the side, his gaze squarely on the bridesmaids. Well, on one bridesmaid in particular. He and Tara had dated in high school, and then he'd left for the service. Upon his brother's death a few months ago, he'd returned home to take care of the kids.

Tara looked up, saw him, and blushed a lovely peach color.

"Interesting," Ella murmured. Should she and Cami start matchmaking? Maybe there'd be more than one wedding this summer.

She couldn't believe she was getting married.

Her mom took her seat up front with Phillip, and the music began. Ella watched as her friends walked down the aisle.

Caden's dad appeared in her doorway. He was just as handsome as Caden with a rugged jawline and laugh lines crinkling out from his vivid green eyes. There was no doubt Caden was his son. "Are you ready, gorgeous?" he asked.

She smiled. "I think so."

He chuckled. "He'll be a good husband to you. If not, I'll take him out back and shoot him."

She laughed. "I appreciate that, Mr. Scott."

He rolled his eyes. "I've told you repeatedly to call me Frank, but if you can't manage Frank, then how about Dad?"

It was one of the sweetest things she'd ever heard. Though she'd invited her own father to the wedding, she'd never heard back from him, which hadn't surprised her. She moved toward the man who would one day be a grand-father to her children. "I could go with 'Dad.'"

His chest puffed out. "Well, now that just made me as happy as happy can be." He held out an arm. "You ready to do this thing?"

Anticipation rolled through her. "I am more than ready." They walked outside the small farmhouse toward the end of the aisle. Somebody had laid down a beautiful white carpet, and pink flowers already dotted the way. The music sounded, and she started walking down the aisle, her gaze seeking Caden up front. He was dressed in a black tux and looked both dangerous and sexy. His hair was cut shorter than usual, and he'd shaved, which only emphasized his hard-cut jaw.

His eyes warmed when he saw her.

She nearly tripped, and his father gently settled her as they continued on their way to Caden. She couldn't look anywhere else. She believed in him, and she trusted him. Life was going to be an adventure, but they'd make it together. While RJ was gone, there was still a search on for the other two men involved in the robberies. They had worn thick masks, and nobody knew their real last names or where they'd gone, but she had no doubt they'd be found.

For now, she was going to enjoy her day. She had almost reached Caden when Harley bounded out of nowhere and skidded to a stop next to him. She halted.

"Whoa!" Frank said, looking at his son.

Caden stared down at the wolf, and some sort of look passed between them. Caden nodded. "Got it."

The wolf turned and bounded away with all the guests watching and a few people gasping.

Frank collected himself and escorted her the rest of the way to Caden, who took her hands immediately.

"What was that about?" she asked.

Caden shook his head. "Harley is part of the family, right?"

She nodded. "Most definitely." The wolf had helped the other day. Who knew, maybe he was a friend.

Caden leaned in and kissed her.

"Hey!" the minister said. "Don't jump the gun there, buddy."

The crowd laughed. Ella smiled up at him. "You can jump the gun anytime."

"Thank you," Caden said, leaning in and kissing her again. "I love you."

Hope and love burst through her. "I love you, too," she said. They'd last forever. She was sure of it.

ONE LAST KISS

⚜

KAT MARTIN

CHAPTER 1

The black-robed judge rapped the gavel, and the courtroom fell silent. As the judge rose and stepped down from the dais, a rising tide of chatter swelled among the wooden pews filled with spectators, miscellaneous family members, lawyers, and their clients.

"I'm sorry, Libby, but the judge has made his ruling. Your uncle's will stands as written. That includes the provisions that apply to you."

The tall doors opened with a clang, and Liberty Hale rose from her place next to her attorney, Bert Strieber.

"As far as the ruling applies to Uncle Marty's greedy family, I couldn't be happier. None of them deserved a nickel more than they received in the will. Uncle Marty's contribution to the Save an Animal Foundation was his business, not theirs. That money will do a lot of good, exactly what my uncle wanted."

Bert waited for her to step into the aisle behind the crowd exiting the courtroom, then followed. He was an older, gray-haired man, a little stoop-shouldered, one of Uncle Marty's best friends. For an instant, Libby's mind strayed to the dignified, handsome older man who had raised her. The only family member willing to assume the burden of providing a home for an orphaned twelve-year-old girl, her grandfather's brother had taken her in after her parents had been killed in a car accident.

Tears threatened. Libby clamped down on her emotions. Martin Hale had died two months ago. Libby was still grieving, trying to accept his death, though after months of battling cancer, Uncle Marty had seen the end as a blessing.

She took a shaky breath. "As I said, I'm glad Judge Barrymore refused to give in to my cousins' outrageous demands. As for me, Uncle Marty left me more money than I ever imagined. It's the provision he created in order for me to get it that I don't understand."

Bert came up beside her as they moved along the aisle. "I can only tell you that whatever your uncle did, he always had your best interests at heart."

It was true and yet . . . "Or else he's still trying to control me."

She loved her uncle as much as the parents she had lost fourteen years ago. Uncle Marty had always been there for her, had always given her anything and everything she wanted. Then he'd fallen ill, and something had shifted between them.

They'd argued about her future—the fact that she really had nothing specific in mind, nothing beyond having a good time and indulging herself in wildly expensive shopping excursions.

Uncle Marty had continually brought up her childhood, reminding her of where she had come from, the small Kansas wheat farm where she was born and raised until the accident.

Somehow that concern had morphed into the strange codicil to the will requiring her to spend part of her summer in the middle of Nowhere, Colorado—on some dude ranch she had never even heard of.

Libby sighed. Trailing behind the grasping family members streaming through the tall mahogany courtroom doors, she and Bert made their way into the anteroom. A few feet ahead of her, Martha Newman, her second cousin by marriage, stopped and turned to face her.

"I hope you're happy, you spoiled little bitch. A bunch of stupid animals are getting half of Martin's fortune. He never should have taken you in when your loser parents died."

A wave of fury hit her so hard her whole body tightened. If Bert hadn't grabbed her shoulder and pulled her back, she would have launched herself at the red-haired witch married to her cousin Ferris.

"Ignore her and keep walking," Bert said.

Since a wrestling match in the foyer of the courthouse was probably a bad idea, Libby kept moving, making her way out through the glass front doors onto Centre Street in Lower Manhattan. The black Lincoln Town Car they had arrived in pulled away from the spot where it had been waiting and drove up to the curb.

As the driver opened the rear door, a rush of warm July wind sent Libby's hair flying, tossing long blond curls over her shoulders. She ducked into the car and slid across the seat, leaving plenty of room for Bert, who climbed in beside her.

"You shouldn't pay any attention to Martha," Bert said. "She's always been a jealous fool."

Because it was true, Libby didn't argue. "Are you sure there's nothing else we can do about the will?"

Bert shook his head. "At this point, Libby, you've got two choices. You can spend a month on the guest ranch, as your uncle's will insists, or you can forfeit your inheritance. I realize you have income from your career as a makeup model, but it's sporadic at best, and let's be honest, your tastes are extremely expensive. Your apartment costs a small fortune." He glanced down at the red leather stiletto heels that matched her outfit. "I would venture to guess the shoes you're wearing cost at least six hundred dollars. Am I correct?"

"Eight hundred." She turned her slim ankle one way and another, showing off her pretty pumps. "These are Louboutins."

"Yes, well, then I suggest you do as your uncle wishes and spend your month at the ranch." He leaned back against the seat. "You know, there is always a chance you might actually enjoy yourself."

Libby scoffed, rolling her long-lashed, heavily mascaraed blue eyes. As a model for some of the top cosmetics companies in the world, she felt an obligation to always look her best. "You have got to be kidding."

Bert chuckled but made no comment.

Crossing her arms over her chest, Libby fell back against the seat. For the first time since Uncle Marty had died, she felt something besides agonizing grief. She was filled with anger and resentment toward the man who was still controlling her, even from the grave. Worse yet, he was determined to put her life in the hands of yet another man.

Libby tried to form an image of the rancher whose orders she would have to follow for the next four weeks. According to Bert, the rancher's father, Chet Bridger, had been close friends with Uncle Marty. Then Chet died, his son inherited the property, and the friendship had continued.

The Bridger Ranch in the mountains northwest of Denver was a working cattle ranch that catered to visitors for a few months in the summer. But the requirements of the will were specific—Libby wouldn't be one of the paying guests; she would be working as one of the employees who served the guests.

Fresh irritation rolled through her. Sam Bridger would be in control of her life—for now. But in a little over a month from now, she would be free to live as she pleased. Libby vowed that from this day forward, no man would ever control her life again.

CHAPTER 2

Sam Bridger stood outside the Vail Valley Jet Center, the executive terminal at the Eagle County Airport, watching a sleek white Citation taxi toward the gate and brake to a halt.

The stairs were put in place, and the door swung open. A well-dressed blonde emerged from the plane, the only passenger aboard. Sam chafed with annoyance as he watched her descend the metal stairs, the spoiled city girl he would be babysitting for the next four weeks.

During the summer, when they opened the ranch to visitors as a means of making extra money, Julio Santiago, his foreman, or Big John Coolwater, his top ranch hand, usually picked up passengers for the hour ride from the airport back to Coffee Springs.

Unlike today, guests usually arrived at the regular passenger terminal, not the fancy private-jet runway. Most of the people with that kind of money flew in during the winter to ski in nearby Vail.

Unfortunately, this was Martin Hale's niece, and Sam considered Marty a friend. In accordance with the man's dying request, Sam had agreed to adhere to the terms Marty set out in the video he'd sent. In exchange for employing his niece, the Bridger Ranch would receive fifty thousand dollars, a sum Sam couldn't afford to turn down.

Not after last year's drought, the drop in beef prices, and the grass fire that had destroyed two of his best grazing pastures.

Sam would have agreed to Marty's request without the money. No way would he have refused a friend's last wish. But Martin Hale wasn't a fool, and Sam was sure the man knew all about the ranch's financial situation. The money was Marty's way of leaving him a bequest.

Sam watched the petite blonde with the beautiful face and gorgeous long hair descend the last of the metal stairs and walk toward him across the tarmac. In a short skirt and matching jacket, she was stunning, with shapely legs, a tiny waist, and a full bosom—the kind of woman who could make a man hard just by looking at him.

Unexpected arousal tightened his jeans, and his annoyance grew. Sam wondered if he had made a bargain with the devil.

CHAPTER 3

Libby looked up to see a tall man in worn cowboy boots and jeans, his blue denim shirt sleeves rolled up to the elbows, revealing muscular forearms. One of the ranch hands, she was sure. Good-looking, she had to admit, with a chest that threatened the snaps on the front of his shirt.

His hair was a shiny dark gold and long enough to curl over the back of his collar. He had a solid jaw and a cleft in his chin. Sun lines crinkled at the corners of his dark brown eyes.

He was better than good-looking, she thought, adjusting her first impression. But—she reminded herself—he was a man. That was reason enough to block him from her thoughts.

She waved as he approached, and he stopped right in front of her.

"Ms. Hale?"

"That's right. I assume you work at the ranch. If you're here to pick me up, my luggage is over there." She pointed a pink, freshly manicured nail toward a stack of leather-trimmed bags on a rolling cart, everything she might need for a month in near isolation in some wilderness outpost.

His gaze followed hers to the cart, and one dark gold eyebrow went up. "All of that's yours?"

She frowned. "If you don't think I brought enough, I can call a friend, have her UPS a few more things."

"Oh, I think you brought enough." He turned toward the valet working behind the concierge counter. "We could use your help over here."

"Yes, sir."

"Take Ms. Hale's luggage out to my truck. It's parked right in front."

"Yes, sir." The young valet couldn't seem to move fast enough. The ranch hand did have a commanding way about him. Uncle Marty had spoken with the same kind of authority. People did whatever he asked without question. She knew it was more than just the billions he was worth, though that clearly added to the motivation.

A memory arose of the warmth in her uncle's eyes whenever they were together and the crooked smile she had come to love. Her eyes misted. Libby blinked away any hint of tears. It was time to move forward, and that was exactly what she intended to do.

Four weeks from now, her life could begin in earnest, she thought as she followed the valet pushing the cart out of the terminal, across the sidewalk to a big black Dodge Ram truck. The weather was warm, but the air was dry, not humid as it had been in Manhattan, and at this altitude, not nearly as hot.

She watched as the tall, blond ranch hand started grabbing luggage off the cart and tossing it into the back of the pickup.

"Be careful, that's Louis Vuitton! It was a gift, customized with my initials."

He clamped his hands on a pair of narrow hips, and his eyes darkened. "You want to load it yourself?"

"Well, no, of course not, but—"

"Then stay out of my way." He loaded the rest of the

bags with only a little more care than the first few, walked over to the passenger side, and opened the door. "Get in."

"How far is the ranch?" she asked.

"It's about an hour's drive from here."

"I guess if we're going to be together for the next hour, I ought to at least know your name. I'm Libby Hale."

"Oh, we're going to be together a lot longer than an hour." When she struggled to climb into the truck, he gripped her waist, hoisted her up as if she weighed nothing, and practically tossed her into the seat. "We'll be spending a lot of time together in the next few weeks. My name is Sam Bridger."

The door slammed loudly as the name echoed through her head. *Sam Bridger.* The man who would determine her fate until she completed the provisions of her uncle's will.

As the driver's side door opened and Bridger slid in behind the wheel, Libby felt the color climbing into her face. She didn't like to hurt people's feelings, and clearly she had.

"I'm sorry, I didn't mean to insult you. I thought the owner would be older, you know, gray-haired, maybe a man a little closer to my uncle's age."

"Sorry to disappoint." Firing the engine, Bridger put the truck in gear and pulled away from the curb.

"It's not your fault. I'm just not used to, you know, being around people like you."

"Country bumpkins, you mean?"

Her cheeks burned. "No, of course not. Rural people. People who live in small towns. I was raised in the city."

He seemed to relax a little, the tension leaving those ridiculously wide shoulders. "With any luck, you'll get used to it out here. Maybe you'll even learn to like it."

"That's what Bert said."

"And Bert is who? Your boyfriend?"

"No. I don't have a boyfriend. I don't date."

For the first time, he actually seemed interested in what she was saying.

"What do you mean, you don't date? A woman who looks like you?" He flicked her a glance that ran from the top of her head to the toes of her five-inch heels. "You have to have men fawning all over you."

She gave him a look. "Exactly the reason I don't date." Men did fawn all over her, but only for one reason—the way she looked. She'd been born with amazing genes, which had given her a near perfect body and a face to go with it. It was nothing more than pure luck.

Men were interested—no question about that. But once a man got what he wanted, he was gone. None of them gave a damn about her beyond sex. Fortunately, it hadn't taken her long to figure that out.

"When you say you don't date, do you mean since last week, last month, or last year?"

She sighed. "I mean I haven't been out with a guy for three years."

"So, what then? You're a lesbian?"

She sighed. "Sometimes I wish I were, but no. Not that there's anything wrong with it and not that it's any of your business."

"True enough."

"What about you? You live out in the middle of nowhere. How long since you had a date?"

Sam laughed. It was the first time she had seen any expression of humor on his face. It changed his looks so dramatically she felt a warm tug in the pit of her stomach.

"Not three years."

No, he was probably another womanizing snake. She seemed to attract them, though so far, Sam Bridger appeared to have no interest in her at all on a male-female level.

They rode along in silence. She was sure she would catch him checking her out. She was wearing a short navy-blue pencil skirt, a pale blue sleeveless silk blouse, and her usual spike heels. Bridger didn't seem to notice.

His lack of interest should have pleased her. Instead, she felt a trickle of irritation. At least the scenery along the route to the ranch kept her entertained: rugged sage-and-mesquite-covered mountains at the lower elevations, tall pine-covered peaks in the distance. The road wound through the country-side, climbing upward, each turn more intriguing than the last.

Just before reaching the tiny town of Coffee Springs—a mile ahead according to a sign on the side of the road—Bridger turned off Highway 131 onto a narrower strip of pavement.

"How far are we from the ranch?" she asked.

"About eight miles."

"So town's not that far away."

His head swiveled toward her. "If you can call Coffee Springs a town."

That didn't sound promising.

Sam kept driving, finally pulling onto a gravel road that led to a wooden gate. A sign read BRIDGER RANCH. Below it was a big wrought iron *B* with a circle around it.

"That's our brand," he explained. "Circle B."

He used a device to open the gate, then continued up the hill, passing lush green pastures dotted with clusters of black steers whose glossy coats gleamed in the sun.

"Black Angus," Sam said. "That's what we raise here on the ranch."

She loved animals. She trusted them way more than people. "They're beautiful."

Sam's gaze swung toward her. "You think so?"

"Don't you?"

"Sure, but that's different. I live here. I deal with them every day."

Her gaze went back to the grassy pastures. "Look at those sweet little calves. Such darling faces."

Amusement touched his features. "On a ranch, you learn very young not to get too attached to them."

Because they grew up and people ate them. "I'm a vegetarian," she said.

Bridger's eyebrows shot up. He cast her a look of pure disbelief. "I can see you're going to fit right in."

Libby's mouth tightened. She didn't have a problem with people who ate meat. After all, humans were carnivores. It was part of their nature. In the back of her mind, she still remembered the taste of a charcoaled hamburger. Her mouth watered at the mere thought of it. It was just that she kept thinking of the animals who provided the nourishment.

She spotted the ranch house ahead, a long, single-story, sprawling wood-frame structure. Huge plate glass windows looked out at the mountains. The view had to be spectacular. A barn sat on one side of the house, and a little farther up the hill, there was a row of wood-framed guest cabins, each with a covered porch out front.

Sam drove up to the house and turned off the engine, then climbed out of the truck.

"Welcome to Bridger Ranch. Let's go inside. Clara's going to need your help in the kitchen."

"Clara's your wife?"

Those piercing dark eyes fixed on her face. "I'm not married."

"Oh." Why she felt a sweep of relief, she didn't know. "So she's your chef?"

He scoffed. "Clara Winslow's my aunt and the ranch

cook." Bridger unloaded her bags from the bed of the truck and grabbed the handles of the two biggest pieces. "Grab a couple of those others and let's go."

She looked down at the bags. Bridger was already walking toward the front door, leaving her to fend for herself. She grabbed two of the other three bags, which turned out to be a lot heavier than they looked. One of the bell staff at her apartment building had carried the luggage down and loaded it into the limo for the drive to the Teterboro jet terminal.

As she entered the foyer beneath a wrought iron chandelier in the shape of a wagon wheel, one of the bags slipped out of her hands and hit the slate floor in front of a pair of long, jean-clad legs in worn cowboy boots.

"Sorry," she said.

"No problem. Just pick it up, follow me, and I'll show you your room. You can come back and get the other stuff later."

She glanced back the way they had come. "I thought I'd be staying in one of the cabins."

"Sorry, those are for paying guests. You're an employee." Bridger started walking.

Libby grabbed the leather handles, hoisted up the bags, and followed him down the hall.

"Your room's at the far end next to the bathroom," he said.

"What do you mean *next to the bathroom*? Are you telling me the bathroom isn't en suite?"

Sam Bridger actually grinned. "Mine is."

Libby swore a nasty oath beneath her breath. She was surprised he even knew the meaning of the French word. She couldn't believe she'd have to stomp down the hall in her nightgown in the middle of the night.

Suspicion crept through her. "Where's your room?"

Sam's mouth edged up at the corner. There was a ruggedness about him that should have made him less handsome but didn't.

"My room's at the other end of the hall."

"Where does your aunt sleep?"

"She's got her own quarters off the kitchen." Bridger opened the bedroom door and stepped back to let her in.

Libby spotted her big bags tossed up on the queen-size four-poster bed, dropped the ones she was carrying, and fought an urge to rub the muscles in her lower back. Her gaze went to the door.

"There's a lock," Bridger said, reading her mind. "But you don't have to worry. I'd never cross the line between employer and employee."

Libby clenched her teeth. Dear God, the man was insufferable. She hated the place already, and she had only just arrived!

CHAPTER 4

Leaving Libby with instructions to change into her work clothes and meet him in the kitchen, Sam strode back down the hall and out the front door, slamming it behind him harder than he intended.

Dammit! If Martin Hale were still alive, Sam would curse him straight to hell.

For chrissake, he wasn't the kind of man who let a woman carry her own bags! Or made her feel anything less than welcome. He'd been raised to treat women with respect, even a certain reverence. He was nearly a foot taller than Libby and at least seventy pounds heavier. It wasn't fair to make the same demands on her that he would make on a man, no matter how sexist that sounded.

But Martin's video had been specific. No special treatment. She must carry her own weight, just like any other employee.

Sam had known Marty Hale for years. When they first met, Sam had been a twenty-year-old kid, just enlisted in the army for a three-year stint after graduating from junior college. Martin had spent two weeks every summer at the ranch for fourteen straight years, even after Chet Bridger died. He knew Sam well enough to trust that if he accepted the fifty-thousand-dollar payment, he would uphold his end of the bargain.

He would treat Liberty Hale the same as any other person who worked on the ranch for the summer. Which, considering she was one of the most beautiful, sexiest females he had ever laid eyes on and he was a red-blooded male, wouldn't be easy to do.

After a couple of deep breaths, Sam walked back into the house, heading for the kitchen. Though the stainless appliances, cabinets, and countertops were new, the room itself was as old as the house, built sixty years ago, a big country kitchen with yellow daisy wallpaper and pale yellow curtains.

An old-fashioned butcher block sat opposite the sink, and there was a long wooden dining table surrounded by ladder-back chairs next to the window.

Both Sam's parents had passed—his dad six years ago, quickly followed by his mother. They'd been a close family, and the loss had hit him hard. Aunt Clara, his mom's older sister, had helped him through the worst of it. She had arrived at the ranch for Olivia Bridger's funeral and never left. Sam was thankful every day to have her there.

Standing at the stove stirring a pot of chili, Clara was a silver-haired woman, still attractive at sixty, with a few extra pounds smoothing out the wrinkles in her cheeks.

She smiled. "So . . . is she as pretty as she looks in her pictures?"

Photos of Libby had been included in the video, along with cosmetic ads from magazines, though Marty had shown Sam pictures of her on his phone over the years.

"They don't begin to do her justice."

Clara smiled. "I can't wait to meet her."

Good luck with that, he wanted to say, but didn't. Liberty, so named because she was born on the Fourth of July, was haughty and overindulged, clearly used to people waiting on her hand and foot. But he would let Clara make up her own mind.

He looked up just as Libby walked into the kitchen in a pair of skintight jeans with silver embroidery and rhinestones on the back pockets and a sleeveless white tank that showed a hint of cleavage. Sam felt the same punch in the gut he'd experienced the moment she had stepped out of the jet and started down the metal stairs.

As if his world had tilted sideways.

He didn't like it. He had a job to do, and it didn't include being sidetracked by a spoiled, rich, city girl. No, he didn't like it, but he was beginning to understand why Marty had sent her to the ranch. She needed a dose of reality, needed to come to grips with a future that no longer included her overprotective billionaire uncle, to prepare herself for a life she would be facing on her own.

"Libby, this is my aunt Clara."

Libby's warm smile surprised him. "A pleasure to meet you, Mrs. Winslow."

"It's just Clara, dear. Or Aunt Clara. That's what everyone calls me. And it's nice to meet you, too. Your uncle always spoke highly of you."

"I really miss him."

"I'm sure you do. He was a good man. It was always a pleasure to have him here."

"How well did you know him?" She flicked a glance at Sam as if the question were actually meant for him.

"Martin came here every summer," Clara answered. "Fourteen years in a row." Her eyes sparkled. "I think he liked my cooking."

Libby smiled. "He did love to eat."

"Marty loved spending time at the ranch," Sam said. "I

think that's why he wanted you to come, to discover the peace he found when he was here."

Her eyes narrowed. "You called him *Marty*?" She had the biggest, bluest eyes he'd ever seen, and the thickest black lashes. He wondered if they could possibly be real, then decided she was probably wearing a lot of mascara.

"We were friends," he said simply.

Libby shook her head. "It's hard to imagine. No one ever called Martin Hale *Marty*. Not even his friends."

"No one but you—is that what you're saying?"

Her chin inched up. "That's right. No one but me." She glanced away, and he thought he caught the sheen of tears. It was probably just the light in the kitchen.

"He never even mentioned this place," Libby said. "He traveled a lot. Two weeks out of town was not unusual for him, but he never spoke about the Bridger Ranch." She sighed. "It's as if he were a different person when he was here."

"I think he *was* different," Sam said. "He told me once that these mountains were the only place he felt completely free."

Libby walked over to the window and looked out at the distant peaks, a few still touched with snow even at this time of year. "It's beautiful."

Sam's gaze followed hers. "Yeah, it is."

Silence fell. It took a moment for him to realize his attention had strayed from the scenery to the woman staring at it.

Anxious to get out of the kitchen and get his thoughts back where they belonged, Sam returned to the subject.

"Part of your duties include helping Clara with breakfast and dinner. She'll take care of the box lunches for the hands and any guests who want them while you clean the guest cabins. Once you're finished, the rest of the afternoon is yours. Your evenings are free after supper is over and the dishes are cleaned up."

One of her eyebrows arched, not golden like her hair, but darkened by a pencil. She was, after all, a makeup model. He wondered how much of her beauty was real and found himself wanting to find out.

"So that's what . . . ?" she asked. "About a twelve-hour workday? Maybe I should have my lawyer negotiate overtime pay."

His lips twitched. Her uncle had had a sharp wit. Apparently, his niece did, too. "What would normal overtime pay be for a makeup model?"

Her gaze sharpened. "How much did Marty tell you about me, anyway? Obviously, you know a lot more of my background than I know of yours, which is nothing."

He shrugged. "Fourteen summers is a long time, and he liked to talk about you."

"Good or bad?"

He smiled. "Both."

Libby flipped a golden curl over her shoulder. "Overtime pay at my level is around two hundred an hour."

Whoa. Plus Marty would have left her a barrel of money. "I don't think that's what your uncle had in mind."

She sighed. "No. For whatever reason, I don't suppose it is. Actually, being a model is a lot like being an actor. Sometimes you work, sometimes you don't. And waiting around for something to turn up can really be boring."

Her honesty surprised him. Then again, everything about her surprised him.

She flicked Clara a glance. "I guess if your aunt is willing to work that hard, I can, too."

Sam would have to see it to believe it. Still, there was a chance she had more grit than he'd first thought.

His gaze went to the rectangular shape in her front

pocket. "One more thing. Your cell phone stays in your room. You're free to use it on your own time when you're upstairs, but you can't bring it down here."

Her hand when protectively to the phone. "You're kidding, right? That's your idea of a joke?"

Sam cast her a pitying glance. "Sorry, no joke. One of the reasons people come here is to escape the outside world. Families want their kids to appreciate the beauty around them. People like your uncle . . . they just want a chance to be free from outside pressures, at least for a while."

Libby grumbled something he couldn't hear. "Fine," she said.

"All right, that's it for now. In the morning I'll show you around. The first guests will be arriving sometime tomorrow. You can help me check them in. Part of your job is to make them feel welcome."

She said nothing.

"Clara can fill you in on what she needs you to do in the kitchen. I'll see you both at supper." Turning, he walked out of the kitchen.

On his way to the barn, Sam spent a full five minutes trying to erase the memory of perfect breasts beneath a sleeveless white tank top and the sexy behind that was impossible to miss with the glitter of rhinestones on each cheek.

He gave a long-suffering sigh. The next month was going to seem like a lifetime.

CHAPTER 5

Libby made it through supper preparations with only a few minor mishaps. She had warned Clara ahead of time that she had no idea how to cook anything more than frozen pizza and an occasional omelet, but she was willing to learn.

"You'll do fine," Clara said, patting her hand, but the woman was smart enough not to give her any difficult tasks.

Libby peeled potatoes, saving the skins to feed the chickens, then washed lettuce and sliced tomatoes for a salad. She hadn't known dicing onions was such a miserable task until Sam walked in and saw tears rolling down her cheeks. His worried expression looked almost sympathetic.

Libby burst out laughing. "Onions," she told him, wiping the wetness from her cheeks.

Sam smiled with relief, and a warm feeling rose in her chest. It had been years since a man's smile had made her feel anything more than wary. She reminded herself not to let her guard down and quickly went back to work.

The meal—roast chicken, mashed potatoes, and gravy—came together smoothly, evidence of Clara's years of experience. There were vegetables right out of the garden and homemade bread, so there were plenty of vegetarian options for Libby.

Sam introduced her to the cowhands who worked at the ranch. Starting tomorrow, while guests were in residence, the men would take their meals in the bunkhouse.

Tonight they sat grouped around the kitchen table: Julio Santiago, the ranch foreman, an older Latino man with leathery skin burnt dark from the sun; Big John Coolwater, Native American, at least six feet six with long, black hair in a single thick braid.

Dare Landon was in his late twenties, a good-looking guy with sandy-brown hair who seemed quiet, capable, and kept to himself. He'd been raised on a ranch in Montana, Sam said, been in the marines before he'd come to work at the ranch. Ronnie Yates was a handsome African American man who struck her as intelligent and friendly. All of them were pleasant and respectful.

Fortunately, her kitchen duties didn't look all that daunting. Libby had worked a lot of different jobs in the city, but her boredom threshold was low and none of them had lasted very long. Sooner or later, she would find her true calling, she was sure, which definitely wasn't cooking or modeling of any kind.

In college at Columbia, she had taken a class in astronomy merely to satisfy a requirement for graduation, then ended up dropping out of school at the end of her third year. Much to her uncle's chagrin.

But the class had sparked an interest that remained. She thought of the hard-sided travel case up in her bedroom that held a Celestron NexStar Evolution portable telescope, one of Uncle Marty's most precious gifts. She planned to find a place outside to set up the scope as soon as she got settled.

She made another pass around the kitchen, paused to wipe up a trace of grease on the counter that she had missed. Clara had already gone to bed, but Libby felt oddly restless.

"The kitchen looks fine." Sam's deep voice rumbled

through her, sending little flutters into her stomach. He had left right after supper, and she hadn't seen him since. "You've had a long day," Sam said. "Why don't you go on to bed? You've got an early start in the morning."

She flicked a glance out the window. She had never seen a night sky so clear. The stars looked as if a huge crystal ball had exploded, scattering diamonds from one horizon to the other.

Libby nodded and untied the apron around her waist. Until that moment, she hadn't realized how exhausted she really was.

She didn't look at Sam as she crossed the room, but she could feel his eyes on her until she disappeared out the door.

Tomorrow would be her first official day. She groaned to think how many more days there would be until this nightmare was over.

The first guests arrived just before noon, when a white four-door Subaru SUV pulled up in front of the cabins. The Dunbar family lived in Denver, a three-hour drive away. It was their second year at the ranch, which Sam considered a sign of approval for a job well done.

As a young man, Caleb Dunbar, the father, had nursed a secret yearning to rodeo. Instead, he'd married, taken an accounting job in the city, and had a couple of kids. Though the man was clearly happy and crazy about his family, being at the ranch revived a little of his long-ago dream.

Sam heard the crunch of sneakers on gravel from somewhere behind and knew Libby had joined him. The scent of orange blossoms gave her away.

"Libby, this is Caleb and Jenny Dunbar." A lean, lanky,

dark-haired man, and his wife, a petite woman with curly, light brown hair. Sam looked down at the couple's ten-year-old son and eight-year-old daughter, miniatures of their parents. "These guys are Jordy and Suzy."

Libby smiled. "Nice to meet you all."

"Libby will be helping with chores while you're here," Sam explained. "She'll be taking care of Cougar Cabin. If there's anything you need, just let her know."

Libby's features tightened. Housekeeping definitely didn't appeal to her.

Too bad, Sam thought. Everyone carried their weight at Bridger Ranch.

Sam gave the Dunbars their keys, and the family went to work unloading their gear. Cougar Cabin was the largest, comprising a living room with a fireplace, a kitchen, two bedrooms, and two baths. There was a queen bed in one room and twin beds in the other.

"We'll see you at supper," Sam said.

Caleb gave a wave, and parents and children hurried away.

"Cute kids," Libby said.

Sam cast her a glance. "You like kids?"

"Sure. But they're a lot of work."

"True enough."

"Animals are a lot less trouble."

Sam just smiled.

The next guests to check in were a pair of older women, both widows, Alice Weeks and Betty Spurgis. Alice was short and plump, Betty slightly taller and thin. Both had short-cropped, iron-gray hair. They were staying in Badger Cabin, a smaller accommodation. It was their first time on a guest ranch, and both were excited.

Betty glanced around. "Oh, it's just beautiful here."

"We think so," Sam said, his gaze automatically going to the mountain range surrounding the pastures, rising toward the endless blue skies.

"We're especially looking forward to the pack trip," Alice said, following the line of his gaze.

Betty smiled. "I haven't been on a horse since I was a little girl." But she was dressed in jeans and boots, ready to go anytime.

"And we get to sleep in a tent," Alice added excitedly.

The corners of Libby's pouty lips turned down, and Sam couldn't stop a grin. "I guess Libby's not as enthusiastic about the trip as you two are. Maybe she'll change her mind once she's up there."

Betty's silver eyebrows went up. "You don't like camping?"

"I don't really know. I'm from Manhattan."

"We're from Phoenix," Alice said. "The photos on the website look wonderful. We can't wait to visit the high country."

"It's beautiful up there," Sam said. "You won't be disappointed." He helped the women with their luggage, then left them to settle in. Libby caught up with him as he strode toward the barn.

"You didn't say anything about sleeping in a tent," she muttered darkly.

"You're here to work. Guests enjoy different activities. Their days are pretty much their own. Some like to fish; others like hiking or sightseeing. One of the add-ons we offer is a camping trip into the mountains. Guests ride in on horseback. We lead a string of pack mules in with supplies, stay two nights, then ride back out."

"Do all the guests go on the trip?"

"Not all of them, no."

"Then I'll stay here and take care of those who remain behind."

If she were anyone else, he might let her. But it wasn't what Marty had wanted, and Marty was paying the bill. "Sorry, that's not going to happen. I'll need you to help with the cooking."

"So Clara's going on the trip?"

He almost laughed at her hopeful expression. "I do the camp cooking. You'll just need to pitch in with the meals and help with cleanup."

"But—"

"But what?" He cast her a glance. "You aren't afraid of horses, are you?"

"No, but—"

"The weather plays a role. At the moment, it looks like we won't be going till the end of next week. That'll give you some time to get used to the idea."

Libby grumbled something he was glad he couldn't hear.

At least so far she'd been pleasant to the guests. Still, she wasn't used to taking orders. He wondered how long her good humor would last.

The afternoon passed more quickly than Libby would have guessed. Between visitor check-ins, Sam had given her a tour of the ranch, or at least a portion of the 5,100-acre property he owned.

Along with the cabins, there were two barns—one with a large tack room—an equipment shed, the bunkhouse, and a metal structure that sheltered huge rolled bales of alfalfa stored for winter feed.

"We're a working cattle ranch," Sam explained. "That's

our main source of income. Having guests in the summer helps raise a little extra money, but it's not really what we do."

According to Sam, along with a thousand head of Black Angus cattle, there were thirty horses, the remuda, he called them. There was also a pigsty and a chicken coop.

Libby paused to watch the black-and-white-speckled hens pecking in the yard around the coop.

"Oh, you raise Plymouth Rocks!" she exclaimed. "And look at that beautiful Rhode Island Red rooster."

Sam's head swiveled toward her in amazement. "You know chickens?"

She shrugged. "I was raised on a farm." But the memories of the first twelve years of her life were buried mostly behind the wall of grief she had built to protect herself after her parents were killed. She remembered almost none of her childhood and didn't really want to.

When he continued to stare, she found herself telling him the truth. "I don't remember much about my life back then. Seeing the chickens sparked a memory of going with my mom to collect eggs from the coop. Some days it was like an Easter egg hunt. My mom had a way of making it fun." Libby swallowed past the sudden lump in her throat. She didn't like thinking about the past. It was just too painful.

Sam said nothing, but she thought that his features softened.

Next they went to visit the pigsty, an open-field enclosure with mounds of fresh straw. Half-round metal shelters offered the small group of pink-and-white pigs shade, and a shallow pond provided a place to bathe and cool themselves.

"We only raise enough animals for our own use, but the visitors enjoy them," Sam said. "We've also got five miniature goats. They're a real favorite with the kids."

Her interest sharpened. "Where are they? I'd love to see them."

Sam pulled out his cell and checked the screen. "Unfortunately, we're out of time. Our next guests should be arriving any minute." He tucked the phone into the back pocket of his jeans, and Libby's gaze lingered on his tight behind.

"Why do you get to use your cell and the rest of us don't?" she grumbled, annoyed with herself for noticing.

"Now that we have guests, I won't use it unless there's an emergency. As I said, people come here to escape the digital world we live in these days."

Sam started walking, and Libby lengthened her stride to keep up with him. "I'm surprised you have any cell service out here at all."

"It's spotty, that's for sure. There's not much once you head up in the hills, but close to the house it's fairly reliable."

At least she could use her phone in her room.

She looked up to see one of the ranch vehicles, a black Ford Expedition, pulling up in front of the cabins. The next guests to arrive had flown from Los Angeles into the Eagle airport, and Big John Coolwater had gone to pick them up.

According to Sam, they were on their honeymoon.

"You must be Brad and Kim Hillman," he said, shaking Brad's hand as Big John unloaded their luggage from the back of the SUV. "It's nice to meet you. I'm Sam Bridger, and this is Libby Hale."

"Good to meet you," Brad said. He was a lawyer, and he looked like one—attractive, with short, perfectly styled dark hair and blue eyes.

"Libby will be taking care of your cabin. If you need anything, just let her know."

Brad slid an arm around his pretty blond bride. "I've got everything I could possibly need right here."

Kim blushed.

"Congratulations to you both," Sam said. "You'll be staying in the Dove's Nest. That's our honeymoon cabin. I think you'll like it."

It turned out to be a one-bedroom with a natural rock fireplace in the living room, a king-size four-poster bed, and a kitchenette. All of the cabins, Libby discovered, were cozy and welcoming and reflected the mountain setting of the ranch.

When Big John set the couple's bags on the pine floor at the foot of the bed, Brad leaned down and brushed a soft kiss over Kim's lips. Warm color crept into her cheeks.

"This looks great," Brad said, his gaze sweeping the room furnished with a pine dresser and nightstands. "The bed looks real comfortable."

Kim's flush deepened.

"We'll leave you two to settle in," Sam said. "Part of the honeymoon package is your choice of supper with us in the main house or having your dinner brought over so you can eat here. You just need to let us know ahead of time."

Brad flicked Kim a heated glance. "We're both pretty slammed after the flight. I think we'll have supper here."

It wasn't hard to read Brad's plans for the evening . . . or the anticipation in Kim's pretty face. Libby's glance strayed from Sam to the big four-poster bed, and a little thread of heat curled low in her belly.

Sam's eyes met hers and seemed to turn a shade darker, but he made no comment as they left the cabin and headed back to the house.

"I don't think we'll be seeing much of the Hillmans," he said. "At least not for the first few days."

Libby glanced back over her shoulder and saw that the curtains had already been drawn. Unexpected longing welled inside her. "They really seem happy," she said.

"They're newlyweds and they're in love. That's the way it's supposed to work."

Libby pressed her lips together. "I suppose."

Sam paused outside the back door. "What? You don't believe in love? Is that the reason you don't date?"

She tilted her head back to look up at him. "I don't date because most men are selfish bastards. I hope Brad Hillman isn't one of them." With that she brushed past him, marched into the house, and closed the door.

CHAPTER 6

After supper, Sam spent a couple of hours in his study. There was always work to do: QuickBooks entries to check, supply orders to prepare, cost analyses to examine. The work was endless. He was grateful for Clara's help, along with the CPA in Coffee Springs who kept everything running smoothly.

Tonight his mind kept straying to Libby. She didn't trust men, that was for sure. Obviously, she'd been hurt badly. He wondered who had done it and felt a surge of protectiveness he hadn't expected.

The house was quiet as he walked down the hall to the kitchen for a glass of milk before heading up to bed. When something glinted on the deck off the dining room, he stepped outside and was surprised to find Libby sitting in a chair peering through a thick tube perched on a tripod.

"You're up late," he said, walking toward her. "Is that a telescope?"

Libby turned away from the scope. Although it was dark, he could tell she was smiling.

"Stargazing is my passion. I got interested in college, and it just stuck with me." She stared up at the blanket of stars overhead. "Isn't it amazing? The sky so black and clear, almost no light anywhere. The stars look like white diamonds on black velvet." She pointed up. "That's the Milky Way. You can just look up and see it. There's nothing like this in the city or anywhere else I've ever been."

Something shifted inside him. He was learning there was more to Libby Hale than he had first thought. "Except for the three years I spent in the army, I've lived in Coffee Springs all my life. You begin to take things for granted, I guess."

"Like being able to see the stars whenever you want?"

"Yeah."

"Want to take a closer look?"

"Sure." But he regretted the impulse the minute he moved closer and inhaled the soft, sweet scent of her.

Libby shifted forward to adjust a few knobs and bring the picture into focus, brushing her breasts against his shoulder and putting her cheek close to his. If he turned his head, he could kiss those full pouty lips.

His body stirred to life, and Sam bit back a groan.

"So what do you think? Isn't it something?"

He forced himself to concentrate. "Spectacular." But he couldn't help wondering if he was talking about the stars or the woman looking up at them.

He took a deep breath and eased away. "Thanks for sharing."

"You think it's safe to leave it set up out here?"

"We're not in New York. If you've got something to cover it and keep out the moisture, it should be fine."

"I've got everything I need."

Sam nodded. "Well, good night then."

He heard her moving around in the darkness behind him. "Good night, Sam."

There was an intimacy in the way she said his name that made his groin tighten. It was impossible to deny he wanted

her. Sam cursed Martin Hale again for putting him in this
position.

The last two guests arrived the next day, a couple of
fishermen. One was a black-haired man named Max Stoddard with a wiry build and darkly suntanned skin. The other,
Vince Nolan, was big and beefy, with straight blond hair
that nearly reached his thick-muscled shoulders.

Libby stood next to Sam as he made the introductions;
then the two men left to unpack their bags and make themselves at home in Wolverine Cabin.

They seemed different from the other guests, Libby
thought, a little less friendly, but maybe it was just her.

By the end of the first few days, she had settled into a
routine, finding the chores less distasteful than she had
imagined. The Dunbar kids picked up after themselves,
while the honeymooners, Kim and Brad, passed on housekeeping for two days in a row and mostly stayed in their
cabin. If Alice and Betty were in Badger Cabin when Libby
arrived, the women both pitched in to help.

In Wolverine, the fishermen, Max and Vince, slept late
and missed breakfast their first morning, picked up sack
lunches, grabbed fishing poles, and headed off to the creek.
At supper, they stayed mostly to themselves. The next day,
they ate and left but declined housekeeping, which was
fine with her.

The guests all seemed to be having a good time, and
Libby had to admit she was enjoying these days away from
the city far more than she had imagined.

This morning she'd awakened early and wandered over
to the window. Noticing the spectacular sunrise taking shape
outside, she quickly dragged on jeans and a long-sleeve

T-shirt, pulled her hair into a ponytail, grabbed her cell to take pictures, and headed downstairs.

Standing at the rail on the deck, she snapped a string of photos, excited to post them on her Instagram page and text them to her best friend, Caroline Thompson, back in the city. Finished, she stuck the phone in her pocket and just stood there watching the light, an array of pink, orange, rose, and gold that reminded her of rainbow sherbet.

Memories tickled the back of her mind—mornings she had stood outside the barn on the farm with her dad, watching the gray dawn brighten to a palette of beautiful colors. She remembered the smell of bacon frying and her mother humming in the kitchen as she cooked.

More memories surfaced. Her first day at school when she was five, getting on the school bus in the winter, her mom reminding her not to lose her gloves. Her chest ached. It took a moment for the sound of bootsteps behind her to register. Libby turned to see Sam, a worried look on his face.

"You're crying. What's wrong?"

She hadn't realized. She swallowed past the lump in her throat, reached up, and wiped the wetness from her cheeks. "It's nothing. I'm fine."

Sam didn't look convinced. His hand covered hers where it rested on the railing, and his touch gave her strength.

"Tell me," he said softly.

Libby dragged in a shaky breath. "I was twelve years old when my parents died. Marty probably told you that."

Sam nodded.

"I was devastated. My world fell completely apart, and I—I just couldn't cope."

"It had to be a terrible time for you."

She swallowed. "I couldn't handle the memories, so I blocked them. Even after I went to the city to live with

Uncle Marty, I refused to talk about my mom and dad or the life I left behind. Over time, it got easier just to forget those years ever happened."

She looked up at him. "And then I came here."

His eyes locked with hers, dark brown and compelling, as if he really wanted to know her thoughts.

"You were raised on a farm. Marty told me that. I guess in a lot of ways, a ranch is similar."

She looked back at the horizon, which had lightened to a soft yellow glow. "We had beautiful sunrises in Kansas. It's not mountainous like Colorado, but I loved living there as a kid. I hadn't realized how much I missed it until I came here."

The hand that covered hers gently squeezed. "Maybe that's why Marty sent you. So you could deal with the past you've tried so hard to forget."

Fresh tears threatened. "Maybe." Not wanting to look weak in front of him, she pulled her hand away and immediately felt the loss. "I need to go in and help Clara."

Sam nodded. As Libby turned away, his expression darkened. "What's that in your pocket? I thought I told you no phones allowed anywhere but your room."

Her mouth tightened. "I was taking a picture. I didn't bring my camera. Next time I'll ask your permission, though I don't think the sun is going to wait." She turned to leave, but Sam reached out and grabbed her arm, stopping her before she reached the door.

"I'm sorry," he said, surprising her. "I should have thought of that. I can't change the rules, but I can drive you into town, where you can buy one of those disposable cameras they sell at the mercantile."

Some of her anger faded. At least he was trying not to be a dick. "That sounds fair."

Sam's gaze went to her bare feet, and his lips twitched.

"You might want to buy yourself a pair of boots while you're there."

One of her eyebrows went up. "You're worried about the camping trip? You don't think my sneakers will work?"

Sam smiled. He had the nicest smile. "It's the horseback ride getting there that's the problem."

Libby smiled back. "I'll give it some thought."

Something shifted in the air between them, heating her from the inside out. Sam's eyes remained on her face, and Libby couldn't look away.

Worse yet, she didn't want to.

Until that moment, she hadn't realized what a danger Sam Bridger posed. As she headed into the house, Libby vowed not to forget again.

Sam thought of the woman taking pictures of the sunrise, and his chest felt tight. He was beginning to understand why Martin Hale had sent his beloved niece to the ranch. Marty hadn't been able to help her deal with her grief. Sam figured Marty was making a last-ditch effort to give her the gift of her past.

And he had enlisted Sam's help to do it.

Sam blew out a breath. Unfortunately, Marty hadn't anticipated the attraction Sam would feel toward his niece. Hell, Sam hadn't expected it, either.

Sure, she was beautiful. Petite and feminine, with miles of shiny blond hair. He wanted to grab a handful and drag her mouth to his, see if those pouty lips tasted as good as they looked. Just thinking about it made him hard.

This morning he had seen her without a trace of makeup, and if anything, she'd only looked more beautiful. At least to him.

He reminded himself there were a lot of beautiful, sexy

women in the world, and he had never had trouble attracting a female he desired. He didn't understand his fierce attraction to this one.

But Libby had caught him completely off guard. He had banked on her being spoiled, selfish, and demanding. He grinned. She was a handful, no doubt. But there was a sweetness to Libby he hadn't expected. It drew him as no woman had in a very long time.

Sam was man enough to know when a woman was equally attracted. And though they'd been at odds at first, that attraction was growing.

He had to put a stop to it. Martin had entrusted the niece he thought of as a daughter into Sam's care. Seducing her was out of the question. He sighed as he checked the repair he had made in the fence, then headed for the barn.

During the summer, the hands all pitched in to help with the guests. Dare was a fisherman, and he was good. He helped rig the poles and showed the men the best fishing holes on the creek.

Ronnie Yates gave riding lessons. As Sam approached the barn, he spotted Alice and Betty, who looked like silver-haired pixies compared to the muscular African American, and Ronnie looked small compared to Big John. The women seemed enthralled with the horses they had been assigned, an older chestnut mare named Biscuit for Betty, and for Alice, a big red Appaloosa named, aptly, Red.

The two horses were circling the ring while Ronnie instructed the women on their position in the saddle and how to hold the reins. Clearly they trusted him to make sure they would be all right.

Sam glanced around for Libby but didn't see her, which was good. The less time he spent with her, the better.

* * *

After finishing cleaning Cougar Cabin, which being the largest took the most time, Libby picked up the bucket that held her cleaning supplies, grabbed the mop and broom, and headed for Wolverine.

The fishermen's car, an older model faded blue Ford Fusion, was parked in front, but the DO NOT DISTURB sign hadn't been hung on the door, so she gave it a quick, firm knock.

Max opened the door. He was shirtless, dressed in jeans, his black hair damp from the shower and sticking to his head. He had a hard, sinewy body and a chest covered by curly black chest hair. There were tattoos on his arms—serpent on one, skull and crossbones on the other.

"We were just leaving," Max said. "Come on in."

Libby stepped into the living room, set the bucket on the floor, and propped the mop beside it, then took the broom and started sweeping in front of the iron stove.

The bedroom door opened, and Vince walked out. "Damned shame," he drawled with a trace of southern accent. "Woman looks as good as you?" He shook his head, moving the stringy blond hair that brushed his shoulders. "You could do a lot better than sweeping floors and cleaning toilets."

Annoyance trickled through her. "It's only for the summer. I've never been on a ranch, so I think of it as an adventure." That was total BS, but why she was there was none of his business.

She started sweeping, and Vince moved up behind her. She stiffened at the heat of his big body standing so close.

"If you're looking for adventure," he said softly, "I could give you a little thrill."

Her mouth tightened. She turned, set her palms on his chest, and pushed him a few steps back. She was used to men like Vince. They all wanted the same thing. She just needed to make sure they understood they weren't going to get it.

"Look, Vince. I'm not interested in anything you're selling, okay? I have a job to do. That's the only reason I'm here. Max said the two of you were leaving. Once you're gone, I can finish my work."

Vince's pale blue eyes fixed on her breasts, and the corner of his mouth slid up. "I like a female with spunk, so I won't take offense. You change your mind, you know where to find me."

Libby gritted her teeth.

"Leave the girl alone," Max said. "We've got things to do. We need to get going."

The men left the cabin, and Libby blew out a breath. She'd been right about those two. They were more secretive, more unapproachable than the other guests. They hadn't tried to make friends, just stayed off to themselves. She'd noticed Vince watching her a couple of times, but she was used to that. Now that she'd stood up to him, she figured he wouldn't give her any more trouble.

Just to be safe, next time she'd make sure they were gone before she went in to do the housekeeping.

Libby made the twin beds, cleaned the bathroom, finished straightening up, and left the cabin. She hadn't done this kind of work since she'd left the farm, but it wasn't that bad and it made the time pass swiftly. She hadn't had a chance to see the miniature goats yet, so she headed in that direction.

As she passed the barn, she noticed one of the stalls standing open and Big John kneeling on the straw inside. Changing course, she wandered over just as he was rising, a small blanket-wrapped bundle tucked into the crook of his thick, powerful arm.

"What happened?"

"It's one of the barn cats. Looks like she ran into trouble last night. Probably a coyote. She got away, but the damage was already done."

"You mean . . . she's dead?"

He nodded, his heavy black braid shifting across his broad back. "I'll take care of her and the kittens she left behind."

Libby's gaze swung to the stall, and she saw a tiny squirming mass in the straw. "Oh my God, she has babies!"

John stopped in the opening, the mother cat still in his arms. "They're too small to make it. It's kinder just to get rid of them."

She dropped to her knees, and her eyes filled as she looked down at the tiny gray bodies. "They just need someone to feed them. I can do it. It won't be that hard."

"You'll be up all hours of the night," Big John said.

"I don't care. You can't just kill them. Please, John, let me take care of them."

John said nothing, just stood there staring as if he was trying to read her thoughts, then nodded.

"What's going on here?" Sam strode up to the open stall door.

Libby put herself between the two men and the kittens. "I won't let you take them. They deserve a chance to live."

Big John looked at Sam. "One of the barn cats died. She just had a litter. They may be too small to survive, but Libby wants to try. I said it was okay."

Sam's gaze swung in her direction. He must have noticed her mutinous expression. "They're going to take a lot of work. Are you sure?"

"I'll take care of them. I can still do my other jobs."

Something moved across his features. "All right. We'll all pitch in if you need help."

"I won't," she said firmly.

Sam nodded. "I think Clara has some doll bottles. She's done this kind of thing before."

Libby felt a wave of relief. "I just need to get them to my room."

Sam found a cardboard box and lined it with straw. They placed the minuscule newborn kittens in the box, and Sam carried it to her room.

Libby had never really thought about backing out of the conditions of her uncle's will and returning to New York, but if she had, the kittens would have ended the notion.

They needed her. It had been a long time since anyone had needed Liberty Hale.

CHAPTER 7

With Clara making preparations for the three-day pack trip coming up tomorrow, Sam had no choice but to drive Libby into Coffee Springs.

The small community, just a little over a block long, had a narrow redbrick post office at one end and Rocky Mountain Supply at the other, and a mercantile and gas station that serviced the area for miles around. The only other businesses were the Coffee Springs Café, the Elkhorn Bar and Grill, Murray's Grocery, the Coffee Springs Bed-and-Breakfast, and Fred's Gun Shop and Dentistry.

Sam helped Libby out of the truck, and they headed into the big metal building that housed the mercantile.

"Mornin', Sam." Fran Tilman, one of the employees, hurried over to help. A stout, older woman with silver hair cut in a bob, Fran knew everyone in town and was always full of gossip.

Just what Sam didn't need.

"Morning, Fran." He turned. "Fran, this is Libby Hale. She's working at the ranch this summer. She needs a few things."

Fran's shrewd gaze went from him to Libby. "Always happy to help." Meaning she was happy to get a chance for fresh gossip.

Fran smiled, and Libby smiled back. "We got just about anything you can think of," Fran said. "What do you need?"

Libby glanced around the big open area that held everything from farm equipment to saddles and horse gear, along with racks of clothing, heavy winter jackets, and Western wear.

"I'll leave you to your shopping," Sam said, eager to escape. "I've got some errands. I won't be gone long." He started to leave, stopped, and turned back. "I don't think I mentioned there's a lake in the mountains where we're camping. If you don't have a bathing suit, you can probably find one here."

Libby's smile widened, betraying the first real excitement he had seen. "A lake. That sounds great. Don't worry, I've got my own suit. I never travel without one."

Sam ground down on the image of Libby in a minuscule bikini, but his body ignored him and stirred to life. He managed to nod as he walked away. Maybe he should have let her skip the pack trip after all.

Libby glanced around the domed-shaped metal structure, taking in the automotive supplies, bags of dry dog food, saddles, bridles, and RV equipment.

"I came to buy a disposable camera." She thought of her cell phone with longing. "If they still make those things."

Fran nodded wisely. "Fujifilm Instax Mini. They come in different colors. There's a rack right over here." The plump woman led the way, and Libby followed.

"Which one's the best?" she asked.

"Well, you can buy the camera bundle, which has some extra goodies, but it costs quite a bit more."

"I'll take it."

Fran eyed her a little differently, plucked a pink plastic

camera off the rack, and handed it over. "So how did you come to be working on the ranch? Are you a longtime friend of Sam's?"

"My uncle was a friend. He suggested I come up for the summer."

"Maybe I knew him. What was his name?"

Libby was there because she had no choice, but the woman didn't need to know that. "Uncle Martin only came for a couple of weeks. He passed a few months back."

"Oh, I'm so sorry." They started toward the register. "You said you have a swimsuit. Is there anything else I can show you?"

She looked over at the Western clothes. "Sam thinks I need a pair of cowboy boots."

Fran grinned. "We have a great boot department. And you might want to look at some Western shirts or jeans. We just got in a new shipment. Oh, and we got some beautiful Montana Silversmith's jewelry: earrings, belt buckles, bracelets, that kind of thing. You're new here, but eventually, you'll probably end up over at the Elkhorn Bar and Grill. They have dances there on the weekends."

"They have a band?"

"Sure do. If you don't know how to country dance, I'm sure Sam can teach you."

The implication was clear, but Libby didn't take the bait, just smiled and made no reply. She followed Fran over to the Western wear department, which immediately captured her interest.

By the time Libby walked out of the mercantile, she was carrying an armload of jeans, boots, shirts, Western tank tops, some pretty silver jewelry, and of course her Fujifilm Mini.

She set the bags down on the sidewalk and began to watch for Sam's truck. Across the parking lot, she noticed

Max and Vince's blue Ford Fusion sitting in front of the gas pumps. Vince filled the tank while Max stood a few feet away, deep in conversation with a bearded man in jeans and a red flannel shirt. There were a few streaks of gray in his reddish brown hair, and above the scraggly beard, a suntanned, weathered complexion.

Preoccupied, they hadn't seen her in an alcove near the front door. Vince finished pumping gas, and he and Max got into the car. Max started the engine while the bearded man took off around the side of the building and disappeared.

They sure didn't look like fishermen, Libby thought, but then what did she know?

As the sedan drove away, Libby spotted Sam's big Dodge truck pulling into the parking lot. Sam got out of the pickup, his eyes widening at the stack of packages at her feet.

"I knew I shouldn't have stayed away so long." He took the armload of bags and began loading them into the back of the truck. Libby tried not to notice the lean muscles shifting beneath his denim shirt, or the way his behind, outlined by faded butter-soft jeans, flexed and tightened with his every move.

The lift in her stomach surprised her. She hadn't felt the least desire for a man in . . . well, years. She'd just been burned too often. But Sam was different. Nothing like the men she used to date in the city.

Or at least that was the way he seemed. Maybe it was all just an act, a way to get her to let down her guard. It had happened before.

"Time to go," Sam said, snapping her out of her dismal thoughts.

Libby climbed into the truck and buckled her seat belt. Tomorrow she was going on a camping trip in the mountains. A memory stirred of her dad promising to take her on

an overnight camping trip with two of her girlfriends. He
and her mom had been killed the week before they were
supposed to leave.

Sadness rose inside her. Libby took a deep breath and
forced it away. She thought again of the pack trip and instead of dread felt an unexpected surge of anticipation.
Maybe a camping trip into the Rocky Mountains wouldn't
be all that bad.

Then she remembered she was a city girl used to five-star
hotels and three-star Michelin restaurants. Not a sleeping
bag on the ground and no bathrooms.

She grimaced. More likely, it would be exactly as bad as
she imagined.

Sam awoke to a sound in the night. He felt restless and
uneasy, probably because he had so much on his mind.
Tomorrow they would be heading out, packing into the
high country. The guests were all excited. Even Libby's attitude had improved. She was ready to go, she'd told him at
supper—after Clara had volunteered to take care of the
kittens while she was away.

Libby trusted Clara. Sam was pretty sure she didn't trust
him. Or any other man for that matter.

He wondered again who was responsible for hurting her
and found himself wishing he could land a punch in the
city-boy's face.

Unable to sleep, he climbed out of bed, pulled on his
jeans, and started down the hall toward the kitchen for a
glass of milk.

A noise sounded at the other end of the hall, and he
turned to see a faint light coming from under Libby's door.
Knowing he should just keep walking, he padded back the
way he'd come and kept going till he reached her room.

Hearing what sounded like crying from the other side of the door, he knocked gently.

"Libby? Are you okay?"

"I'm okay," she said, but her voice sounded shaky and a notch too high.

Sam opened the door, peered into the dimly lit bedroom, and saw Libby sitting on the bed, holding one of the kittens against her chest. Tears streaked down her cheeks.

She looked up at him, and her lips trembled. "He's dead, Sam." She swallowed. "He was the smallest, so I named . . . named him Tiny. I couldn't get him to eat, and now . . . now he's dead."

Sam felt a tug in his heart. He sat down on the bed beside her. "It's not your fault. You knew it could happen when you brought the kittens here to the house. He was just too little to survive."

She wiped a tear from her cheek. "I know."

Sam gently took the minuscule gray body from her hands, went into the bathroom and grabbed a hand towel, wrapped up the kitten, and carried it downstairs to the mud room. He'd bury it in the morning. In the meantime, he needed to get back to Libby.

He found her where he'd left her, sitting on the edge of the bed in her shorty nightgown. Thank God it was cotton and not transparent, though he could clearly make out the soft swells of her breasts. He managed to keep his mind out of the gutter and tamp down any forbidden thoughts.

The bad news was she was still crying. Sam returned to his place beside her.

"It's all right, honey. Sometimes bad things happen. You did the best you could."

She looked up at him with big, tear-filled blue eyes. "Why does everything I love have to die? My parents, Uncle

Marty. Now Tiny is dead." She sobbed, bent over double, and started crying even harder.

This wasn't just about the kitten, he realized. This was about her parents and Marty and the grief she had managed to keep bottled up until now. He hadn't meant to touch her, but somehow she was in his lap and sobbing against his shoulder.

"It's okay." He gently smoothed a hand down her back. "Just let yourself go."

Libby's arms went around his neck, and she clung to him, her body shaking with the force of her tears. He was bare chested, and he could feel the dampness on his skin. Sam let her cry until her tears turned to hiccups and she finally relaxed against him.

"You okay?" he asked, brushing pale damp strands from her cheeks.

She nodded but didn't let go. Instead, she drew a little away, looked up at him, and pressed a soft kiss on his lips.

For an instant, Sam went still. God help him, so far he had managed to stay away from her, but with her body so warm and feminine against his, nothing could hold him back now. His mouth claimed hers, and the soft kiss deepened into something more, something hot and fierce.

Libby made a sound in her throat, urging him to take the hot kiss even deeper. Tangling his hands in her hair to hold her in place, Sam ravaged her mouth, taking everything she offered, giving her what she wanted in return.

"Libby," he whispered, forcing himself to slow down. "If we don't stop, I'm going to want more. In the morning you'll regret it."

"I need you, Sam," she said, kissing him until he groaned. Her waist was tiny before it flared into a pair of womanly hips. Her breasts felt soft and full against his bare chest.

He eased down the bodice of her nightgown and found

that each perfect breast exactly filled his palms. Her skin was smooth as silk, the small tips as hard as berries. He yearned to take them into his mouth and taste the sweetness.

God, he wanted her. Ached to bury himself inside her.

He kissed the corners of her mouth, her nose, her eyes, tasted the wetness of her tears, and felt a sharp pang in his chest that finally pierced his conscience.

His heart was hammering, the arousal beneath his fly hard as stone.

Sam released a shaky breath. "Libby . . . honey. I can't do this."

She looked up at him, her eyes glazed with passion.

"Your uncle was my friend. I can't betray his trust."

She stared into his eyes. "I know you want me," she said. "Men always want me."

His chest tightened. "I want you. I won't lie about it. But this isn't what Marty had in mind for you."

She stiffened, pulled up her nightgown, slid off his lap, and turned to face him. "I don't care what my uncle had in mind. He's gone. He's dead, just like everyone else. I'm my own person now. Uncle Marty doesn't control my life anymore."

"Libby . . ."

"Get out, Sam. Go away and leave me alone."

He didn't want to go. He wanted to hold her again, pick up where they'd left off. He rose from the bed and started for the door.

"I probably would have disappointed you anyway," she said softly from behind him. "I'm not very good at sex."

Sam turned and walked back to her. Leaning down, he cupped her face in his hands. "You don't have to be good at it, Libby. You just have to be with the right man." He kissed her softly one last time. Sam warned himself not to say the words but couldn't seem to stop himself. "This isn't over. We'll have time to figure things out."

Turning away before he could change his mind and show her exactly how good sex between them could be, Sam opened the door and walked out of the bedroom.

CHAPTER 8

As soon as breakfast was over, Libby ran upstairs to change into her riding clothes. She pulled on the jeans she had bought at the mercantile, which were snug but comfortable, the boots Fran had assured her wouldn't hurt her feet even the first time she wore them, and a pale yellow Western shirt with pink roses embroidered on the yoke in back.

The final touch was the straw cowboy hat Fran had insisted she needed as protection against the sun. She grinned as she looked in the mirror. *Not bad,* she thought, *for a city cowgirl.*

She grabbed the small overnight bag of necessities she had packed from the list Sam had given each guest and headed out of the house.

The horses were saddled and waiting, along with three mules to carry the supplies. Sam had explained that he would ride in front while Big John rode at the back of the group, leading the pack string. She spotted him talking to his foreman, Julio Santiago, who was staying behind with the rest of the hands to handle the cattle and any ranch problems that might come up.

So far Libby had managed not to think about what happened with Sam in her bedroom last night. It was a moment of weakness because of the kitten, she told herself. It didn't mean anything. But dammit, why did the man have to look so incredibly hot this morning?

Just the way he carried himself turned her on, his shoulders so straight, his strides so relaxed and confident. In his dusty straw cowboy hat, khaki T-shirt, snug jeans, and worn boots, he looked as if he'd just stepped out of a city girl's Western fantasy.

Libby hated him for making her want him all over again.

His eyes raked her from head to foot as he walked up, taking in her hat and boots. The look in those intense dark eyes said she wasn't the only one who remembered last night.

"You ready?" he asked, his eyes carefully fixed on her face. Libby knew she looked good. Score one for her.

Pasting on a smile, she tipped her head back to look at him from beneath the brim of her hat. "Which horse is mine?"

Sam pointed to a little palomino mare with the sweetest long-lashed brown eyes she'd ever seen. "That's Sunshine," he said. "Most of the others have ridden at least once or twice since they got here, so they're ready to go. I wish you'd had the chance, but you don't need to worry. Sunshine's good-natured and easy to handle, and you'll be riding right behind me."

Oh, lucky me! She could watch his broad back and tight buns all the way to the top of the mountain.

"You were raised on a farm," Sam said. "You know how to ride, right?"

"We used to have a couple of horses, but it was a long time ago."

"I'm sure it'll come back to you, but I can give you a quick refresher course."

Sam walked her over to Sunshine, who turned a patient look in her direction.

"All you have to do is grab the horn, stick your boot in the stirrup, and swing up into the saddle."

She bent to the task, saddle leather creaking as she settled herself in the seat.

Sam adjusted the position of her boot. "Stirrups are just about right." He lifted the reins over Sunshine's head. "She's got a soft mouth, so keep your touch light. You remember how to use the reins?"

Surprisingly, she did. And sitting on a horse again felt good. Really good.

He smoothed a gloved hand down Sunshine's sleek neck, and she remembered his palm kneading her breast. A rush of heat hit her that had nothing to do with the warm sun and everything to do with how good he'd made her feel.

Sam rested a hand on her thigh, then hastily jerked it away. "Just relax and have fun, okay?"

Ignoring a fresh rush of heat, Libby focused on the day ahead. She had decided to make the best of the situation. Other people were there to have fun. She wasn't going to spoil it for them.

Or so she thought until she saw Max and Vince come out of Wolverine Cabin and walk toward them.

"I thought they were staying behind to fish," Libby said.

"They changed their minds at the last minute and decided to join us. Fishing's always good up at the lake."

Libby said nothing. But as the men walked past, she felt Vince's pale eyes skimming over her, and a chill slid down her spine. Max nudged Vince toward the barn, where a pair of bay horses stood saddled and waiting.

Sam tied a bedroll on the back of Libby's saddle, took her overnight bag, and packed it in one of the mule panniers. According to Sam, each side of the box had to be weighted exactly right in order to keep the load from shifting and creating a problem for the mule.

* * *

"Everybody's mounted and ready," Sam said. He swung up into the saddle of a sorrel quarter horse with a thick chest and bowed neck and turned to give her a last reassuring glance. "You have any kind of problem, don't be afraid to let me know, okay?"

Libby nodded. "Okay."

"Let's go."

They set off single file, with the Dunbar family on the trail behind Libby, Caleb looking nearly as comfortable in the saddle as Sam. The perky black horse Caleb rode had plenty of energy, dancing from side to side and tossing his pretty head. Jordy and Suzy followed, grinning from ear to ear, Jenny smiling as she rode behind them.

Betty on Biscuit and Alice on Red were clearly enthralled. Kim and Brad Hillman mostly grinned at each other, barely noticing the spectacular scenery. Max and Vince rode in silence. They didn't look particularly happy to be there, but maybe their attitude would improve once they reached the lake.

Big John led the pack string, three mules plodding along in a line tied together with a length of rope. The riders made their way along the main ranch road, then turned onto a trail across one of the pastures. Clusters of curious Black Angus watched them; then Sam dismounted and opened a gate, and they headed up into the hills.

Libby shifted in the saddle, but it didn't take long to get familiar with the roll and sway of the horse, and she found herself relaxing. It was hard to admit, but she was glad she had come. If she didn't have to look at the broad shoulders and narrow hips of the man in front of her, the dark gold hair that curled over his collar beneath the brim of his hat, she might have thought the day was perfect.

By lunchtime, she wasn't so sure. Her legs and bottom were aching, and sweat trickled down the back of her neck. She was working up the courage to swing down from the horse, when she felt Sam's big hands wrap around her waist and lift her down to the ground.

Pain traveled up her thighs, and Libby inwardly groaned. Sam smiled, and she wanted to hit him.

"You'll get used to it," he said. "If you walk around a little, your muscles will loosen and some of the stiffness will ease."

He walked off to help Betty and Alice, but they had been riding in the arena next to the barn every day. Libby had been sure she could talk Sam into letting her stay back at the ranch. Now she was paying the price.

Eventually, the ache in her legs and behind began to fade. She took one of the sack lunches and sat down on a log next to Jenny, a cool breeze ruffling Jenny's light brown hair.

"Where are the kids?" Libby asked.

"Caleb took them for a walk. The two weeks we spend up here is like heaven for him." She sighed. "If he hadn't married me, his life would have been completely different. Sometimes I feel bad about that."

"Caleb loves you and the kids. You can see it every time he looks at you. Maybe someday you'll find a way to give him his dream, and both of you will be happy."

Jenny smiled. "We're saving for a weekend home in the mountains. We've almost got enough."

"That's wonderful."

They chatted as Jenny ate one of the thick ham-and-Swiss sandwiches Clara had packed. Libby enjoyed one of the cheese sandwiches, and there were ample helpings of apples, orange juice, and chocolate granola bars.

Sam walked up when they'd finished. "If you need to

make a pit stop, there's an outhouse on the other side of the clearing. I'll see you back here in fifteen minutes."

"We better go," Jenny said, rising. "We might not get another chance till we get to camp."

Libby reluctantly followed, thinking how much easier it was for men out here in the middle of nowhere. She and Jenny joined the other women in front of the wooden outhouse door. When her turn came, she held her breath and fought down her gag reflex.

"Not exactly the Ritz," she grumbled as she walked back outside.

Next in line, Betty laughed and disappeared into the wooden shed.

As she started back toward the horses, Libby spotted Vince on the other side of the clearing. He was looking over his shoulder at her as he urinated in the grass behind a tree. He turned so she could see that his fly was open, his dick in his hand.

Heat rushed into her face. Libby turned away and kept walking. She thought about telling Sam. He'd be furious, she was sure, but if Sam confronted Vince, anything could happen, and she didn't want to ruin the trip for everyone else.

Besides, she'd known Vince was a dick. Seeing it just proved the point. She grinned. In her line of work, men often made fools of themselves. No way was she letting an asshat like Vince Nolan get to her.

Besides, she wasn't really afraid of him. Uncle Marty had insisted she take a self-defense class in Manhattan. She wasn't particularly good at it, but she'd passed the course. If Vince pressed her again, maybe she'd get a chance to use what she had learned.

She smiled at the slim possibility the moves she'd discovered would actually work.

Making her way back to the horses, she pulled out the

half of an apple she had saved for Sunshine, held her hand out flat, and let the horse pick it up.

Sunshine chewed the treat and gave a soft whiffle of thanks. Libby swung up in the saddle, ignoring a twinge of pain. She ached in places that had never ached before, and once they got to camp, there would be chores.

And it was only day one. Libby groaned as Sam settled into the saddle of the big sorrel in front of her, and they headed up the trail. She wanted to curse Uncle Marty.

Then they reached a turn in the trail, and she looked down at the lush green valley below and the tiny speck that was the ranch house and found herself smiling instead.

CHAPTER 9

Night had settled in. The steaks Sam had grilled on an iron grate over the cooking fire had been a big success. And the fresh vegetables from the garden he cooked in foil next to the meat satisfied the hunger Libby felt after the long ride in the saddle.

Bridger Camp was a permanent fixture in a clearing just above Wolf Lake. Besides the cooking fire, there was a portable stove that had been packed in earlier and assembled.

The tents had also been set up days ago, each furnished with a pair of cots. There was an outhouse in the forest not far away and a solar shower that could be filled with water from the lake.

The most popular spot was the fire pit, where the flames were currently blazing into the clear night sky. It was surrounded by a circle of logs that made the perfect spot for everyone to gather after the meal.

Sam smiled. As campsites went, it definitely wasn't five-star, but it wasn't completely primitive, either.

Big John and Caleb had unpacked the mules and tended the horses; then Big John had wandered off somewhere, as he liked to do.

The honeymooners had taken a blanket and disappeared into the forest, but not without a word of caution from Sam not to wander too far away. With their dad's help, Jordy and Suzy were shaving branches off sticks for marshmallow roasting. Vince and Max sat drinking beer on one side of the fire pit, with Betty, Alice, Jenny, and Libby on the other.

Sam thought of the way Libby had gone to work when they reached camp, pitching in with the cooking, determined to pull her weight. She was exhausted, he knew, and part of him felt guilty. Libby wasn't used to this kind of hard labor, or riding, or any of the things she'd been exposed to on the ranch.

But aside from the money, Marty had been a friend, and Sam knew the man believed sending Libby to work on the ranch was the right thing to do.

"Time for marshmallows!" Jordy hollered, racing back to the fire.

Caleb and little Suzy followed, Caleb passing around the marshmallow-roasting sticks they had made.

Sam headed for the camp kitchen set up beneath a canvas awning, took out a couple bags of marshmallows, and returned to the fire. Everyone loaded their sticks with the puffy white balls and stuck them into the flames.

Sam's gaze went in search of Libby. She'd been quiet all evening, and though every lustful part of him wanted a repeat of what had happened in her bedroom last night, Sam had forced himself to stay away from her. Even so, he found himself watching her, wanting to make sure she was okay.

Feeling a tug on his belt, he glanced down to see little Suzy looking up at him, blond ponytail drooping to one side of her head.

"My mars-mallow keeps falling off." Suzy handed him her stick. "Can you fix it?"

Sam smiled. "Sure." He grabbed the stick and a couple of marshmallows and slid them on just right. He walked her over to her mom. "Hold it right here, but don't get too close to the fire, okay?"

Suzy bobbed her head, ponytail swinging precariously up and down. Jenny gave him a grateful smile. Unconsciously, Sam's gaze went in search of Libby again. She was standing a few feet away, leaning over the fire to help Jordy.

Sam saw the flames racing up her pant leg at the same instant she screamed.

"Libby!" He hit her like a linebacker tackling the quarterback, taking the brunt of the impact as both of them went down. Sam rolled her beneath him, back and forth, back and forth, till the flames running up the side of her jeans were out.

Her eyes were huge and frightened as he jerked out his knife, flipped open the blade, and sliced open her pantleg. Her calf was red but not badly burned, and Sam felt a sweep of relief.

"I-I'm okay," Libby said, her voice wobbly. "I'm okay."

Sam pulled her to her feet and straight into his arms. She was shaking, but so was he. He didn't let go, couldn't force himself to let her go.

"I-I'm okay," she said again, holding him tight, her face pressed into his chest until the trembling in her body began to ease.

Sam took a slow, deep breath and turned to see they were surrounded by everyone in the camp.

"She's all right," he said. "She's going to be okay. I'll put some aloe on the burn, and she'll be fine." But instead of going after the medicine, he swept her up in his arms and carried her into his tent. The flap fell closed behind him as he set her on one of the cots and grabbed the medical kit, took out a bottle of the clear, gooey cactus salve that was the best burn healer he knew.

Sam looked at her pretty face and those incredible blue

eyes, and anger swept in to hide how frightened he had been.

"What the hell did you think you were you doing? Surely you know enough to stand back from a blazing fire!"

Libby stiffened and tried to stand up, but Sam shoved her back down.

"Sit still. You aren't going anywhere until I take care of that leg."

"Give me the bottle, and I'll do it myself." She held out a hand Sam ignored.

He took a tortured breath and slowly released it. "Look, you scared me, okay? You could have been burned very badly." Crouching beside the cot, he gently smeared on the cooling medicine, then turned her ankle to make sure the red streak running up her calf was completely covered with the gel. "I don't think it's going to blister."

"I was trying to help Jordy," Libby said. "I didn't realize we were standing so close. I'm sorry."

Sam reached up and framed her face in his hands. He looked into those beautiful blue eyes, leaned over, and very softly kissed her. "I should have been paying closer attention. I usually do, but . . ."

Libby leaned in and kissed him. "It's not your job to babysit me. No matter what you think."

Sam kissed her one last time, then pushed to his feet. "I need to get back out there. They're all worried about you."

Libby stood up from the cot. "Sam . . . ?"

He turned. "Yes?"

"My first day of camp? It wasn't really so bad. At least not until I set myself on fire."

Sam laughed with sheer relief. "Good to know."

He opened the tent flap and held it while Libby walked outside, where even the kids stood silently waiting.

"I'm fine," Libby said to them. "Sam put some salve on

my leg, so it barely hurts. Thanks for worrying about me, but I'm okay. I'm going to take a couple of Advil and go to bed. I'll see you all in the morning."

"Good night, Libby," Jenny said, and the others chimed in.

She flicked Sam a last glance, then crossed to the tent she'd been assigned. The crew tents were set a little apart from the others to give the guests a feeling of privacy. As the group dispersed, Sam glanced over to see Libby disappear into her tent.

A shadowy figure stood in the darkness not far away, and unease filtered through him. The man in the shadows was Vince.

Libby awoke in the middle of the night. It was pitch-dark, so black she couldn't tell the front of the tent from the back.

Outside, a soft shuffling and occasional sniffing sound moved along the bottom of the tent. Her hands tightened around the sleeping bag. Exhausted, she had forgotten to zip the tent when she'd gone to bed.

The shuffling and sniffing continued, the animal moving toward the open tent flap. Was it a bear? Oh God, what should she do? If she didn't sound the alarm, was she putting everyone in danger?

Her heart was pounding so hard she could feel it in her temples. The shuffling was getting closer. Sam would know what to do. She slipped out of her sleeping bag. It was now or never.

Libby bolted through the tent opening and rushed out into the darkness and over to Sam's tent, which fortunately wasn't zipped, either.

She ducked inside. "Sam . . ." she whispered, leaning down to shake his shoulder. "Wake up. There's a bear—"

He was already awake, she realized as he sat up in the dark and swung his long legs to the side of the cot.

"It's not a bear," he said quietly as he drew her down beside him. "It's a raccoon. They won't hurt you."

Libby breathed a sigh of relief. "I was afraid it might attack someone." Her eyes had finally adjusted, and she could see him sitting there, shirtless, in just a pair of boxers. He had a beautiful body, all smooth muscle, just a dusting of gold on his hard, amazing chest. Soft heat curled low in her belly.

"I've never seen a raccoon," she said, forcing her mind back where it belonged. "Except on TV."

She caught a flash of white as he smiled. "They come looking for food scraps. That's one of the reasons we keep everything packed up."

"I guess I screwed up again. I'm sorry I bothered you."

"You didn't screw up. You've never been camping. When we get back, I've got a book you can read on animals in the area. Next time you'll know what it is, and you won't be afraid."

Next time. Something warm blossomed inside her. She wasn't leaving yet. She would still have time with Sam. The warmth inside her swelled. She wanted to reach out and touch him.

"How's your leg?" he asked barely above a whisper, and yet she thought his voice had roughened.

"The aloe worked. I'm okay, but . . ."

"What?"

"But maybe you should . . . umm . . . take a look." Oh God, had she really said that? Was she making a fool of herself again?

Sam took her hand and placed it over his heart. It was

beating as hard as hers had been when she rushed into his tent.

"If I touch you, Libby, I won't want to stop. I'll want to touch you all over."

It was dark and quiet, the whole camp dead asleep, the other tents some distance away. Libby ran her hand over the muscles on his chest. "That's how I feel, Sam. Every time I look at you, I want to touch you."

A low sound came from his throat. Sam framed her face between his palms, and his mouth came down over hers. It was a soft, sweet, melting kiss that went on and on until she was clinging to his shoulders. Then suddenly it was more.

Desire rose inside her, turning her body hot and damp. She was wearing only a sleep-tee, no panties, no bra. It would be so easy just to . . . Libby slid her arms around Sam's neck and pushed him backward on the cot. She started kissing him again, and he groaned.

Sam took it from there, lifting her astride him, pulling the sleep-tee off over her head and taking her breasts into his mouth. A rush of heat hit her, spreading like fire through her body. She could feel his erection pressing against her, big and hard, his calloused hands gliding over her skin, moving down to her hips, then sliding between her legs to stroke her.

Sam kissed her again, and the fire inside exploded into white hot flame. It had been years since a man touched her this way, and it had never felt so good. Libby came with a violent, unexpected rush that had him silencing her cry with a deep, penetrating kiss.

Libby rested her head on Sam's chest, and he held her as she drifted down, held her for what seemed like forever. Then he pressed a kiss on her forehead.

"No condom," he said, and she realized he was still hard.

"Oh, Sam, I'm—"

"For God's sake, don't say you're sorry." He traced the outline of her lips. "We'll make up for it next time."

Next time. The words he had said before washed over her like a balm.

Sam eased her off him, and she noticed it was getting light outside. Apparently, it was later than she'd thought.

"You better get back to your tent," he said softly. Then he slid his hands into her hair to hold her in place and kissed her one last time. "I'll see you at breakfast."

Libby just nodded. Every bone in her body felt limp and pliant without the stress that she had been feeling ever since her uncle died. A smile hovered on her lips. She had never been so bold with a man. She had always let the guy set the pace and just gone along with it. With Sam, it was different. Everything about Sam felt different.

Hurriedly, she slipped out of his tent and made her way back to her own. The sky continued to lighten. As she lifted the canvas flap, she spotted a hulking shape in the shadows.

Vince stepped out where she could see him and cupped the bulge at the front of his jeans. The faint curl of his lips said he knew what she and Sam had been doing in the tent. In the hazy dawn light, something dark and cold flashed in his eyes.

Fear slid through her, but Libby forced it down. She wasn't letting Vince Nolan or any other man intimidate her again. Disappearing into the tent, she zipped the flap.

She'd decide what to do about Vince in the morning.

In the meantime, she would have to figure out what to do about Sam.

CHAPTER 10

Sam wasn't a man who spent much time on regrets. If he made a mistake, he left it in the past and moved on with his life. Last night, he had made a huge mistake, but so far he hadn't figured a way to move past it.

Instead, all he could think of was finishing what he'd started. Or more accurately, what Libby had started. He almost smiled. He wanted Libby in his bed, and not for just one night, but even thinking about it wasn't fair to Libby. And it wasn't fair to him.

In a couple of weeks' time, Libby would return to the city. With any luck, she would be a better, happier person for the experiences she'd had on the ranch. Libby would go back to the lavish, glamorous life she'd lived in New York, and Sam would stay here on the ranch, the only place he could ever be happy.

There was no chance of a relationship, no future for the two of them.

Hell, how had the word *relationship* even entered his mind?

He shook his head and concentrated on cooking breakfast, which everyone waited eagerly for Libby to serve. The bacon sizzled in a giant frying pan, and next to it a pan of scrambled eggs turned a perfect fluffy yellow. There was even a batch of biscuits he'd cooked in a Dutch oven over the open flames.

A thought that reminded him of Libby, the fire last night, and the terror he had felt. Sam shook it off. Accidents happened. He knew that. Still, it was Libby, and the idea of her being hurt in any way sent a ball of dread into his stomach.

"Everything ready?" Libby asked. She was surrounded by Suzy and Jordy and the rest of the guests, all wearing eager, hungry expressions.

He nodded. "You got the plates?"

"Right here." Libby handed them over one at a time, Sam filled them, and Libby passed them around. The kids ate first, then everyone else. It took three batches in all, the last for him, Big John, and Libby—though she passed on the bacon.

The weather had been warm and would be even warmer today. As the guests wandered off to explore the area, Sam worked with Libby to clean up the breakfast dishes. Libby had barely looked at him all morning. He tried not to wonder what she was thinking, but it was impossible to do. He had promised her sex would be good between them, but he hadn't really had a chance to show her. He hoped she at least liked the sample he had given her.

Sam inwardly smiled.

"It's warming up," he said as they finished drying the last metal plate and tin coffee mug and put them away. They'd already dealt with the trash, put away the leftover food, and hoisted the food box into a tree. No bears in camp last night, but he sure as hell didn't want to attract them, or more raccoons.

"You going swimming?" he asked.

Libby smiled. "Absolutely." Was there an impish tilt to those big blue eyes? Because just thinking about Libby in a bathing suit was enough to make him hard. "What about you?" she asked.

"Maybe. I've got some chores to take care of first."

She glanced up at the sky. "It's eleven o'clock. I think I'll go change."

Sam cocked an eyebrow. "Was that just a guess, or can you actually tell time by the sun?"

"I can navigate by the stars, and yes, I can use the sun to tell time. My dad and I made a sundial once when I was a kid." She glanced away, shadows in her beautiful eyes. "I still remember how it works."

He knew the memories must be painful. But he deeply believed remembering the past was the only way Libby could move forward toward a happy future. As she walked away, he glanced over to see Big John standing in the shadows. The man was as silent as a cat.

"Your woman . . . she is different from the others you have known."

The muscles across Sam's abdomen contracted. John had a way of knowing things that was almost spooky. "She isn't my woman. She'll be leaving in a couple of weeks. And you're right. She is different." He tossed the last of the cold coffee he had been nursing all morning and set the tin cup aside. "She belongs in the city. Soon as her time here is over, she'll be going back to the life she lives in Manhattan."

John said nothing, just gave him a pitying stare out of eyes as black as onyx. Turning, he walked away.

Forcing thoughts of Libby aside, Sam worked around the camp for a while, then changed into his swimsuit, grabbed a towel, and headed down to the lake. The water was clear enough to see the round multicolored rocks at the bottom. On the camp side, there was a long stretch of sandy beach. Sunlight glistened on waves slapping lightly against the shore.

Sam's gaze roamed over the guests enjoying the water. One of the camp rules was that one person stayed out of the lake at all times to observe and make sure everyone was safe. At the moment, Caleb sat on a log on a low hill above the beach, a pair of binoculars beside him on the grass. His wife and kids played in the water. Betty and Alice were splashing around and laughing. Kim and Brad were both sunbathing on a flat rock a little way down the shore.

Sam glanced around for Libby, spotted her as she emerged from the lake a few feet away. Water streamed over her perfect breasts, tiny waist, and curvy hips. She was wearing a one-piece white swimsuit cut high on the sides and low in the front and back, tasteful, and yet she was the sexiest woman he'd ever seen.

His mouth went dry while his skin felt hot and tight. *Jesus*. He'd learned the shape of her body last night, but seeing her half naked stirred an erection he fought to conquer. He clamped down on his lust but still had to concentrate on something else to bring himself under control.

"You should join us," Libby said. "The water feels great, once you get used to it." Her gaze slid over the front of his swimsuit, and her pouty lips edged up. Sam had no doubt she knew exactly the effect she was having on him.

"I think I'll spell Caleb, let him go swimming with his family."

Libby propped a hand on her hip, drawing his attention to the sexy curves he had touched last night. "Are you sure I can't convince you?"

At the moment, there was almost nothing she couldn't convince him to do. "Maybe later," he said gruffly, and forced himself to walk toward the hill.

"Why don't you take a swim?" he said to Caleb. "I'll take a turn watching for a while."

"Great. Thanks." Caleb whipped off his shirt and tossed

it on a bush, adjusted his swimsuit, and walked down the hill. He grinned as he waded into the water to join Jenny and the kids.

Sam sat down on the log, his gaze skimming the water for any sign of trouble. This was a job he took seriously and expected the same attitude from everyone else. The only people missing from view were Max and Vince, who had gone fishing on the other side of the lake.

Sam picked up the binoculars and scanned the shoreline, saw the two men reclining on towels spread open on the ground, both of them asleep.

They had come to fish, or so they'd said. A lot of places along the creek were catch-and-release, but the fish in the lake were keepers. So far neither man had brought back any photos of trophies they had caught, and there was no sign of a fish near their poles, which lay abandoned against the trunk of a tree. They had to be the worst fishermen he'd ever seen—or they weren't there for the fishing.

Unease filtered through him. So far they hadn't given him any reason to be concerned, and yet there was something about them he just didn't trust. Over the years, he'd had lots of different people as guests. That was what made life interesting. Most of them had been really great people, but there had been a few troublemakers in the crowd.

The good news was the men would be leaving in three more days. He would just have to keep an eye on them until then. He checked the water, counted heads, then focused the binoculars back on the men across the lake. Neither Max nor Vince was anywhere in sight.

Apparently nap time was over.

It was time to return to camp and help Sam get ready for supper. There was always work to do in the camp, Libby discovered. Big John handled the livestock, but Sam took care of the rest. He needed her help, and she was glad.

The evening meal went smoothly, a combination of fried lake trout Brad and Caleb had caught, hot dogs, potato salad, and chili beans. Libby ate more than she should have, fish not being a problem for her conscience, and Clara's potato salad was delicious.

Afterward everyone sang songs around the campfire. Tomorrow morning they would pack up and head back to the ranch. Libby was enjoying herself, but a long hot shower sounded like heaven, and a comfortable mattress beat a narrow cot any day. She had to admit she'd be glad to get home.

A soft pang echoed in her heart. Not that Bridger Ranch was actually her home.

In a couple more weeks, she'd be leaving, returning to her life in the city. All she'd have left of Sam and the ranch were the memories she made while she was there. Her throat tightened. She wanted Sam, and he wanted her. Libby vowed to make a memory that would stay with her through the years after she left.

As everyone dispersed to their tents, she glanced toward the tent that belonged to Sam. She wanted to spend the night with him, wanted him to finish what they had started last night. A sigh of frustration escaped. No way was she being the aggressor again tonight, and she knew Sam wouldn't come to her.

He had duties, responsibilities. Once they got home, maybe they could find a way to be together.

The thought hovered deliciously in the back of her mind as she headed for the outhouse before she went to bed. The moon was out, bright enough that she didn't need a flashlight to find the wooden building in the woods.

Finished, she descended the two wooden steps and

walked down the trail back to camp. It was darker here among the pine trees. She gasped as a tall, bulky figure stepped into the trail, blocking her path.

Libby stiffened. "Get out of my way, Vince."

His teeth flashed in a smile more wolfish than friendly. "I've been looking for you. I figured you'd have to come here sooner or later." His blond hair glinted in the moonlight, paler than Sam's, long and stringy, not thick and silky.

Libby stiffened her spine. No way was she letting the guy intimidate her. "I'm warning you, Vince. If you don't get out of my way, I'm going to scream."

Instead of backing off, he moved closer. She caught the sudden flash of silver, saw the knife in his hand, and shock rolled through her. She opened her mouth to scream, but Vince's thick arm wrapped around her neck, dragging her back against him and knocking the breath from her lungs. She felt the edge of the blade at the side of her neck.

"You aren't going to scream," Vince said. "Not if you're smart. You're going to give me what you gave Sam Bridger last night, and you're going to keep your mouth shut. If you don't, Bridger's throat will be the next one I cut."

Libby was shaking as Vince pressed the knife a little deeper, forcing her off the trail into the forest, spilling a drop of blood that ran down her neck. He was big, more than twice her size, and the hard look in his eyes said he wasn't bluffing.

She thought about her self-defense classes, but as long as he held the knife, he was in control. She had to wait, bide her time. She stumbled as he dragged her farther into the forest, turned her around, and forced her up against the trunk of a tree. He sheathed the knife, but his big hand remained around her throat, holding her in place.

Libby whimpered as he popped the snap on the waistband of her jeans and unfastened her zipper.

"A smart woman would relax and enjoy herself."

Bile rose in her throat. It was now or never. Taking a deep breath, she jerked her knee up into his groin hard enough to make him grunt, but the impact wasn't hard enough to make him stop.

His mouth tightened. So did the thick fingers around her neck. "I like a little fight in a woman, but not too much." He ran a finger over her cheek. "Just give me what I want, keep your mouth shut, and you'll be okay."

He used his free hand to unzip his pants, and Libby started struggling. No way was she giving in to this animal without a fight. The moment he lowered his head to kiss the side of her neck, she drew back and head-butted him as hard as she could. Pain shot into her skull, and stars appeared behind her eyes. The next instant, Vince was flying backward, landing in a heap on the ground, and she was free.

Big John Coolwater stood over him, a giant hand balled into a fist. "You can leave now, you and your friend. Or you can ride down with us in the morning and face the sheriff. The choice is yours."

Vince worked his jaw. A trail of blood oozed from a cut at the corner of his mouth. "We don't know the way back."

"The horses do. Give them their heads, and they will find their way home. If you have other ideas or plan to make trouble when you get there, I'll be somewhere behind you. You won't like what will happen if you make me angry."

Max walked out of the woods just then, his gaze running over them as he took in the scene. He was smaller than Vince, dark and wiry instead of blond and beefy. "What the hell have you done, Vince?"

"Take him and go," Big John commanded. "Or face the law tomorrow."

Max eyed Big John, assessing the situation. Then he

turned and nudged Vince's shoulder with his boot. "Get up, goddamnit. I told you not to make trouble."

"Fine." Vince rolled to his feet, wiping the blood off his lips with the back of his hand. "I'm sick of these fucking hillbillies anyway. Let's get our asses on the road."

They stumbled off toward the horses, Big John right behind them. He stopped and turned. "I will be back in the morning." He started walking and didn't turn around again.

Libby took a moment to compose herself. She was trembling all over, her head aching, her mind still spinning. Nausea rolled in her stomach. She took a deep breath and waited until she could control her shaking limbs. Then she adjusted her clothes and started through the trees back up the trail toward camp.

By the time she got there, she had made a decision. If Big John wanted Sam to know about Vince, he would have said something. Sam was responsible for all the people in camp. If he knew what Vince had done, Sam would go after him. If he did, anything could happen while he was gone.

Libby decided to wait, tell Sam in the morning. She prayed Big John would be okay, but there was a calm certainty about the man that assured her he would be.

The camp was quiet when Libby crawled into her tent. A few minutes later, the flap lifted and Sam appeared in the opening.

"I was starting to worry," he said.

She hoped her voice didn't tremble. "I was . . . umm . . . stargazing," she lied, hoping he wouldn't see the moisture in her eyes.

Sam lingered in the doorway, and she thought for a moment he might come inside. It was what she wanted most and the very last thing she wanted.

"Good night, Sam," she said.

A long moment passed. "Good night, Libby." Sam left the tent, zipping it behind him.

Libby could hear his soft footfalls as he returned to his tent. Then everything went quiet.

Tears burned her eyes. If Big John hadn't shown up when he did, Vince would have raped her. More tears welled and spilled over onto her cheeks. She muffled her sobs with the sleeping bag.

As the hours slipped past and sleep wouldn't come, Libby thought of Sam and wished he had stayed.

CHAPTER 11

Something was wrong. Sam could feel it in his bones. He'd spent a lousy night in the tent, sleeping off and on, worried and not sure why.

He climbed out of bed well before dawn and packed up his things for the trip back down the mountain. Big John would be tending the livestock, getting the horses and mules watered, fed, and ready for the journey. Sam felt anxious and unsettled, eager to get back home. He needed to start breakfast, get everyone fed, make sandwiches for lunch on the trail, then get the guests on their way.

He looked over at Libby's tent. She'd been up early every morning, but no sign of her yet today. He headed in her direction, paused as he heard movement inside the canvas walls. The zipper went up, and Libby stumbled out.

She looked up at him, and there were dark circles under her beautiful eyes. "Sam," she said as he walked toward her. "Sam . . ." Libby burst into tears and threw herself into his arms.

"I knew it!" Sam pulled her closer. "I goddamned knew it!" His heart slammed hard inside his chest. Libby was trembling. Sam didn't let go. "What's happened? What's going on?"

Libby clung to him a few seconds more, then eased away to look into his face. "I-Is Big John back? Is he okay?"

"I don't know. I haven't seen him yet this morning." He drew her over to a fallen log, sat down, and pulled her down beside him. "Tell me what happened."

Libby dragged in a shaky breath. "I wanted to tell you last night, but I . . . I knew it was the wrong thing to do." She leaned against him, and he wrapped an arm around her shoulders.

"Tell me, baby. What's going on?"

A slow breath whispered out. "Vince followed me last night. He was waiting in the forest. He had a knife. He tried . . . he tried to rape me, Sam. Big John came . . . and . . . and he stopped Vince before he could hurt me."

Sam felt a wave of fury unlike anything he had ever known. If he'd had Vince Nolan's knife in his hand, he would have killed the son of a bitch right there.

"Tell me the rest," he softly commanded, forcing himself under control.

"Big John hit Vince hard enough to knock him down. Then Max showed up, and Big John gave the men an ultimatum. Leave right then, ride down the mountain last night, or face the sheriff when we got back. The men left, and Big John followed them to make sure they didn't cause trouble at the ranch." Libby slid her arms around his neck and leaned into him. "I'm afraid for him, Sam."

Sam kissed her temple. Libby was worried about Big John Coolwater. This petite woman who'd been attacked and nearly raped was worried about a man three times her size with skills Sam couldn't begin to match. It made his chest feel tight.

"I've known John Coolwater for years," he said. "The man has skills you wouldn't believe. He may have followed them, but they would never know he was there—not unless he wanted them to. And if something happened, he could handle it. I promise you."

She wiped tears from her cheeks. "He said he'd be back this morning."

"It's a helluva ride down and all the way back, but if Big John says he'll be here, he will be." He stood up from the log and drew Libby up beside him, had to force himself not to pull her back into his arms. "Are you sure Vince didn't hurt you?"

Libby rubbed her forehead. "I head-butted him. I learned it in self-defense class. The teacher forgot to mention how bad it hurts."

Sam hadn't noticed before, but there was a bump near her hairline the size of an egg. "Jesus, honey."

"I took some Tylenol. I'll be okay."

"You could have a concussion. Any blurred vision? Anything like that?"

"No, nothing like that."

"We'll get you checked out as soon as we get home."

She touched her forehead. "It hurts, but I don't think I hit him hard enough to do any real damage. I think I might have helped Big John a little, kind of gave him an opening, so I guess it was worth it."

Sam's jaw clenched. "Vince Nolan assaulted you. You have the right to press charges. Is that what you want to do?"

"No. Oh God, no, Sam. Please. I don't want to talk to the sheriff. I only have a short time left here. I don't want to spoil it."

He swallowed, pulled her close. "A guy named Glen Carver is the Eagle County sheriff. He plays things close to the vest. I'll let him know what happened. Glen can check on Nolan. If Nolan tried that with you, maybe he's done it to someone else. There may even be some kind of warrant for his arrest."

Libby glanced away.

Sam didn't push it. They still had to get back home. "In the meantime, I've got some things I need to take care of so we can get out of here. Then I have to cook breakfast. Why don't you go lie down while I take care of everything?"

Libby shook her head. "No way. I've been lying there staring up at the canvas half the night. I need something to do." She glanced toward the portable camp kitchen. "I'll peel the potatoes and start breakfast while you handle whatever you need to do."

"Are you sure you're up to it?"

"I'm okay. Really."

Sam watched her walk away, and feelings he didn't know he had welled up inside him. He had underestimated Libby Hale from the moment he watched her getting off that fancy jet airplane. His feelings swelled, mixed with the anger he felt at himself for not being able to protect her. His jaw hardened. No one, he vowed, was ever going to hurt Libby again.

Dragging in a steadying breath, Sam forced himself to concentrate on the work that had to be done. Heading for Caleb's tent, he found the dark-haired man ducking through the flap in his boots and jeans, his cowboy hat pulled low.

"'Morning, Sam." Caleb finished popping the snaps on the front of his plaid Western shirt.

"Caleb, we had some trouble last night, and Big John had to make a trip down the mountain. I could sure use your help."

Caleb's head came up. "Is he okay?"

"Far as I know. John plans to come back. Just not sure when he'll get here."

"Anything you need me to do, I'm glad to help."

Sam nodded. "You're good with livestock. Think you

could manage to water the horses and mules and get them saddled and ready to leave?"

"You bet."

"Thanks, Caleb."

"No worries." Caleb grinned, clearly in his element. "I'll take care of everything."

Sam had to smile.

Once people realized he was shorthanded and Vince and Max never appeared, everyone began to speculate. Sam said nothing. Libby had been through enough. The good news was everyone pitched in to help, so breaking down the camp went faster than it usually did.

Sam left Libby to finish cleaning up and went to find Caleb. They needed to get the mules loaded, not a job for a novice. He found Big John there, already hard at work.

"I'm glad you made it back safely," Sam said, relieved, though he knew how well John could take care of himself.

"Libby told you?"

Sam's hand unconsciously fisted. "She waited till this morning. She figured I had responsibilities here, and you could handle Vince and Max on your own."

Big John grunted. "Smart woman."

"I don't know whether to be pissed off or thankful."

Big John looked stoic, as if Sam would eventually figure it out. He thought of what Vince Nolan had tried to do, and his jaw clenched hard.

Sam forced his muscles to relax. "She said you got there before Vince hurt her."

Big John spat on the ground. "I was watching him. I saw the way he looked at her. When I noticed she was gone and so was he, I followed."

"I'm damned glad you did. Thanks, John, for looking out for her." He owed his friend a debt he could never repay.

Just thinking of what could have happened made an ache throb in his chest.

"We need to get back," Big John said. "He could still cause problems."

Sam nodded. "I'll round up the rest of the gear. We'll ride out as soon as you've got the mules packed and ready."

As he headed back to camp, Sam thought again of what Vince Nolan had done, and a shot of anger hit him so hard perspiration rose at the back of his neck.

He wasn't done with Nolan.

Not by a long shot.

CHAPTER 12

They arrived back at the ranch late that afternoon. Tired, needing a shower and a nap before supper, everyone headed for their cabins. Big John and Caleb tended the animals while Sam strode toward Wolverine Cabin.

Libby hurried to catch up with him. "I don't see their car," she said, searching for the older Ford Fusion that had been parked in front. Sam opened the door, which wasn't locked, and found the cabin empty. He checked the bedroom, looked in the closet, and checked the bathroom.

"Their gear is all gone."

"Good riddance," Libby said, her hand touching the scab that had formed on the spot where Vince had pressed his knife against her throat. She suppressed a shiver.

Sam's gaze went around the empty cabin, and his jaw tightened. "I almost wish they were here." He urged her back out the door and closed it behind them. "Clara will have supper mostly done. Why don't you go and shower, maybe catch a nap?"

She didn't protest. She was exhausted, and after her fight with Vince, her body ached all over.

"How's your head?" Sam asked. "You haven't had any nausea or blurry vision?"

"No, nothing like that."

"Still have a headache?"

"I took some more Tylenol. That helped. Mostly, I'm just tired."

"All right, then." He reached out and touched her cheek. "Go, get some rest. I'll check on you in a while just to make sure you're all right."

Libby nodded and hurried toward the house. She was eager to see the kittens, make sure they were okay. Her overnight bag was still packed in one of the mule panniers, but she had plenty of clothes, makeup, and everything else. Funny, she didn't seem to need all that stuff anymore.

She sighed. She probably shouldn't get used to not wearing makeup. It was part of her life in the city, an essential part of her job. She'd done magazine ads for Revlon, L'Oreal, Maybelline, all the big cosmetic firms. She felt kind of guilty when she went au naturel.

In truth, wearing a little makeup made her feel feminine and pretty. She enjoyed looking pretty, especially for Sam.

Memories stirred of their encounter in his tent, but she forced them away. She thought about Sam way too much. She didn't want to get hurt, and there was every chance she would if she fell for Sam.

Libby paused as she walked into the kitchen. She must have looked awful—dark circles under her eyes, her hair a rat's nest, and a bump on her forehead—because Clara hurried over and hugged her.

"You must be exhausted. What in the world did Sam do to you?"

A faint smile touched her lips. *Not enough,* she thought. "It was a hard trip but mostly good." Except for Vince Nolan attacking her. "I . . . umm . . . hit my head." She touched the lump on her forehead. "Sam said it would be okay if I took a nap before you'll need help."

"Oh, honey. Of course it's okay. I've had all day to get

supper ready. You just run along now and don't come back until you're feeling better."

"What about the kittens? Are they all okay?"

Clara smiled. "They did just fine. Their box is still in my room if you want to check on them."

"Thanks, Aunt Clara." It was the first time Libby had ever called her that, but everyone else did. In that moment, it felt right.

Libby headed to Clara's room to check on the kittens, who looked bigger already, and healthy, their gray fur shiny and beginning to fluff out. She didn't want to wake them, so she continued to her room, stripped off her dirty clothes, and took a hot shower. As soon as she climbed into bed, she fell asleep.

Morning sunlight streamed through the windows when she awoke. Shocked she had slept through the night, she grabbed her clothes and hurriedly dressed. Glancing out the bedroom window, she spotted a black-and-white SUV parked in front of the house; *Eagle County Sheriff* was painted on the door.

Dread rolled through her. Libby steeled herself for the conversation ahead, but by the time she got down the hall, the sheriff's car was driving off toward the gate.

"I'm sorry," she said as she walked into the kitchen. "I can't believe I slept so late. I should have set my alarm." Breakfast was over, everyone gone.

Clara tossed aside the potholder in her hand. "Don't you worry about it. You needed the rest or you wouldn't have slept so long. How are you feeling today?"

"Good. No headache." Libby smiled. "I slept straight through. I feel great this morning."

"A good night's sleep can work miracles," Clara said.

Still half asleep, Libby headed for the coffeepot on the kitchen counter and poured herself a mug.

Clara returned a baking pan to the cupboard. "Sam told me you had trouble with one of the guests. *Vince.*" She said the name as if it burned her tongue. "I tried to like him, but he was never really friendly. Are you sure you're okay?"

"I'm all right." She didn't want to think about it. She especially didn't want to talk about it. "It's over and they're gone."

Sam walked through the back door just then and spotted her next to the sink. He strode toward her in that sexy way of his, long legs moving with power and confidence. There was an air of authority about him that always made her feel safe.

He poured himself a cup of coffee. "The sheriff just left. Let's go into the living room where we can talk." Reaching out, he took her hand, and they started in that direction.

The living room was large, a beautiful high-ceilinged room with big plate glass windows looking out at distant snowcapped peaks. Sam led her over to the seating area in front of the river rock fireplace, and they sat down on the brown leather sofa.

"Sheriff Carver was here," Sam said. "I called him to report what happened on the mountain."

Libby nodded, coffee mug cradled in her hands. "I saw his car through the window."

"Carver ran a check on Vince Nolan and Max Stoddard, but nothing turned up. No outstanding warrants, nothing like that."

"That's good, I guess."

"Maybe. Max had an apartment in Denver, where apparently Vince was staying, but Max recently moved out. Neither of them left a forwarding address."

Sam ran a hand over his jaw. He had shaved that morning, exposing the cleft in his chin. "I checked Max's driver's license when he arrived. Address matched the one in

Denver he used when he booked the cabin online. That's our usual procedure." He shook his head. "Even if I'd dug deeper, nothing would have turned up."

"It wasn't your fault, Sam. There's no way to tell if you can trust someone just by looking at them. They're gone now. That's the important thing."

Sam said nothing.

"I need to get going," Libby said. "The cabins need to be cleaned. I want to make sure Wolverine is thoroughly scrubbed. Before we left on the trip, I smelled cigarette smoke in there."

A muscle ticked in Sam's jaw. "No smoking allowed. They agreed to that when they booked the cabin."

"I'll air it out before the next guests arrive."

"I had a bad feeling about those two," Sam said. "I should have listened to my instincts."

"What happened wasn't your fault," Libby said again.

Sam exhaled a slow breath, and Libby could tell he was trying to hold on to his temper.

"Why don't you take the day off?" he suggested. "You deserve it. I'll have Dare or one of the other hands fill in for you."

Libby shook her head. "No way. I already missed supper and breakfast. I can't just sit in my room." She took her mug and rose from the leather sofa. "I'll see you later." She took off before Sam could try to persuade her. Sitting around all day wouldn't make her feel any better.

She worked through the morning and had the afternoon to herself. With nothing to do until it was time to help with supper, she wandered outside.

The first time she had seen the tiny, miniature goats, she had completely fallen in love. Some snowy white with black legs, some brown and white, others black and white, they were funny and sweet and were beginning to recognize her because she sometimes sneaked them treats.

Libby headed in that direction. Shoving open the gate, she went into the pen and sat down on the grass beneath the tree to watch them leap and play and butt their heads in mock battles. It was a sunny, beautiful Colorado day as she leaned against the tree trunk and let the sun warm her.

The little goats came up to nuzzle her hand, and she smiled in pleasure. She would only close her eyes for a moment, she told herself. Just a few seconds to feel the sun on her face and the goat's silky coats beneath her hands.

She smiled as she drifted to sleep.

Sam had been looking for Libby all over. Finding no sign of her, he was beginning to worry. He had no idea which rock Stoddard and Nolan had crawled back under or whether they might return to the ranch. Vince seemed to be obsessed with Libby. Sam didn't trust the man not to cause more trouble.

He spotted Big John and headed in his direction. "I'm looking for Libby. Have you seen her?"

The big man nodded. "I will show you where she is."

Sam followed John's long strides toward the pen that held the pygmy goats. Libby sat on the ground at the base of a tree, her legs out in front of her, a tiny goat curled up on each side of her, another in her lap. Her golden hair streamed over her shoulders, her eyes were closed, and there was a soft smile on her face. All of them were asleep.

For a moment, Sam thought he must have fallen down the rabbit hole and stumbled across Alice in Wonderland. He looked at this woman he had reluctantly accepted into his life, and his heart simply turned over.

Big John grunted low in his throat. "I wonder if she knows yet that she is home."

Sam glanced over at his friend. "What?"

"This woman, she does not belong in the city."

His chest clamped down. "What are you talking about? Libby lives in Manhattan. In a couple of weeks she'll go back, and we'll probably never see her again."

Big John cast him a glance that was far too perceptive, then turned and walked away.

What the hell? But when Sam looked back at Libby, emotion tightened his throat. *You can't have her,* his mind warned. *She's a city girl. She could never be happy here.*

But for the first time since Libby's arrival, Sam wasn't so sure.

One thing he knew—he was setting himself up for heartache if he didn't get his feelings in check.

Instead of waking her, Sam left her sleeping with the tiny goats and headed back to the house.

CHAPTER 13

"Why don't you go to bed," Libby said to Clara when supper was over. Clara's rooms off the kitchen were comprised of a living area with TV, bedroom, and bath. She enjoyed crocheting and reading in the evenings and usually headed off as soon as supper was over.

"I'll make sure everything is put away before I tuck in for the night," Libby finished.

Clara yawned. "Are you sure?"

"Of course. I'll see you in the morning."

Clara shuffled off to her rooms, and Libby finished putting away the last of the supper dishes. After sleeping so late that morning, then napping in the afternoon, she wasn't ready for bed. She went out on the deck to look at the stars through her telescope for a while, secretly hoping Sam would join her.

He'd been distant all day, saying very little, working with the ranch hands longer than usual, then heading for his study as soon as supper was over. She wondered if he was avoiding her. Maybe he regretted what had happened in his tent, or maybe he hadn't enjoyed it as much as she had.

Her eyes burned. She had warned Sam she wasn't that

good at sex. When he never came out of the house, she finally gave up, went inside and to her room.

As she undressed and pulled on a sleep-tee, she thought of Vince Nolan and what had almost happened. She liked to leave the windows open at night so she could see the stars and feel the evening breeze, but tonight she felt restless and edgy, and the breeze didn't help.

It was almost midnight, and she was still wide-awake. She felt lonely in a way she hadn't since she had first come to Bridger Ranch. She glanced up at the sound of a quiet knock at the door. It swung open, and Sam stood in the hall-way, tall and broad-shouldered, his dark gold hair gleaming in the moonlight streaming through the open window.

"I heard you moving around in here," he said. "I thought maybe I should check, make sure you're okay."

She tossed back the sheet and sat on the edge of the bed. "I'm glad you came."

Sam moved closer, and she could see the day's growth of beard along his jaw.

"Are you?" he asked. "Because this thing that's happening between us . . ."

"Yes . . . ?"

"If we don't stop it now, it isn't going to end well for either one of us."

Sadness rolled through her. "I know." Sam was right, but she no longer cared. Sam wanted her. That was all that mattered.

"I want to make love to you, honey, but it's only going to make things more difficult when it's time for you to leave."

Her throat felt tight. She rose from the side of the bed and stepped into his arms. "I don't care."

Sam pulled her closer. "I want you, Libby. I want you so damned much."

Her eyes burned. "Sam . . ."

She felt his fingers sliding into her hair; then his mouth came down over hers. It was a soft, sweet kiss that went on and on, slowly turning hot, wet, and erotic.

Libby gripped the front of Sam's denim shirt and took the kiss even deeper, inhaling the sexy male scent of leather and horses. His big hands moved down to the hem of her sleep-tee, and he pulled it off over her head, then eased away to look at her.

"So beautiful." He cupped her breasts and caressed them as he kissed his way down the side of her neck.

Desire burned through her. His mouth took the place of his hands, and she thought she had never felt anything so sensual as the tug of his warm lips, the zig of pleasure when his teeth grazed her nipple.

A soft moan escaped. She tipped her head back to give him better access, and Sam trailed kisses over her neck and shoulders. It wasn't enough. She wanted him naked, wanted to see his amazing body, see the heavy male part of him that had been hidden from her too long.

"Please, Sam, I want to touch you."

He kissed her one last time and began to strip off his clothes. In moments he was naked, more beautiful than she had imagined, all taut muscle, his erection thick and hard against his flat belly.

She had never wanted to give a man oral pleasure before, but she wanted to give that gift to Sam. He stopped her before she made the first move.

"I want this to last, baby. Just the thought of you touching me that way is enough to make me go off like a schoolboy." He flashed one of his devastating white smiles, bent his head, and kissed her.

The next thing she knew they were lying in bed, Sam

trailing kisses along her neck, over her breasts, moving lower.

"I want to feel you inside me, Sam. I want to feel your weight on top of me while you make love to me. I've never wanted anything so much."

Sam kissed her as he came up over her, kissed her until she was hot and achy, damp and needy all at once.

"Please, Sam."

"Soon, baby." He touched her, stroked her, filled her, then held himself in check until she was squirming beneath him, silently begging for more. She arched her back, taking him deeper, riding the edge of climax, which Sam clearly knew.

He drew himself out and sank in. Pulled out and sank in. Stars exploded behind Libby's eyes, and sweet pleasure burned through her. Sam didn't stop, just moved faster, deeper, harder, driving her up all over again. Gripping his muscular shoulders, she clung to him, her body tightening around him as Sam followed her to release. Head thrown back, muscles straining, he clenched his jaw to hold back a sound of passion.

Libby's eyes filled as Sam eased down on top of her. He was heavy, but she didn't want to let him go. She toyed with a strand of golden hair, and her heart throbbed. She loved him. She had tried not to let it happen, but she loved him, and there was nothing she could do to save herself from the heartbreak ahead.

"Are you okay?" Sam asked, lifting himself away from her.

Libby blinked back tears she hoped he wouldn't see and managed to smile. "Better than okay."

Sam kissed her softly one last time and left to deal with the condom she had barely noticed him put on. He returned and settled her in the crook of his arm, her head on his powerful bicep.

"You were right, Sam." She traced a finger over the muscles on his chest. "It just has to be the right man."

Sam caught her hand and brought it to his lips. She could feel him smile. "The right man is just getting started, honey."

Sam kissed her long and deep, arousing her once more. Proving his point even better than he had before.

CHAPTER 14

Sam was in trouble. The kind he had given up on long ago. Sam was in love with Liberty Hale, and there was no way it could ever work.

He knew she cared about him, maybe more than cared. But Libby was a beautiful, sophisticated woman who had studied at Columbia University, part of a wealthy, high-society family in New York. He couldn't ask her to give all that up, no matter his feelings for her. It wouldn't be fair to Libby.

He tried not to think of last night and how good it had been between them. Tried not to think about how he wanted to spend tonight—and every night until she left—in her bed.

Instead, he concentrated on the work he needed to do. He had a ranch to run. He didn't have time to spend mooning over a woman.

It was checkout day for the current group of visitors. With group two arriving next week, it was amazing how quickly time passed. Which meant his time with Libby would soon come to an end.

The thought cast a dark pall over an otherwise spectacular day.

The weather was warm, heading toward hot, the heat

nice for a change. Betty and Alice had already checked out, hugged him, vowed to come back next year, and driven off with a teary smile and a wave. The honeymooners were gone, too, thrilled with their stay in the Dove's Nest and their adventures these past couple of weeks.

Sam had seen Libby earlier that morning, but not lately. He figured she would want to be there to say goodbye to Jenny, Caleb, Jordy, and Suzy.

His cell phone rang. He always felt a little guilty using it, but it was his job to run the place and keep everyone happy and safe.

"Bridger."

"Sam, it's Glen Carver. I've got some news you need to hear."

"What is it?"

"Max Stoddard and Vince Nolan had another room-mate. His name is Deacon Mitchell. Last month, Mitchell robbed a bank in Denver. Shot two security guards and got away with more than two hundred thousand dollars. One of the guards died, the other is in critical condition, but it looks like he'll make it. There were three men involved in the robbery, but only Mitchell was identified. All three fled the scene."

Dread formed a knot in his stomach. "You're thinking Vince and Max are the other two men?"

"There's no evidence at this point, but as I said, Mitchell was living in the apartment with them, and now they're in the wind. We've got an arrest warrant out for Mitchell and a BOLO out on Stoddard and Nolan as persons of interest."

"Anything else?"

"That's it for now. I'll keep you posted."

"Thanks, Glen." Sam made a mental note to tell Big John, Julio, and the rest of the hands to be on the lookout for the men. They were likely miles from the area, but he didn't like taking chances.

Shoving the phone back in his hip pocket, he headed for Cougar Cabin, where the Dunbars would be getting ready to leave. Sam stopped at the bottom of the porch steps when the door swung open, and everything inside him went cold.

Vince Nolan stood in the opening, his arm around Libby's waist, holding her in front of him like a shield. A big semiautomatic pistol was pressed against the side of her head.

Vince's lips curled into a smirk that was far from a smile. "I've got something that belongs to you, Bridger. You want her back—and the happy little family inside—you'll do exactly what I tell you."

The knot in Sam's stomach tightened. "What do you want, Nolan? Name it and you've got it. Just let them go."

The smirk faded. "You think I'm an idiot? We'll let them go when we get what we came for."

"And that is?"

"This rich bitch brings in the family jet to fly us the fuck out of here."

How the hell did they know about Libby? But Libby and Jenny were friends. A memory stirred of the two of them sitting around the campfire talking about their families. He remembered Libby saying Martin Hale was her uncle. Either Vince or Max must have overheard.

Libby's gaze met Sam's across the distance between them. There was fear in her eyes but also determination. "I told Vince I could help them get away. I said I could arrange it if they would let the Dunbar family go."

He should have known. It was exactly like Libby to risk herself to save the people she cared about.

"All right," Sam said. "That sounds like it could work. You let the Dunbars go, and we'll work out the details."

Vince laughed, a harsh, grating sound. "I don't think so. I think we all stick together till the jet's on its way. We'll leave the Dunbars here when we go. We're taking Libby with us to the airport."

Sam wondered where they'd parked their old blue Ford. Too bad no one had spotted it.

"Once we're on the plane and the pilot's been told what to do," Vince continued, "you can have her back."

Sam clenched his jaw and fought to keep his hands from fisting. He could read the lie in Vince's face. No way was he letting Libby go. He'd wanted her from the start.

"Why did you come back here, Vince?"

Vince smoothed a finger down Libby's cheek. "The bitch and I have unfinished business." The criminal ran a hand over Libby's breast, and Sam felt a fresh shot of rage.

Libby's eyes slid closed, and Sam wanted to kill Vince Nolan.

Max Stoddard stepped up beside him in the doorway. "We figured Libby might be useful. Turns out we were right."

Libby's gaze met Sam's. "I need my phone, Sam. All my contacts are in there."

He didn't want to leave her. He was afraid of what Vince might do while he was gone. He didn't have any choice. "I'll be right back."

"One more thing." Vince's gun pressed more firmly against Libby's head. "You call the cops, and we start shooting."

Fear tightened Sam's chest. He didn't doubt Vince meant every word. "No cops," Sam said, forcing himself to turn and walk back to the house.

Clara's worried gaze met his as he stormed into the kitchen. "What's going on?" she asked.

"Vince and Max are holding Libby and the Dunbars

hostage. They're bank robbers, Clara. They want Libby to arrange for a jet to pick them up and fly them somewhere safe."

"Oh my God, Sam. What are we going to do?"

"We can't call the police, or they'll shoot someone." He glanced toward the window. "See if you can make your way around back. Find Big John and tell him what's going on."

He started for the hallway, stopped, and turned. "And call Kade Logan." Kade owned the biggest spread in the region, the Diamond Bar Ranch, just down the road. Kade was Sam's best friend. "Tell him we're in trouble and explain the situation. Kade may be able to help."

Clara nodded, her face as pale as glass.

"And tell him definitely *not* to call the sheriff." Sam raced down the hall.

Libby sat next to Jenny on the sofa. Jordy sat close to Libby on one side, while Suzy sat curled up next to her mom. Caleb was lying on the floor in the bedroom, his ankles bound, his hands tied behind his back. Blood trickled from the corner of his mouth, and his right eye was swollen almost shut.

By the time Libby had arrived at Cougar Cabin to say goodbye to the family, Vince and Max were already there. Another man was with them, the bearded man she had seen at the gas station. Caleb had put up a valiant fight against the men to protect his family, but he was battling three hardened criminals.

Libby had walked into their trap, and now all she could do was try to protect her friends. Her lips trembled. Vince was there because of her. Her looks had always attracted men, some good, some bad, but nothing like this. She was terrified of what was going to happen, but she couldn't let the Dunbars down.

She heard Sam's voice outside, met Jenny's gaze for an instant, then rose from the sofa and hurried to the door. Vince drew his weapon and shoved it into her back. He cast her a warning glance as he opened the door.

"I've got your cell," Sam called out to her.

"Set it on the porch and back away," Vince commanded.

Sam complied. Vince kept the gun on Libby while he picked up the phone; then he hauled her back inside the cabin. Libby flashed Sam a last glance, hoping he could read the love in her eyes before Vince closed the door. The bearded man—Deke, Max had called him—lounged in a chair near the sofa as if he belonged there.

Max walked toward her, his lean, wiry body moving with purpose. He was smarter than Vince, but Vince was stronger. "Make the call," Max demanded. "And don't say anything more than necessary. Just tell them you need to leave early and arrange for the jet to pick you up as soon as possible."

Libby swallowed and nodded. She phoned Bert Strieber on his personal cell. "Hi, Bert." She hoped her voice didn't tremble.

"Libby. It's good to hear from you. How are things going at the ranch?"

She took a deep breath. She hated to lie, but there was nothing she could do. "Unfortunately, things aren't going too well. I need to come home, Bert. I'm not going to be able to stay. I want you to send a jet to pick me up as soon as possible."

"Are you sure, Libby? You know you'll be giving up your inheritance."

"I know. Please, Bert. Just do it. We can talk about it when I get back."

Bert sighed. "If you're sure it's what you want, I'll arrange for a charter to pick you up at the Eagle County jet terminal. I'll call you back as soon as everything's set."

"Make it a priority, Bert." She flicked a glance at Max, who looked harder than she remembered, with tight lines around his mouth and a dark edge in his eyes she hadn't noticed before. "How long do you think it'll be?" she asked.

"You're close to Denver. Shouldn't be more than a couple of hours. I'll let you know." Bert ended the call.

She knew he was disappointed in her. Libby wished she could tell him the truth, that she wasn't ready to go back to New York. That the ranch was exactly where she wanted to be.

The thought struck her like a blow. Did she really want to stay? Did she want to give up her glamorous life in the city to live in the middle of nowhere with Sam?

And even if she did, would Sam want her to stay?

Whatever the answer, she didn't have time to think about it now.

"The jet should be here in a couple of hours," she said. "My attorney is going to call me back as soon as he has everything arranged."

Vince walked over to where she stood near the window, slid an arm around her waist, and pulled her close. "We've got a little time. Why don't you and me go have a little fun?"

She tried to unwind his arm, but he was built like a bull and she couldn't break his hold. "Get away from me, Vince."

Jenny shot up from the sofa. "Leave her alone, Vince!"

"Mommy!" Suzy's eyes welled with tears.

"Leave Libby alone," Jordy said, standing up next to his mother, clearly Caleb Dunbar's son. The tension in the room was thick.

The bearded man, Deke, spoke up. "Use your head,

Nolan. You don't have time for that now. You can have her when we get where we're going."

Libby's insides crawled. Vince released his hold, and she took a step back. At the same time, her cell phone rang.

"It's Sam," she said as his contact info popped up on the screen.

Vince jerked the phone out of her hand. "What do you want, Bridger?"

She could only hear half the conversation, but it was enough.

"They're fine," Vince said. "For now." Sam must have demanded to talk to her because Vince handed her the phone.

"Are you okay?" Sam's worried voice eased some of the fear inside her.

"I'm okay."

"What about the Dunbars?"

She needed to give him as much information as possible. "Caleb tried to fight, and the three of them beat him pretty badly. He's tied up in the bedroom. Jenny and the kids are in here with me, and they're okay."

Vince jerked the phone out of her hand and pressed the button ending the call. "You better hope Bridger keeps his cool and doesn't call the cops."

"He won't." At least Libby didn't think he would. But Sam wouldn't sit around waiting for something to happen. He would be taking action to try to resolve the situation. She trusted Sam. Libby just wished she knew what he was planning to do.

CHAPTER 15

Sam paced the living room. Libby had relayed valuable information. Deacon Mitchell was in the cabin with Vince and Max, and Caleb was hurt and unable to give him any help. Across the room, Clara sat on the sofa while Big John stood next to the fireplace.

"We have to *do* something!" Clara said, breaking the silence.

"I plan to," Sam said. "I'm going to try to get Vince to release the Dunbars in exchange for me."

Clara leaped up from the sofa. "No, Sam, you can't do that. It's too dangerous. Surely there's another way."

A sharp knock at the door drew everyone's attention. Sam walked over and checked the peephole, saw Kade Logan standing on the porch. A dark brown Stetson rode low on his forehead. There had been no engine noise to signal his arrival.

Sam pulled open the door. "How the hell did you get here?"

"The old-fashioned way," Kade said, taking his hat off as he walked into the house. "I rode my horse. Clara called and gave me a rundown. Now tell me what the hell is going on."

Kade was a few years older than Sam, just as tall with the same hard-muscled build. He had short dark hair, dark eyes, and a square-jawed, ruggedly handsome face women seemed unable to resist.

"We've got a hostage situation, a young woman named Libby Hale and the Dunbar family: mother, father, and their two kids. Three armed men in the cabin: Vince Nolan, Max Stoddard, and a guy named Deacon Mitchell. They're bank robbers, Kade. Killed a guard and put another in the hospital."

Kade's jaw tightened. "What do they want?"

"They want Libby to arrange a jet so they can escape."

"She can do that?"

"It's a long story, but yes, she can."

"So what's the plan?"

"I'm going to try to exchange myself for the family. I'm responsible for the people who stay here, and I want them safe. Aside from that, Vince is obsessed with Libby. I need to be there to protect her as much as I can, but I've got to have someone to run a rescue operation from here."

Kade assessed him shrewdly, probably guessing Sam's interest in Libby ran deeper than he was saying. His friend was right. Sam loved her. He'd do anything to keep her safe.

"Just tell me what you need," Kade said.

Sam scrubbed a hand over his jaw. He sighed. "Even if Libby gets them a jet, there's no way they're letting her go—and I'm not letting them take her. I'm thinking we arrange a little party to stop them somewhere along the road to the airport."

Kade mulled the idea over, seemed to approve. He flashed a glance at Big John. "You in?"

John grunted. "You couldn't keep me out."

Kade nodded. He knew Big John was former military, some kind of undercover reconnaissance, though John had never actually said. Kade knew the man had skills.

"Anyone else we can bring in on this?" Kade asked.

"Dare Landon was a marine," Big John said. "He will help if we ask."

Sam had already considered it. He shook his head. "We can't risk too many people knowing. If Vince gets wind of it, they might kill someone just to make a point. We need to handle this ourselves."

Big John started nodding. "You are right. With scum like these, the three of us should be enough."

Sam almost smiled. "I need to get back out there. If the jet's flying in from Denver, it could be here in an hour or two, maybe less. That gives us a little time, not much."

"Leave it to Big John and me," Kade said.

Sam gave him a nod and headed for the kitchen. He walked out the back door, making himself obvious to whoever was watching from Cougar Cabin. None of the hands were around. John would have made sure they stayed away.

Sam stopped in front of the cabin. "I need to talk to you, Nolan!" he called out. "I want to make a deal!"

Vince pulled open the door but didn't step out on the porch. "What kind of deal?"

"Sooner or later, the kids and their parents are going to be a liability. They need to be fed and looked after. You let them go, and in their place, I'll be your hostage."

Vince laughed. "No way. They leave here, they'll call the cops."

"No, they won't. They can stay in the house with Clara until you're safely on the jet and on your way."

"What's the matter, Bridger? You worried about your woman?" His lips curled in the smirk Sam hated. "If you haven't figured it out yet, she's going with us. She stays till we reach our destination—then you can have her back." The smirk broadened. "She might be a little shopworn, but she'll be alive."

Sam fought down a surge of fury as Vince stepped back inside and closed the door.

Sam bitterly cursed.

For the next half hour, he, Kade, and Big John made plans. They decided to intercept the vehicle at a spot John suggested, a curve in the road where the vehicle would have to slow down. The trees were dense on one side of the road, and big granite boulders covered an area on the hill on the opposite side.

Sam would stay behind to orchestrate the men's departure. At that point, the Dunbar family would be a burden rather than an asset. Sam believed the men would leave the family behind. Libby was all they needed to insure their escape.

The knot returned to Sam's stomach. Libby would be in the car when the trap was sprung.

The plan was for Kade, the best shot in Eagle County, to take a position in the rocks about fifty yards from the road, armed with his .243 hunting rifle, a smaller caliber weapon that was less likely to be heard with the windows up and the air conditioner running. Kade would shoot out the rear tire of the sedan, causing a blowout and forcing the vehicle to stop.

Sam would be following the Ford, staying as close as possible without being spotted. As soon as he reached the ambush spot, he would park out of sight and come up on the men from the rear. Big John would be somewhere among the trees while Kade moved down off the hill into a closer position.

If everything went as planned and luck was on their side, all three men would get out of the car to change the tire, and Sam, Kade, and Big John would take them down.

If everything went as planned, Libby would stay safely inside the car.

The problem was, *everything* never went as planned.
Sam silently cursed.

On the coffee table in front of the sofa, Libby's cell
phone rang. She glanced at the screen. "It's my attorney
calling about the jet."

"Answer it," Max demanded. He'd been getting more
and more edgy. It seemed that dealing with Vince was bad
enough, and now Max was exerting himself. "Put it on
speaker."

Libby pressed the button. "Hi, Bert. Did you get it done?"

"The jet's on its way. It's coming from Denver, so it
won't take long. The airport is an hour from the ranch—the
plane will be there by the time you arrive."

"Thanks, Bert. I'll see you in New York."

"Are you sure about this, Libby?"

"I've got to go, Bert. We'll talk soon." *Unless she was
dead.* Because there was no way she was getting on a plane
with Vince Nolan and his criminal friends. Vince jerked the
phone from her hand and tossed it back down on the table.

Earlier she had overheard him and Max talking about the
man who had come with them. Vince had said something
about the *big haul* they scored and that Deke had brought
the money. Now that they had a way to escape, they didn't
have to worry about the guy double-crossing them.

"Time to get rolling," Max said. "Vince, you go get the
car. We'll be ready to leave when you get back." He turned
to Jenny. "Get your kids and go in the bedroom with your
husband."

Deke scratched his scraggly beard, pulled his pistol, and
pointed it at Jenny. "You know what's good for you, girl,
you'll keep your mouth shut and do what Max says."

Vince flashed Libby a lascivious glance as he lumbered

out of the cabin. Deke turned his gun toward Libby while Max urged Jenny and the kids toward the bedroom.

Jenny paused long enough to hug her. "Sam won't let you down," Jenny whispered, her eyes full of tears.

"I know," Libby said, her own eyes misting.

"Get in there," Max commanded Jenny. "And don't come out till Bridger comes in to get you."

Jenny cast her a last worried glance and herded the kids into the bedroom.

"Leave the door open," Max called out. "You want your man to stay alive, don't untie him until we're gone."

Deke kept the gun pointed at Libby while Max made his way to the window to watch for Vince. The car must have been parked somewhere nearby. Libby heard the sound of an engine and the crunch of wheels rolling over the ground; then the vehicle came to a stop in front of the cabin.

Max opened the door. "Time to go." He motioned with the pistol, which looked big and deadly. As Libby walked out on the porch, Max stuck the gun in her ribs. The Ford Fusion idled in front of the cabin. Libby's heart jerked as Sam emerged from the house.

"Stay where you are, Bridger," Max warned. "You try to follow us, she dies. You call the cops and they try to stop us, she dies. When we reach our destination, we'll let her go."

Sam's hand balled into a fist. Libby knew he was holding on to his temper by a thread. Her heart was quaking with fear for him. "Do what they say, Sam. I'll be all right."

Sam took a deep breath and slowly released it. "Seems like I don't have any choice." But the look in his eyes said there was no way he was letting her get on that plane.

She wanted to tell him she loved him. There was a chance she would die, or maybe Sam would. But saying something like that might distract him from whatever it was he planned.

Max opened the rear passenger door, shoved Libby inside next to Deke, slammed the door, and jumped in the front passenger seat.

"Let's go," Max said, and the car rolled off toward the front gate.

Libby's heart beat hard. She turned to look out the rear window for a last glimpse of Sam, but he was no longer there.

CHAPTER 16

Sam raced into the house. The Smith & Wesson 9mm pistol he'd bought years ago waited on the kitchen table. Sam clipped the holster onto his belt, then grabbed his Winchester .30-30 hunting rifle lying on the table beside it.

"Don't worry, I'll take care of the Dunbars," Clara said. "You just get our girl back."

Sam gave a quick nod as he ran for the door. His pulse was pounding. Adrenaline poured through his veins. He waited for the sedan to roll through the gate toward the single-lane road leading to the highway. As soon as the car took the first turn out of sight, Sam raced for his truck. Behind him, Clara ran out of the house, heading for Cougar Cabin.

Sam trusted Clara and prayed the Dunbars were safe as he fired the engine on his big black Dodge, put the pickup in gear, and drove away.

By now Big John and Kade would be in position. Sam forced himself not to slam his foot on the accelerator and rocket down the road after his quarry. The timing had to be perfect, or one of them could die.

Or Libby could be killed.

His chest constricted. He thought again of calling the

sheriff, as he'd considered half a dozen times, but if the police got involved, anything could happen. He trusted Big John and Kade.

And he trusted himself. He would do anything to protect Libby. Even give up his own life.

He hit the button on his cell phone, and Big John picked up. "They're on their way and I'm right behind them, close as I can get without being spotted. You both in position?"

"We're ready," John said. "Kade will be able to see the car before I can. Soon as it rolls around the curve, he'll take the shot. Keep the line open. I'll let you know when to move in."

"Will do." Sam drove at the speed he figured Vince would be driving, fast, but not so fast he'd lose control on the curvy mountain road.

The spot they had chosen was four miles from the front gate, so it wouldn't take long for the sedan to get there. Sam maintained his speed, though every cell in his body screamed for him to catch up with Vince and drag Libby out of the car to safety.

Time seemed to crawl. A couple of deer leaped into the road ahead of him, and Sam swerved to miss them. The curve in the road was just ahead.

Sam's phone came to life. "Kade hit the target. The tire exploded. The driver had to fight the wheel some, but the car is slowing, pulling to a stop. Kade's on his way down the hill to his secondary position."

"I'm on my way." Sam drove the pickup to a stop off the side of the road and opened the door. Tucking the phone into his pocket, he grabbed the rifle and took off into the trees, careful to stay above the road, out of sight, as he moved into position.

So far no sign of the old Ford Fusion. Then he caught a

flash of oxidized blue. The car had pulled off the road just as they'd planned.

Sam ducked lower and moved silently closer. Vince was already out of the car, swearing as he rounded the trunk to examine the left rear tire. Max stepped out on the passenger side, leaving Mitchell in the backseat with Libby.

Spotting the shredded tire, Vince swore a foul oath. "Looks like we got a blowout. A bad one."

Max's head came up. "You think it could be a trap?"

Sam ducked even lower as Max surveyed the area around the car. Vince followed Max's gaze. Nothing moved but a few pine branches stirred by the afternoon breeze.

Vince grunted. "This old piece of shit car? Just bad luck, more likely. But get the girl out here just in case."

Sam silently cursed. *Everything never went as planned.*

They would have to go to plan B. Which meant waiting for an opening.

Crouched behind a boulder, Sam wedged his rifle into a crevice in the shade where it wouldn't reflect sunlight and give away his position. He leveled the barrel at Vince, who moved to the rear of the car and opened the trunk.

Deacon Mitchell hauled Libby out of the backseat, his pistol pressed into her ribs, head swiveling one way, then the other, on the lookout for a trap.

Big John and Kade held their positions on the other side of the road. Sam sighted down the barrel, but as long as Mitchell held Libby at gunpoint, there was nothing any of them could do.

Vince reached into the trunk, pulled out the spare tire and the jack while Max kept watch.

Vince leaned down to set the jack in place. "Get your ass over here, Max, and help me. We need to get this fixed and get the hell out of here before Bridger has the law breathing down our necks. Get me that lug wrench."

Sam waited, his gaze fixed on Libby, willing her to know he was there. As if she had heard him, her gaze swung in his direction. Mitchell took a step, Libby kicked back hard, slamming her foot into his knee, then turned to flee.

Sam took the shot, the sound echoing across the road. Mitchell's gun went flying. He went down and didn't get up. Libby started running, but Vince grabbed her arm and hauled her back against him, his forearm locked around her neck. Pistol drawn, Max fired toward Sam's position at the same time another shot rang out. *Kade.* A scarlet stain appeared on Max's chest. He swayed and sagged to the ground.

Sam was up and running, taking big leaping strides down the mountain, pistol gripped in his hand.

Vince tightened his hold on Libby. "Stop right where you are!"

Sam came to a sliding halt, his gun leveled at Vince's head. He itched to pull the trigger, but there was too much risk of hitting Libby. A few feet away, Max lay groaning, wounded but not dead, his pistol well out of reach.

"I can break her neck as easy as snapping a twig," Vince said. "Take one more step and I'll do it."

Sam's fingers tightened around the trigger. "You hurt her, I'll kill you."

"You can shoot, but she'll be dead. I don't think you'll take the chance. Where's your truck?"

Sam looked at Libby. Her face was bone white, her fingers digging into the muscular arm pressing into her windpipe.

"It's parked around the curve," Sam said.

"Toss your keys over here."

Sam fished the keys out of his pocket and tossed them in

front of Vince, who dragged Libby with him as he reached down to scoop them up. "Now the gun."

Sam's jaw clenched. He didn't want to give up his weapon. If Vince got the gun, he could kill them both. His gaze went to Libby. The trust in her eyes made his chest ache. Sam crouched and set the pistol on the pavement, took a steadying breath, and backed away. Kade and Big John were still out there. He was trusting his life and Libby's to his friends.

On the hill, sunlight flashed on the barrel of Kade's rifle, but he still didn't have a shot. Sam's gun lay a few feet in front of Vince, tempting him to pick it up, but reaching for it would make him a target.

Vince hesitated. "Use your boot to ease the pistol closer," he commanded.

From the corner of his eye, Sam caught movement in the shadows and spotted Big John moving silently up behind Vince. Sam's shoulders tightened. He took a slow step toward the pistol and eased it toward Vince with the toe of his boot. It was still too far away.

"Closer!" Vince demanded, squeezing until Libby fought for a breath of air. The wind blew Vince's stringy blond hair against the side of his thick neck.

Hold on, baby, Sam silently pleaded, his gaze fixed on Libby.

Vince screamed as John's big fist slammed into the back of his neck, breaking several vertebrae and sending the bank robber crashing to the ground. Libby twisted free as Vince hit the pavement, dead before he reached it.

"Sam!" Libby raced toward him, and Sam swept her into his arms.

"I've got you," he said, a tremor of relief running through him. "You're safe, honey. They can't hurt you anymore."

Libby's arms tightened around his neck. "I love you, Sam." She was shaking, but so was he.

"I love you, too, sweetheart."

"I don't want to go back, Sam. I want to stay here with you."

Love for her washed through him, and emotion clogged his throat. "If you stay, I'm never letting you go."

"Oh, Sam." Libby went up on her toes and kissed him, and Sam kissed her back. From a few feet away, Big John stood watching. The look in his onyx eyes said what the big man had known all along.

Libby had found her way home.

Read on for an excerpt from *One Last Chance,*
Kat Martin's next spellbinding novel.

ONE LAST CHANCE

**New York Times bestselling author Kat Martin
mixes high-octane adventure with sizzling romance
for an explosive thriller featuring an ex–Green Beret,
a dangerous cult, and a female private investigator
who will let nothing stop her from rescuing
her missing sister.**

Former Green Beret Edge Logan has made a new life
for himself at Nighthawk Security in Denver, using his
finely honed skills to neutralize threats of all kinds.
When he overhears friend and fellow agent Skye Delaney
discussing a new case involving her missing sister and
a mysterious cult, he offers himself as backup. With her
own military background, Skye is gutsy and more than
capable, but a cult like Children of the Sun is too
risky for anyone to investigate alone.

Skye is grateful for Edge's experience, even though
she is aware of the attraction simmering between them.
Her battle scars make her reluctant to get involved with
anyone, much less a coworker—even a warrior like Edge.
But infiltrating the cult's compound is more complicated
than expected—and something much more sinister than
worship is clearly going on behind its walls. As the pair
works against the clock to unearth high-stakes secrets,
the personal barriers between them begin to crumble.
Together, can they unmask the face of evil
before their time runs out?

CHAPTER 1

May
Sunderland, England

The old house creaked and groaned. Eve shivered and pulled her robe a little closer around her. She'd told herself that in time she'd get used to the place, grow accustomed to the ominous sounds and eerie, shifting movements in the shadows, but she had lived in the home she had inherited from her uncle for more than two months, and the unsettling disturbances had only grown worse.

Uncle George's former tenant, Willard Dobbs, an old family friend who used to rent a room upstairs, believed it was just her imagination, the wind playing tricks on her, the movement of the wood inside the walls of the hundred-year-old home. But the ghostly moans, whispers, and cruel laughter, the sound of running footsteps in the hallway, were impossible to ignore.

Since Willard had moved out three years ago, he wasn't around when the darkness came alive, when the air in the room seemed to thicken and pulse, when it took all her will just to make herself breathe.

Eve shivered as the howl of the wind outside increased, rattling the shutters on the paned-glass windows, but no wind she had ever heard sounded like angry words being whispered in the darkness.

Rising from the antique rocker in the living room, she moved the chair closer to the fireplace, hoping to dispel the chill. The smokeless coal she was required to burn wasn't the same as a roaring blaze, but the glowing embers somehow made her feel better.

A noise in the hall caught her attention, and she went still. It was the whispering she had heard before, like men speaking in low tones somewhere just out of sight. Time and again, she had gone to see who was there, but the hall was always empty.

Goose bumps crept over her skin. Today she had finally done something about it. Setting aside her closed-mindedness, she had gone on the internet and googled information on ghosts, haunted houses, anything she could think of that might give her some answers.

It didn't take long to realize she wasn't the only person who had trouble with spirits or ghosts or whatever they turned out to be. Willard Dobbs might not believe in ghosts, but there were people out there who were convinced they were real.

Eve had sent an email to a group in America called Paranormal Investigations, Inc., a team of experts who traveled the world to research problems like hers. Their website was discreet. No photos of the people who worked there, no names, just a picture of the office in a redbrick building near the waterfront in Seattle. At the bottom, the page simply read, *If you need help, we are here for you.*

Interested but not satisfied with the limited information provided, Eve continued her research. The man who had started the company was a billionaire in Seattle named Ransom King. King owned dozens of extremely profitable corporations, including several hotel chains, one of them the five-star King's Inns, various high-rise buildings, and real estate developments around the country. He was a good-looking, broad-shouldered man, tall, with blue eyes and wavy black hair.

Paranormal Investigations wasn't a business King ran for profit. According to one of the myriad articles she'd read about him, researching paranormal phenomena had become his passion, a hunger for knowledge that seemed to have settled deep in his bones. He had founded the company after losing his wife and three-year old daughter in a car accident. King had been driving the night a violent rainstorm had sent the car careening off the road into a tree.

Eve could only imagine how grief-stricken he must have been.

Intrigued and desperate for help, Eve had filled out the brief contact information form on the website, giving her name, phone number, and address. Her message simply said:

My name is Eve St. Clair. I'm an American living in England. I think there is something in my house, something dark and sinister that is not of this world. Can you help me? I live alone. I'm not crazy and I'm not making this up. Please help me if you can.

She glanced over at the burgundy settee where she had been sleeping for nearly a week. On the surface, it seemed ridiculous, but she couldn't face going upstairs to her bedroom. Down here, she would at least be able to run if something bad happened.

She reminded herself to put away the blanket and pillows in the morning before her weekly housekeeper, Mrs. Pennyworth, arrived. The older woman was a notorious gossip. Eve certainly didn't want her knowing she was too frightened to sleep in her own bed.

A scratching noise sent a chill sliding down her spine. It

was probably just branches outside the window, scraping against the glass. At least, that's what she told herself.

Eve settled back in the chair and started rocking, the movement easing some of the tension between her shoulder blades. When what sounded like a dozen footsteps thundered down the hall, she prayed she would hear from the Americans soon.

Ransom King sat behind the computer on his wide, glass-topped desk in the King Enterprise's high-rise building in downtown Seattle. The office was modern, with all the latest high-tech equipment, from a top-of-the-line iMac Pro to a seventy-inch flat screen with a wireless HDMI transmitter and receiver kit.

A gray leather sofa and chairs provided a comfortable conversation area with a chrome and glass coffee table, and a wall of glass overlooked the harbor and the blue waters of Elliott Bay.

On the computer screen in front of him, he reread the most recent email message that had come in from Eve St. Clair. They had corresponded several times. Her case looked interesting. Part of her note read,

I keep praying this isn't real. If it is, at least I'll know.

Ran understood the words in a way few people could. In the months following the accident that had killed his wife, Sabrina, and their daughter, Chrissy, he had seen Rina and Chrissy's faces in his dreams a hundred times.

In his dreams. That's what he'd told himself. But a person didn't dream in the middle of the afternoon with his eyes open.

Talking to a shrink hadn't helped. Every explanation centered around the overwhelming guilt he felt for the death of his wife and child. Which was true, but not a satisfactory explanation of the visions that had continued to plague him.

Desperate to do something—anything that would give him peace—he had finally gone to a psychic. He had managed to keep his visits secret, but in the end, it hadn't mattered. Lillian Bouchon had turned out to be a fraud.

The woman was a fake and a con artist, like most of the charlatans who supposedly possessed supernatural abilities. He had run through a list of them, but during his pursuit of the truth, he'd met people whose abilities were real.

In a move that had caused him endless ridicule, he had assembled a team of paranormal experts. People with open minds, an interest in the field, and a determination to find answers to age-old questions—or some version of them.

Kathryn Collins and Jesse Stahl had been his first hires. The best in their fields, Katie handled the video equipment while Jesse handled audio and other miscellaneous instruments. Ran dug up background information on each case, and probed the history, looking into past events that might have influenced whatever was happening on the premises they were investigating.

A woman named Caroline Barclay had been the first psychic on the team. On certain occasions, she'd been able to sense and communicate with unseen energy, but she wasn't always successful. Other people followed, mostly women, who seemed to be more intuitive than men.

Aside from the members of the team he kept on payroll, including a team coordinator to handle the logistics, Ran also brought in part-time help on occasion: a psychometrist named Sarah Owens, who could touch an object and know its past, and a former priest named Lucas Devereaux, formerly known as Father Luke.

What Ran had seen in the years since his formation of the team had convinced him that spirits were real, and though he'd never made contact with Sabrina or little Chrissy, the visions and dreams had finally faded, allowing him to find a fragile sort of peace.

Two years ago, he had hired Violet Sutton, a woman he had met in an online chat room for gifted people. Tests supported her claim that she was a sensitive, and occasionally clairvoyant. He had watched her work and hired her.

Ran glanced back at the screen and thought of the case in England. What the team did could be perilous. It could be wildly exciting, a rush like nothing he had ever felt before. But under certain circumstances, it could be deadly.

And there was Eve St. Clair, a woman he found surprisingly intriguing. He liked her intelligence and what seemed to be sincerity in her emails. From photos he'd seen on social media, she was attractive, with a slender figure and very dark hair. He liked the open-mindedness she had shown in reaching out for help.

And there was the fear she worked so hard to hide. If what she was reporting was true, Eve might have good reason to be afraid.

Making a sudden decision, Ran called his executive assistant and asked her to clear his schedule for the next three days. If the team found something or encountered some kind of trouble, he would be there.

Ran checked his gold Rolex. Ten a.m. in Seattle. Six p.m. in Sunderland, England. He'd go out, maybe walk down to the Bell Harbor Marina, where he kept his forty-foot sailboat. He loved that boat, loved being out on the water, loved the solitude and the peace that usually eluded him.

Maybe when he returned, he'd find a message on his computer.

Maybe he'd have another email from Eve.

THE GHOST ILLUSION
KAT MARTIN

**In this spine-tingling tale, *New York Times*
bestselling author Kat Martin melds
psychological thriller and ghost story
as one woman's daring search for the truth behind a
historic British tragedy tests the dividing line
between life and death.**

If you need help, we are here for you.

Eve St. Clair desperately needs help sorting reality
from her fearful imaginings when ghostly voices seem
to haunt the Victorian house in Sunderland, England,
that she inherited from her uncle.
Online research leads to a group that claims to offer just
the aid she's seeking. But can Ransom King's handpicked
team of investigators truly banish Eve's night terrors?

Since the deaths of his wife and daughter, Seattle
billionaire Ransom King has devoted himself to
researching parapsychology and debunking the frauds
who prey upon the bereaved. But Eve is a psychologist
herself, clearly sane, and her sincerity is palpable.
King senses a very real danger stalking the beautiful
divorcée. As his interest in her case turns deeply personal,
he will move heaven and earth to uncover the truth—
no matter how shocking—and save the woman he loves.

They shall not grow old, as we that are left grow old.
Age shall not weary them nor the years condemn.
At the going down of the sun and in the morning, we
shall remember them.

Laurence Binyon

ABOUT THE BOOK

I wanted to write a ghost story. The two I had previously written were both challenging and interesting to write, so I began my usual search for a place to set the novel. England, I thought. Plenty of ghosts in England. I began searching abandoned historic buildings, and that was the beginning of a journey that led me to a place I did not want to be.

More research pulled me deeper. I am bringing you a tale I felt compelled to write. It is not one I would have chosen. But I believe it is a story I am meant to tell.

Soon you will understand why.

CHAPTER 1

The old house creaked and groaned. Eve shivered and pulled her robe a little closer around her. She'd told herself that in time she'd get used to the place, grow accustomed to the ominous sounds and eerie, shifting movements in the shadows, but she had lived in the home she had inherited from her uncle for more than two months, and the unsettling disturbances had only grown worse.

Uncle George's former tenant, Willard Dobbs, an old family friend who used to rent a room upstairs, believed it was just her imagination, the wind playing tricks on her, the movement of the wood inside the walls of the hundred-year-old home. But the ghostly moans, whispers, and cruel laughter, the sound of running footsteps in the hallway, were impossible to ignore.

Since Willard had moved out three years ago, he wasn't around when the darkness came alive, when the air in the room seemed to thicken and pulse, when it took all her will just to make herself breathe.

Eve shivered as the howl of the wind outside increased, rattling the shutters on the paned-glass windows, but no wind she had ever heard sounded like angry words being whispered in the darkness.

Rising from the antique rocker in the living room, she moved the chair closer to the fireplace, hoping to dispel the chill. The smokeless coal she was required to burn wasn't the same as a roaring blaze, but the glowing embers somehow made her feel better.

A noise in the hall caught her attention, and she went still. It was the whispering she had heard before, like men speaking in low tones somewhere just out of sight. Time and again, she had gone to see who was there, but the hall was always empty.

Goose bumps crept over her skin. Today she had finally done something about it. Setting aside her closed-mindedness, she had gone on the internet and googled information on ghosts, haunted houses, anything she could think of that might give her some answers.

It didn't take long to realize she wasn't the only person who had trouble with spirits or ghosts or whatever they turned out to be. Willard Dobbs might not believe in ghosts, but there were people out there who were convinced they were real.

Eve had sent an email to a group in America called Paranormal Investigations, Inc., a team of experts who traveled the world to research problems like hers. Their website was discreet. No photos of the people who worked there, no names, just a picture of the office in a redbrick building near the waterfront in Seattle. At the bottom, the page simply read, *If you need help, we are here for you.*

Interested but not satisfied with the limited information provided, Eve continued her research. The man who had started the company was a billionaire in Seattle named Ransom King. King owned dozens of extremely profitable corporations, including several hotel chains, one of them the five-star King's Inns, various high-rise buildings, and real estate developments around the country. He was a good-looking, broad-shouldered man, tall, with blue eyes and wavy black hair.

Paranormal Investigations wasn't a business King ran for profit. According to one of the myriad articles she'd read about him, researching paranormal phenomena had become his passion, a hunger for knowledge that seemed to have settled deep in his bones. He had founded the company after losing his wife and three-year old daughter in a car accident. King had been driving the night a violent rainstorm had sent the car careening off the road into a tree.

Eve could only imagine how grief-stricken he must have been.

Intrigued and desperate for help, Eve had filled out the brief contact information form on the website, giving her name, phone number, and address. Her message simply said:

My name is Eve St. Clair. I'm an American living in England. I think there is something in my house, something dark and sinister that is not of this world. Can you help me? I live alone. I'm not crazy and I'm not making this up. Please help me if you can.

She glanced over at the burgundy settee where she had been sleeping for nearly a week. On the surface, it seemed ridiculous, but she couldn't face going upstairs to her bedroom. Down here, she would at least be able to run if something bad happened.

She reminded herself to put away the blanket and pillows in the morning before her weekly housekeeper, Mrs. Pennyworth, arrived. The older woman was a notorious gossip. Eve certainly didn't want her knowing she was too frightened to sleep in her own bed.

A scratching noise sent a chill sliding down her spine. It

was probably just branches outside the window, scraping against the glass. At least, that's what she told herself.

Eve settled back in the chair and started rocking, the movement easing some of the tension between her shoulder blades. When what sounded like a dozen footsteps thundered down the hall, she prayed she would hear from the Americans soon.

Ransom King sat behind the computer on his wide, glass-topped desk in the King Enterprise's high-rise building in downtown Seattle. The office was modern, with all the latest high-tech equipment, from a top-of-the-line iMac Pro to a seventy-inch flat screen with a wireless HDMI transmitter and receiver kit.

A gray leather sofa and chairs provided a comfortable conversation area with a chrome and glass coffee table, and a wall of glass overlooked the harbor and the blue waters of Elliott Bay.

On the computer screen in front of him, he reread the most recent email message that had come in from Eve St. Clair. They had corresponded several times. Her case looked interesting. Part of her note read,

I keep praying this isn't real. If it is, at least I'll know.

Ran understood the words in a way few people could. In the months following the accident that had killed his wife, Sabrina, and their daughter, Chrissy, he had seen Rina and Chrissy's faces in his dreams a hundred times.

In his dreams. That's what he'd told himself. But a person didn't dream in the middle of the afternoon with his eyes open.

Talking to a shrink hadn't helped. Every explanation centered around the overwhelming guilt he felt for the death of his wife and child. Which was true, but not a satisfactory explanation of the visions that had continued to plague him.

Desperate to do something—anything that would give him peace—he had finally gone to a psychic. He had managed to keep his visits secret, but in the end, it hadn't mattered. Lillian Bouchon had turned out to be a fraud.

The woman was a fake and a con artist, like most of the charlatans who supposedly possessed supernatural abilities. He had run through a list of them, but during his pursuit of the truth, he'd met people whose abilities were real.

In a move that had caused him endless ridicule, he had assembled a team of paranormal experts. People with open minds, an interest in the field, and a determination to find answers to age-old questions—or some version of them.

Kathryn Collins and Jesse Stahl had been his first hires. The best in their fields, Katie handled the video equipment while Jesse handled audio and other miscellaneous instruments. Ran dug up background information on each case, and probed the history, looking into past events that might have influenced whatever was happening on the premises they were investigating.

A woman named Caroline Barclay had been the first psychic on the team. On certain occasions, she'd been able to sense and communicate with unseen energy, but she wasn't always successful. Other people followed, mostly women, who seemed to be more intuitive than men.

Aside from the members of the team he kept on payroll, including a team coordinator to handle the logistics, Ran also brought in part-time help on occasion: a psychometrist named Sarah Owens, who could touch an object and know its past, and a former priest named Lucas Devereaux, formerly known as Father Luke.

What Ran had seen in the years since his formation of the team had convinced him that spirits were real, and though he'd never made contact with Sabrina or little Chrissy, the visions and dreams had finally faded, allowing him to find a fragile sort of peace.

Two years ago, he had hired Violet Sutton, a woman he had met in an online chat room for gifted people. Tests supported her claim that she was a sensitive, and occasionally clairvoyant. He had watched her work and hired her.

Ran glanced back at the screen and thought of the case in England. What the team did could be perilous. It could be wildly exciting, a rush like nothing he had ever felt before. But under certain circumstances, it could be deadly.

And there was Eve St. Clair, a woman he found surprisingly intriguing. He liked her intelligence and what seemed to be sincerity in her emails. From photos he'd seen on social media, she was attractive, with a slender figure and very dark hair. He liked the open-mindedness she had shown in reaching out for help.

And there was the fear she worked so hard to hide. If what she was reporting was true, Eve might have good reason to be afraid.

Making a sudden decision, Ran called his executive assistant and asked her to clear his schedule for the next three days. If the team found something or encountered some kind of trouble, he would be there.

Ran checked his gold Rolex. Ten a.m. in Seattle. Six p.m. in Sunderland, England. He'd go out, maybe walk down to the Bell Harbor Marina, where he kept his forty-foot sailboat. He loved that boat, loved being out on the water, loved the solitude and the peace that usually eluded him.

Maybe when he returned, he'd find a message on his computer.

Maybe he'd have another email from Eve.

Explore the world of Rebecca Zanetti in digital format!

WARRIOR'S HOPE
THE DARK PROTECTORS

New York Times **Bestselling Author**
Rebecca Zanetti
**An explosive love triangle comes to its passionate
conclusion and decides the fate of battling nations in
award-winning and *New York Times* bestselling author
Rebecca Zanetti's Dark Protectors . . .**

As the only female vampire ever born, and the heir to
two powerful immortal families, Hope Kayrs-Kyllwood
has always felt the weight of fate and destiny. Now her
heart is torn between two men and two different futures.
It's a choice between duty and love, peace and war, with
the fate of everyone she loves hanging in the balance.

As the leader of the Kurjan nation, Drake has always
known that mating Hope is the best path to avoiding
war. He's counting on her to know the same. . . . Paxton
has been Hope's best friend and protector since they
were children. He would kill and die for her without
a second thought. In fact, he's always known
that would be his path . . .

With deadly factions at her heels, Hope must decide
whom to trust and where her loyalty lies—before the
choice is taken away from her . . .

PRAISE FOR THE DARK PROTECTORS SERIES

"Spicy romantic interplay; highly recommended."
—*Library Journal* on Vampire's Faith

"Sizzling sex scenes and a memorable cast."
—*Publishers Weekly* on Claimed

"If you want hot sexy dangerous romance with
powerful alpha vampires who rule the Realm,
this series is for you."
—*Paranormal Haven*

UNFORGOTTEN
DEEP OPS

NEW YORK TIMES BESTSELLING AUTHOR
REBECCA ZANETTI

"Zanetti is a master of romantic suspense."
—*Kirkus Reviews*

Puzzles. Brilliant and inquisitive, Serena Johnson has spent her entire life solving puzzles and deciphering patterns in the world around her. Seeking a new challenge, she accepts a job with a private organization, thinking she's helping to protect the company against dangerous threats. But all too soon, those dangers turn against both her and the Deep Ops team that has taken her in. And the pattern she discerns promises a deadly end . . .

Passions. Tate Bianchi is a cop from a long line of cops. He likes his routine, he likes his job, and he likes his weekends free. He also likes his relationships casual. When Serena needs help, he follows his duty to protect her. But he's soon shocked by the wild feelings the awkward but adorable genius inspires in him. For the first time in his life, he's ready to go all in—no matter the cost . . .

Perils. The passion between Serena and Tate overwhelms them both. But as the threats against her become even more deadly, their friends and families are caught in the crosshairs. And when Tate is forced to make a fateful choice, it might be too late . . .

PRAISE FOR DRIVEN

"Zanetti still makes time to dig into her characters' psyches in the midst of the action, adding nuance to the exciting plot."
—*Publishers Weekly*

"The story moves fast, and there's an unexpected twist or two, as well as a scene-and-booze-stealing German shepherd that provides a little levity to this dark and satisfying romantic thriller."
—*Bookpage*

Read more of Rebecca Zanetti's
Redemption, Wyoming, series in the anthology

He's My Cowboy,

coming soon!

CHAPTER 1

Scarlet and golden leaves lit the trees on both sides of the country road as Tara Webber drove her convertible, singing *American Girl* at the top of her lungs. It had finally stopped raining, and the sun shone down at the perfect temperature for late September.

She had just reached her second rendition of the song when a massive ball of fur jumped across the country road. Shrieking, she hit her brakes and spun out, careening off the road and sliding into a thick meadow bogged down with mud and weeds. Only locals even knew this low spot existed. Tourists often pulled off the road voluntarily here and then got stuck. She came to a stop and collected herself.

Her head rang and she took several deep breaths, prying her fingers off the steering wheel. She was okay. Everything was okay.

A quick glance to the other side of the road confirmed that a massive wolf had leaped in front of her car. He sat looking at her, his head cocked. His eyes were deep green and his fur a light gray.

She shoved open her door and looked down at the muddy mess all around her car. This was a disaster. She knew she shouldn't have worn heels to church today, but they had looked so cute with her yellow dress that she couldn't help herself. "Darn it, Harley," she yelled. "When are you going to stop causing accidents in this town?"

The wolf snorted, turned, and ran between the colorful trees, soon disappearing from view.

She sighed. Now what? She reached over for her massive purse and dug around for her cell phone, pulling it out. Nope, no service. That just figured.

She turned to look in the backseat to make sure the two casserole dishes were still intact and covered. They were. She was taking them out to Henry Jones, who had lost his nephew a couple months previous and hadn't been to church in a while. She didn't think he cooked much, so she delivered food to him at least once a week. He lived quite a distance from town on his ranch. She should have known to at least bring a pair of boots with her just in case. But she'd been late that morning, as usual, so she'd hurried to church and then figured she'd visit Henry. Now she was stuck in the mud wearing heels and with no phone service.

She kept her door open and looked around for a rock or something to step on. Both sides of the dirt road were filled, right now, with muddy grass from the continuous rain they'd had. While the trees looked happy for the rain with their sparkling leaves, the wet grass was an absolute disaster for her shoes. There were no rocks anywhere near her.

The rumble of a truck down the road caught her attention, and she sat back in the car, wincing. There were only two ranches this far out of town, and one was owned by Henry Jones. Hopefully Henry had headed to town earlier and was now going home. She cranked her neck to see around the bend but could only hear a diesel truck. Finally, it rounded the turn and her heart sank. It was not Henry Jones. "Oh, man." She was not ready for this.

The truck pulled to a stop in the middle of the road right where Harley had been and the driver's door opened. Greg

Simpson stepped out, all six foot four of him. She'd seen him in the back of the church earlier, and she'd smiled as usual, but other than that, she hadn't gone near her ex.

He'd worn his black boots, dark jeans, and a white button-down shirt to church, and he looked every inch the long and lean cowboy he'd become. Yet the edge was still there in his movements and in his eyes when he flicked them in her direction. His time as a soldier had marked him hard, and she was positive she didn't know the half of it.

He tipped his Stetson back and walked closer to the edge. "You okay?" His voice was a low rumble that licked across the distance between them.

"I'm fine," she called out, looking around at the muddy swamp.

His grin was a quick flash of teeth and then it was gone. Even so, she blinked. When was the last time she'd seen him smile?

He'd been home for three months to take over the family ranch after his brother had died, and she'd only seen him around town a few times. Not once had he smiled. Though she couldn't blame him. Life couldn't be easy at the farm raising three teenagers who'd lost their mother a decade ago and their father this year.

"I'm kind of stuck," she called out.

"I can see that, darlin'." He looked down at the mud and then shrugged his shoulders, heading straight for her.

"Wait." She held up both hands. "No, no, no. I—"

He reached her before she could finish the sentence. "You what?"

She had no clue what she was going to say. Instead, she tipped her head back, looking way up into his handsome face. He'd been good-looking in high school, but the years had honed him into raw, animalistic sexiness. There was no other way to describe Greg Simpson.

WILL SHE FIND THE ANSWER

Teenager Lia Porter shouldn't have been anywhere near the railroad bridge that night. Sneaking home after a party in the fields outside Pike, Wisconsin, she glimpsed a woman in a leather jacket, running in terror. Lia puts the incident from her mind—until a body is found near the same spot fifteen years later, wearing the same jacket. The police rule it a suicide. Lia knows different. The woman she saw was trying to save her own life, not end it. But whatever she was fleeing from found her first . . .

BEFORE THE KILLER

The stranger who arrives at Lia's store shares her suspicions. Hollywood stunt driver Kaden Vaughn has come home to Wisconsin to learn the truth about what happened to his brother's fiancée years ago. The leather jacket, the timing—he believes the dead woman is Vanna, and that Lia may be the only person who can help. Together they retrace Vanna's steps, but the more they dig, the darker the secrets become.

FINDS HER?

The killer is still out there, stalking the streets of Pike again, willing to do whatever is necessary to keep the truth locked in mystery. One by one, all those who know something about that night must be silenced, until there is no one left to tell . . .

Please turn the page for an exciting sneak peek of Alexandra Ivy's
DESPERATE ACTS

Now on sale wherever print and e-books are sold!

PROLOGUE

Pike, WI
December 14, 2007

Tugging her coat tight around her shivering body, Lia Porter scurried down the dark pathway. It was past midnight, and the late December air was cold enough to burn her lungs as she sucked in deep breaths. This was so stupid. She should never have crept out of her house to attend the party. Even at fifteen years old she knew that a gathering of kids in an old barn in the middle of winter was a lame idea. Some of her friends might enjoy shivering around a small fire, listening to country music and drinking cheap beer, but she'd been bored out of her mind.

So why had she allowed herself to be cajoled into going?

Lia wrinkled her nose. She'd told herself that she was tired of being called Lia-Killjoy by her classmates. Okay. She liked to follow the rules. She wasn't a maverick. Or a risk-taker. She didn't cheat on tests or skip classes. She didn't even go skinny-dipping at the local lake. In fact, if she wasn't at school, she was helping her mother at the family-owned grocery store in the center of town. But that didn't mean she couldn't have a good time, right?

But deep in her heart she knew that wasn't why she spent an hour straightening her strawberry-blond hair until it fell in a smooth curtain down her back. Or added a layer of mascara to the long lashes that framed her green eyes. Or why she'd snuck out of her room and trudged two miles to the middle of the frozen field.

She'd been hoping to attract the attention of Chuck Moore, the guy she'd nursed a secret crush on for an entire year. He wasn't the most popular boy in class. Or the cutest. He had frizzy black hair and an overbite that was prominent despite his braces. But he was one of the few guys who at least pretended to listen when she spoke. That was far more attractive to a girl who'd spent her school life in the shadows than perfect features or bulging muscles.

Unfortunately, she'd had to wait until her mother was asleep before sneaking out. They lived above the store and she couldn't just climb out a bedroom window. She had to creep down the squeaky stairs at the back of the two-story brick building. By the time she arrived at the barn the party was in full swing, and Chuck was already in the hayloft with her best friend, Karen Cranford.

Calling herself an idiot, she'd forced herself to stay long enough to drink a beer and pretend to laugh at the antics of the guys who thought it was a great idea to try to push one another into the fire. As if nursing second-degree burns was a hilarious way to spend the evening. Then, assuring herself that she'd proved whatever stupid point she'd come there to make, she'd slipped out the door and headed across the dark field.

Lia muttered a bad word as she slipped on a patch of ice. Pike, Wisconsin, wasn't the best location to take a midnight stroll. Especially in the middle of winter. If she fell and broke a leg, she was going to be in so much trouble.

The thought of her mother made Lia grimace. Trina Porter

had only been sixteen when she'd given birth to Lia. That had been tough enough, but Lia's father had disappeared just months after she was born, and her grandparents had died in a tragic car accident eight years later. Trina was forced to work endless hours to keep a roof over their heads and food on their table. She'd sacrificed everything to give her child a warm and loving home.

Lia felt the constant weight of those sacrifices pressing down on her like an anchor. If she knowingly added to her mom's daily struggle, she would never forgive herself.

Rounding a bend in the pathway, Lia breathed a sigh of relief. Ahead, she could see the soft glow of streetlights. Soon she would be back in her room, tucked in her warm bed with one of the books she'd borrowed from the library. Exactly where she wanted to be.

Lost in the fantasy of being curled up beneath her thick comforter with a cup of hot cocoa, Lia came to an abrupt halt. She heard a sound in the distance. Not a car. Or an animal. It sounded like . . . like running footsteps.

More curious than alarmed, Lia watched as a shadowed form appeared from the shadows. It didn't occur to her that she might be in danger. This was Pike. Nothing bad ever happened here. The figure neared, moving down the path toward her. As she grew closer, Lia could make out the delicate features of a woman with long, black hair that flowed behind her. She was wearing a heavy leather jacket and pants that looked like some kind of uniform. Lia could also see the glitter of gold in the moonlight. The woman had a large badge pinned to the upper shoulder of her jacket. Like a cop.

Oh no.

Lia sucked in a sharp breath. Had her mother awakened and found her missing? Had she called the sheriff's office? No. She sternly squashed the urge to panic. She would recognize anyone local. Pike was too small to have strangers. This woman was from somewhere else.

So why was she running from town in the middle of the night?

It was a question that was to haunt Lia for the next fifteen years, as the woman suddenly spotted her standing in the middle of the pathway. She'd just reached the bridge that spanned the railroad tracks.

A scream was ripped from her throat, as if Lia was a monster, not a fifteen-year-old girl sneaking home from a party. Then, with a shocking speed, the woman turned toward the edge of the bridge, climbing onto the stone guardrail.

What the heck was she doing? Lia took a startled step forward, lifting her hand as the woman wobbled. It was at least twelve feet to the tracks below. Not even the local boys were stupid enough to jump from there.

"Wait!" she called out, but she was too late.

With a last, terrified glance toward Lia, the woman leaned forward and disappeared into the darkness.

CHAPTER 1

It was mid-December and the town of Pike, Wisconsin, looked like an image on a postcard. The ground was coated in pristine layers of snow and the trees sparkled with Christmas lights. The town square was draped in garland that filled the crisp air with a scent of pine. There was even a miniature North Pole set up in the park where Santa perched on a chair from six to seven in the evenings for the kids to take pictures.

The downside to the winter wonderland, however, was the brutal windchill that whipped through the narrow streets despite the clear blue skies and bright morning sunlight. The cold kept most sensible people snuggled in the warmth of their homes. A shame for the local businesses that depended on the holiday season to pad their yearly income, but for Lia Porter, the quiet was welcome. The grocery store was never a hot spot in town, not even during Christmas, but she was there alone and she didn't want to be disturbed.

Seated at her desk in the private office she'd claimed at the back of the building, Lia kept one eye on her computer and the other on the surveillance monitor that kept guard on the front of the store. She wasn't afraid of shoplifters. The four short aisles with wooden shelves were stocked with basic supplies. Flour, sugar, bread, and canned goods. There was also a cooler with dairy products and a section for frozen foods. If someone was desperate enough to steal food, she would be happy to hand it over to them. She just wanted to keep watch in case a customer entered and needed her help.

Something that wouldn't be necessary if Wayne had arrived on time. With a sigh, Lia returned her attention to the computer screen, where she'd downloaded the portfolio of an online retailer who was trying to attract new investors. Lia was interested. She preferred putting her capital in businesses just starting out. Getting in on the ground floor meant she would make the most profit. But she was still reviewing the business model and debt-to-equity ratio before she agreed to meet with the founder.

High risk/high return didn't mean recklessly tossing her money around. She devoted weeks and sometimes months in research before she agreed to invest. That had been her motto since she'd taken the trust fund she'd inherited from her grandparents at the age of twenty-one and invested it with a local carpenter who wanted to flip houses. Her mother had been horrified, but soon she was making a profit, and she'd taken that money to invest in another company. And then another.

Within five years, she had tripled her trust fund and proved that she could not only support herself but could build a large enough nest egg that she didn't have to worry about her future. It'd also given her mother the opportunity to concentrate on her own life. Within a few months, the older woman had married a man who'd loved her for years and whisked her away to a secluded cabin in Colorado.

Lia had been delighted that her mom could find happiness, and she hadn't minded taking over the store that had been in their family for over a hundred years. It was as much a part of Pike as the surrounding dairy farms and the stone courthouse down the street. It rarely made a profit, but the store wasn't about creating money. It was keeping the tradition that her great-great-great-grandfather had started, as well as providing much-needed provisions for the older citizens who didn't feel comfortable driving to the larger town of Grange. Not to mention offering the necessities during the winter months, when the roads could be closed for days at a time.

Scribbling a few notes she wanted to double-check before continuing her interest in the potential investment, Lia heard the familiar tinkle of a bell. Someone had pushed open the front door. She glanced toward the monitor, watching the tall, lanky boy with short, rust-brown hair and a narrow face enter the store.

Wayne Neilson was a seventeen-year-old boy who'd asked for a job the previous summer. Lia already had a part-time helper who'd been there for forty years, but Della was getting older and her health wasn't always the best, so Lia had agreed to give Wayne an opportunity. He was being raised by a single mother just like she had. She understood the need to earn extra money.

He'd proven to be remarkably dependable, arriving right after school to put in a couple of hours and on Saturday and Sunday mornings.

Until this Saturday morning.

Rising from the desk, Lia headed out of the office and firmly shut the door. Only her mother knew about her investment skills. And that was how she wanted to keep it. Pike was a small town where everyone was always snooping into everyone's business. It was even worse for someone like her.

She'd always been different. She didn't have a father. She didn't mix easily with the other kids. And now she'd vaulted past her scary thirtieth birthday with no marriage proposal in sight. It made people study her as if she was a puzzle that needed to be solved. Or maybe fixed.

She wanted something that was just for herself.

She entered the main part of the store and walked toward the front counter, where Wayne was hanging his heavy parka on a hook drilled into the paneled wall.

"Hey, Ms. Porter. Sorry about being late," he said, his narrow face flushed and his blue eyes sparkling with an intense emotion.

"Is everything okay?"

"Fine." He shifted from foot to foot, as if he was having trouble standing still. "At least for me."

Lia studied him with mounting concern. Usually he was shy and subdued to the point she could barely get more than two words out of him. This excitement was completely out of character.

"What's going on?"

He glanced around the store, as if making sure it was empty. Then, he sucked in a deep breath.

"Drew and Cord found a body."

"A body of what?"

Wayne leaned toward her; his voice lowered to a harsh whisper. "A human body." He grimaced. "Or at least a skeleton."

Lia snorted. She knew both Drew Hurst and Cord Walsh. They were known around Pike as the local bullies. Clichéd but true. And their favorite target was usually Wayne.

"Are you sure they weren't messing with you?"

Wayne grimaced, no doubt recalling a thousand different

insults, humiliations, and even physical blows he'd endured over the years.

"Yeah. They're usually being jerks. Especially to me," he conceded. "But they aren't smart enough to set up an actual prank. They just shove people into lockers and steal stuff out of backpacks." He shrugged, the bones of his thin shoulders visible beneath his T-shirt. "Besides, they couldn't fake looking pale as ghosts when they climbed over the bridge railing. Or Drew puking up his guts when he told me what they'd seen. For real, I thought he was going to pass out."

Lia jerked, as if she'd just touched a live wire. And that was what it felt like as the shock zigzagged through her.

"What bridge railing?" She had to force the words past her stiff lips.

Wayne was thankfully oblivious to her tension. Like any teenage boy, he rarely noticed anything that didn't affect him directly.

"The one over the railroad tracks."

"The railroad bridge," she breathed, battling back the image that had haunted her for the past fifteen years. "I thought the whole area was closed off while they put in new railway tracks."

"It is. That's why they were there. It's a perfect time to sled down that steep hill without worrying about a train coming by and squashing them."

Lia shook her head. Both Drew and Cord had to be eighteen, or close to it. They were seniors, after all. But neither bothered to use their brains. Assuming they had one.

"So what happened?"

"Drew said he hit an icy patch that threw him off his sled and he rolled into a ditch next to the tracks. That's when he saw something under a bunch of old branches."

Lia shoved away her opinion of Drew and Cord. Right now, nothing mattered but the wild claim they'd made.

"And you're absolutely certain they found a body?"

"I can show you."

Lia took an instinctive step backward, as if he was about to pull a rotting corpse out of his pocket.

"What?"

Wayne held up the phone that was a constant fixture in his hand. "I had to see for myself."

"You went down to look at the body?"

"Of course." He swiped his finger over the screen, seemingly searching for something. "Nothing ever happens in this town. I wasn't going to miss the one nanosecond of excitement." He turned the phone around, a hint of pride on his narrow face. "Even if it was a little gruesome."

Lia glanced at the screen, realizing he'd pulled up a photo. She sent him a sharp glance.

"You took pictures?"

"Yep. And I posted them on my Instagram account. I'm hoping they'll go viral."

"Wayne."

He hunched his shoulders in a defensive motion. "Like I said, It's my one nanosecond of excitement. And it's not hurting anyone. Whoever the skeleton belongs to is dead and gone." He continued to hold out the phone. "Look."

Lia didn't want to look. She wanted to scurry back to her office and shut the door. Maybe then she could pretend it was just another day. A regular, boring day like every other regular, boring day.

A strange compulsion, however, had her leaning forward, studying the image Wayne had enlarged. Her gaze went immediately to the skull that peeked out of a layer of ice. It didn't look real. Instead, it appeared to have been carved from aged ivory, with empty eyes sockets that were shadowed, as if hiding unbearable secrets, and perfectly intact teeth that appeared too large and weirdly threatening. With a shudder, Lia forced her gaze to take in the rest of the skeleton. Or at least what was visible.

The upper torso was covered by what appeared to be a weathered leather jacket. She hissed, enlarging the picture until she could see the gold badge that had dulled over the years but remained unmistakable.

"Oh my God." Lia pressed a hand to her heaving stomach. Any hope of returning to her office and acting as if everything was normal was replaced with a burning urgency to take some sort of action. She didn't know exactly what that action was going to be, but she couldn't sit around and do nothing. "I need you to cover the store for an hour or so," she muttered.

"Okay." Wayne climbed onto the stool behind the cash register. "But if you want to take a look at the skeleton, it's too late. The mayor is there and he won't let anyone near the place. He's such a jerk."

Lia bit her lip. The mention of the mayor jolted her sluggish brain. That was what she needed to do. Speak with a law official. Unfortunately, Zac Evans, who'd proven to be an outstanding sheriff, had left Pike a week earlier to take his wife on an overdue honeymoon. He refused to tell them where he was going, only that it involved a cruise ship and that he was shutting off his phone and refusing to think about work until after the holidays.

Good news for him. Awful news for her.

For now, Pike was without a full-time sheriff, and until Zac returned, the local mayor was filling the position. Tate Erickson was barely capable of performing his duties as mayor, let alone taking on the sheriff's job.

Still, what choice did she have?

"I'll be back later." She scurried to the back of the narrow building, using the private staircase to head up to the apartment above the store.

It was a wide-open space arranged with a living room and kitchen and bedroom with an attached bathroom. The furniture hadn't changed since her mother moved out. The leather couch and chairs were worn and sagging in places, but they were comfortable, and that was all that mattered. Grabbing her purse, Lia slid a heavy parka over her casual jeans and bright red sweater before pulling on a thick stocking hat. She'd cut her strawberry-blond hair into a short, pixie style that was easy to take care of but did nothing to keep her warm. Then, heading back down the narrow staircase, she left the building to climb into the SUV with PORTER GROCERIES painted on the side. Once a month she delivered groceries to the customers who were housebound.

Driving out of the alley, she turned away from the center square and headed toward the outer road. The streets were slick from the most recent snowfall, but she was too impatient to creep along at a cautious pace. She slid past the old drive-in, where the framework of bare wood from the screen had managed to survive. Next to it was an indoor skating rink that hadn't been so lucky. It had collapsed years ago. Farther on was the bowling alley, which had been converted into a charity shop.

At last, she turned onto a narrow path that led toward the rolling fields that surrounded Pike and drove until she reached a curve in the road. She parked the SUV and switched off the engine. Ahead, she could see the barricades that had been put up along with glowing yellow police tape. A shiver raced through her as she watched the thin plastic flap in the stiff breeze.

Climbing out of the vehicle, Lia headed toward the short, heavyset man in a brown uniform standing guard against the gathering crowd.

Anthony was the same age as Lia and had been a sheriff's deputy for several years. He'd never been overly ambitious in school. He was the kid who sat in the back so he could sleep. At least, when he bothered to show up for school. Most days he skipped to go hunting or fishing. But she assumed that he was decent at his job.

She halted directly in front of the man. "Hey, Anthony. Is the mayor here?"

"Unfortunately." He nodded toward the steep bank behind him that led down to the railroad tracks. "He's down there."

"I need to talk to him."

"Can't. He's busy right now."

"This is important."

"Sorry, but it's going to have to wait."

"Anthony—"

The deputy held up a pudgy hand, interrupting her protest. "Trust me, Lia, this isn't the time." He glanced over his shoulder, making sure the mayor wasn't lurking behind him. "Erickson's been pissy since he became a fill-in for the sheriff, but today he's off the charts. He's been storming and stomping around ever since he caught sight of the skeleton. I assume he finally realized that being sheriff is more than getting free coffee at the diner."

Lia ground her teeth, not bothering to argue. Anthony might not have displayed ambition when he was young, but he'd always been stubborn as a mule. There was no point in beating her head against a brick wall.

"Thanks."

Turning away from the barrier, Lia stepped off the pathway and headed toward the snow-packed ridgeline. There was more than one way to get down to the tracks.

"Lia!"

Lia halted at the sound of her name being called out, glancing to the side to see a woman hurrying toward her.

Bailey Evans was Lia's best friend, and the sheriff's cousin. She was thin with brown hair pulled into a messy bun on top of her head. She was currently wearing a thick coat, but as usual she'd forgotten a hat and her gloves. Bailey was a fantastic caregiver at the local nursing home, but she could be remarkably absentminded. As if she was so occupied with tending to others that she didn't have time to worry about herself.

"Did you hear the news?" Bailey asked, halting next to Lia.

"Just that they found a skeleton."

"It's thrilling, isn't it? Horrible, of course." The flecks of gold in Bailey's dark eyes sparkled with eager curiosity, her cheeks flushed. "But absolutely thrilling."

Lia hid her grimace. She couldn't blame Bailey for being excited. Although Pike had endured more than its fair share of murders over the past five years, there was something morbidly intriguing about a mysterious death.

"Do they know who it is?"

"I don't think so." Bailey wrinkled her nose. "Tate is being more of an ass than usual. I miss Zac."

Lia sighed. "Who doesn't? He's the only decent sheriff we've had since Rupert retired." Lia was still in school when Rupert Jansen was forced to leave his position after being shot on the job, but everyone knew he'd been legendary. "Did Tate say anything?"

"He told me to keep my nose out of his business." Bailey made a sound of disgust. "Idiot. I'm the town gossip. My nose belongs in everyone's business." She glanced toward the nearby field, which was crammed with emergency vehicles. "I did hear one of the EMTs call it a 'her' when they loaded the body bag into the ambulance. Other than that, it's a complete mystery."

"A woman," Lia breathed.

"I've been trying to imagine who it could be." Bailey reached up to push back her thick hair, which was being tossed by the breeze. "I don't know any missing women. Not unless you count my Aunt Misty, who traveled to Paris thirty years ago and never came home. Really, who could blame her? Sipping café au lait in a cute little bistro certainly beats sucking down a cup of joe in a local dive, am I right?"

Usually Lia would smile at Bailey's chatter. The fact that they were complete opposites was what made their relationship so much fun. This morning, however, she was too tense to appreciate her friend's humor.

"It could be one of Jude's victims," she pointed out.

Bailey's amusement died at the mention of the monster who'd lived in Pike nearly thirty years before.

"That was my first thought as well. There's always a chance that one slipped through the cracks," she agreed, her tone doubtful. "But Zac was pretty certain they'd located all of them. Otherwise, he would never have left town."

It did seem doubtful. Zac had spent endless months searching through the stacks of evidence left behind by the serial killer. If there'd been any hint of a missing victim, he would never have closed the case.

Which meant the woman she'd seen that night hadn't

been fleeing a madman. At least not a madman who'd already faced justice. Honestly, that only made things worse.

"I need to talk to Tate," she muttered.

Without warning, Bailey reached out to grasp her arm. "I wouldn't if I were you."

"Why not?"

"He not only snapped at me. The jerk." Her jaw tightened at the memory. "He's been on a rampage with everyone, including the deputies. Last I heard, he was screaming about 'crime scenes' and 'preservation of clues.' I'm guessing he's been watching reruns of *Law & Order*. Or, more likely, *The Andy Griffith Show*. He certainly has a Barney Fife vibe."

Lia bit her lower lip. She hated confrontations. It didn't mean she didn't have a spine. She could be ruthless when necessary. But she preferred to avoid messy arguments. Maybe she should wait until . . .

No. Lia squared her shoulders. The last time she'd decided to avoid revealing what she'd seen, a woman obviously had ended up dead. She wasn't going to risk letting anything bad happen again. Not if revealing the truth could prevent it.

"He'll just have to scream," she said in grim tones. "I need to talk to him."

"Fine." Bailey nodded, easily sensing Lia's determination. Still, she kept a tight grip on her arm. "Don't forget we're having a Friends of Pike meeting Tuesday night. We need to discuss the Fourth of July festival. Jolene already sent me an email." Bailey rolled her eyes. Jolene was married to Tate Erickson. Her position as the mayor's wife meant she considered herself an authority on everything Pike. Or what she envisioned Pike should be. And while Tate possessed a brash, outgoing sort of charm that had allowed him to keep getting reelected for the past twenty years, Jolene was just the opposite. She was a soft-spoken woman with deep dimples and a cloud of blond hair. But in her own way she was just as ruthless. She used her supposedly fragile health to avoid unpleasant confrontations or to manipulate others into giving in to her every demand.

"Now what does she want?" Lia asked.

"She suggested that we replace the greased pig run with an afternoon tea and cakewalk. She's afraid we might get in trouble with the PETA people." Bailey did more eyerolling. "As if anyone would know what's happening in Pike. We can barely interest the locals in noticing the events, let alone attract the attention of anyone else."

"I doubt PETA would be showing up to complain," Lia agreed. "But then again, I'm not opposed to getting rid of the greased pig. It's kind of disgusting."

"Agreed, but it's been a part of the Fourth of July celebrations for a hundred years. The rest of the committee is going to have a cow." Bailey heaved a sigh. "Greased pigs and cows. That's my life."

Lia managed a small smile of encouragement. "I'll be there."

"Thanks, Lia." Bailey gave Lia's arm a squeeze before dropping her hand and stepping back. "I can always depend on you."

Lia swallowed a sigh as she turned away. That was her. Dependable Lia.

Tate was frantically pulling aside the dead branches and chunks of frozen snow that were piled near the skeleton. He ignored the destruction of his expensive leather gloves. Jolene was going to bitch when he went home and she saw them, but what the hell? If it wasn't his gloves, she'd find something else to bitch about. She was nothing if not consistent. And right now, he didn't have time to worry about anything except making sure there was nothing around he didn't want found.

When he'd first gotten the call that a bunch of boys had found a skeleton by the railroad tracks, he'd been more annoyed than concerned. This sheriff thing was a short-term gig. Just until Zac Evans returned to Pike. He assumed it would be an easy way to add an accomplishment to his résumé as mayor. It was never too early to start thinking about his reelection. And claiming he'd stepped in as sheriff to keep his citizens safe was going to make a great headline. He hadn't anticipated having to climb through the ice and snow to look at a bunch of stupid bones. And certainly not on his day off.

Reluctantly, he'd wrangled into layers of thick clothing and pulled on a pair of heavy boots. Then, driving to the location, he'd slipped and cursed his way down the steep incline to where a group of gawkers were gathered around the bones.

He'd been on the point of ordering one of his deputies to take charge of removing the skeleton when he'd caught a glimpse of gold on the faded leather jacket.

It was a badge. One he recognized.

His chest tightened and his mouth went dry, and just for a horrifying second, he feared he was having a heart attack. This couldn't be happening. Not after all these years.

Forcing himself to step forward, Tate ordered everyone to leave, including his own deputies. Unfortunately, the police photographer continued taking pictures of the scene, while the EMTs fussed and argued over the best means of removing the bones without disturbing evidence. Tate was ready to scream in frustration before he was finally alone.

Now he searched for a purse or briefcase or a computer memory stick that might have survived. Anything that might reveal why the woman had been in Pike.

Rolling aside a large rock, Tate was abruptly interrupted by the sound of boots crunching through the thin layer of ice. Muttering a curse, he spun around to confront the young woman who was closer than he expected. Dammit. Had she seen him scrambling through the brush?

"No one is allowed down here," he barked out. "How many damned times do I have to say it?"

Lia Porter acted as if she hadn't heard him, continuing forward until she was standing just a few inches from where the body was found.

"I have some information."

Tate frowned. Lia was thirty. Give or take a year. He had a vague memory of handing her a diploma when she'd graduated. Too young to have any actual information. At least none that could affect him.

"I don't care if you have the Holy Grail," he retorted, his tone harsh. "Not now."

"It's about the skeleton you found."

A small niggle of concern wormed its way through Tate's heart. Maybe he should find out what she knew.

"Make it quick."

Lia licked her lips. "I think I saw her the night she died."

Tate hissed in shock. "What?"

Lia glanced up the steep hill, her gaze locked on the nearby bridge.

"Fifteen years ago I was walking home from a party in the middle of the night and I saw a woman up there."

Tate forced himself to take a deep breath. No need to

panic. "You risked contaminating my crime scene to tell me that you stumbled home drunk in the middle of the night fifteen years ago and thought you'd seen something in the pitch dark?"

Her green eyes flashed with outrage. "I wasn't drunk, and there was enough moonlight to know it was a woman."

"Did you talk to her?"

"No. When she caught sight of me, she turned and jumped off the railing."

Tate's momentary urge to throw up vanished at her clipped words. She knew nothing.

"Sounds like a figment of your imagination."

"I know what I saw."

Tate clicked his tongue, not having to fake his surge of impatience. "Even if it wasn't a drunken illusion, we don't know if this woman jumped off the bridge or off a passing train or if she was wandering along the tracks and tripped over and broke her neck. We don't even know how long she's been here. She could have died a hundred years ago. So, if you don't mind . . ."

"I recognize the badge."

The nausea returned. "What?"

"The woman I saw jump from the bridge was wearing a leather jacket with a gold badge pinned on the front." She pointed to a place over her left breast. "Right there."

Tate's brows snapped together. "How do you know about the jacket?"

"Wayne Neilson showed me a photo of the skeleton."

"Shit." Tate knew those stupid kids were going to be trouble as soon as he caught sight of the skeleton. "I told those boys to erase any pictures they took."

Lia shrugged. "By now they're being shared around social media."

She was right, of course. And worse was the knowledge

that once the pictures started circulating, the local interest story would quickly become a shitshow.

"Damned internet," he muttered.

"Do you want to hear what I saw that night?" the woman stubbornly demanded.

"Not now, Lia," he snapped. "If you want to make some sort of formal report, you can come to the office on Monday. Right now, I'm too busy."

"This is ridiculous."

She threw her hands up in the air, but thank God she turned to climb up the steep incline. He couldn't deal with Lia Porter. Not now.

After waiting until she was out of sight, Tate pulled his cell phone out of the pocket of his coat. He'd sent a quick text the moment he recognized who had been found. Now he needed to share that this was going to be more than a passing inconvenience.

He pressed a familiar number and grimaced when his call was answered with a sharp demand to know where he was.

"I'm still at the scene," he said. "The EMTs just took away the body." He listened a second. "Of course I'm sure. There wasn't any identification, but she had the badge on her jacket. It has to be her." Another pause. "No. I couldn't destroy it. Those dumbass kids had already taken pictures. You don't think people would ask questions if it magically disappeared?" He blew out a heavy breath, the puff of icy vapor reminding him that he was freezing his ass off. "And it gets worse. Lia Porter came charging down here claiming she'd seen the woman the night she died." He flinched as a sharp reprimand drilled into his ear, as if he was somehow responsible for Lia being in the wrong place at the wrong time. "I don't know. She was babbling about a woman jumping off the bridge and recognizing the jacket. She'd seen a picture one of those inbred brats took. I told her I'd talk to her later." He made a sound of impatience as the reprimand continued. "How was I supposed to distract her? I'm cold, I'm tired, and I'm done playing sheriff for the day. I'll deal with Lia after I've made sure there's nothing out here that can point back to us." He held the phone in front of his face, his tone sarcastic. "Oh, and you're welcome. Once again I'm stuck trying to clean up your messes."